THE THIRD SECTION

Jasper Kent

BANTAM PRESS

LONDON · TORONTO · SYDNEY · AUCKLAND · JOHANNESBURG

TRANSWORLD PUBLISHERS
61–63 Uxbridge Road, London W5 5SA
A Random House Group Company
www.transworldbooks.co.uk

First published in Great Britain
in 2011 by Bantam Press
an imprint of Transworld Publishers

A CIP catalogue record for this book
is available from the British Library.

ISBN 9780593065372

Addresses for Random House Group Ltd companies outside the UK
can be found at: www.randomhouse.co.uk
The Random House Group Ltd Reg. No. 954009

The Random House Group Limited supports The Forest Stewardship
Council® (FSC®), the leading international forest certification organization.
All our titles that are printed on Greenpeace approved FSC® certified paper
carry the FSC® logo. Our paper procurement policy can be found at
www.randomhouse.co.uk/environment

Typeset in 11/14½pt Sabon by
Kestrel Data, Exeter, Devon.
Printed and bound in Great Britain by
CPI Mackays, Chatham, ME5 8TD.

2 4 6 8 10 9 7 5 3 1

For my parents

AUTHOR'S NOTES

Measurements
A verst is a Russian unit of distance, slightly greater than a kilometre.

Dates
During the nineteenth century, Russians based their dates on the old Julian Calendar, which in the 1850s was twelve days behind the Gregorian Calendar used in Western Europe. All dates in the text are given in the Russian form and so, for example, the coronation of Alexander II is placed on 26 August 1856, where Western history books have it on 7 September.

Characters
A list of characters in the Danilov Quintet appears on page 475.

Thanks to Stéphane Marsan and Hilary Casey for assistance with French and German.

Selected Romanov Family

Reigning tsars and tsaritsas shown in **bold**
Dates are birth–[start of reign]–[end of reign]

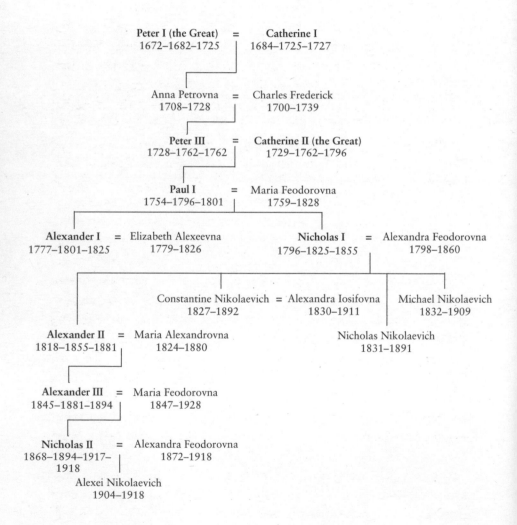

Peter I (the Great) = Catherine I
1672–1682–1725   1684–1725–1727

Anna Petrovna = Charles Frederick
1708–1728   1700–1739

Peter III = Catherine II (the Great)
1728–1762–1762   1729–1762–1796

Paul I = Maria Feodorovna
1754–1796–1801   1759–1828

Alexander I = Elizabeth Alexeevna
1777–1801–1825   1779–1826

Nicholas I = Alexandra Feodorovna
1796–1825–1855   1798–1860

Constantine Nikolaevich = Alexandra Iosifovna
1827–1892   1830–1911

Michael Nikolaevich
1832–1909

Alexander II = Maria Alexandrovna
1818–1855–1881   1824–1880

Nicholas Nikolaevich
1831–1891

Alexander III = Maria Feodorovna
1845–1881–1894   1847–1928

Nicholas II = Alexandra Feodorovna
1868–1894–1917–1918   1872–1918

Alexei Nikolaevich
1904–1918

THE CRIMEAN WAR

In 1853 Russia went to war with the Ottoman Empire for the eleventh time in three hundred years. The difference on this occasion was that Great Britain and France allied with the Turks, leading to a European war on a scale not seen since the time of Napoleon. There were major engagements around the Danube, in the Baltic and the White Sea, in the Caucasus and even in the Pacific, but the most significant theatre of conflict was the Black Sea, where the Allies attempted to destroy the Russian fleet harboured in Sevastopol on the Crimean Peninsula. Hence in the West at least, the conflict became known as the Crimean War.

The immediate cause of the war was the argument over who should have control of the Christian holy sites within the Muslim Ottoman Empire; the Catholic Church, championed by France, or the Orthodox Church, by Russia. More generally, antagonism between the two sides was due to fears of Russian expansion into the British Empire. Russia had the potential of reaching British India over land, while Britain's access was by sea, over the circuitous route around the Cape of Good Hope. Turkish influence in the east acted as a buffer against Russian ambitions, but the anticipated collapse of the Ottoman Empire – nicknamed by Tsar Nicholas I as the 'Sick Man of Europe' – would mean that Russia could gain much of the Turkish territory and take a step closer to the subcontinent.

While the French had little interest in this dispute, the French Emperor, Napoleon III, was, like the British, concerned over Russian naval access to the Mediterranean, through the Black Sea. Moreover, Napoleon III saw that making a stand against

Russia might consolidate his recently acquired position (he became emperor in the coup d'état of 1851) as well as offering a chance to take revenge for his uncle Napoleon Bonaparte's defeat by Russia in 1812 and Tsar Nicholas' failure to properly recognize Napoleon III's claim to be emperor.

To test Turkey's determination during negotiations over the holy sites, Nicholas I ordered the Russian occupation of Moldavia and Wallachia – autonomous principalities within the Ottoman Empire and historically the lands over which the two nations had often clashed. The Conference of Vienna led to a proposed compromise which gave Russia limited authority over the holy sites. This was enough for Russia, which began to withdraw from the principalities, but not for Turkey, which declared war on Russia. The remaining players began to take sides.

Austria and Prussia remained neutral, but in March 1854 Britain and France jointly declared war on Russia. Within six months their troops landed in the Crimea and had soon besieged the naval base of Sevastopol. By the end of 1855, Sevastopol had fallen, and in 1856 the Treaty of Paris brought the war to an end. The most significant result was the demilitarization of the Black Sea, which applied equally to Russia and Turkey. However, the Turks had coastline on the Mediterranean itself, whereas Russia was denied a southern fleet for a quarter of a century.

TE DEUM!

Tsar Nicholas I, in a *Punch* cartoon by John Leech from January 1854

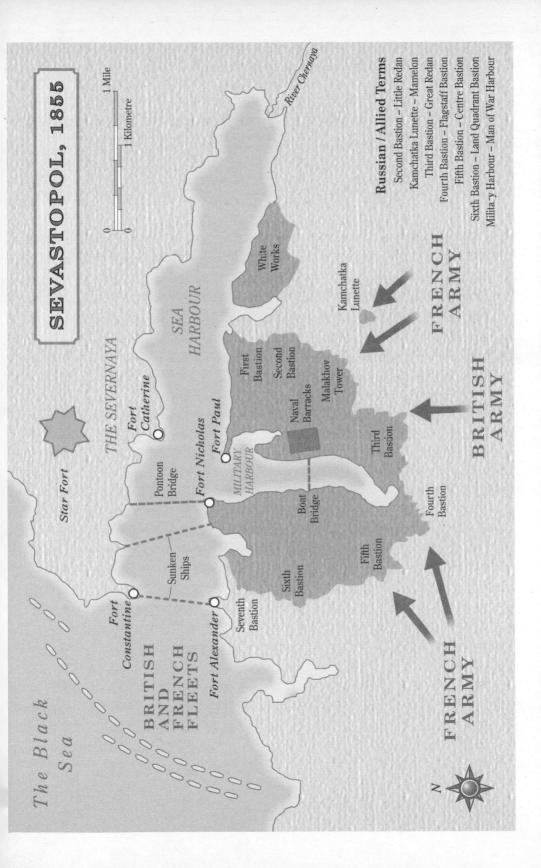

SEVASTOPOL, 1855

The Black Sea

Star Fort

THE SEVERNAYA

Fort Catherine

SEA HARBOUR

River Chernaya

White Works

Fort Nicholas

Fort Paul

Pontoon Bridge

Sunken Ships

Fort Constantine

MILITARY HARBOUR

First Bastion

Second Bastion

Kamchatka Lunette

BRITISH AND FRENCH FLEETS

Fort Alexander

Seventh Bastion

Sixth Bastion

Boat Bridge

Naval Barracks

Malakhov Tower

Third Bastion

FRENCH ARMY

BRITISH ARMY

Fifth Bastion

Fourth Bastion

FRENCH ARMY

N

Russian / Allied Terms

Second Bastion – Little Redan
Kamchatka Lunette – Mamelon
Third Bastion – Great Redan
Fourth Bastion – Flagstaff Bastion
Fifth Bastion – Centre Bastion
Sixth Bastion – Land Quadrant Bastion
Milita-y Harbour – Man of War Harbour

1 Mile

1 Kilometre

0

HIS IMPERIAL MAJESTY'S OWN CHANCELLERY

Following his ascension to the throne in 1825, Tsar Nicholas I consolidated his personal authority by taking powers away from individual ministries and incorporating them into a body known as His Imperial Majesty's Own Chancellery. The chancellery was divided into several departments, or sections.

The First Section of His Imperial Majesty's Own Chancellery dealt with imperial decrees and orders. The Second Section was responsible for the codification of law; the Fourth for the administration of charitable and educational institutions.

The Third Section was in charge of political crimes, censorship, espionage and internal suppression. It was the tsar's secret police.

1854

PROLOGUE

The valley of death lay far behind.

Even so, Owen could still hear the rhythmic thump of cannon fire – four tightly grouped reports, then silence, then four again, and again, and again. He looked over his shoulder, but could see nothing – no men, no horses. There must have been over six hundred of them at the beginning. All dead now, probably. Owen slowed his own horse to a canter.

The rhythm of the cannon changed – volleys of three now, rather than four. Owen laughed, briefly. There were no guns, not here. Back in the valley they might still be firing, but not here. He slowed his horse even more and the rhythm of hoofbeats changed again, quietening to almost nothing. There had been a point when the cannon had been loud enough to engulf the sound of twenty-four hundred thundering hooves, but not any more. He halted Byron. The horse breathed noisily. Byron had been at the gallop from the beginning, never questioning what he was instructed to do, just as Owen had never questioned. None of them had.

They'd charged down the valley behind Lord Cardigan, not for a moment pausing to query his command, even as canister hailed down from the hills to the left and right of them. Ahead had been the guns, the guns that they must take at any cost, because that was what they had been told to do. Cannonballs spun and bounced towards them along the valley floor, threatening to rip the brigade into tatters, but that only went to prove how essential it was to capture the position. Men and horses fell on either side, the blood of both spattering Owen's face and uniform, but he kept going. Cardigan had kept on too – Owen remembered

19

that much – as did everyone else, all those who hadn't lost their mounts, or their lives. They got as far as the Russian guns; Owen, Cardigan, maybe a few hundred others. And once among them, it was child's play to cut the gunners down, sabres making easy meat of men on foot, trained to fight targets at a distance of a thousand yards, not face to face. The Russians ran like cowards, and those who didn't run perished. British casualties were heavy, but the guns had been taken.

And then realization had dawned upon them, realization of the futility of the whole charge. They were in Russian territory, and unsupported. They could never hold what they had gained, even if reinforcements arrived – and there was no sign of that. The retreat was sounded and the survivors of the Light Brigade had turned their horses, but there was only one path of escape – the corpse-strewn valley down which they had come. And there were still gun emplacements on the hills on either side, and when they left, the guns here would soon be manned once again. As many would die as had been lost already. Even so, it was the only way to go.

But not for Owen; he did not retreat. Instead he'd carried on at full tilt through the guns, through the cavalry behind, shocked into inaction by the futility of the British attack. Some might have seen him as brave to ride on further into enemy territory, others as a coward who had disobeyed orders and abandoned his comrades, but he was neither. Fear had made him incapable of any rational action – for both cowardice and bravery required decisiveness. He had done nothing, merely allowed Byron to continue his onward gallop, leading them where he might.

But no one need know that. When the count was taken, the name of Lieutenant P. E. A. Owen of the 17th Lancers would be among the hundreds missing, presumed dead. If he could make it back to the British lines soon enough, there would be no questions as to what had happened. They'd just be happy to know that there was one more healthy soldier – and healthy horse – able to fight another day. One less man dead or captured.

Though that wasn't a certainty yet. He'd survived the battle, but was deep behind enemy lines. He was a good way north of Balaklava now, and heading north-east. That was for the best.

He'd need to make a wide arc to get back to the British camp. If he circled left, he'd end up going past Sevastopol, which wouldn't be clever. So he'd curve round to the right towards the coast and talk his way past the French – or even the Turks, God help him. But at least you knew where you were with the Turks; it was hard to break the habit of thinking of the French as the enemy.

Already the hills on his right were beginning to look intimidating. The land he was going through was pretty flat – mostly used for growing vines, though all hope of that seemed to have been abandoned for the time being with the arrival of armies from four nations. But Owen knew the line of the rocky hills ran from south-west to north-east and that if he didn't venture across that line within an hour or so, then he'd be spending the night out in the open. He scanned the terrain, looking for an easy route between the peaks.

The pounding noise came again, but this time he wasn't fooled into thinking it was gunfire. Anyone on horseback around here was likely to be Russian and a glance over Owen's shoulder confirmed it. He cursed his stupidity at not having made some effort to disguise his uniform, but it was too late now. Byron showed no reluctance to break into his fastest gallop and they raced onwards, forced further from the prospective safety of the British lines with every yard they went. It was five minutes before Owen slowed the horse a little and risked turning to examine his pursuers.

There were three of them, over half a mile behind him. They weren't going fast enough to get close very soon, but in this terrain they were unlikely to lose sight of him. Moreover, they knew the deployment of the other Russian troops in the area. They didn't need to catch him – simply corral him.

The road, such as it was, forked, the less trodden path leading into the hills. This seemed the better bet, with more than enough twists in the road to put him out of their sight.

He quickly began to doubt his decision. He was coming to a town. If there were troops stationed here, he was finished. So far, he could see only peasants – Tatars by the look of them. He doubted that they could even tell a Russian from an Englishman, with or without the uniform.

The road weaved on ahead and began to steepen as the hills

on either side turned into cliffs. Owen looked behind him again, but could not see the three horsemen. That didn't mean they had given up. With the cliffs now rising on both sides, he had no choice over the direction he took. They didn't need to see him to know that.

He was at the centre of the town now. On his right was a palace, in the Tatar style. Two towers – minarets, he supposed – strained elegantly towards the sky. From the roadside a woman stopped to look at him. She was old, and it was hard to tell whether the darkness of her skin was a result of dirt, or its natural hue. She showed no surprise at his arrival, making him fear that she was used to the presence of soldiers. On his left, the cliff ran alongside the road now, hanging over the palace. At one point natural weathering had shaped it into what could almost be interpreted as a face – a skull perhaps. He thought of the skull and bones of his regiment's insignia on his cap badge. Death or Glory, it meant; and he'd abandoned any hope of glory.

He was soon out of the town and into the hills. The last building he saw was some kind of monastery, built into the cliffside itself. It was an odd contrast, so close to a Mohammedan village. The road had switched to the right-hand side of the valley and the hill dropped steeply away to his left before rising as a cliff on the other side. On his right the wooded slope towered above him. He was reminded of the valley he had ridden into at Balaklava. This was narrower and steeper, but he had no doubt the whole of the Light Brigade – what was left of them – would have merrily charged in here if so commanded. If there were any cannon lurking on the brow of the hill, waiting to fire down on him, then he was doomed.

He drew to a halt and looked ahead. Now he could see what his pursuers must always have known. It was a dead end. The track curved round the head of the valley and then wound up the other side to some sort of settlement. From here he had a reasonable view back down the route he had come, the leafless trees allowing glimpses of the path. The three horsemen were still there – advancing slowly towards him, but closer than when he had last seen them, before the village. They knew he was trapped.

He dismounted. The route ahead was impassable for Byron, or

for any horse. He loosely tied the reins to a tree and patted the creature's neck in a casual way that might fool both of them into believing their separation would be only temporary. The path tacked from side to side on the grassy slope, all of a sudden too steep for trees or bushes to find purchase. He would be a sitting duck if he followed it, so instead he scrambled directly up the steepest incline, towards the buildings he had seen.

It was more of a citadel than a settlement. The top part of the slope was a vertical cliff of perhaps twenty or thirty feet, making the buildings at its summit unassailable. Where there was no cliff, a wall had been built in its stead, with a gateway to which the path led. If Owen could get inside, then he might have some hope of defending himself. If he could get inside.

He tried the gate, but it was chained shut. He had no time to attempt to break through. To the right, where the wall and the natural cliff merged, there had been a rock fall. He scrambled up the collapsed boulders and was soon level with the top of the wall. At that moment he heard a shot and a bullet slammed into the rock, just yards away from him. He threw himself over the wall and on to the stone pathway below, landing badly, but not so badly that he couldn't walk.

Inside was quite a sizeable town – a cave city where habitations had been built from naturally occurring structures in the rock. A few buildings were entirely manmade, but most owed their existence half to man, half to nature.

He heard voices from outside and peeped back over the cliff. The three Russians were approaching. Like him, they had dismounted. Two of them carried pistols, but Owen knew how primitive their weapons were. The other must have been the one who had fired and would have to reload before he could do so again. Owen squeezed his fingers around the grip of his Dean and Adams revolver and smiled. Five shots without reloading – and only three targets.

The men approached the rock fall that had been Owen's path over the wall. They spoke to each other briefly, but he could make nothing of it. The one without a gun began to climb and the others eyed the cliff top, ready to take aim at anything that dared raise its head.

Owen's shot rang out before they even saw his movement. The Russian climbing towards him made no sound, but fell away limply from the rocks, landing at the feet of his comrades. Owen stood and fired again, aiming at the one nearer to him. The bullet missed, but before the men could turn Owen was able to squeeze the trigger again and get off another shot.

He felt a searing pain in his hand and forearm. The powder had blown back from the chamber and he could see the black scorch-marks on the skin of his arm. He didn't even realize he'd dropped the gun until he heard it clattering against the rocks below. It was well out of his reach, and thankfully out of theirs too. But now they were emboldened, and the two began climbing up towards him.

Owen ran. The citadel – abandoned by whoever had once lived here – stood on a narrow plateau, just a few hundred yards across. On the far side it was even less accessible. Another cliff dropped away vertically for twenty feet and then a steep, grassy slope descended hundreds more into the valley. There was no sign of a path on this side. In times of invasion, the place would have been impregnable.

He heard a sound behind him and turned. There was only one of them, picking his way between the cave mouths that covered this part of the plateau, pistol in hand. Owen drew his sword. The man fired, but missed. Owen charged across the rocky ground. Where the Russian stood was actually the roof of a cave. Several holes, quite large enough for either of them to fall through, were scattered in the rock around him – manmade, to guess by their shape. Beneath them the cave floor could be seen, six feet down.

The Russian had drawn his own sword and their blades clashed with the full force of Owen's charge. The Russian stepped back, nearer to one of the gaps in the rock. Owen brought his blade down again, and again the Russian parried, spotting the trap that Owen had hoped would catch him and leaping over it, landing on the far side with both feet together. Now it was Owen who risked falling, his momentum carrying him forward so that he teetered on the edge, swinging his arms to keep his balance and having to abandon any defensive stance.

The Russian lunged at him, and even though he was falling,

Owen managed to direct himself away from the blade. In an instant he was ready to counterattack. His opponent, overconfident in his assault, had been forced to step over the opening in the rock beneath him. Now he was in no position to bring his feet back together. He stood there, steady but ungainly, one foot on either edge of the aperture, as though a parade-ground march had been frozen in mid-step.

He would have done better to fall. Owen raised his sword in a feint to bring it down on his adversary's left arm, but the intent was only to draw away the Russian's own sword. Owen changed the direction of his blow and the blade embedded itself in the inside of the man's leading thigh, slicing through the rough material of his uniform and sliding smoothly into the flesh beneath.

The Russian fell instantly, with no strength in his leg to support him. The ground seemed almost to swallow him up as he dropped into the cave below, and Owen heard a nauseating crack as his head caught the stone lip.

Moments later, he heard another sound – the report of one more pistol firing – and felt in the same instant a bullet hit his arm, just below the right shoulder. It was a flesh wound, but it would be enough to limit his ability with a sword. The last of his pursuers approached warily across the plateau. Owen stepped backwards, glancing at the ground behind him to avoid the fate that had so recently befallen his opponent. The surviving Russian, able to see where he was going, moved faster, but was still some yards away when Owen reached the cliff edge and knew he could go no further. He raised his sword, trying not to show the pain that it caused in his arm. There was little he could do to fight, and he knew he could not retreat.

But Owen had one advantage over his foe – he had already surveyed the terrain.

The Russian seemed hesitant to approach, but Owen knew it would be his only chance of survival. He clenched his left fist and shook both arms, baring his teeth to shout.

'Come on, you fucking coward! Fight me!'

He doubted the Russian had understood a word, but the meaning must have been clear. The man ran towards him, sword in the air. He wasn't a fool, and didn't run so fast that Owen needed merely to sidestep to see him fling himself, arms flailing, over the precipice. But Owen's plan was more subtle than that.

As he approached, Owen threw his sword to the ground and then, in a single motion, grabbed the soldier's lapels and took a step backwards off the edge of the cliff. The Russian might have been able to stop himself alone from falling, but he had not been prepared for anything so suicidal.

The drop was not far – four feet at most. Owen had seen the ledge running just below the cliff top when he first looked out over that edge of the plateau. He landed heavily, feeling his head hit stone, but managed to remain conscious. With the Russian's momentum still behind him, it was easy for Owen to roll and propel him those few extra feet which meant there would be no hidden ledge to save him. Owen felt fingers tugging at the sleeve of his tunic, but they could find no grip.

It took him a few seconds to crawl over and look down. The Russian's body had hit the steep grass slope below the cliff and was now rolling over and over down to the valley beyond. It must have been thirty seconds before he came to a stop. As Owen watched, the Russian tried to pull himself to his feet, then collapsed. He would be horribly bruised, but perhaps not fatally injured. But even if he could walk, it would take him hours to get back round to the accessible side of the citadel, and by then it would be dark, and Owen could easily slip past him.

It was not too tricky to get back on to the plateau. A little way along the ledge were some roughly cut steps leading up. The cliff face itself was marked with a number of cave mouths to which the ledge gave access. Most of them were blocked by rubble, but even had they been open, Owen would have felt no desire to explore.

He made his way back to the scene of his swordfight and peered into the hole through which his opponent had fallen, but saw nothing. Now that the sun was low, he could not even make out the ground beneath. He scouted around and soon found another set of rough-hewn steps that led down to what seemed to be the more normal entrance of the cave. Inside, the man's body lay on a pile of rocks. He was dead. It would not have been pleasant. The loss of blood from his leg would have been slow, but unceasing. Owen was surprised how little of it there was to be seen, but the boulders on which he lay were not tightly packed, and the blood would easily have found its way between them, to drip down on to whatever lay below. With luck, the man would have been knocked out by the fall, and not felt the life draining from him into the ground.

Owen walked back to the cave entrance and sat beside it, leaning against the wall. He put his hand to his arm. It was damp with blood, but he doubted the wound was serious. The pain in the back of his head from where it had hit the ground was more of a concern, and he could feel it blurring his senses. All he needed now was to get off the plateau and, in the shadow of darkness, make his way back to the British camp. With luck, Byron would still be there to carry him.

But first he would rest.

Owen didn't know how long he had dozed, but it was dark now. The moon outside was a thin crescent, shining its light through the doorway and through the several holes in the ceiling, cutting through the cave in glowing, ethereal columns. The skin of the dead Russian, lying in one such ray of moonlight, looked as grey as the rocks beside him.

Next to the body stood the figure of a man.

Owen was instantly alert, afraid that one of his enemies had somehow survived, but fear soon gave way to confusion. The man was tall, and looked very old. Or perhaps more aged than old. He stood like a young man, proud and upright, without any hint of frailty, but his skin was wizened and wrinkled. He was dreadfully thin – emaciated. Owen could count every rib. His lips were dark, almost black.

He spoke. It sounded like Russian.

'*Ya nye gavaryu pa ruski*,' stammered Owen, using the one, self-contradictory fragment of the language that he knew.

'*En quelle année sommes-nous?*' said the man. Owen understood the language well enough, but it was a strange question.

'1854,' he replied, using the French with which he had been addressed.

27

'1854?' The man stuck with the same language. 'Twenty-nine years.'

He said nothing more, but seemed to smile. Owen noticed that behind him a dark tunnel led downwards to more caves. When he had first arrived that afternoon, there had only been rubble lying there.

'Who are you?' Owen asked.

The man paused, thinking. Perhaps it had been twenty-nine years since anyone had asked him such a question. Perhaps he was the only remaining inhabitant of this citadel, abandoned when the others left.

'I am called Prometheus,' he said at length.

'That's a strange name.'

'I'm a strange creature.' Prometheus glanced at the body of the dead Russian. 'Did you slaughter him?'

Owen nodded.

'Thank you,' said Prometheus. 'But it will not be enough for all of us.'

'Enough?'

Prometheus continued as if Owen had said nothing. 'We must learn to share.' He walked across the cave towards Owen at tremendous speed. 'It will taste better if not filtered through the rocks.'

Prometheus opened his mouth wide and Owen saw for the first time his fang-like teeth. Owen raised his sword, but Prometheus grasped it by the blade and wrenched it from his grip. He felt a hand grab his head and another his arm and Prometheus' mouth fell upon his neck. He could not see what was happening, but it felt as though his skin were being tightly pinched before suddenly yielding.

There was little pain. A sense of light-headedness filled him and he lost both the strength and the will to struggle. The most horrible part of it was the slurping sound as, gulp by gulp, the blood left Owen's body and entered Prometheus. And at the same time, some splinter of Prometheus' mind seemed to enter Owen's. He could taste blood on his tongue, and knew it was his own. He could sense the gradual satiation of an ancient thirst. It was a strange but not unpleasant way to die.

And yet he did not die. Not straight away. After a few minutes, Prometheus stopped, and laid Owen gently down on the cave floor. He turned and called over his shoulder into the dark tunnel from which he must have come. Shadows moved and more figures emerged into the cave. And Owen knew – because he knew Prometheus' mind – that they would not be so gentle with him.

1855

CHAPTER I

LIGHT TUMBLES FROM THE STARS, RUSHING DOWNWARDS, heading for wherever it might fall. Some will be lost in the darkness of the sky; some will land upon planets where no eye can witness its arrival; some will hurtle towards the Earth. And as it looks down upon the Earth, it will see the land as though it were a gigantic map, laid out to be read by the stars themselves. Great cities, illuminated by the flames of candles and lamps, shine back at the starlight, and dark, straight lines stretch between them. Closer still, points of light travel along those lines, between the cities, as flames and sparks billow into the darkness, testimony to the power that man has harnessed.

Behind the flames, a procession – a train of candlelit windows dragged across the countryside by the fiery engine, and behind each window, people. Behind one such sits a little girl, her curls – the colour of fire – cascading over her shoulders. She looks up and smiles at the two adults opposite – her beloved parents – as the starlight hits their faces, augmenting, however slightly, the light from the candle at the window. The little girl frowns, but the starlight can do no more than it already has to help her see what she so desperately wants to see. But it has not done enough.

The little girl looks from her mother to her father and back to her mother, but their faces are unchanged. They remain what they have always been to her – a smooth, perfect, unrecognizable blank.

*   *   *

Tamara Valentinovna Komarova awoke. She was alone. There were a few other passengers in the second-class carriage but none near her – none she knew.

She often dreamed of her parents – her real parents – more even than she dreamed of her husband and children. The faces of Valentin and Yelena Lavrov rarely troubled her mind, awake or asleep. They had been good to her and no child could have asked for more, but Tamara had carried with her for as long as she could remember the conviction that they were not her true parents. The house she grew up in had been haunted by ghosts – memories of two people for whom she cherished the most unutterable love, whose presence in her mind could only be explained if they were her father and her mother. But they came to her not as true recollections but as dark reflections in a looking glass, memories not of reality but perhaps of a game she had once played; a game in which she conjured up idealized replacements for those who had loved her and raised her. It was the remembrance of a child's foolishness.

And yet she knew the Lavrovs were not her parents.

It had distanced her from them, which wasn't fair to anyone, but whenever she had tried to raise the issue they had dismissed her suspicions as absurdity. She was thirty-three now, and couldn't remember a time when they hadn't been there, teaching her, nurturing her, doting on her as any true parent would; but neither could she remember a time when she had not been certain she was not their child.

There was a brief moment when she thought she had identified her true father: Prince Pyetr Mihailovich Volkonsky. It might be the whim of many a little girl to believe that her father was a prince, but the idea had not come to Tamara until she was seventeen, and was no whim. She had been idly rummaging – as she presumed all girls of that age did – through her official father's desk when she had discovered a note from Volkonsky confirming the delivery, that year as every year, of the sum of three thousand roubles for her upkeep. Specifically for her. She couldn't think of anything other than it must have something to do with her parentage.

But if Volkonsky was her father, who was her mother? It was

34

possible that it might still be the woman who had raised her – Yelena Vadimovna Lavrova. Could she and Volkonsky have had an affair? But if that were so, then the annual payments to Valentin Valentinovich would imply that he knew about it, and Tamara could hardly imagine him being happy to raise so obvious a reminder of his own cuckolding. Perhaps she was the daughter of some unknown paramour of Volkonsky's – given to the Lavrovs to raise as their own. That seemed more feasible – and a little more romantic.

But now she knew better. Prince Volkonsky had died two years ago and Tamara had felt no qualms about using her official position to gain access to at least some of his private papers, as kept in the archives in Petersburg. It had taken her six months, and in the end she had found only one letter that made any mention of her – not even by name, simply a reference to 'a girl in Moscow in the care of V. V. Lavrov'. It made clear that Tamara was not his daughter, but that he was providing money for her care on behalf of her father, whom Volkonsky regarded as 'a brother and an unhailed hero of the nation'.

For a little while Tamara had felt quite proud, but her thoughts soon turned to a darker possibility. As far as she could tell – this time from studying Valentin Valentinovich's papers – Volkonsky had first taken an interest in her upbringing when she was five, in 1826. That was just after the Decembrist Uprising, when three thousand soldiers – officers and men – had taken it upon themselves to decide who should be tsar. Thankfully they had failed, but among them had been another Volkonsky – Sergei Grigorovich, related to Pyetr Mihailovich as a cousin and a brother-in-law – who had been a leader of the uprising and had as punishment been sent to Siberia as an exile. Could Pyetr Mihailovich be paying to support his cousin's child? Could Tamara be the offspring of a Decembrist? It was an odious thought, but she had never been able to dismiss it.

But whatever she might think, she evidently did not believe in her heart that either of the Volkonskys was her father, or that Valentin Valentinovich was her father or Yelena Vadimovna her mother. Otherwise, why did she not see their faces in her dreams?

The train had slowed, as it always did, to climb the Valdai Hills. It was the steepest incline on the route from Petersburg to Moscow. The line had only been open for five years, but already there were plans to reroute it – to follow a longer, shallower path around the hills. And already there were plans to use that for propaganda against Tsar Nikolai. The story would be that Nikolai had drawn the route between Saint Petersburg and Moscow himself, using a ruler on the map to find the shortest distance. But his thumb had lain over the edge of the ruler and caused a bump in the line, just at the point of the Valdai Hills. And none of the tsar's cronies had dared make a correction.

She had never met the tsar, but knew people who had, and though he might be resolute in his judgements, he was not a fool. Anyone who had seen the surveyors out, in all weathers, trying to determine the most practical route for the line, would know that Nikolai was in no position to make such detailed decisions. But she also knew that there were many in the government and beyond who would like to make him out to be a despot, even those close to him – perhaps even his own sons.

The train was late already. She smiled to herself. Five years ago she would have had to take a coach on the paved chaussée that ran between the old and the new capitals, and it would have taken days. Now, the journey was less than twenty-four hours, and still everyone complained over a couple of hours' delay – including Tamara.

The train reached the top of the hill and began to speed up again. This wasn't the first time she had taken this journey, nor was it likely to be the last, but today it did have a sense of permanence to it. Today, she was leaving Petersburg and going to live once again in Moscow. Moscow was the town where she had been born – if any of the details of her early life could be believed – and where she had grown up. The Lavrovs still lived there. Petersburg was the town where she had married and where she had borne three children. But it was not a city that could tell her what she needed to know.

Only Moscow – the city of those dim remembrances – could do that. It was where she was most likely to find any records relating to her lineage. She had exhausted the archives of Petersburg and her contacts there, and now she must move on. There was no certainty that she would discover anything, but she had to try – otherwise, what was she for?

She had been fortunate to get work in Moscow that would give her the possibility of access to the great library of letters and documents that lay hidden within the Kremlin. Only a government official would have a chance of gaining entry and for a woman that kind of work was rare. But she had carried out such work – however distasteful – in Petersburg and she doubted whether she would find its nature very much different in the old capital. Besides, she needed the money. After she had married, her father had always forwarded her the payments from Volkonsky – 'a little gift from Papa', as he had called them, as if forgetting that he had admitted where they truly came from – but with Volkonsky's death that had stopped. Tamara wasn't destitute, but a regular income was a blessing.

She stood up. It would be an hour until the next stop, and she desperately needed a cigarette. Even if smoking were allowed on the train, there would be frowns to see a woman partaking of that pleasure in public. She walked down the carriage, opened the door at the end and stepped into the cold night air. A railing surrounded the narrow platform at the end of the wagon, with gates that would allow her to the next one or on to the station when they stopped.

She reached into her reticule and took out a cigarette, lighting it with a match. The junior conductor, standing at his post by the brake, glanced at her, but raised no objection to her breaking the rules. He had probably witnessed it a hundred times. And even if he had thought of calling a gendarme at the next station, he had seen her authority to travel when he looked at her ticket, and would guess that the police would not interfere.

Tamara drew deeply on the cigarette, enjoying the sensation of the smoke clutching at her lungs, and glanced up at the starry sky, then gazed out across the flat, snow-covered countryside as it raced past her. She exhaled. The train – this miracle of Russian modernity, built by American engineers and running on English rails – pressed on into the night, carrying her, for all its faults, at a speed of almost forty versts every hour, towards the truth that she had forever yearned to know.

Tverskaya Street was much as Tamara remembered it, its neat columns of trees naked of leaves and with the February snow clinging to their branches. It was less than a year since she had last visited Moscow, but even in the twelve years since she had made the move to Petersburg, there had not been much that had changed. She crossed Strastnaya Square with its cluster of churches and headed north-west, away from the Kremlin – her first port of call on arriving in the city. The gate and bell tower of the Convent of the Passion, which gave the square its name, were new, though she had seen them slowly rise up over the past few years. Now they were complete, she couldn't say that she admired the rose-pink walls. But Moscow had to be renewed. Her parents – the Lavrovs – often spoke of how things had been before the war, before the fires that had destroyed two-thirds of the city, but back then they too had lived in Petersburg, and knew the old capital only as tourists.

It was dark now, even though it was still early. The snow here in the city had melted under the persistent tread of feet and wheels of traffic, but it would come again soon; the worst of winter was not over. She crossed a side street on the right and knew that the next would be her destination – her new home as well as her new job.

She turned off the main street and into Degtyarny Lane. The building was easy to spot, on the north side, its plaster walls painted a pale lilac, as garish as those of the convent, but in this case seeming entirely appropriate. This part of town had avoided the fires of 1812. Opposite the building stood a little bench, but the street was empty of people. Although it was dark, it was still too early for there to be much likelihood of business. That would change over the next few hours.

Tamara lifted the heavy iron knocker and rapped on the door. Moments later a little wooden flap at eye level, covered with a grille, was opened from the inside and Tamara was faced with a pair of the most scintillating blue eyes. The hatch closed and Tamara heard the sound of bolts being drawn back, then the door opened to reveal a young woman. She was somewhere in her early twenties, the blonde of her hair as perfect as the blue of her eyes. She was a little shorter than Tamara and dressed as though for a party. At her throat was a simple black-velvet choker.

She looked Tamara up and down. 'You must be Tamara Valentinovna,' she said.

'That's right. And you?'

'Raisa Styepanovna,' replied the girl with a smile.

She led Tamara inside.

Tamara had been told, not an hour earlier, that Raisa Styepanovna was the only one of the girls she could fully trust. Her first appointment of the day, direct from stepping off the train, had been inside the Kremlin. In Petersburg, the location of the offices of the Third Section of His Majesty's Own Chancellery was well known; the 'building beside the chain bridge' as it was usually called, the bridge being the one that crossed the Fontanka at the southern end of the Summer Garden. But in Petersburg, the leaders of the Third Section – Count Orlov and General Dubyelt – believed that a secret police force was most effective when it was least secret; that fear was a more effective weapon than surprise. In Moscow the organization was run by Actual State Councillor Yudin and though technically he was subservient to both the count and the general, Moscow was far enough from Petersburg for them to let him do things his way.

And his way, it seemed, involved the utmost secrecy.

Tamara had known only to report to the gate in the Nikolai Tower at the northern end of Red Square. From there the guard had led her into the Kremlin and its chaotic clutter of buildings erected by tsars and tsaritsas through the ages, each determined to make their own mark, none daring to expand beyond the walls established centuries ago. They walked between the Arsenal and the Senate, both relative newcomers to the citadel, and then turned, as if intending to leave via the Trinity Gate. At the last moment, the guard turned again and took them along the inside of the thick defensive outer wall, to a small wooden door, just beside the corner of the newly built Armoury. There a small, precise, balding man named Gribov had met her and escorted her down a short flight of stairs that led into the foundations of the wall itself.

At its bottom, sitting quietly in his subterranean office, she had met Vasiliy Innokyentievich Yudin. He deliberately ignored her arrival – a common enough trick to ensure that a subordinate did not feel at ease. Instead he continued to read the magazine that he clutched close to him, hiding his face from her. Tamara looked at the cover, but could not make sense of the writing. Then she realized it was in the Latin alphabet. The title was *Punch*, though she couldn't guess what language the word came from.

Yudin turned a page and laughed loudly; in doing so, he pretended to notice for the first time that Tamara was there. Without asking who she was, he handed the magazine across to her, pointing to a cartoon at the bottom of the page. It portrayed a man playing a church organ. It took a second look before she realized that the figure portrayed was intended to be Tsar Nikolai. The oddity of it – the point, she presumed, of the joke – was that he was sporting a large pair of bat's wings and, when she looked closely, had pointed ears, again seemingly meant to be suggestive of the animal.

It was clearly some kind of test. She returned the magazine to Yudin, considering her response. 'Why would they portray His Majesty as a bat?' she asked.

'Why indeed?' Yudin was still smirking from whatever humour he had seen in there. 'Makes you wonder if they know something we don't.'

She considered for a moment whether it was appropriate for him to be reading the enemy's propaganda in the middle of a war, but she could easily see that it fell within the purview of the Section.

Yudin indicated that she should sit down. As she complied, he slipped the magazine into a drawer of his desk. 'You come on the highest recommendation of Leontiy Vasilievich,' he said, referring to the man that she had only ever spoken of as General Dubyelt.

The office was dark, dank and old – certainly no recent addition to the complex. Here beneath the surface, windows were meaningless. Yudin's desk was lit by a single oil lamp, and a similar one stood on one of the crowded bookshelves behind him.

Anyone who lived in a city where in the winter there were almost sixteen hours of darkness became accustomed to operating in such gloomy conditions, but few would welcome it as Yudin seemed to have done in his choice of rooms. A strange smell hung in the air that Tamara put down to damp. They must be close to the level of the Moskva here, and she wouldn't have been surprised if the room had been flooded more than once.

'Thank you, Your Excellency,' she replied. Given the role Dubyelt had recommended her for, it was difficult to know whether to take what Yudin had said as a compliment.

Yudin raised his hand with an air of humility. 'We are not in Petersburg now, Tamara Valentinovna. I think we can be a little less formal.'

He was a younger man than she had been expecting. She guessed he was in his late forties, but as she looked at him she realized he might be ten years older than that, or more. It was his hair that confused her. It was of such a deep and uniform shade of black that it was quite obviously dyed, in a way that suggested a much older man. But the tone of his skin was not that of a man with greying hair. He was clean-shaven – as the law dictated for a civilian – and had gone to the trouble of dyeing his eyebrows the same dark hue. Only his eyelashes were pale, glittering as they caught the lamplight.

He picked up a sheet of paper from his desk and glanced at it. 'Some very impressive names,' he said. 'And some impressive information that you've wheedled out of them.'

'Men think power makes them attractive, and powerful men have secrets.'

'And how can they demonstrate that they have secrets without whispering a few of them to you?'

'That's how it works,' she said blankly, trying to avoid any possibility of him thinking she might enjoy her work.

'Do you find it attractive?' Yudin asked, as if making small talk. 'Power?'

She had heard it all before. All her superiors – all of them men – had a fascination for what drove her, unable to believe that her work was to her as monotonous as theirs was to them; a necessity in order to live. Even so, she thought about his question for a moment. The image of her husband, Vitya, came to her mind and she felt her face redden. It would not be noticed in the darkness. 'Not that kind of power,' she replied.

Still he persisted. 'You were certainly in a position to choose to sleep with these men. You must have found them in some way attractive.'

He understood nothing; nor should she have expected him to. 'General Dubyelt led me to believe that my role here would be somewhat different,' she said.

'He did?'

Yudin knew it perfectly well. Tamara had seen the letter that Dubyelt had sent him, but clearly he wanted to hear how Tamara would describe her work.

'I'm not young any more, Vasiliy Innokyentievich.'

'You're still very attractive.' He said it as though he had read the information in her file.

'He told me I'd be in charge,' she said firmly. There had always been the possibility that the nature of her work might change by the time she got to Moscow. If it had, there was not much she could do about it, but now was her best chance to try.

'An officer, rather than a foot soldier?' suggested Yudin.

'If you like. He said it was a new venture in Moscow; that a woman would be able to manage things less conspicuously.'

Yudin nodded slowly. 'We've acquired a house in the north of the city. It's an established bordello – been going since before the war.' He stopped for a moment. 'The Patriotic War, I mean.' While the distinction between the current war and that of 1812 might have been necessary, Tamara couldn't help but note the implication that the current war was in some way less than patriotic. 'The former owner got into some legal trouble,' continued Yudin, 'and we took the establishment off his hands. It has a very respectable clientele.' He picked up another list of names and handed it to her. 'Just the sort of men you like to . . . rub shoulders with.'

'So the girls there know what they're doing?'

'Most of them were there when we took over. They know one side of the job – how to get their man to bed – but they're less acquainted with the other – how to get him to talk once he's there.'

'So I'm to teach them everything I know?'

Yudin shrugged. 'You're in complete control – at least on a day-to-day basis. You'll have your own rooms there and you'll run the place as you see fit. All I want from you is regular information.'

Information was all that interested Tamara – though not of the kind that Yudin sought to learn from sweaty generals and libidinous privy councillors. But it was too soon to mention her interest in the archives. She felt a sense of relief washing over her at the fact that Yudin's view of her job matched Dubyelt's, and she wasn't going to push her luck.

'About anything in particular?' she asked.

'Broadly, there are three categories. Foreigners, for a start. They may well be wary, and of course there are not many English or French around just now, but it would be useful to know which way Austria is going to jump. Among our own people there are two sorts. Some you've been dealing with already: soldiers and ministers who just talk too much. We need to know which of them are loose-lipped and put a stop to it.' He paused. 'And finally there are those who tell us things that we don't know.'

'Such as?' Tamara could already guess what he was talking about.

'It's been almost thirty years since the Decembrists were rounded up. That's long enough for people to start to forget. You remember '48?'

Tamara's eyes flashed at him. She wondered how he could know, how he could be so cruel, but then realized that the year 1848 meant to him, to most of the world, something very different from what it did to her. She nodded.

'Half of Europe went mad with revolution,' he continued. 'It didn't happen here, but it might have. That's our biggest fear. That's what I want you to listen out for. Even within our own government there may be revolutionary voices. Perhaps even in this department.'

'So I report only to you?'

'Has Leontiy Vasilievich told you otherwise?'

Tamara shrugged. Dubyelt had said nothing on the subject, but she knew well enough the internal politics of the Section to understand that it was best to keep everybody guessing.

'Then I won't contradict him,' said Yudin. He pushed an envelope towards her. 'Here are details of the place and its employees. The only other one of our people in there is Raisa Styepanovna Tokoryeva. You can speak freely to her, but she's under your command.'

He said nothing more and Tamara took it that the interview was at an end. She stood up to leave. 'Thank you, Vasiliy Innokyentievich,' she said. 'I'll be in touch.'

She was almost at the door when he spoke again. 'Oh, and you'll need this.'

She turned. His arm was held out across the desk, proffering a sheet of paper – a yellow sheet of paper. She took it from him, but did not need to look closely to see what it was: the yellow ticket that identified a woman formally as a prostitute. She guessed that one of the girls had not yet been issued with it; perhaps Raisa Styepanovna.

'Who's it for?' she asked.

Yudin said nothing, but nodded his head towards the ticket. Tamara looked. The name on it was her own: Tamara Valentinovna Komarova. She had never needed such a thing before, despite meriting it, but this made things seem official. Yudin had been toying with her earlier. She looked questioningly at him.

'Even senior officers have to pitch in with the troops sometimes,' he said, 'particularly in time of war.'

She cursed herself for thinking things might be any different, then turned and left.

CHAPTER II

DMITRY FELT ENTOMBED. THE SNOW SURROUNDED HIM, filling his nostrils, lashing against his eyes and inveigling its way between his lips. It was as if he had been buried in it, but he had not. It was merely a flurry within a storm that would soon die down again and then he would be able to see. Somewhere out there in front of him, across the river, stood the enemy. It might be the French, or the British, or the Turks. It could even be the damned Sardinians, now that they'd chosen to join in, sucking up to the French in the hope of support in their own war. Dmitry could not see to tell. He couldn't even see the river, but he knew it was there.

'Major Danilov!'

Dmitry turned. A young *poruchik* was standing beside him, a dispatch clutched in his gloved hand. Dmitry could only guess how the youth had managed to find him in the blizzard. He took the paper from him and tried to read it, holding it away from him so that he could focus. The driving snow flickered between his eyes and the scrawled writing, but it was not difficult to make out. There were only two words.

Save ammunition.

Dmitry screwed the paper into a ball and was about to throw it to the ground when he thought better of it. He slipped it into his pocket. What would the French make of it if they found orders like that?

'Any reply, sir?'

Dmitry smiled to himself. Had he been both wittier and more reckless he might have sent a response that expressed his true

45

feelings. 'No reply,' he said. The *poruchik* saluted and dashed away, disappearing in an instant behind sheets of falling snow.

It was the enemy's first assault of the year, and a foolish one. The allied lines were to the south of Sevastopol, stretching inland from the coast. The city was their target, but it was well if hastily defended. Dividing it like a jagged wound was the harbour, wherein were anchored the remains of the Black Sea fleet – the whole reason that the British and French were here. The harbour was fed by the Chernaya river, continuing the natural line of defence out to the east. To cross it was the enemy's best hope of encircling the city. But they had chosen the wrong day to attempt it.

Dmitry mounted his horse and trotted down the Russian lines. The wind had dropped, and although the snow was still falling, it was now possible to see a little further, almost to the far side of the river. The enemy weren't making much progress. Their attack had begun with a bombardment. The intent had been to drive the Russians back from the north bank of the river, but while it had achieved that goal, it had also warned them of the impending advance. Some might question why Dmitry was even here. He was a staff officer, deemed too senior in more senses than one for service in the field; it was an assessment that sickened him, and when the attack had come he'd been among the first into action. He had the desire neither to die nor to kill – but either was better than remaining at headquarters, reading reports of both.

He didn't bother to forward the orders he had been given. The men knew that ammunition was short as well as he did, and knew that it was down to the rotten supply lines from Moscow. Even the enemy, sailing through the Mediterranean, could get supplies quicker than the Russians. And now the English had built a railway up from the docks at Balaklava. There were no locomotives for it yet – the wagons were pulled by horses – but it meant that food, ammunition and even artillery could come all the way from the factories of England to the red-coated British infantrymen on the front line without ever travelling along anything so primitive as a road. If Tsar Nikolai had chosen to build a railway from Moscow to Sevastopol, or Simferopol or even Odessa, then the enemy wouldn't have got a toehold on the peninsula. But the line from Moscow to Petersburg had more prestige – and that's what mattered to a tsar.

On the far riverbank Dmitry could just see French sappers trying to control the segmented pontoon bridges that they hoped would allow their fellow troops to march straight across. They made easy targets, but the weather was as effective a hindrance to them as any bullet. Even as he watched, one of the ropes that they were heaving on broke loose, whipping across the pontoon and knocking a man into the river. His comrades reached down for him, but then the blizzard blew up again and Dmitry could see no more. He remembered his father's stories of the Battle of the Berezina, when Napoleon had desperately organized the bridging of the river so that he could lead his remaining troops out of Russia. His father had not attempted to hide his admiration for the sappers then, who stood chest deep in the freezing water, constantly shoring up the construction they had built from scavenged wood. But Dmitry could not feel a similar sympathy for his enemy. They at least came here by choice, whereas the Russian soldiers – the men, if not the officers – were serfs; owned either by the tsar or by other rich nobles and obliged to do their masters' bidding, be it to die of exhaustion toiling in the cornfield or to die from a bullet in the field of battle.

'Boat coming!'

Dmitry could not tell which eagle-eyed spotter had made the call, but as he looked out over the river, the prow of a landing craft began to emerge from the cascading snow. Dmitry was about to shout an instruction, but the captain of the company beat him to it.

'Muskets only!' he shouted. 'Fire at will!'

'Hold fire!' Dmitry countermanded instantly, raising his hand in the air. 'Let them get close.'

The captain corrected his instructions without the slightest complaint, just as Dmitry would have – each of them was merely a link in the chain of command. The corrected order was passed down the line. The men on the boat began to fire, and a number of the Russian infantrymen fell. Dmitry felt a bullet whistle past close to his ear and was surprised that he did not flinch. At least half the British and almost as many of the French had *shtutser*s,

47

which reloaded faster and were more accurate than muskets. In the Russian army, they were almost non-existent. Dmitry remembered the discussions about introducing them, decades before, and recalled one senior officer's opinion that faster-loading guns would only encourage the men to use up more ammunition instead of relying on their bayonets. That point of view had won out. It was the same attitude that encouraged men to deliberately loosen the ramrod and the keeper-rings on their muskets so that they rattled during drill. It was a fine thing for five hundred guns to sound together in perfect time on the parade ground, another to see that not one of them could hit a man in the field.

Still Dmitry held his hand in the air, like the conductor of some orchestra, holding off for as long as possible the delicious resolution of a suspended chord. When the boat was close enough – close enough for the men on board to dream that their assault might be successful – he dropped his hand, and accompanied the motion with a shout of 'Fire!' Again the order was echoed down the line, followed eagerly by the report of gunfire. At that range, not even a Russian musket could miss its mark – and there were far more muskets than there had been men on the boat.

With a slight thump, the vessel hit the northern bank of the river, but no one was able to disembark. They were fools to have attempted a landing in this weather. For all his faults, Tsar Nikolai understood how Russia fought a war and had expressed it very clearly. 'Russia has two generals in whom she can confide – Generals *Janvier* and *Février*.' It was true, even as far south as this. It was the Russian winter that had defeated Napoleon, and the same winter that, so far, was holding off this new French assault. But January was over, and February was the shortest month, and then there would be ten more when the Russians would have to fight alone, without the assistance of Nikolai's two favourite generals.

Another shout came from further down the line. Dmitry spurred his horse and rode on to see what was happening. This time it was a minor success by the pontoniers – they had managed to lash together two sections of a bridge, spanning perhaps a tenth of the total width of the river. Russian artillery fire quickly saw off the attack, destroying in seconds the work of many hours, along with most of the workers. Dmitry sat and watched impassively. The snow was stopping now, but it had done its work. It would soon be dark, and the enemy would not attack at night. Sevastopol was safe; until tomorrow.

The storm had settled down overnight and the following day was calm and clear, though it was still cold and the ground remained blanketed in snow. There had been no word of a further attempt to cross the river – the enemy had lost enough men and equipment to make them think twice about trying that route of attack again. Today Dmitry was off duty, back in the centre of the city. He sat in the mess at the Nikolai Barracks, trying to write a letter.

Dear Papa,

That was as far as he got. He knew precisely what he wanted to express. The problem was he had written the same thing in a hundred different ways before, and always with the same response: no response at all. He rested his head back against the chair and tried not to think too hard. As ever, when he relaxed, music came to him. It had been so since he was a child, whole orchestras playing in his head, music that was familiar and yet strange. The harmony was harmony that he knew. The rhythms and counterpoints were all of a kind that would be accepted as correct by a professor of music, though perhaps frowned upon for being a little too avant-garde. But it was all original. Certainly Dmitry could summon up a well-known tune, but when he simply let the music flow through him, it was a creation of his own, something that neither he nor anyone else had ever heard before. In the whole of his forty-seven years, he didn't believe it had ever repeated itself. But neither in that time had he ever managed to write a single note of it down on paper.

Perhaps one day it would happen, but he wouldn't attempt to force it. Today it was with words that he was trying to express himself. The last time he had heard from his father had been in 1847. Neither of them had corresponded with enormous frequency, but it had been common for there to be one or two letters in each direction every year. Of course, 1848 had its significance. That was the year Dmitry's mother had died. Many people in Petersburg had died, when both famine and cholera had struck the city. Marfa Mihailovna had been wealthy enough to have no concern over the famine, but disease was no respecter of status. Dmitry had not even been at home to comfort her, or to bury her.

But it was hard to see why that should have stopped Dmitry's father from writing. Marfa had not been his wife in any real sense for years. It was his mistress, Domnikiia Semyonovna, who had followed him into exile after his participation in the Decembrist Uprising, thirty years before. Dmitry had loved his father for his stance against the tsar, but hated him for choosing his lover over his wife. But as the years had passed, the heroism of the former had eclipsed the human failing of the latter. And in truth it was Marfa who had made the choice, in not following her husband to Siberia. Long before her death she had forgiven her husband his infidelity, and urged Dmitry to do the same.

And so Aleksei's distant silence made even less sense. There was the possibility that it was down to censorship. Dmitry was well aware that the Third Section read all letters to and from exiles; and a few more besides, he would guess. But he'd always been careful not to write anything that would cause them to be intercepted, and his father had been wise enough to do the same. Neither of them ever made mention of military matters, or politics, or mentioned Tsar Nikolai without expressing the deepest and sincerest affection for him – and without any hint of irony.

Dmitry looked down at the paper again, but still could not think of a way to express himself. It was simple enough; he just needed to say, 'Please write, however little you put, however you wish to insult me, just to let me know you're alive.' But Dmitry already knew his father was alive. If he had died, Dmitry would have been informed. He knew other sons of Decembrist exiles who had been. By his reckoning, there could only be a score or so of them left alive – but his father was undoubtedly one of them.

He tried to stop thinking and listen again to the music in his head, in the hope that it would help him. Instead, all he heard was a vaguely familiar gypsy melody, played on the mess's out-of-tune piano. He did not need to look round to know that Prince Galtsin had come into the room and gone straight to the instrument. The rivalry between them was unspoken. Dmitry was convinced he was the better pianist, but Galtsin had the more popular repertoire; around here at least. Dmitry had seen the appeal of peasant music in his youth, but as he had grown older it had struck him as increasingly trivial. But Dmitry's tastes did not chime with those of the common – or even the noble – soldier. He found his playing more in favour among the ladies of Saint Petersburg.

Eventually Galtsin finished the piece and a round of applause broke out through the mess. '*Bis*! *Bis*!' cried a voice that Dmitry did not recognize, but he did not look round for fear that he might seem to agree with the sentiment.

'Perhaps Mitka would like to play for us,' said Galtsin, raising his voice to be sure Dmitry would hear him.

'The regiment seems spoilt for talent,' said the unknown voice.

'Come on, Mitka,' said Galtsin. 'You know you want to.'

Dmitry stood and turned, his eyes immediately fixing on the figure standing beside Galtsin at the piano. It was a naval lieutenant of perhaps thirty-five years. What many would immediately note in him was his height, but as Dmitry approached, he realized that their eyes were on the same level. Dmitry was a tall man, and this newcomer matched him exactly. What struck Dmitry was his leanness. He was thin, but not skinny, as though every limb was composed solely of muscle, from what Dmitry could judge through the uniform. Certainly on his neck and jaw the flesh was sculpted as though part of some ancient statue.

'Anatoliy Vladimirovich Tyeplov,' said Galtsin, introducing them. 'Dmitry Alekseevich Danilov.'

They shook hands. Tyeplov's grip was as firm as Dmitry had expected.

'Danilov?' said Tyeplov. 'Son of Aleksei . . .'

'Son of Aleksei Ivanovich Danilov,' Dmitry completed. 'The Decembrist.' Nobody had ever held Dmitry's father's actions against him. For all his faults, the tsar had been scrupulous in announcing that no stain should attach itself to the innocent relatives of any of the conspirators, however close the relationship might be.

'Of course,' said Tyeplov happily. 'I knew I'd heard the name somewhere.' As he spoke, he fiddled with the fingers of his left hand, as if toying with a ring that he evidently did not possess.

'Play for us,' he added, indicating the piano as Galtsin vacated the seat.

Dmitry sat down and considered. He was not going to pander to the crowd, as Galtsin had. There was one composer whom Dmitry loved above all others, and over whose early death he still sometimes felt the desire to weep. The officers in the mess would be bored with his work, if they knew enough to recognize Dmitry's obsession. Even so, Chopin it would be. But what piece? He let his hands fall to the keyboard, his left little finger and right thumb falling on two low Cs, an octave apart. Then his hands wandered upwards over the keys, always with the same interval between them, before the piece settled into the slow, sublime six-four of Chopin's first ballade.

He lost himself in the music, enjoying the fast, complex arpeggios and the huge, understated main theme, letting it flow into him as well as out of him. The music seemed to tell him a story of mystery and joy, of adversity and victory, that he could never quite remember once it had ended, like the details of a dream. It was a story of which he was the narrator, but as with his own music, he could not both create it and consume it at the same time. He felt as though he had scarcely begun when he heard that the music had come to an end. His hands were still, sustaining the final low Gs. He breathed deeply. He had lost any sense of time, but he knew that the piece usually took him about ten minutes. He resisted the urge to move on to the second ballade, hearing the pa-pom, pa-pom of its opening notes only in his head. Galtsin was standing over on the far side of the room with a glass of vodka in his hand, chatting in a low voice. Others were displaying the minimum of polite interest that they could get away with.

Only Tyeplov remained, leaning on the piano and staring at Dmitry with a look of surprised rapture that would only be expected from a man who was listening to Chopin for the first time in his entire life.

Dmitry paced angrily through the slush-filled streets of Sevastopol. Winter was departing, sooner than he had expected, but then he was used to the weather in Petersburg, far to the north. When the siege had first begun, the previous autumn, he had wondered whether in winter the harbour itself might freeze over, making the journey between the north and south of the city easier. But it was a foolish idea, now he knew the climate. He'd even imagined the possibility that if the harbour did freeze then the enemy might be able to march across its icy surface and into the city. He'd soon dismissed the fear. A few well-aimed cannonballs would break up the ice and send the troops fleeing back to land.

His mind went back, as so often, to 14 December 1825. He'd not seen it but he had heard how many of the fleeing rebels ran out on to the frozen Neva to escape, only for Nikolai to order just the same tactics. The ice over the river was broken into pieces, and many brave men froze or drowned. For months Dmitry had believed that his closest friend had thus perished. Vasiliy Denisovich Makarov had been like a second father to Dmitry, often understanding him better than his own father did. After the uprising Vasiliy had gone into hiding and written to both Dmitry and his mother from Prussia. And when he finally returned to his homeland, it had been under a different name: Vasiliy Innokyentievich Yudin. Tsar Nikolai had a long memory, and was not likely to forgive anyone who could be identified as having stood in Senate Square that day. Dmitry was lucky not to have been so identified – he had both his father and Yudin to thank for it, but in saving him, they had made him a coward.

Today Dmitry was heading to the Severnaya – the northern part of Sevastopol, a region of the city which held no real danger, not for the moment. When the Allies had first landed, they had come at Sevastopol from the north, but believed the defences were too strong and so circled round to the south, only to be met by Lieutenant-Colonel Totleben's improvised but utterly effective fortifications. Now, it was Russian troops that occupied the territory here and all the way to the isthmus at Perekop, the narrow link to the mainland. But things could change.

There were many boats waiting on the harbour shore, eager to transport both soldiers and civilians across to the north. Dmitry stepped into the nearest and sat down on the thwart. Without a word, the oarsman cast off and began the slow, short journey. There had been talk of assembling a pontoon bridge to make the crossing easier, but nothing had come of it yet. There was more than one general who suspected the men would fight with greater bravery if they knew there was no prospect of retreat. Even so, desertions were commonplace, as was demonstrated by Dmitry's duty today.

The water was calm, and the only sound was that of the oars as they dipped in and out of it. It was a moment for Dmitry to relax. He looked out across the water. To his right the harbour split. The main part – the Sea Harbour – stretched out east, while pointing south there was a smaller branch known as the Military Harbour. The British, so he had heard, called it the Man-of-War Harbour.

But it was to the west that the real interest lay. Out to sea, only versts away, the British and French fleets stood, waiting. It was from them that the real threat came; their guns that had caused the severest damage during the first bombardment back in October. There were big guns on land too, but they were as nothing compared to what the ships had. The fleet had remained quiet, mostly, for months now, but in the spring they'd be heard again. At least they couldn't simply sail into the harbour and land marines. Two narrow strips of white, breaking waves stretching across the water were testimony to that, one only a little way from the dinghy, the other at the very boundary between the harbour and the Black Sea.

The breakers gave only a clue to what lay beneath – sunken ships, anything that the navy had been able to get its hands on to float out there and scupper. Occasionally, when the sea was calm, as today, a mast or the line of a bow could just be seen breaking surface, enough to act as a reminder that to sail into the harbour would result in serious if not terminal damage to any craft that attempted it.

Dmitry stepped on to the northern shore, handing the ferryman a few copecks for his trouble, then continued on foot towards the Star Fort. This was the other thing that kept the enemy fleets out of the harbour, and the reason that their armies had chosen to attack from the south. At a guess the building occupied almost a quarter of the entire Severnaya; an eight-pointed star of solid stone and brick – far more forbidding than any of the rushed fortifications in the south. It loomed out over the land and the harbour itself, threatening the annihilation of any force that dared to approach from the north or from the sea. But it could do no more than threaten. The structure was almost forty years old; under-maintained, undermanned and under-gunned. If the Allies had chosen to attack, they would have occupied the Severnaya within days, but thankfully the fort's reputation had deterred them – that and a little disinformation spread through the local populace.

Dmitry followed the ramparts around anticlockwise, noting that what had seemed imposing at a distance was so obviously decrepit now he was close. He came to the gate. 'Major Danilov,' he said to the guard. 'Here to see Captain Shulgin.'

It took some time to track down Shulgin. When he eventually arrived, he seemed flustered. Dmitry noticed how dirty his hands were, with soil under his fingernails. He led Dmitry across to the northern corner of the fort.

'So you've had a couple of desertions, Captain,' said Dmitry as they walked.

'I think the word I used in my report was "disappearances".'

'It amounts to the same thing.'

'Perhaps among your men, Major,' snapped Shulgin, seeming to forget the difference in their ranks, 'but not mine. These were engineers – some of the best-trained men in the army. They're not the sort to absent themselves at the first whiff of cannon smoke.' Dmitry could only admire the captain's faith in his men, but he knew it was misplaced. He knew that fear could affect any man – some just learned to hide it better than others.

They had come to a wooden doorway on the inside of the thick outer wall of the fort which towered above them, fragile and decaying. The sense that it might topple inwards and crush them was not entirely fanciful. Shulgin opened the door and indicated that Dmitry should lead the way. Inside, a narrow flight of wooden steps led down within the wall.

'Anyway,' continued the captain as they descended, 'they're not absent any more.'

'But I don't suppose I'd be here if they'd been discovered safe and sound.'

'No,' was Shulgin's brief response.

At the bottom of the steps a low tunnel headed north, out of the Star Fort. Even Shulgin had to stoop, and Dmitry was virtually bowing. He felt instantly trapped. In general he had no fear of enclosed spaces, unless the enclosure came from above as it did now, giving him an unnerving sense of being buried. The tunnel was built like a mineshaft, with walls of loose earth and the fewest possible boards of wood used to shore up the sides and roof. He had been inside similar earthworks beneath the bastions.

'Why are you building this?' he asked.

'Partly in the hope of undermining the enemy – more so we can listen out for them digging to undermine us.'

Dmitry had been in the army quite long enough to know that much. He tried not to show his annoyance. 'I mean why here? The enemy's nowhere near.'

'Oh, we dug this long before we knew where the French would attack,' explained Shulgin. 'And once they're dug, we have to maintain them.'

'Or else this happens?'

'Exactly.'

They had been forced to halt. In front of them the tunnel was blocked by a pile of earth and rocks. Such clear evidence of how real his fears of entombment could become made Dmitry even more uneasy, but also revealed just how close to the surface they were. The tallow lamps that had lit their way so far now became quite unnecessary as daylight shone through the gaping hole that the cave-in had created. Fresh air blew on Dmitry's face. He breathed deeply and relaxed, though he still felt the oppression of the tunnel's roof, undamaged above where he stood, forcing him to bend.

Two sappers – as many as could be fitted into the narrow space – were digging at the pile of debris, and Dmitry could already see what lay within. The pink hand and forearm of a man lolled incongruously from the dark earth.

'So they were killed when the tunnel collapsed,' said Dmitry, squatting down so that at least his torso could be upright.

'I think not,' said Shulgin. 'They'd already been missing two days when it happened.'

'Are you sure it's them?'

Shulgin shouted at one of the sappers, who stopped his work and pulled back a tarpaulin that was draped at the edge of the mound. Beneath it lay the upper half of a soldier's body – the remainder still buried. The figure revealed beneath the tarpaulin was caked in mud, but enough had been cleaned away from his face to make his identity clear to anyone who knew him.

'So they deserted and hid down here,' suggested Dmitry, 'and then the cave-in got them.' A better fate than to be shot by their own comrades, as Dmitry would have been obliged to command.

'There was a man working down here when it happened. He got away, thank God. He swears there was no one else here.'

Shulgin gazed up at the hole in the ceiling. Dmitry looked too, judging how far it was to the surface.

'They fell through?' he asked.

'Then they'd be on top.'

Dmitry thought for a moment, though only one conclusion remained. 'So the bodies had been buried, just above the tunnel.'

'I reckon. Whoever did it wouldn't have expected them to be found for years – and then they'd just be taken for casualties.'

Suddenly the two sappers stepped back, standing up as best they were able. Another arm had been revealed. The men took hold of one limb each and hauled at the body. Slowly at first and then with a sudden collapse as the earth around it gave way, the corpse spilled out. Dmitry took a step back, fearful of further damage to the tunnel and another cave-in, but all seemed steady.

The body lay on its back on the mound of earth, its feet still buried in the loose soil. The arms lazed on either side of the head, where the sappers had dropped them, as if the dead man were surrendering. Dmitry looked into the mud-covered, upside-down face, out of which a pair of blue eyes, sparkling and clean, gazed back.

Water splashed on to the face and Shulgin's hand began to rub the dirt from it, like a brutal nanny cleaning up her charge ready for tea. When this face was as clean as the other one, Shulgin stopped and stared, twisting his head to see it the right way up.

'That's him,' said Shulgin. There was nothing in his voice to suggest that he'd ever doubted it.

'What killed them?' asked Dmitry.

Shulgin shrugged.

Dmitry reached out and took the bucket of water that Shulgin had used to clean the man's face. He tipped more over the chest and neck and began to clean off the rest of the mud, trying to show a little more deference than had Shulgin, but knowing that circumstances could give the dead man no great hope of dignity. Around the throat the encrustation of dirt was particularly thick. Dmitry managed to get his fingernails beneath – silently acknowledging the reason for Shulgin's dirty hands – and pulled it away. It came easily, only to reveal another layer of mud.

Dmitry stared at what he saw, and then looked up at Shulgin, whose face revealed the same confusion that Dmitry felt. The surface of the mud on the man's neck, smoothed by Dmitry's fingertips, was now concave, dipping below the level at which the skin should show – and yet no skin was visible. Dmitry reached forward again and scraped at the soil with his fingers, pulling more away as though cleaning out a crevice in a rock, except that the distinction between earth and rock would have been easier to discern than that between earth and flesh. Shulgin poured on the remainder of the bucket of water, washing all but the last few grains of dirt away.

Dmitry stood up. His head bumped slightly against the ceiling, but it would take more than that to distract him from what he was looking at.

'My God!' hissed Shulgin. Dmitry remained silent. 'Have you ever seen anything like that before?'

Dmitry had already asked himself that question. In his mind he was back in a street in Moscow, outside the Maly Theatre, thirty years before. A dead soldier lay in a pool of his own blood, the pathetic victim of a creature that Dmitry had hoped could be left in the past. Today only traces of blood were visible, mingled with the mud that they had washed away. Dmitry doubted whether this time very much of it had been allowed to go to waste. The wound was of the same nature as back then, but far, far deeper. Still flecked with dirt, torn vein and sinew and even bone could be clearly seen in the deep laceration beneath the chin, ensuring that neither Dmitry nor Shulgin could doubt what had happened.

Half the man's throat had been torn away.

CHAPTER III

IT WAS A MATTER OF BLOOD – ROMANOV BLOOD. IT HAD BEEN FOR the past 143 years.

Yudin stared across his desk at Raisa Styepanovna. She knew none of it; he had been careful to see to that. But he had known about it for – what? – forty-three of those years, ever since Zmyeevich had explained it all to him before sending him out into Russia to do his will.

Zmyeevich. Yudin felt a thrill of fear course through him just at the thought of the great vampire. Once they had been allies – though neither had seen things as being quite on equal terms. Even then, Yudin had been afraid; afraid that he might take a step too far, either deliberately or in error, and find himself facing the wrath of a creature that had learned to kill – learned to enjoy killing – centuries before Yudin had even been born. Eventually, inevitably, their alliance had come to an end, and Yudin had barely escaped with his life. But escape he had, defeating Zmyeevich if only for a moment. And that gave him hope that if it came to it, he might defeat him again. And more than that, he knew Zmyeevich's secret.

Zmyeevich had been there 143 years before, in 1712, as had Tsar Pyotr – Pyotr the Great. It was the year Petersburg became the capital of Russia. The two of them had done a deal. Yudin had heard the story from both sides, from Zmyeevich and from the Romanovs – the descendants of Pyotr – and he believed neither of them, not fully. But the two had come to some sort of arrangement.

However they liked to dress it up, Pyotr had agreed to join

59

with Zmyeevich as one of his own kind, a *voordalak* that lived by night and feasted on blood. But Pyotr had tricked Zmyeevich and only gone halfway with the process, gaining from Zmyeevich his vast knowledge, but not falling under his power.

But Zmyeevich had taken blood from Pyotr and that gave him hope, hope that if a Romanov of any generation could be persuaded to drink Zmyeevich's own blood and then to die with it still in his body, the transformation begun with Pyotr would be complete. That Romanov would be reborn as a vampire and would be subject to Zmyeevich's will. And if that Romanov were himself tsar, then the whole of Russia would be Zmyeevich's plaything.

Raisa knew little, but she had her part in it. What she had just handed to him, tiny though it was, might make all the difference between success and failure. Yudin studied her in the dim light of his underground office, but she turned away from him to gaze, as she always did, into one dark corner of the room. There stood a large wooden chest of map drawers. On top of it was an item that neither of them could see, but both knew was there. A dark blanket was draped over it, to prevent accidents.

Yudin had known Raisa for many years, more years than the unenlightened observer might think possible for a woman of her evident youth. When they had first met, in 1818, she had been just seventeen years old, the fifth daughter and eighth child of a Kievan prince. He had not gone by the name of Yudin then. When they were first introduced he had been Vasiliy Denisovich Makarov.

After they had become friends and – briefly – lovers he had told her his true name, Richard Llywelyn Cain, though by then she knew him well enough to doubt the truth of anything he told her. More recently she had been happy to accept that he had, for the time being, become Vasiliy Innokyentievich Yudin. The one name that she had never associated with him was that for which, of all his pseudonyms, he had the most affection – the name of Iuda.

Sadly, he knew of no country on Earth where he could pass himself off with the name of Christ's betrayer and not raise an eyebrow – no country in Christendom at least. Perhaps one day he would travel to the orient, but in Russia, to call himself Yudin was the closest he could safely come to it. The name Iuda had been a deliberately obvious alias when he had worked as one of a group of twelve vampires who, disguised as mercenaries and assuming the names of Christ's apostles, had come to Russia to feed on the remnants of Napoleon's invading army, although Yudin had had his own agenda. That had been a long time ago – before he had ever met Raisa Styepanovna. Before he himself had become a *voordalak*.

'How did you get this?' he asked, gazing down at the glass vial cupped in his hand. It was small, perhaps the size of the top two joints of his middle finger, and the dark liquid that flowed from one end to the other as he moved his hand scarcely half filled it. But that did not matter – it was a question of quality, not quantity, and this blood was of the highest quality imaginable. It excited him just to know that it rested in his palm. This was Romanov blood.

'He let me kiss him,' she said lightly, still looking at the blanket as if she could see what lay beneath.

'The tsarevich let you kiss him? As simple as that?'

She turned her head to look at him. 'He's a goat – they all are. He expected more.'

'Did he get it?'

'Not after I'd taken what I wanted. Anyway, he had a party to get back to.'

'He didn't notice?' Yudin again looked at the vial and at Aleksandr's blood within.

'Perhaps later. I took it from his lip. They never feel it, do they?'

Yudin had carried out many experiments to determine that. To say 'never' was an overstatement, but a *voordalak* could secrete a substance that numbed its victim to the superficial pain. For himself, he had never had the desire to save anyone pain; neither had Raisa. But in this case it was a necessary concession.

'How much did you take for yourself?' he asked.

'About twice as much again.' She turned her head towards him and gave a little pout. 'I have my needs too,' she said.

It was easy to understand how Aleksandr had been tempted by her, even though any such emotion was lost to Yudin. The party had been given by the American ambassador in Petersburg. There had been no problem for Yudin in procuring an invitation for Raisa. It wasn't certain that she'd be able to get anywhere near the tsarevich, but she'd clearly proved her abilities. That little vial of blood was the result. He slipped it into a drawer of his desk.

'What do you make of Tamara Valentinovna?' he asked, changing the subject.

She turned back to the desk, sitting opposite him. 'I despise her.'

'Is that wise?'

'Oh, she doesn't know.' Raisa was a little more enthusiastic now, then switched to a tone of mockery. 'She thinks we're friends.'

'Keep it that way.'

'For how long?'

Yudin considered, but he had no answer. His plans were not yet fully formulated. 'For the time being,' was the best reply he could offer. 'And then, she can be yours. They all can, if you want them.'

Raisa's eyes grew distant. Yudin could guess what she was thinking, and the idea aroused him just as it must have done her. Young blood was always to be relished, and Raisa worked and lived in a house that brimmed with it. Images of death and terror and blood-smeared flesh washed through his mind, delighting him. Perhaps, when the time came, he would not let Raisa have them to herself. Perhaps he would make her share.

'You pretend you're different, but you're not,' said Raisa, both guessing and interrupting his thoughts. There was no joining of their minds as there would have been if one had created the other, but after so many years she understood him better than he found comfortable.

He smiled slightly. 'You and I are both different. That's why we're alive.'

'What do you know of her?' asked Raisa.

'Tamara Valentinovna?' He skimmed through the files on his desk and found Tamara's, although he could remember perfectly well the basic information it conveyed. 'Born in Moscow in 1821. Daughter of Valentin Valentinovich Lavrov – a cloth merchant – and Yelena Vadimovna. Married. Moved to Petersburg. Had children. Began affairs with *numerous* gentlemen of varying nobility. One of them was a senior figure within the Third Section – not myself, I hasten to add – and so we were soon making good use of her; just as all those others had been. Recently she requested a move to Moscow . . .'

'Enough!' said Raisa abruptly.

'You asked.'

She stood and walked back over to the chest, reaching out her hand to pull off the blanket. As she grasped it she paused, looking back towards Yudin. 'Aren't you going to stop me?' she asked.

Yudin shrugged.

She tugged at the cloth and it fell to the floor, revealing a mirror. There was nothing special about it. The frame was of gilded wood. Its three sections were joined with hinges, like a triptych. It would grace any lady's dressing table – as once it had.

> 'Spieglein, Spieglein an der Wand,
> 'Wer ist die Schönste im ganzen Land?'

Yudin smirked as he spoke the words of the Grimms' fairy tale. It was utterly apposite, as Raisa gazed into the mirror, searching for her lost beauty. But it was not original. He must have uttered the words a hundred times, on every occasion he caught her standing despondently in front of a looking glass, which was often. He hated to repeat himself, but he knew how much it annoyed her, so he continued to say it.

She ignored him, or at least put on a good show of doing so. He got out of his chair and stood behind her, gazing like her into the glass. The windowless room was lit only by lamplight, but still every detail could be seen. His desk, his chair, the shelves upon shelves of books, the stairs up to the world outside, the doorway down to what lay below. The only thing missing was any trace of either him or Raisa.

'You promised me,' she said.

'I'll keep my promise,' he replied – and he meant it, though he knew she had little basis for believing him.

'When?'

'When I know how.'

'It's been thirty years.' Her voice bore the weariness of those years. 'Thirty years in which I've never been able to look upon my own face.'

Yudin's eyes scanned the mirror, coming to rest at the point where he imagined his reflection should be. It was there – he knew it. Years ago he had carried out experiments that proved that the reflected image of a vampire could be seen by man and vampire alike, but that the minds of both for some reason blocked out that image and replaced it with nothing – or rather with what the mind expected to see. He knew that the image he saw, behind where his body should be, was a construction of his own intellect, formed from memory and guesswork. He could see a door that was closed, but that was because it had been closed when he last glimpsed it. If, somehow, one of those sad wretches from the chambers below were to ascend the stairs and silently open the door, intent on revenge for what had been done to them, then he would be quite oblivious to it. His own imagination would continue with the happy illusion that the door remained safely shut.

He turned and looked, but the door – the real door – was still closed.

'I'm getting close,' he said, almost forgetting that it was Raisa and not himself he was speaking to.

'I have no reason to believe you,' she said, 'except that I know you're even more curious than I am.' She understood him perfectly. He wasn't in the least curious to see his own face in the mirror, but was desperate to understand the mechanism that prevented it.

'I'm expecting a delivery soon,' he explained. 'A new piece of equipment. From Iceland!' His enthusiasm was real – dimmed, but still surviving from when he had been . . . from before. But he also knew he had been down similar roads already, always to find a dead end. It was a simple idea: a looking glass that could reflect the face of a vampire. And yet it had eluded him for a quarter of a century.

She turned away from the mirror to face him. 'So am I still beautiful?' she asked.

'Of course,' he said. He wondered if she even thought it worth listening to him. For one thing, he could so easily lie, and for another, he did not know whether he any longer had the ability to judge. Every sensation, every human desire, had been dimmed when he had made that transition and become a *voordalak*. The hunger for food and the thirst for drink were gone, as was the desire for the touch of female flesh. For Yudin, such things had always been weaknesses – base, animal desires that acted only as a distraction from what truly interested him. But with hunger came the appreciation of the work of a great chef; with thirst came a palate that recognized a fine vintage; with lust came the admiration of a beautiful face. His intellect understood that Raisa Styepanovna was beautiful, but his heart felt nothing. He saw her as though through a glass, darkly, and was glad of it. He had lost all his visceral human yearnings and replaced them with one: a taste for blood that he could easily control. But what had remained of him? The only thing in himself that he had ever loved: his curiosity.

Raisa raised her hands and put them to her face, running her fingertips across her pale skin. 'I feel . . . old,' she said.

Yudin peered at her. He genuinely couldn't see it, but he knew that he could not trust himself. And it was a possibility. A vampire could be forever young, but only if it remained well fed. He looked into her eyes and saw a smile in them. He knew what she was asking, and since he had not completely banished his own corporeal desires, he was happy to indulge her – and himself. Their conversation had given him a thirst.

He turned and went to the door behind them, unlocking it with a key that he kept inside his jacket on a chain. He opened the door and held out his hand, showing Raisa Styepanovna that she should lead the way. She lifted her skirts slightly and began to descend the narrow stone staircase. Yudin closed the door behind them and followed her down, down to a department of the Third Section that not even Dubyelt had the first inkling existed.

It was a journey Tamara knew she had to make. The house where she had grown up, still her parents' home, was scarcely two versts from where she now lived – and worked. She certainly wasn't going to make the suggestion that *they* should visit *her*. She hadn't written to say she was moving back and so they had not heard of her by any means for quite some time. They knew as well as she did that they were not her parents, but she had no doubt they possessed as much love for her as they did for her brother, Rodion Valentinovich – whose pedigree she had no reason to question.

She crossed Great Nikitskaya Street, the halfway point of her short journey, and felt suddenly more nervous. She stepped back into a doorway to light a cigarette, taking off her mitten so that she could hold it. The match flared brightly, illuminating her face, but nobody was near to see it. She breathed in, enjoying the noxious, sulphurous smell in anticipation of what it portended. She felt instantly calmer. A man walked past and glanced at her through the dancing snowflakes. She noticed a look of outrage beginning to form on his face, but then he walked briskly past. People could object as much as they wanted. A word from her could have him arrested. She enjoyed the sense of power, even though she had never used it so trivially.

Emboldened, she stepped out into the street and continued walking, cigarette in hand. In the case of the gentleman who had just passed, she realized, there would have been no need to threaten arrest. He had recognized her, and she him. She had seen him at least twice at Degtyarny Lane – he might even be heading there now. Tobacco was nothing in comparison with *his* vices.

Would Valentin Valentinovich and Yelena Vadimovna ever have the slightest chance of understanding her, she wondered. She hoped she would never find out. Yelena at least would be prepared to listen, perhaps to sympathize, but it was difficult to envisage in similar circumstances her doing the same, even to protect her own husband.

Vitaliy Igorevich had been Tamara's first love, and her only love. She had moved to Petersburg to be with him when they married, in 1840, when she was nineteen. He had been twenty-eight. On the eve of their wedding he had, a strict traditionalist, presented her with his diary. She had stayed up almost the whole night reading it, reading of the seven lovers he had previously known, of his feelings towards her as expressed to himself and of his hope for the future, not only for them, but for Russia. By morning she had discovered ways in which she loved him that she had never guessed, without any diminution of the ways in which she already loved him. That evening she discovered yet another way to love him, and for him to express his love for her.

It was in 1844, when Milenochka was three and Stasik was nearly one – Luka not even dreamed of – that things changed. Up until then Tamara had always felt a liking for Prince Larionov, not least for the fact that he was her husband's most enthusiastic sponsor. Vitaliy was a physician. He did not come from a wealthy family – Tamara herself had probably brought more money to the marriage – and so he spread his work between meagre employment at the Army Medical Academy and more lucrative private practice. Prince Larionov, a regular patient, recommended Vitya's services widely to his friends, and even occasionally paid for those services when his friends saw fit to ignore their medical bills.

But in 1844 Larionov had called on Tamara during the day, while Vitya was at the Academy. There was nothing so unusual in that, but the story he told her was concerning. There had been a death a few weeks earlier in the Academy hospital. A young soldier had been horribly burned when a cannon exploded near him. The tragedy was that it had not even taken place on the battlefield, merely during artillery training at Volkovo Polye. Whether much could have been done to save him was a moot point, and Vitya had been just one of several doctors who had tried, but the soldier had come from a noble family and his death might have ramifications. Tamara remembered the word as it had formed on Larionov's lips – 'ramifications'.

Essentially, as Larionov had tactfully explained, it was possible that rumours might spread that would mean Vitya was never welcomed again as a doctor in a private house, either in Petersburg or in Moscow. And then Larionov had added that there also existed the possibility that such rumours might not spread.

In retrospect, Tamara realized that Larionov was probably a little taken aback by the naivety of her response. She was genuinely touched by his concern and desperately hoped that together they could find some way to save Vitya's career.

'What can we do?' she'd asked.

Larionov had smiled, and Tamara saw in him for the first time the hint of something vile. 'How well you put it,' he said. 'Because your husband's fate depends very much upon what you and I do – together.'

At the same moment Larionov had placed his hand upon her

leg and his smile had widened, but only on one side, and Tamara had understood everything. When Larionov left her house, seconds later, he could have been in no doubt as to how she felt about his proposal, but he displayed no diminution in his self-confidence. She should have told Vitya, but she could not imagine the words on her tongue. She didn't have the openness that Vitya had shown when he gave her his diary. All she could do was hope that Larionov would accept defeat.

It was three weeks before Vitya mentioned that a number of patients – four, to be precise – had told him they no longer required his services. It was no great financial loss – Vitya never charged more than he knew his patients could afford, and these families were on the outer fringes of the aristocracy – but it troubled him that people who had once put so much trust in him could suddenly turn him away.

Tamara understood immediately. This was just Larionov flexing his muscles. Those families were not significant of themselves, but as soon as Larionov whispered his lies into the ears of a more respected household there would be no stopping the gossip.

The following day, Tamara had gone to visit Prince Larionov. He had screwed her there and then, in his salon, having told the footman to step outside. Tamara had tried to think of Vitya, but that only made it worse. As the weeks and months went by, she learned to think of nothing. But Vitya lost no more clients, and even gained a few, thanks to Larionov's enthusiastic recommendation, as he never failed to explain to her. It was intended to make her feel worse, to feel more controlled by him than she already was – and it succeeded.

After about a year Larionov grew tired of her and passed her on to a friend – passed her on, like a book he had enjoyed and was pleased to recommend to another. But already she had heard things from Larionov's lips that he would hope never made it to the ear of the tsar, but never dreamed she would be in a position to tell. It was through her fourth lover that she became connected with the Third Section. By then Larionov had long forgotten her, but she had acquired a reputation among men in a certain stratum of society, and while no one was as barefaced as Larionov about it, Tamara could not doubt that Vitya's new-found success was in some way down to her own. And when she thought that, she hated herself more. Vitya was a brilliant man – he didn't need her help to succeed.

The fourth man for whom Tamara acted as a harlot was Actual State Councillor Popov, of the Third Section – assistant to Dubyelt himself on all matters related to censorship. Tamara told Popov and Popov told Dubyelt and Dubyelt told Orlov and Orlov told His Majesty. Prince Larionov's fall from favour was rapid, but not widely publicized. He was allowed to retire to his smallest country estate – a mere fifty serfs. Somewhere near Kazan, Tamara recalled. If he returned to Petersburg or Moscow he would be arrested. She would have liked that.

Popov tired of her body too, but not of her mind. He introduced her to General Dubyelt and her status as a courtesan became officially sanctioned. There was no way out of it for her now – whatever power Larionov might have had to destroy her and Vitya's lives was as nothing compared with what Dubyelt might achieve. And, she convinced herself, she was acting for her country – and risking less in that cause than the common soldier did every day.

And then 1848 had come.

She stopped. She was outside the Lavrovs' home – her home – in the south of the Arbat. She threw what remained of her cigarette to the ground and it hissed as the snow melted and then extinguished the glowing tip. Five weathered stone steps separated her from the front door of the house in which she had grown up. She looked up to the window above – the window of what had once been her bedroom – and then turned and gazed out across the snow-blanketed street. She always remembered it as snowy, and always remembered watching and waiting. Sometimes it was to stare longingly at the figure of a man departing, sometimes eagerly, knowing that he would soon return. And then the memory came to her of the man just standing there in the street, almost at the spot where she stood now, his neck craned, like hers, to look up at the window. But that had been a different man and the more she tried to recall him the more the memory made her feel afraid, and also protective; protective of . . . her mother?

The door opened, banishing her recollections.

'Hello, Dubois,' she said with half a smile to the butler who had evidently spied her presence before she had even needed to knock – the same French butler she had known since she was seventeen.

'Madame Tamara.' His speech was as understated as ever, but she could tell that he was surprised, and pleased.

He took her hat, coat and mittens and almost – but not quite – ran to announce her to her parents. They had changed little, in her eyes at least. Yelena Vadimovna was now sixty-two, but did not show it as she ran across the room to greet her daughter. Valentin Valentinovich moved more slowly, partly due to his age, partly due to his generally more restrained manner, but his embrace was as tight as Yelena's had been.

They talked a lot about very little. At first they spoke of the war and of Rodion, Tamara's brother. He was stationed at Helsingfors. Apparently, the British fleet in the Baltic was even larger than in the Black Sea, though the waters were unnavigable until spring. The whole family had been back for the New Year and they'd left the eldest boy, Vadim Rodionovich, to stay with his grandparents to be educated in Moscow – it was a shame he'd already gone to bed when Tamara arrived. Then, realizing perhaps that it revealed too much if they spoke only of her brother's side of the family, they began to turn the conversation on to her.

They asked her where she was living and Tamara was vague. They asked if she was still working for the government, and she said she was. They asked which department, and she said His Imperial Majesty's Own Chancellery. They asked which section and she said the fourth. They were pleased – working to help educate the poor was an ideal job for Tamara.

'I must admit though,' Yelena had eventually said, 'to a little surprise that you've come back to live in Moscow after all these years. Not that we're not both delighted.' She glanced at her husband, as if to verify his agreement. Tamara seized the opportunity to turn the conversation in the direction that she both feared and yearned for.

'I came to research my parents,' she said. She almost felt herself flinch in anticipation of their response. She knew how they always reacted, yet still she kept on doing it.

'"Research" us,' said Valentin. 'That's a nice way of putting it.' But his laughter was forced – a last-ditch attempt to avoid hearing what he knew she was about to say.

'My natural parents, I mean.' Tamara put every effort into making it sound unimportant. Only at the last moment did she manage to say 'natural' instead of 'real'. The mood of the room changed instantly.

'Oh, for heaven's sake, Toma, haven't we been over this enough?' Yelena stood as she spoke, and began to pace across the room.

Valentin shook his head sadly, and rubbed his hands against his thighs. 'Insulting. Most insulting,' he mumbled to himself. 'Ungrateful.'

Tamara felt like a little girl again. She'd always hated to upset them, but she'd grown to learn it was often a trick. Whenever she was naughty, the easiest way to punish her was to make her feel that she had let them down. She felt the tears rising in her, but held them back. On this occasion they were probably being genuine, to a degree. She *was* being insulting, and ungrateful – but that didn't diminish the fact that what she was saying was true.

'I don't love either of you any less for it,' she said, hearing the sudden emotion in her own voice. 'I probably love you even more.'

'It's a madness in you,' said Yelena. 'An obsession.'

'A serpent's tooth,' muttered Valentin.

'All that you've done for me counts for even more if I'm not your flesh and blood.' Now Tamara felt she was pleading.

'Exactly,' said Yelena, coming to a halt in front of Tamara. 'How could we – why would we – if you're not our daughter?'

'Because you're good people.'

'Ha!' said Valentin, louder than before. 'It's too late for flattery now.'

'What about Volkonsky's money?'

'He is not your father.' Valentin's voice was firm.

'I know that now – he was paying on behalf of someone else.'

'I've explained,' he replied with forced calm. 'He knew your grandfather. They fought together in the war. He wanted to do something for you.'

'For me and not for Rodion?'

'A man can make his own way in life,' Valentin persisted. 'Volkonsky even wrote to you, telling you just the same.'

'And how would you know that?' asked Tamara. Valentin looked flustered. The fact that he was such a poor liar was another reason to suspect he was not her father. 'Anyway – I've seen Volkonsky's papers, and they tell a very different story.'

'I think you'd better go,' he said stiffly.

Tamara was taken aback. It was an unusual reaction from him, but perhaps it was all he could think of now she had pushed him into a corner. She looked across the room, but Yelena's eyes were glued to the floor, daring to look neither at her husband nor Tamara.

'Very well then,' she said, standing. 'Perhaps it's for the best. Mama. Papa.' Her looks to both of them were returned by averted gazes. It was a moment before she saw the irony of the words she had used to address them; they seemed so natural on her lips. She turned and left. She was almost at the front door when she heard Yelena's footsteps catching up with her.

'Why do you keep bringing it up?' her mother asked. She was calm now – determinedly rational.

'Because you keep denying it,' said Tamara simply.

'And why would that ever change?' Her eyes flicked across Tamara's face, studying it, but also trying to communicate something unspoken. 'If Prince Volkonsky went to his grave without telling you what you seem so keen to hear, then why do you think we'll do any different?'

It was the closest thing to an admission that Tamara had ever heard from either of them, but still she wanted more. 'But how can you both pretend all the time?'

'We're not pretending. But if you think we're capable of it, why can't you be?'

Tamara nodded. Yelena pulled her close and kissed her on each cheek. Tamara turned and opened the door.

'You will come again, soon, won't you?' said Yelena.

Tamara nodded.

'And when you do, pretend, for all our sakes.'

'I'll try.'

She left, closing the door behind her. She stood there on the stone steps, thinking for a moment or two, and then set off, marching through the snow with a deliberate air of determination and pride that she hoped would fool anyone who saw her. She needed a safe place to run to, somewhere she would feel accepted. Every child should have such a place, even a child of thirty-three. Only an orphan could not run to her parents and ask them to take away all the troubles of the world and to make it stop – whatever 'it' might be. And at least an orphan could be consoled by the knowledge that she was a victim of circumstance. For Tamara, it was all down to her own stupidity.

Her cheeks tingled as her tears froze against them.

CHAPTER IV

DMITRY THREW HIMSELF TO THE GROUND AS A SHELL EXPLODED not far in front of him. The huge earthworks, so recently and hastily erected, protected him and those nearby from the blast, but he felt the ground shake. He waited only a moment and then pulled himself back to his feet. He peeped through a small hole in the earth towards the enemy beyond. They were French, all of them as far as he could tell, but it wasn't surprising – the British lines were further to the south. The French had advanced a little way, but were now close enough to be in range of the Russian musket fire. They were making the best use of what little cover there was while their artillery once again attempted to soften up the Russian defences. But despite the twilight their dark blue uniforms stood out unmistakably against the snow, so that even the inaccurate Russian musketeers eventually got lucky. Dmitry watched as first one, then another and then another distant figure collapsed to the ground. It was some consolation to be fighting a mortal foe. He tried to push the thought from his mind, but he could not. It lurked there, waiting to taunt him, that simple, inescapable fact.

There were vampires in Sevastopol.

It was a preposterous idea, but his urge was more to scream than to laugh at it. The thought of it made him feel like a child, desperate to run to his father and be assured that everything was safe. It was more than a regression to a childhood need for security. Dmitry's father was truly the only person on the planet who would not, quite rationally, laugh at his fears. Even Yudin, whom Dmitry loved almost as a father, would scoff at the very idea of the existence of the *voordalak*. But Aleksei would not have laughed. He had met vampires before: once in 1812 and again in 1825. That second occasion was when Dmitry too had encountered them, and when Aleksei had told him the horrible truth of it all. For thirty years, Dmitry had hoped such monsters could be forgotten.

There was no way Dmitry could have told anyone here his suspicions as to how the two engineers beneath the Star Fort had really died. Even in his own mind, in the day since the bodies had been found he had fluctuated between the rational conviction that some lunatic had torn out the throats of those two men, and the heartfelt certainty that he had once again seen the scraps of humanity that remained once a *voordalak* had satisfied its hunger. Dmitry had no doubt that such creatures existed, but existence was not the same as presence. It had been a long time, just as it had been a long time since Russia had warred with France. But after forty years, the French were back. Perhaps they had brought the *voordalak* – *le vampire* – with them.

He and Captain Shulgin had quickly agreed that the killings were the work of a madman. For Dmitry the distinction was moot. A vampire was in many ways just a man with his own particular kind of madness. But at least a madman could die – die by a bullet or a blade. A vampire required more specialist methods. But if Dmitry started suggesting any of those then it would be *he* who was deemed mad. Instead he prepared, quietly and alone, just as his father had done. All the officers were warned that there was a killer on the loose, and a few chuckled at the thought that one more way of dying would make any difference. Dmitry bit his tongue and did not suggest what a difference it really could make. At least there had been only two deaths. Perhaps the creature had been merely . . . passing through.

For the moment, Dmitry's worries concerned a more tangible foe. Since the enemy's abortive attack across the Chernaya, the tide seemed to have turned a little in Russia's favour. They had taken the round hill to the south-east of the city just two days before, and it had already been fortified by the men of the Kamchatka Regiment – hence the hill's newly assumed name of the Kamchatka Lunette. The French apparently called it Le

75

Mamelon, observing immediately, as any Frenchman would, its resemblance to a nipple. New defences had been built close to the hill, the most northern of which was the White Works, and it had been while Dmitry was inspecting these – simply to have some idea of their layout – that the French had attacked. It was a bold move, and the right thing to do – attempting to dislodge the Russians while their defences were still incomplete.

The attack had come two hours ago, and as darkness had fallen Dmitry had had ample opportunities to retire back to the city, but he had not taken them. There was much that he could learn by observing the French tactics – not to mention the faulty tactics of his own side – but that was merely an excuse. The truth was that Dmitry had spent the last half-decade waiting for something to happen, for something to change and make his life interesting. God knew it wouldn't be at headquarters. Being out here was a throw of the dice. If it ended in death – hateful though it was to admit it – he would not mind. He did not want to die, but it was a gamble he was prepared to take against the prospect of . . . something new.

Another shell came in, closer, and this time Dmitry's descent on to the earth was involuntary. He lay there for a moment on his stomach, his face pressed close against the pale clay that had been exposed when the White Works' defences were dug, giving it its name. He was uninjured. He had escaped death. But still there was nothing new.

'You promised to tell me of Chopin.'

Dmitry turned his head and couldn't help but grin. Tyeplov stood over him, looking calm and in control despite the noise of battle around him. He was holding out his hand towards Dmitry. A sensation of embarrassment ran through him, at being discovered in so vulnerable a position. It was hard to discern whether the feeling was better or worse for the fact that it was Tyeplov who towered above him.

'Now?' he asked, accepting the hand and letting Tyeplov effortlessly pull him to his feet.

Tyeplov tilted his head to one side. 'I could ask Prince Galtsin instead.'

Before Dmitry could respond, Tyeplov had begun to climb the

rickety wooden stairway that led up to a platform just below the parapet of the earth defences. Dmitry followed him, feeling suddenly invigorated by his presence. At the top, Tyeplov hoisted his gun from his shoulder and positioned himself between two gabions – the earth-filled wicker baskets that made up so much of Sevastopol's defensive front line. He fired a shot and then stepped back behind the gabion to reload. Within seconds he was ready to fire again.

'That's a *shtutser*!' exclaimed Dmitry.

'A Minié,' said Tyeplov, pulling back to reload once more, pouring both powder and bullet into the barrel in what seemed like a single action and then swiftly ramming them home.

'Where did you get it?'

'From a Frenchman,' Tyeplov explained. 'A dead one.'

Dmitry laughed, more to please Tyeplov than because he found the idea amusing. 'Serves him right,' he said, without quite understanding what he meant by it. He looked through the next gap between gabions. The French were in full attack now, running forward towards the defences. Somewhere to his right, Dmitry could just make out a breach – perhaps blown by their artillery, perhaps not yet fully built in the rush to defend the Kamchatka. That was where the infantrymen were heading. He heard the report of Tyeplov's gun, and saw one of them fall. Tyeplov ducked in again, but within seconds was once more taking aim. Another man tumbled to the ground.

'You want a go?' asked Tyeplov as he loaded.

Dmitry grinned and took the offered rifle. It reminded him of the first time his father let him hold a gun – though then the target had been nothing more dangerous than a pheasant. He leaned out between the gabions and tracked the figure of a running Frenchman, scarcely visible through the gloom. He squeezed the trigger and felt the gun recoil, but the soldier carried on.

'You're aiming a little high,' said Tyeplov as he took the gun from Dmitry and reloaded it before handing it back.

Dmitry had never been a good shot – it wasn't an essential skill for a horseman – but with a weapon like this, shooting became the sort of skill any officer could aspire to. He tracked another of the enemy, taking Tyeplov's advice, and fired again. It seemed like the same instant that the man fell. Dmitry could see the blood draining from his neck and staining the snow as his arms flailed, as if trying to drag him onwards in his attack. Dmitry laughed and felt Tyeplov pat him on the back. He handed over the gun again and Tyeplov reloaded.

'Your father killed quite a few Frenchmen in his time, I hear,' said Tyeplov as Dmitry aimed once more. 'A true Russian hero.'

Dmitry let the barrel of the gun drop as he fired and his bullet implanted itself harmlessly in the snow. Realization came to him – and with it disappointment. So that was what it was all about. Tyeplov was fishing, most likely for the Third Section. Tsar Nikolai might claim that the families of Decembrists were guiltless of any offence, but that didn't mean he wouldn't try to trap them into revealing their sympathies. But none of that quite explained the depth of Dmitry's regret at discovering Tyeplov's true interest.

'He was for a while,' said Dmitry, 'but he ended up disgracing us all.' It was an absolute inversion of the truth. When Dmitry had thought Aleksei to be a soldier, and worse, a spy, just like Tyeplov, he had had little respect for him. Only when he had discovered that Aleksei was a member of a society dedicated to bringing Russia the government it deserved had he seen him as a hero. Tyeplov offered the gun back to Dmitry, who raised his hand in refusal. He felt sickened at his own actions, at the pleasure he had taken in killing a man in so impersonal a way. That wasn't Dmitry; he'd done it only to please Tyeplov – to be with him and to be like him.

Tyeplov shrugged and aimed the gun himself. 'You don't believe that,' he said with quiet conviction, then fired again.

'I do.' Dmitry knew better than to attempt to play any games. These government agents were not subtle, so he'd heard, though he had never before met one. It was best to counter their suggestions with simple certainties.

The French were in retreat now. Evidently the breach had been successfully defended, and now they had no hope other than to flee the Russian guns. Tyeplov happily fired at their backs, his aim unerring.

'I have friends who say your father was the bravest man they ever met.'

'They knew him?' Dmitry could not hide his surprise, or his curiosity.

Tyeplov fired again, and another man fell. 'Oh, yes. Long time ago, of course.' The battle was over now. The French – all but a few stragglers – had gone back to their lines. Tyeplov fired again and there was one straggler fewer. 'Though he was never much use with a gun, was he – your father?' Tyeplov stepped away from the gabions and made his way back down the steps, clearly deciding there was no more to be done.

'What do you mean?' Dmitry's voice sounded indignant, even though he knew that his father had always been more comfortable with a sword than with a musket.

'Because of his hand,' explained Tyeplov. He turned and aimed the rifle back up the steps at Dmitry. He waggled the muzzle up and down to highlight the odd way he was holding the forestock. The last two fingers of his left hand were curled into his palm, and he allowed the gun simply to rest on his index finger, with his thumb steadying at the side. It was just the way Aleksei held a gun, having lost the last two fingers of his left hand to a Turkish blade.

'That's what they used to call him,' said Tyeplov, still pointing the gun towards Dmitry, 'long before they knew his real name.'

'Call him?' Dmitry came down the steps, pushing the barrel of the gun to one side. It was quiet all around now, and he wanted to get back to the city and away from Tyeplov, but he was fascinated to learn more.

'Because of his hand,' Tyeplov said again. 'That's where he got the nickname.'

'What nickname?' asked Dmitry.

Tyeplov glanced from side to side and spoke softly, almost reverently. 'The three-fingered man,' he replied.

To whom it may concern,

Please grant the bearer, Tamara Valentinovna Komarova, full access to the information she requires regarding Prince Volkonsky.

L. V. Dubyelt

Tamara held out her hand and Gribov returned the letter. She did not want him looking at it for too long, lest he notice it was undated. It had once borne a date – 2 October 1852 – but if she had left that on there it might have diluted the sense of urgency that was conveyed. The simple stroke of a knife had removed it from the top of the page. Questions over the date might also have led to questions as to precisely which source of information Dubyelt had been granting access. He had meant the archive in Petersburg, but Tamara could think of no reason why he might not also have meant the one in Moscow. She certainly wouldn't suggest anything to the contrary to Gribov. Nor would she point out the ambiguity over exactly which Prince Volkonsky was meant – the Decembrist exile, Sergei Grigorovich, or the Minister of the Imperial Court, Pyetr Mihailovich – a distinction she had not made clear even when Dubyelt had originally signed the authorization. Tamara was interested in both princes, and much more besides.

Gribov stood, picking up a lamp that had been glowing dimly on his desk, and went to the door. Tamara turned her head to follow his movements, but did not realize that he intended her to accompany him until his curling finger beckoned her. She rose and walked out of the office after him.

'I hope you don't mind my natural sense of discretion,' he said as they walked along the dim corridor.

'Not at all. It does you credit,' she told him. She had not been sure that it would work, but in the end he was like any official – afraid of his superiors. At first she had asked him, and he had said no. Then she had shown him the letter. She had verified that Yudin was away from his office, otherwise Gribov would have gone straight to him, unwilling to let the decision rest on his shoulders. But in Yudin's absence, a letter from General Dubyelt, with the general himself too far distant for personal verification, had seemed certain to sway Gribov. In the end, he had reacted just as she had hoped. She understood men like Gribov – she understood men.

'If it were down to me, I would allow anyone in,' he explained as they walked. 'Such a beautiful library should not be kept a secret.' They had come to the top of the dark stone stairway down to Yudin's lair, opposite which the door led out to the open air of the Kremlin. In front of them was a dead end, decorated with a hanging tapestry, a copy of something French and medieval – a virginal woman attended by a unicorn and a lion. The red of the woman's hair reminded Tamara a little of herself, but the slight figure and diminutive bosom of the tapestry were more akin to Raisa than Tamara. The unicorn gazed vainly into a mirror held in the woman's hand, but Tamara had only a moment to study the reflection before Gribov pulled the curtain aside to reveal a door that Tamara had not known existed. He unlocked it with a heavy iron key.

Beyond lay a staircase, longer, narrower and far, far older than the one that would have taken them to visit Yudin. Gribov led the way and the path twisted and turned until the memory of daylight above was forgotten and all sense of direction was lost. The stairs ended in a long straight corridor that Tamara could only guess led beneath the Kremlin, since to lead out of it would be nonsensical. Other corridors connecting, presumably, to other entrances split off, but Gribov ignored them. At last they came to another door, which Gribov unlocked with another key. Now he allowed her to enter first. The room was too dark for her to make out any detail, but she sensed a vast space in front of her. Then Gribov stood beside her and turned up his lamp, suddenly illuminating all that was around them.

Tamara clicked her tongue in a mixture of astonishment and admiration, but was able to form no articulate sound.

'Beautiful, isn't it?' said Gribov, after a considered pause.

Tamara could only nod. The chamber stretched out further than she could see. Brickwork pillars, from which sprouted the vaults of the roof, were regularly spaced throughout, perhaps fifty or more of them, sharing between them the entire weight of whichever of the Kremlin's buildings stood above. Tamara guessed they must be as old as the citadel itself. But what was most enthralling was what lay between the pillars: documents – thousands of them, if not millions, piled on to tables and crammed into shelves. There were ten times as many as she'd seen in Petersburg.

'This was built to the instruction of Ivan the Fourth,' she heard Gribov say, correcting her estimate of the library's age. 'Built to hold the Liberia – the collected knowledge of the whole of Byzantium.'

Tamara had heard tales of such a thing, but believed them to be myths. It was designed to bolster Moscow's claim to be – after Byzantium and Rome itself – the Third Rome, the newest heart of Christendom, wherein resided knowledge that could be trusted neither to the Turks nor, worse, to the Pope.

'This is it?' she whispered. 'Here?' Her own interest lay in far more recent documents, but she could not help but be thrilled by the thought of what she might find. She thought of her adoptive father, Valentin Valentinovich, and realized how much his love of books had become a part of her. He would envy her presence here.

'No.' Gribov chuckled as he answered her, as if this were a routine he followed with everyone he brought down here. 'Perhaps once, but not for many centuries. The documents from Byzantium have been removed. My guess is that there is another similar room, near here, perhaps just the thickness of a wall away from us' – he reached out and caressed the brickwork as he spoke – 'where they are housed, but I don't know how to get to it. Perhaps His Majesty does. Perhaps one of his ancestors once did, but forgot to hand the secret down.'

'But this has the records I want?' asked Tamara, her mind just able to focus on its purpose.

'It contains everything we've collected since the time of Pyotr the Great; everything that's not in Petersburg.'

'That's just what I need.'

'I'll leave you to it,' said Gribov. There was more than a hint of victory in his voice – the knowledge that too much information was as unhelpful as too little. But Tamara was thrilled. Ever since she had been allowed the freedom to roam through her father's library she had loved books in an almost physical way: the smell of them, the feel of them, the anticipation of what new worlds she might find within. This place was like a dream to her.

'Thank you,' she said, only slightly exaggerating the relish she felt at the idea with the intent of deflating Gribov's sense of victory. 'Where do I find Volkonsky?'

Gribov waved his hand in front of him. 'Who can say? Some

of the material is sorted, some not. Most remains where it was placed when it arrived. Towards the back it's very ancient indeed.' From a table near to the door he picked up a candle and lit it from his lamp. 'I'd stay to help, but I'm sure you understand, this is not my only duty.'

She heard his footsteps receding behind her, and then the slamming of the door. He had taken the candle to guide him, but left her the lamp. She felt suddenly entombed, but looking around she saw that he had left the key on the table beside her. She took the lamp and ventured out into the chamber – into the past. It was an overwhelming task, but she felt more hopeful than she had done in years. If the truth about her parents did not lie somewhere beneath that high, vaulted ceiling, then she could not imagine anywhere that it might be.

The sound of some gigantic bell resonated across Red Square, and was ignored by most. Climbing the hill from the Moskva Bridge past Saint Vasiliy's, Yudin reacted perhaps more than those around him; he hadn't realized it was so late. Time could be a vital matter for a *voordalak*. To return tardily to his coffin, or at least to some place of dark seclusion, and to be caught in the first rays of the dawning sun would be a foolish and unpleasant way to die. But he didn't need clocks to tell him the position of the sun. Around dusk and dawn, he could feel its presence, like a wolf, lurking below the horizon, hoping that the laws of physics might momentarily change so that it could pounce unexpectedly and take him. But Yudin trusted the laws of physics more than anything in the whole world – more than his own instincts.

Currently those laws dictated that the sun was somewhere on the far side of the Earth and so although Yudin might be late, he had little to fear from it. He looked up at the clock on the Saviour's Tower, having to strain his neck since he was almost directly underneath it. It wasn't the hour, or even the quarter, and the single stroke of the bell sounded nothing like the distinctive, newly restored chimes of the clock. Most likely it was from a church – one of the many inside the Kremlin.

He tightened his grip on the wooden box under his arm and strode through the gateway beneath the tower, eager to make use of its contents. It was his most treasured possession: his microscope – one of the few things he had rescued when he had fled his laboratory in the caves deep beneath Chufut Kalye. Out there in the Crimea, the war had been going on for months, but he had heard of no action anywhere close to his old haunt. What would anyone find if they went there now, he wondered. He had fond memories of the place, but now he kept his scientific paraphernalia at his house. It was a place he rarely visited, to the south of the river in Zamoskvorechye, but it was useful. He stored most of his possessions there, and in the cellar was a coffin where he could lie during the day if unable to reach his more regular sleeping place beneath the Kremlin. It was not his only bolthole in the city.

It had been almost a week since Raisa had handed him the sample of the tsarevich's blood – a sample which she had so expertly drawn from him without his even noticing. Perhaps afterwards he had felt the cut to his lip, and connected it to his stolen encounter with her. But even if he did, he would put it down to unbridled passion overcoming her in the presence of so powerful a figure. But how much did he know about the Romanov Betrayal? His uncle and namesake, Aleksandr I, had understood it all. Surely that knowledge would have been passed down to those most in danger. Would the younger Aleksandr have made the connection when he raised his hand and discovered the blood on his lips? It did not matter. Yudin had his sample, and in a moment he would be able to examine it.

Yudin had made most of his discoveries years before, when working in those caves. Zmyeevich possessed the Romanov blood – blood which Pyotr the Great had willingly allowed to be drunk from him. With that came the risk for any Romanov that, merely by drinking a few drops of Zmyeevich's blood, they might become like him. With Yudin's help he had almost succeeded with Nikolai's brother, Tsar Aleksandr I. But Aleksandr's death had saved him.

And there lay the problem. Yudin had discovered that within each generation of Romanovs there was only one chance of success. Zmyeevich had attempted to exert his power over Aleksandr and had failed. That meant that he could not attempt it with Nikolai, or any of Aleksandr's other brothers. The chance had moved to the next generation: Aleksandr, Konstantin and the others.

Yudin smiled. Tsar Nikolai was a sentimental man. His father, Tsar Pavel, had had four sons and named them, in order, Aleksandr, Konstantin, Nikolai and Mihail. Nikolai had four sons and named them, in order, Aleksandr, Konstantin, Nikolai and Mihail. The first set of brothers bore the patronymic Pavlovich, the second Nikolayevich. It was to the Nikolayevichs that Zmyeevich would turn his attention – but not yet. Not until one of them became tsar. It would most likely be Aleksandr, but who could tell? If Zmyeevich shot his bolt too soon, the young tsarevich might never live to be tsar, and the chance would be lost for another generation. Zmyeevich would wait until there was certainty.

And what would Yudin do? He and Zmyeevich were no longer allies – far from it – and Zmyeevich was not to be taken lightly as an enemy. For Yudin there seemed only two options: to win Zmyeevich's favour, by helping him, or to defeat him for ever.

He had not yet decided. And in order to decide he needed knowledge. There was no rush to it. Nikolai was healthy and had many years of life before him. When he did die then his son's blood would take on the highest importance, but for now it was merely a matter of interest. Yudin revelled in such matters.

The bell sounded for a second time. Now that the sound was not deflected by the walls of the Kremlin, Yudin could get a better idea of where it was coming from: almost straight ahead of him – the Assumption Belfry. It was the Assumption Bell itself that had been rung. A few passers-by stopped to look, surprised that the bell should be sounded at that time of day, but Yudin pressed on. He had his microscope and he had his blood sample and he was eager to make use of them. He was right in front of the belfry now, and his office was only a few minutes away.

At the back of his mind, a memory lurked – almost like the sun, prowling below the horizon, waiting. There was some tradition about that particular bell that he could not remember. It had to strike three times. It had happened once before in his lifetime, or at least since he had been in Russia, but he had not been in

Moscow to hear it. It marked an event that happened rarely – an event that would change everything.

The bell was struck for a third time and memory rushed back to Yudin. He continued to walk, but only because he lacked the willpower to make himself stop. His mind focused solely on the awful realization, closing out the world around him and attempting to calculate the ramifications for Russia, for the Romanovs and most of all for himself. When the Assumption Bell tolled three times it conveyed a precise and unmistakable message – that the tsar was dead. The last time it happened had been in 1825 and Yudin had been far away in the south, in Taganrog, close – and it was no coincidence – to the deathbed of Tsar Aleksandr. He had been on a boat with Zmyeevich and seen the flag lowered to half-mast. He remembered his horror as Zmyeevich announced that he could sense no connection with Aleksandr, that the tsar would not be reborn as a *voordalak* and that he had died a normal death.

That moment had marked the parting of the ways for Yudin and Zmyeevich, and had almost cost him his life. For Zmyeevich the cost had been merely a postponement – a knowledge that the Romanov Betrayal could not be avenged for another generation, not before the day when Aleksandr II held sway as Tsar of All the Russias. That day had arrived – and Yudin was quite unprepared.

He broke into a run.

He was the spitting image of his father and had the same temperament. Tamara's nephew burst into the Lavrovs' drawing room without knocking, shouting the phrase, 'Have you heard?' and then stopping to catch his breath.

'Vadim Rodionovich, how dare you!' Valentin's stern shout at his grandson reminded Tamara of her own youth, when Valentin would shout at her and Rodion, and with equally good reason. She was relieved, however, at Vadim's arrival, which had broken the uncomfortable silence of her visit.

Vadim was too out of breath to speak and instead just stood there, panting. It had been four years since Tamara had seen him last. He reminded her of how her own sons, Stasik and Luka, might have grown up, and she was surprised to find such thoughts

86

more of a pleasure than a cause for tears. Yet the tears still came often.

'But have you heard?' Vadim asked again.

'Heard what, Vadya?' she asked him, with a little laughter in her voice.

'The news. It came on the railway telegraph – from Petersburg.'

'What news?' Yelena's voice was more irritated than Tamara's.

'He's dead,' panted Vadim. 'His Majesty – he's dead.'

There was a moment of silence as the three adults looked at the boy's face, trying to judge whether he was telling the truth and praying that he wasn't, but they quickly realized it was a thing that no Russian, not even a child, would joke about. Yelena covered her face with her hands and let out a moan.

'The poor man,' said Valentin. 'That poor family.'

Tamara was surprised by her own reaction to the news. Her first thought had been for the political implications; the fact that Aleksandr Nikolayevich looked far less kindly upon the Third Section than had his father. Beyond the obvious personal problems that any weakening or even disbandment of it would cause, she truly believed that it would be to the benefit of the country's enemies. But then she noticed the moisture in her eyes, and the tightness of her stomach. Valentin Valentinovich was right, about both the man and the family. Nikolai had been so strong, such an appropriate man to lead his nation. He had been only fifty-eight.

Tamara glanced around the room. It was a very Russian scene, one which would be played out across the country as the news spread – in each home a private grief, as though a member of the family had been lost. It was quite insane and quite beautiful. She went over to kneel beside her mother, taking her hand. No one spoke. Her mother forced a smile and stroked her hair. Her father sat very still with his hands resting on his thighs, shaking his head slowly from side to side. Vadim seemed confused, trying to reconcile his excitement at the news with the sorrow that it had brought to everybody.

Suddenly, Tamara was four years old again. She knew the age precisely because it was the time they had heard of the old tsar's death – Aleksandr I. News travelled more slowly back then, but it had reached them within days. She had been like Vadim was now, too young to understand the grief of others, but she remembered Yelena and Valentin being very much the same as they were now.

For perhaps the first time she appreciated the magnificence of their old age and understood why they were so affected. They were not just grieving for Nikolai, but for their memories of the death of Aleksandr, and of his father Pavel before him – perhaps even the death of Yekaterina. They would have been as young then as she was at Aleksandr's death. Perhaps they realized too that they would not live to see the end of this new tsar's reign – or at least hoped it.

And from the distant reaches of that four-year-old mind came another thought – the memory of a hope, but not of its fulfilment. What had affected her most as a child on hearing of the death of the tsar had not been a sense of sorrow, but a realization that the news also meant that her father – her real father – would be coming home.

CHAPTER V

THE IMPERIAL ARMY WAS TAKING THE NEWS SURPRISINGLY well. The death of the tsar made no difference to daily life in the besieged city of Sevastopol. The enemy guns had not fallen silent in deference to the departed emperor, nor had they fired a salute in honour of the succession of the new one. Many were pleased that Tsar Aleksandr had at last relieved the woeful commander-in-chief, Prince Menshikov, and replaced him with Prince Gorchakov, but those who bothered to read the dates on the dispatches soon realized that this had not been the first act of the new tsar, but the last of the old one. Some of the men had shed a tear for their departed emperor, but among the officers it was only those who knew him personally who showed any real emotion at his passing.

Dmitry had never met the late Tsar Nikolai, but had seen him on several occasions, the first being in December 1825 as he sat astride a horse just to the south of Senate Square and ordered his cannon to open fire on the thousands of good men who had dared raise objections to his absolute power. Nikolai's power had won out – and Dmitry had never forgiven him.

But neither had Dmitry ever done anything about it. He'd fantasized over the idea of himself as a lone assassin, liberating Russia by annihilating her dictator, but he had never acted, or even begun to formulate a plan. He guessed that there were others like him – in the army and elsewhere – but it would need them to work together for anything to come of it. And since the fall of the Decembrists, there were few who dared talk like that. The Third Section was everywhere, or at least that was what people – what

Dmitry – believed, and that was enough. No one had acted. In the end Nikolai had died of a winter chill. General *Février* had turned traitor.

'You're the last man I expected to see moping over the death of Impernikel.'

Dmitry looked up. It was Tyeplov. In each hand he held a glass of brandy. He offered one to Dmitry.

'You shouldn't call him that,' said Dmitry, his voice kept low. The name, a simple contraction of '*Empereur Nikolai*', was not particularly insulting in itself, but it was the favourite epithet of the tsar's long-time critic, the exile Aleksandr Herzen.

'Nobody here cares any more than you or I do,' said Tyeplov, sitting down beside him. Dmitry looked around. It was probably true. If anyone here held the same strength of opinion as Dmitry, they kept it to themselves, but few would object to so trifling an insult.

Two weeks ago, Dmitry would have suspected that Tyeplov was trying to lure him into saying something even more treasonous, which he could report back to his masters in the Third Section, but now he had come to doubt it. Tyeplov was too obvious for a government spy – and far too engaging. They had already dined together several times. Anatoliy Vladimirovich Tyeplov – Tolya, as Dmitry now addressed him – was wonderful company. In many ways, Dmitry found him like a child, his mind an empty vessel into which Dmitry could pour so much of his knowledge and fascination and taste. Tyeplov was in no way stupid, but there were some huge gaps in his education. On the other hand, there were areas in which he had ideas of which Dmitry had never dreamed. Talking to him was like talking to an open-minded father – someone from whom he could learn but who did not object to learning from him. Dmitry had lost his own father, Aleksei, at an age when such communication could only really be one way. Even with Yudin there was a sense that there was little Dmitry could tell him that he did not already know.

But there were other ways in which Tyeplov was nothing like a father. For a start, he must have been a good fifteen years younger than Dmitry. And neither Aleksei nor Yudin had ever occupied Dmitry's mind quite so exclusively as Tyeplov did.

'Anyway,' said Dmitry, sipping his brandy, 'I wasn't moping. I was remembering.'

'14 December 1825,' said Tyeplov, simply.

'How did you know?'

'It's what everyone's thinking. At the end, we think of the beginning.'

'I was there,' said Dmitry. It was a foolish admission, but for some reason he blurted it out.

'With your father?'

Dmitry nodded. 'And a friend – someone who was almost like a father to me.'

'What happened?'

Dmitry looked over to him. It wasn't something he had spoken of to anyone before, apart from Yudin, but the concern that displayed itself in Tyeplov's eyes made Dmitry's urge to unburden himself irresistible.

'My father and I were both there, in Senate Square, with the others – prepared to die for what we believed in. And then Vasiliy Denisovich – this friend – came and joined us.'

'He was a revolutionary too?'

Dmitry smiled at the thought. 'Oh no. Vasiliy had no interest in that sort of thing.'

'Had?'

'He died – on that day.' It was odious for Dmitry to lie to Tyeplov, but it was a promise he had made to Yudin on discovering that he was alive and that he had changed his name.

'Go on.'

'Both Papa and Vasiliy begged me to leave – Vasiliy even brought Mama into it – and so I did. I walked away and left them to it.'

'It must have been a great relief to them.'

'You think so?' asked Dmitry eagerly. Yudin had always said as much to him, but he knew nothing of Aleksei's thoughts. Even a hint of where Dmitry had been that day would be pounced upon by the censors.

Tyeplov nodded firmly. 'So what did you do?'

'I went home – by a roundabout route. There were troops everywhere, some loyal to Nikolai, others on our side, but I didn't want to run into either. I went out across the Neva, over to Vasilevskiy Island, then on to Petrogradskaya and finally back across the ice to the mainland. The shooting was over by then. Vasiliy was dead and Papa had been arrested.'

'How did he die?'

'He was shot. I heard about it long after. My father tried to help him. But then when the ice broke up, his body was lost in the water.' That much was true. Dmitry had managed to piece it together from various witnesses and in the end from Yudin himself. His father had never written of it.

'Did they find the body?'

Dmitry shook his head, staring down into his drink. He could not look Tyeplov in the eye and lie so blatantly. Though it was in a sense true. They didn't find a body because Yudin had survived. The bullet wound had been superficial and he had been pulled from the water moments after falling in. He had managed to escape the city and flee. He told it all to Dmitry when he returned, years later.

'And your father?'

'Arrested. Tried. Exiled. I never saw him again.'

'Not even when he was in prison?'

'No.' Everyone, Aleksei included, had said it was for the best, to avoid any suspicion of where Dmitry's sympathies lay.

'So what did you do?'

Nothing, thought Dmitry, before churning out the usual list. 'I stayed with the army. Became a loyal subject of Impernikel. Suppressed those who rose up against him. Looked after my mother. Got married.' Nothing. Nothing. Nothing.

'Children?'

Dmitry shook his head. 'What about you?'

'Never even married.'

'No, I meant the whole life story thing.'

'Ah!' said Tyeplov. 'Now there's a tale.'

Dmitry was not to hear it, not then. The shout of 'Anatoliy' flew across the room. Tyeplov looked, and Dmitry thought that he saw a momentary scowl cross his friend's face. It was a reflection of Dmitry's own annoyance, of his jealousy of Tyeplov's company.

'I'm sorry,' Tyeplov said, standing. 'Come. Join us.'

Dmitry considered, but the thoughts of Aleksei and Yudin and the events of thirty years before had thrown him into a dark humour. Instead he went over to the piano and began to play Beethoven – it suited his mood and he knew Tyeplov enjoyed it. He watched as Tyeplov chatted with the two officers who had hailed him; a *Shtabs*-Captain and a *poruchik*. He had no need to look at the keyboard and kept his eyes fixed on his friend, playing with just a fragment more passion whenever Tyeplov's eyes flicked towards him.

Yudin had chosen to savour the moment. He'd been busy in the days since the news had arrived, but not so busy that he couldn't have spared the hour or so that it would have taken to set up his microscope and finally gaze upon the exquisite detail of what Raisa had provided for him. But so august an observation merited better than time that was spared; it required time that was dedicated. There was no rush. If Yudin could have observed Aleksandr's blood at the very moment of his father's death, then he might have seen something uniquely wonderful, but in the time it had taken the news to reach Moscow – even via the magnetic telegraph – that moment had passed, and a delay of days was no worse than a delay of minutes.

Yudin checked himself. That was an assumption. For him to believe that it took but an instant for the knowledge of Aleksandr's new-found status to be transferred from his body in Petersburg to the sample of his blood in Moscow was as foolish as the belief that light travelled at an infinite speed – which was to say that it did not travel at all. A new experiment was needed to establish the speed of that transfer, but now was not the time. Yudin had better things to interest him: the blood of a Romanov – the blood of a new tsar.

What secrets might it reveal? Might he find a way to hurry the process of transformation, to make Aleksandr into a *voordalak* with none of the machinations that their failed attempt on the first Aleksandr had involved? If he could present such a mechanism to Zmyeevich then all would be forgiven. Or perhaps what he discovered might lie in a different direction. Perhaps he could even find out that it was possible to completely reverse the process and

93

thereby cure the Romanovs of their affliction for ever. He had no affection for the rulers of Russia, but they would pay mightily for such a cure – and would protect him from Zmyeevich. On the other hand, Zmyeevich would pay for it too, if only to keep it from them. Yudin saw the auction price rising and rising before his eyes.

He allowed himself one more moment to savour the idea, then got to work. He cleared his desk and took the microscope out of its case. The brasswork was a little tarnished, but he would see to that later. Next, he gathered together every lamp and candle he had – even going up to Gribov's room to fetch more – and lit them, assembling them as close together as he could at the opposite end of the desk from the instrument. Then, from a small drawer in the bottom of the microscope case, he produced a lens. It was an ordinary magnifying glass, quite a large one, mounted on a stand. He placed it between the lamps and the microscope and began adjusting its position.

It had been one of the most horrible realizations after he had become a vampire. For a moment he had feared he might never be able to look into a microscope again. A microscope required light – an abundant commodity for most in the form of sunlight, but unusable for a vampire. Any microscope – Yudin's included – was fitted with a small mirror beneath the viewing platform. The mirror could be adjusted to any angle and was meant to be positioned so that sunlight reflected from it up through the specimen, through the combination of lenses that did the work of magnification and into the observer's eye.

Yudin had tried it once. It had been the most delectable agony he ever experienced. He only opened the curtain a fraction, so that sunlight fell upon the mirror, not on him, but the light that came from the microscope and entered his eye had been as intense – more intense – than any example he had seen of light falling directly upon a vampire's body. In the caves beneath Chufut Kalye, when he had been merely human, he had carried out many experiments to discover the effect of light on vampires. But times had changed, and this one he had been forced to perform upon himself.

He had gone completely blind in that eye. Raising his hand to it

he could find only a bloody gap, which he knew was already healing. He could not look in a mirror to see the effect. He had put
his hand to the back of his head and felt a gap there too. The light
had burned all the way through his skull. And yet, within less
than a minute, he was as normal. The wound was healed and his
sight restored, with no scar to hint at the horrible disfigurement
he had so briefly endured. It was the knowledge that there would
be no permanent damage that made the pain bearable.

Using artificial light was a sufficient solution, which Yudin had
come upon with only a little further experimentation. The light
was not as bright as the sun would have been, but it was clear
enough for him to examine his specimens. He made final adjust-
ments to the magnifying glass so that it focused the image of the
lamps and candles close to the mirror. Then he prepared his slide.

He poured out just a drop of Aleksandr's blood. He corrected
himself – of the tsar's blood. It was still liquid thanks to the anti-
coagulant that Raisa had naturally introduced with her bite. He
added a thin film of mica which the blood sucked eagerly down
on to itself until it was thin enough for light to penetrate. He
put the slide under the microscope and peered down through the
eyepiece.

The blood appeared perfectly normal.

That was to be expected. While Yudin had never had the chance
to examine Romanov blood like this before, the circumstances
that had created it were not unique. He had reproduced them in
his laboratory in the Crimea. He had allowed a vampire to drink
a man's blood almost to the point of killing him, but not quite.
He'd then let the man breed, and examined the offspring's blood.
It had looked like that of any human – and yet when the child
was given the blood of the original vampire to drink and then
killed, it became a vampire. It was just as they had planned
with Aleksandr I – just as Zmyeevich was undoubtedly planning
with the new Aleksandr.

Yudin surmised that there was a change in the blood at some
level, but it was an internal change, or perhaps something too
small to be seen by the microscope. It did not matter – his
experiments had not ended there and neither would this one. He
went over to the map drawers and opened the top one. In it lay

several vials, each neatly labelled. He picked one out. It was larger than the vial of Aleksandr's blood, but then it had been donated voluntarily. Even as he held it in his hand he felt awed by it. This was why Zmyeevich hated him so, and yet feared to act against him. It felt almost sacred to cradle it in his fingers: the blood of the vampire Zmyeevich. What power it gave him. He needed only to wait until day and then hurl it out into the light to inflict the most terrible pain on Zmyeevich, wherever he might be in the world, as the sun burned that small fragment of him. It would be as if the blood within his own veins were burning. But he would quickly recover, and Yudin would become suddenly vulnerable, his only power over Zmyeevich lost for ever. Along with his ability to experiment.

He mixed a drop of Zmyeevich's blood with the sample of Aleksandr's and re-examined the slide, licking his lips in anticipation of observing this once-in-a-generation moment. This was what would happen, on a much vaster scale, within Aleksandr's own body if he were to ingest Zmyeevich's blood. Yudin opened his notebook on the desk beside him and picked up a pencil, ready to make notes.

The red cells of Zmyeevich's blood were quite distinct from Aleksandr's. This was simply a difference between vampires and humans that Yudin had observed many times before. Aleksandr's were disc-shaped, with a slight depression in the middle. The *voordalak* cells were larger – almost half as large again – and completely smooth.

The next observation was important – although it was more a lack of an observation. If the blood had been merely human – not Romanov blood that had already been taken by Zmyeevich – then the vampire cells would have attacked the human cells. In numbers as great as this, they would have been victorious, although a strong human could fight off a small dose. Yudin used the word 'attack', but the exact mechanism wasn't clear; again too small to be seen in the microscope. The human cells merely withered. But that did not happen here.

What did happen was far more spectacular. The cells merged. It was almost – though Yudin knew he was being fanciful – as if the vampire cells seduced the human cells. They buffeted against them and then, being larger, began to surround them. And then, with the silent 'pop' of two droplets of rain on a window pane forming into one, they merged into a single cell – perfectly spherical. Within two minutes, Yudin could see no other kind of cell in his sample.

The third stage would come soon, when each spherical cell would redivide, regenerating the two cells from which it formed, except that now both cells would be larger and would lack the indentation in the middle. Both would be vampire cells. He had seen it a hundred times before, but never with such illustrious bloodlines. The idea that he was about to witness the spawning of the blood of a Romanov thrilled him.

He waited.

He checked his watch.

The process should have begun within a minute of the spherical cells forming.

He waited again.

After five minutes, he stood up. He began to pace around the desk, staring angrily at the microscope, as though it were to blame. He wished he had all his old notebooks with him, but they were back at the house. He went through the possibilities in his mind.

One consideration jumped at him. Aleksandr was not a Romanov. It was no secret that Russia's tsaritsas could be as promiscuous as her tsars. It had been a constant fear for Zmyeevich – that the throne would one day be taken by a bastard child who did not carry the Romanov blood and over whom he had no chance of taking control. The most likely candidate had been Tsar Pavel, whose mother, Yekaterina the Great, had had countless lovers and shown no affection for her supposed son. But Pavel's son, Aleksandr I, was beyond doubt a Romanov. He had seen through Zmyeevich's eyes and the *voordalak* had in turn been able to influence his mind. But that did not prove that Aleksandr's brother Nikolai was a true Romanov, nor that Nikolai's son was.

But Yudin was being an idiot. If the blood he had seen had not been Romanov blood, then the spherical cells would not have formed. The red blood cells would have been destroyed, as when any normal human blood met vampire blood. So if this was Romanov blood, then perhaps it was not Aleksandr's. If it had come from his brothers, or his son, then it would have shown the full reaction, just as it should for Aleksandr. Could it be Nikolai's? That would fit the observations. Nikolai came from a generation of Romanovs that could no longer be affected, thanks to the attempts already made on his brother – Zmyeevich could only focus his power on one child in each generation. That would mean the spherical cells formed but did not divide, wouldn't it? Yudin cursed not having his books to refer to. But why should Raisa take Nikolai's blood and pass it off as his son's? She wouldn't risk lying to Yudin. And the chances of her stealing a kiss from the tsar were far more slight than that she should manage it with his son.

Then, in an instant, all was clear. Yudin froze as the realization came upon him. He had eliminated every other possibility and now only one explanation remained, unlikely though it seemed.

If Aleksandr was not properly affected by Zmyeevich's blood, then – and it was as preposterous as it was inescapable – Tsar Nikolai could not be dead.

Yudin looked down at his own watery grave. It had been almost thirty years, but he remembered the cold. The surface of the Neva had been frozen then – frozen solid. Today there were still chunks of ice, floating out towards the Gulf of Finland, but also stretches of clear blue water in between. He turned round and looked behind him. The Bronze Horseman stared into the sky, oblivious to his presence. The statue had not gone by that name in 1825. It was only after Pushkin had written his poem that the statue of Pyotr the Great picked up its now familiar epithet. Yudin was one of the few who understood the statue's meaning.

Trampled beneath the hooves of Pyotr's horse lay a serpent, defeated by him as though he were Saint George and it was a dragon. In truth, the serpent represented Zmyeevich – his name literally meaning 'son of the serpent'. It was on this very spot, in 1712, that Pyotr had tricked the vampire and stolen his knowledge, but in doing so had condemned his own descendants to be victims of a blood curse.

It was here too that the Decembrists had stood against Tsar Nikolai. Yudin had been among them, along with his old adversary, Aleksei. They had been near the statue when the guns opened fire. Yudin traced their steps from there. He'd been ahead, suspecting that Aleksei had something planned for him, though nothing so lacking in subtlety as a mere pistol. He'd thought to run down Galernaya Street, but one glance at it told him that if the imperial guards caught up, it would be a shooting gallery. Instead, he had turned to the river, where many were already fleeing across the thick, steady ice.

This evening there was no one around. Beneath him, in the river, ice clung to the embankment, but where he had jumped down all those years before there was a gap through which he could see the cold dark water. He stepped forward, feeling the sensation of falling for only a fraction of a second before the icy water engulfed him. If anyone had seen, they would have taken it for a suicide, but his body would not be found, just as it had not been found thirty years before. Neither had Zmyeevich's, 113 years before that.

Yudin swam forward, under the water, barely able to see, remembering that Zmyeevich too, after his confrontation with Pyotr, had thrown himself into the river somewhere hereabouts, in fear for his life. There were myths that vampires hated the water, but in reality they had many of the attributes required to be good swimmers. They had no trouble with the cold – until it was enough for the fluids in their bodies to actually freeze solid – and they had little need for air. To be sure they needed to breathe, but they could survive without it, just as they could survive without consuming the blood and flesh of humans. Eventually lack of any of those things would cause them to slip into unconsciousness, but it would not kill them. If Yudin remained beneath the water too long he would lose strength and sink to the river bed, there to remain undisturbed. Perhaps centuries from now some fisherman would dredge him up, and on the first gulps of cool, fresh air he would come spluttering and coughing back to this world, hungry and grateful to find in that fisherman both his saviour and his first repast.

But Yudin would not be so foolish. He knew he could make

his planned journey by surfacing a mere two or three times for breath. It would mean that his approach was unobserved. It was a hard swim though, upstream against a strong current. He had no idea which direction Zmyeevich had headed on entering the water, but he would guess it was out to sea. His aim had been to depart Russia by the quickest conceivable route. As for Yudin, in 1825, there had been no aim – no intent. He remembered that Aleksei had shot him as he fled across the ice, mortally wounding him, but not killing him outright. Then Aleksei had begun his play-acting for the crowd, pretending to comfort his fallen friend, victim of one of the soldiers' muskets. They had talked and Aleksei had teased him over some trick that he had pulled, but the details were hazy. Yudin had drunk the blood that he had taken from the *voordalak* Kyesha, who had previously drunk *his* blood. It was Yudin's only hope of survival – to become such a creature himself. Then, with death, memory stopped.

He surfaced and took a gulp of air, glad of the opportunity to check his bearings. He was between the Winter Place and the lighthouses, just at the point where the Greater and Lesser Nevas split. He could just see his destination in the distance. He submerged again, and remembered his soggy restoration to life.

The persistence of memory had been his greatest fear. All the *voordalaki* he had ever spoken to claimed that they were the same being – the same person – that they had been before being transformed into that new state. It was easy enough for them to say, but Yudin had always wondered if the vampire might not be some other creature that took over the physical body of its victim, discarding its previous owner and taking from him only sufficient memories to pass itself off as a continuation of the original. He could think of no experiment that could prove things one way or another, except one that he would have to perform on himself, and that he delayed until the only other possibility was his own death.

He had returned to consciousness somewhere to the east of Helsingfors on one of the many islands that were scattered along that stretch of coast. It had been a little over a month since his death. That was a not untypical period for the transformation. Ideally a vampire would awake in its human grave, safe from the light of day and able to dig itself out when night fell, but Yudin's body had simply lain on a beach, exposed to the rays of the sun. Thankfully, nature guarded against such risks. The final stages of the transformation, when the vampire's flesh changed its nature so as to become susceptible to even the dimmest sunlight, always occurred at night. Yudin had known it by experimentation, and had learned it for himself. He had scuttled into a cave long before the dawning of his first day as a *voordalak*.

He popped his head above the water again. He was very close now. The Peter and Paul Fortress stood ahead of him. He was directly in front of the jetty from which the Decembrists, Aleksei among them, had begun their journey to the east. He could see two guards, some distance apart. Neither of them seemed particularly alert. There would be more of them on the far side, where an attack from the land could take them by surprise, but from the river an enemy could only approach by boat and would be easily spotted before reaching the fortress walls; or so they thought.

When he next surfaced he was under an arch of the jetty itself – the one closest to land. He could hear the footsteps of one of the guards above him. The water was shallow enough here that he had no need to swim.

'Help!' he shouted weakly. He heard the guard's feet move, but nothing more. 'Help me!' A little louder this time.

'Who's there?' shouted the guard.

'Please!' cried Yudin plaintively, then squatted down so that he was entirely submerged, with his face just inches below the surface.

He saw the blurry silhouette of the guard, peering out from the edge of the jetty and into the cold water, searching for the source of the sound. Yudin launched himself upwards, pushing against the firm river bed beneath his feet. He reached out with both hands and grabbed at the man's head. One hand caught his collar, the other an ear. In a moment, Yudin was falling back into the water and the soldier, off balance from leaning over, came with him. There would have hardly been a splash. Once beneath the river surface, the man attempted to struggle for a few seconds, but Yudin's teeth soon found their mark and he felt the delicious warmth of fresh blood filling his mouth, diluted but unmistakable, mixed with the river water.

He didn't wallow in the indulgence. He floated the body under the jetty, hoping that the current would not spit it out again too soon. A dark trail meandered through the water, staining the blocks of floating ice where it touched them, but it would take a keen eye for the other guard to notice it – and a good deal more time than he had available to him.

Yudin peered out of the water. On the other side of the jetty, the second guard was just disappearing around the corner of the Naryshkin Bastion. Yudin pulled himself up on to the pathway and ran lightly along it, hoping the splat, splat, splat of his wet feet would not attract attention. He stood with his back pressed against the ravelin, listening for the man's return, estimating his height.

He heard steps approaching and then glimpsed the soldier's leading foot emerging from behind the stonework. Yudin threw out his fist with a single, determined backhand blow. He heard a crunch as the man's nose collapsed. Yudin had been aiming for the throat, but it did not matter. The guard crumpled and Yudin caught him before he hit the ground – any observer might have thought it an act of concern. Out of the water, and with less prospect of being disturbed, Yudin took the opportunity to feed. He bent over the unconscious guard, listening to uneven breaths that were sucked into the mouth and then spluttered out through the broken nose.

Yudin's teeth easily penetrated the man's throat and from then on it was a simple matter. The human heart, desperate to cling on to life, continued to pump, forcing the blood out of the newly created wound. Yudin merely had to swallow occasionally and he became nourished.

Sated, he left the body half empty, rolling it into the river with an indifferent shove towards the jetty where it might be hidden beside its former comrade. He was glad the man had been unconscious, or he would have been tempted to linger too long in enjoying his pain. To drink as he had done was merely the scratching of an itch – the yielding to an obvious temptation from which no pleasure but the visceral could be taken. And while the blood that he had consumed would, over the next few days and even weeks, make him feel stronger and appear younger, its immediate effect was to render him tired and slothful; satisfied – it was an odious sensation.

But it could be overcome. Yudin looked at the stone wall. It was perhaps six times his height, with an overhanging ledge at the top. Arched openings allowed cannon to aim out into the river, but gave no access to the interior of the fortress. Occasionally, deliberate gaps in the stonework allowed a view through the entire thickness of the wall, but were too narrow for anything larger than a rat to make use of.

He began to climb. It was a fascinating skill that he had dis-covered – and needed – within hours of awakening as a vampire, as he climbed his way up the cliffs that surrounded the beach where he had found himself. He clung close to the wall, allowing his fingers to take his entire weight as they insinuated themselves into even the tiniest crevice between the straight-cut stones. He moved quickly, despite his wet clothes, leaving behind him a damp trail soaking into the granite. He pictured himself as a slug.

Once on the top of the fortifications, he glanced around. His final destination was the Pyetropavlovskiy Cathedral – dedicated to the same two saints who gave the fortress itself their names. Its spire soared into the air, disproportionate for the whole island, not merely the church beneath it. He could see no one, but knew there would be guards patrolling the interior. He could deal with them, but he did not want to be again distracted by his baser needs.

He dropped to the ground and crept through the shadows between the mint and the commandant's house, smiling at the thought that it was in there that Aleksei, along with the other Decembrists, had been interrogated and, hopefully, tortured to reveal the names of all the other conspirators he knew. Aleksei would have held out, to protect one name at least: that of his son. Even then, he would have had some idea that Dmitry was lost to him, taken in hand by Yudin himself when Aleksei was away with his mistress, just as Aleksei's wife, Marfa, had been. Aleksei knew that too. It was a delightful torture for Aleksei now, far away, cut off from any communication, to wonder how the relationship between his son and his most bitter enemy had developed. One day, Dmitry would face the final humiliation – and Yudin would ensure that Aleksei learned of it; better still, witnessed it. But that day would have to be soon – like Yudin, Aleksei was an old man now. Yudin wore it better.

He dodged a couple of guards easily and was soon in front of the cathedral's yellow walls, at the foot of the bell tower. Pyotr had founded it in 1712. Some in the Romanov family, who pretended they knew, said he did so specifically to give thanks to God for his defeat of Zmyeevich, but as with so much of that story, it was a mixture of myth and propaganda. It was a quite un-Russian church, better suited to Rome than Petersburg, wherein one might expect to hear ancient superstitions intoned in Latin by an old man who knew nothing of the world. In reality the language would be Church Slavonic rather than Latin, but the inanity of the content would be the same. The cathedral was not built for defence – the walls of the fortress saw to that – but it might still be guarded; to walk in through the door would be unwise.

Yudin scaled the wall of the bell tower with much the same ease as he had that of the fortress. Soon he was higher than the roof of the main building. The gilded spire stretched skyward above him, topped by an angel clutching a cross and pointing towards heaven. Yudin had no need to go that far. He smashed a window and was soon inside the bell tower. From there, he found a stone stairway spiralling downwards to the body of the church.

For any Russian who loved his tsar, it would have been a magnificent sight. The illumination of a thousand candles shone on the marble columns and brightly decorated walls and ceiling. The iconostasis – not simply a flat wall but an entire structure in itself – towered over the sanctuary. But it was all mere decoration. In the middle of the nave, in front of the iconostasis, surrounded by candles, on a pedestal, in a coffin, lay the centrepiece – a cold, still, silent corpse. This was what Yudin had come to see.

He heard the murmur of a voice. Over by the main door stood two soldiers, chatting softly. Yudin again felt on his lips the taste for blood, even though he had already consumed more than enough for his needs. He resisted. If they noticed him, he would deal with them, but it would be wiser to let them live. Tomorrow the church would be filled with almost every living member of the Romanov family – come to pay homage to one of their own. At least one of them would know of the ancient pact with Zmyeevich – Yudin was not sure who, but they would not be so stupid as to let the story be lost and so leave their children ignorant of what might befall them. To find bodies that so obviously bore the mark of the *voordalak* would raise their suspicions, and their defences, unnecessarily.

He skirted around the nave, along the northern aisle, until he was as close as possible to the late Tsar Nikolai. At least, that was whose body officially lay there. Yudin had his suspicions. Why, though, should Nikolai fake his own death? Did it have something to do with the Romanov bloodline, or was it unrelated? Was he even a willing participant, or had the new tsar, Aleksandr, taken power from his father by force and imprisoned him somewhere, lacking the stomach for parricide? If it were true then Aleksandr II was breaking with centuries of familial tradition.

But it all hinged on the fact or otherwise of Nikolai's death. Yudin stole a glance at the two guards, still deep in conversation, and crept out towards the centre of the nave, ducking down so that the coffin itself obscured any view they might have of him. Soon he was beside it. He stood up, and gazed in.

It certainly looked like Nikolai. He was older than when Yudin had last seen him, and a little fatter, but that could be put down to the process of embalming. His moustache was neatly waxed and his hair brushed forward, as it usually had been in life, to hide the great expanse of his balding head. Yudin placed his hand on the body's forehead, enjoying its coldness, and confirming beyond doubt that it was dead.

It could, of course, be a doppelgänger. Any man of approximately the correct height and appearance could have easily been persuaded to perform this duty of ultimate sacrifice for the sake of his tsar, and probably wouldn't have been given the option. The blood would tell, but Yudin understood enough of the mechanisms of preservation to know that the first step would have been to drain the blood from the body. The ruddy hue of the cheek was purely the effect of external make-up, to hide the work of entirely legitimate, if wasteful, vampirism. But a sample of flesh would be just as informative.

Yudin reached into his pocket, stiff and unyielding from its earlier soaking, and withdrew a small leather case. Inside was a scalpel. It was a delicate instrument; ideal for the task. The fragment of tissue need not be large, but still had to be taken from somewhere that would not be noticed. But why be so subtle? Yudin felt the sudden urge to desecrate the body in a way that would be unmistakable to all the Romanovs when they came to bury their beloved – to carve into his forehead a single word: Zmyeevich. That would scare them, the thought that the arch-*voordalak* could get in here, so close to the heart of their power.

Yudin chuckled quietly, but resisted. He lifted the corpse's left arm and turned it so that the hand was palm up, pulling back the sleeve to reveal the pale skin between it and the glove. They had not thought to apply make-up here, where no one would look. He cut away a sliver of skin and a little of the fat below, and slipped it into a glass tube, which he returned to the leather case.

He turned away. Tomorrow, before a vast crowd, Nikolai would be interred beneath the cathedral, beside his father Pavel and his grandmother Yekaterina and countless other tsars and tsaritsas, most but not all of whom shared that same Romanov blood and its curse. Pyotr III had been willing to join with Zmyeevich, but Yekaterina, his wife, had prevented it and herself become empress. Her blood was not Romanov, though her spirit was. With Aleksandr I they had come closest. He had even drunk Zmyeevich's blood, but had lived long enough to be free of it. His body was down there too, having taken the long slow journey across Russia from Taganrog, where death had found him.

One day, if Zmyeevich got his way, there would be a tsar who, although buried, would awaken in the crypt of the cathedral and would ascend to take his place beside his master to rule Russia for eternity. Would that tsar be Aleksandr II? Yudin did not know. He did not understand what he had seen in his microscope, but that fragment of tissue in his pocket would explain things. He was eager to examine it.

He left the way he had come.

CHAPTER VI

'**W**HY DON'T YOU HAVE A MIRROR?**'

Tamara had been into Raisa's room – as she had all the girls' rooms – more than once over the weeks since she'd arrived, but the absence of that otherwise universal item of furnishing had not previously occurred to her. She was seated on the bed, watching Raisa from behind as she brushed her long, blonde tresses. In front of her was a dressing table, much the same as in any of the other rooms – except that it had no mirror.

'Vanity,' said Raisa simply.

'Vanity?' Tamara would not deny that Raisa was vain – any woman who was so consistently well turned out would always be suspected of that – but it didn't explain the lack of a mirror. 'If you were vain, surely you'd have more mirrors.'

'Like Irina Karlovna?' Raisa briefly nodded towards the door that connected her room with that of her colleague, though Tamara doubted either of them had ever used it – Raisa and Irina were not friends.

Tamara laughed. 'Exactly!' The walls of Irina's room were covered with mirrors. She'd even asked to have one fixed to the ceiling, but Tamara had still to find an opportunity to discover whether Yudin would stump up the money.

'And whose benefit do you think those mirrors are really there for? Irina's?'

'For her clients', obviously.' Otherwise Tamara wouldn't have agreed to paying for any of them.

'And what do you suppose those gentlemen are looking at in the mirrors?'

'Irina?' suggested Tamara, though she knew already where Raisa was leading.

'They don't need a mirror for that. What those men are gazing at, through the entire process, is themselves. They find it so hard to believe that Irina has coaxed them into achieving something that they haven't managed with their wives for years, that they need to keep looking over her shoulder and checking.'

Tamara laughed.

'I'd rather have them looking at me,' continued Raisa. 'Hence no mirrors. Pure vanity.'

It was a good story, if not a good explanation. 'But what about doing your make-up?' asked Tamara.

Raisa swivelled round on her stool. In her hand she had a dainty pot of rouge – Rallye and Company's finest. She picked up a brush and dabbed it in the pot, then began to apply it to her lips. Her hand never wavered, and within seconds her lips were a perfect cherry red, the line between pale, powdered skin and rouged lip as precise as the boundary between two nations, drawn on a field marshal's map. She picked up another pot and with another brush applied pale blue shading to her eyelids, enhancing the natural sapphire of her eyes. Again she made not one slip.

'Practice,' she said when she had finished.

'I'd like to see you do that on the train,' said Tamara.

Before Raisa could reply there was a knock at the door. It was Nadia Vitalyevna. She was a curious thing. She had no qualms about the nature of the work that most of the girls in the brothel were called upon to perform, and yet despite her youthful charm, there was some quality about her that made her quite unappealing to the majority of the clientele. Those men who did show an interest, Tamara distrusted profoundly, and so Nadia had fallen into the necessary role of a simple housemaid. Perhaps she would grow into a more suitable creature for the work to which she aspired.

'Lieutenant General Yelagin here for you,' she said.

Raisa rolled her eyes, but Tamara knew that Yelagin was no ordinary customer. 'He's on Yudin's list,' she said. There were certain officers that Yudin insisted should be allowed every

108

indulgence. It wasn't because he liked them. She stood and walked over to the door as Nadia departed to fetch Raisa's guest.

'Anything for the motherland,' said Raisa, giving a mock salute.

Tamara glanced at her and grinned, then left her to her work.

It was Nikolai's body.

At least, it was the body of a Romanov and of Nikolai's generation – and that left little room for other possibilities. Back in Moscow, in his office beneath the Kremlin, Yudin had examined the small fragment of fatty skin that he had taken from the body in the cathedral. The body had been buried now, and the remainder of the family had bid their tearful farewells, and Yudin was as sure as they that it was truly Nikolai.

He had ground the sample to a pulp with a pestle and mortar, then mixed it with oil to form a liquid from which he could make a slide for his microscope. Then he'd added a few drops of Zmyeevich's blood and watched. Each time now that he used any part, however small, of that precious blood supply, he became nervous. It would not last for ever. He had eked it out over thirty years, expecting that it would be ultimately useful at the time of Nikolai's death; and useful it was proving, but not in any ultimate sense. Each discovery that Yudin made only led him on to further questions.

The current observation was a dull one – but informative. Nothing happened. With normal human flesh, as with normal human blood, the blood of a vampire should wreak immediate destruction, causing the human cells to wither and die. Here, there was no reaction. Vampire and human cells coexisted. They did not merge, as he had previously observed with Aleksandr's cells, because they were not blood, but the lack of immediate decay was enough.

He went over to his notebooks and checked again. He had brought them all here from his house in Zamoskvorechye now – all the secrets he had discovered from years of experimenting on the creatures. Some of the books were in a sorry state, battered and dog-eared not only from his regular use of them, but from being stored underground, hidden away at times when mobility had been his only means of survival. There were benefits to the settled life he had here in Moscow.

Two of the books though – including the one he was now consulting – had withstood the years remarkably well. They were covered in a light, flexible and phenomenally durable material. All the books had been bound in such a way to begin with – bound in the skin of a living vampire. He'd begun it more for amusement than because he thought it particularly practical, but it had turned out that there were only two ways that the skin could be damaged: it could be exposed to sunlight – which Yudin was incapable of causing without risk to himself – or the vampire from which the skin had originally come could perish. There had been three that he had used for the purpose. Two of them were dead – one killed by Yudin's own hand, and to save the life of Aleksei, of all people.

The third creature, whose skin still covered those last two volumes, remained where Yudin had left him – entombed beneath the cave city of Chufut Kalye, which Yudin had been precipitately forced to leave. He had used explosives to seal all the tunnels that led down there, and the *voordalaki* on whom he had been experimenting were thereby entombed. They would starve, but they would not die. Instead they would simply become dormant, unconscious of the world around them until such time as they could once again taste human blood on their lips and be given strength enough to revive. It was an unlikely scenario, despite the war so nearby. Far more probable was that some explorer would one day dig his way back into those caves and, in doing so, expose those emaciated bodies he found to the light of the sun, destroying them for ever. But Yudin's notebooks were still neatly bound, and so he knew that deep within those caves his former captive was still, in some sense, alive.

He checked the entry he was looking for. It was dated April 1824. It described exactly what he had just observed. The human flesh had not been Romanov and the vampire blood had not been Zmyeevich's, but that did not matter. Neither that family nor its nemesis was in any way special in terms of their biology – only in their status. He read through the details and could find no difference between what he had done then and what he was doing now. He tried to think back, but could find no memory whatsoever of actually carrying out the experiment he could now see described in his own handwriting – one of dozens he had conducted at the time. He silently complimented himself on his own assiduity in taking notes, not then knowing for sure how long he would live, or how poor his memory would become.

But there was always the possibility that he had made an error back then. He couldn't see how, but he was not fool enough to think himself infallible. It would be easy enough to reproduce, to confirm that his notes were correct. For vampire blood he could use his own, or that of Raisa or one of the several other samples he had collected over the years. As for human blood, he had an ample supply of it – how else did he live?

He collected a few items from his desk and then took out a key and went across the room to the heavy wooden door that stood opposite the covered mirror. He unlocked it, revealing the stone steps that descended to that deeper, older level of the building. He carried out one last check on the equipment he had picked up: a porcelain bowl, a scalpel and a thin glass rod, hollow on the inside, like a reed. It was all that he needed.

He descended the steps.

It was April now – two months since the late tsar's death – and spring was clearly on its way. There were only a few mounds of snow left waiting to melt, regularly located at street corners where they'd been piled up as the roads and pavements were cleared. Even though it was dark, it was still warm enough for Raisa and Tamara to walk through the Moscow streets without heavy over-coats or gloves.

But it was spring in another sense too, in the sense of hope and optimism that seemed to be shared among so many in the city. It was not unusual at this time of year, but now it was a feeling of expectation for not just a new season but a new era. Tamara did not share the belief herself. She preferred the certainty that Nikolai had brought with him. Aleksandr wanted change – just like his uncle and namesake had. There was even talk of freeing the serfs. So many of Tamara's generation dreamed of it, but during Nikolai's reign had not spoken, knowing he had spies on

111

every corner. None suspected that she might be one of them, so they did talk to her, but she didn't report them; not over matters like that.

What none of them seemed to consider was that freedom was the freedom to starve. Certainly plenty of the more able emancipated serfs would prosper and rise in society, but who would pay for it? It wouldn't be their former owners; the rich would always take care of themselves. Those they left behind – those they stepped over – alongside whom they had toiled for decades, would be the ones for whom life would be intolerably worse. Tamara preferred order. The tsar was there to protect them, all of them, serf and noble alike. How would he do that in the chaos that emancipation would bring? Aleksandr I had been persuaded to leave things be, against his own instincts. Perhaps the same could be achieved with Aleksandr II.

'It's getting late,' said Raisa.

'Are you expecting someone?' Tamara asked.

'No, but . . .' Raisa could find no 'but'.

'They'll manage,' said Tamara.

Even so, she increased her pace. She had already been hurrying when she had seen Raisa on the other side of Tverskaya Street and hailed her. They had been walking together now for only a few minutes. Tamara took a step out into the road to make room for a family who walked past, heading down Tverskaya Street towards Red Square. The adults were around Tamara's age. The little boy, clutching a parent's hand in each of his and scarcely needing to bear his own weight on his legs, must have been about nine. Tamara let her head turn to follow them as she passed.

'You like children, don't you?' said Raisa.

Tamara nodded. 'I had three in Petersburg.' She had said it before even thinking. It was her business and she longed to keep it so. On the other hand, there were times when she equally yearned to speak of it. The Lavrovs knew, of course, but how could she talk to them of her children when she had rejected them as parents?

Raisa stole a glance at her. The wind had strengthened and it was easier to walk with their heads down. It suited Tamara. She needed to talk, but it would help her to remain detached if she could not see any reaction in the person to whom she spoke.

Raisa could be dispassionate at the best of times, but this would be even less uncomfortable.

'You left them there?' asked Raisa.

'Left them? I suppose I did. It took me six years to get away.'

'You only lived there for six years?'

'No, I lived there for fourteen years,' Tamara explained. 'I wanted to leave for the last six.'

'What happened?'

'1848.'

'The year of revolutions?'

Tamara gave a brief laugh. 'What did that matter to us?' She paused, but knew that she would tell Raisa everything. Almost everything. 'In 1848 we were living in a house on Vasilevskiy Island, overlooking the river. My husband, Vitaliy, was a doctor and we had three children, Milena, Stanislav and Luka. Luka was just two.'

'Sounds idyllic.'

'It was.' It was true, though there was little in Tamara's voice to convey it. She had moved on from Larionov by then, and seen his downfall, and was sleeping with whoever Dubyelt said she should – not so many in number. But whenever she could forget that, whenever she was with Vitya or the children, she had been happy.

'Was Vitaliy successful?'

'Very – he was a good doctor.'

'So what happened?'

'Cholera.' Tamara whispered the word.

'I see.'

'It was everywhere. Every street had its deaths – every house in some areas.'

'Couldn't you have gone out of the city?'

'Vitya begged me to. He had to stay – it was his job. He saved lives, I know he did.'

'But you didn't go?' asked Raisa.

'I wanted to be with him, but eventually he won out. It was when the riots started, in June. I saw them all, crowding together in the Haymarket. Vitya said that would make it worse – all those people gathered together. Tsar Nikolai himself spoke to them – tried to calm them down, but by then we were already packing.

'Vitya was so confident – he made it difficult to believe that anything would go wrong if we did what he said. I remember him holding me, telling me that he'd be all right, that doctors rarely caught the disease. He was lying – but he was right.'

'So you left him?' said Raisa.

Tamara nodded. 'We went to Pavlovsk, but we hadn't been on the train long when Stasik started showing symptoms.' She remembered the foul stench of his diarrhoea inside the hot stuffy coach as she'd hugged him close to her, hoping that the conductor wouldn't notice and throw them off for fear of catching the disease himself. She'd forced him to drink water, as Vitya had recommended, and made sure the other children did as well. But it did no good.

'He was dead before we got there.' She had climbed down from the carriage, holding him in her arms, shouting for a doctor, but no one would even approach her. At last someone came and looked at him and told her he was dead. She laid his body down on the platform where she stood and kissed his forehead in the way her father – and for a moment she had almost been able to recall his face – used to kiss hers. She wept, feeling a pain within her belly where Stasik had grown, as though he had been ripped out of her. But eventually, when she did stop crying and found they had taken his body away, the pain inside her didn't stop. It kept growing and growing – a knife digging into her guts – even as they put her to bed.

'I went down with it too,' she told Raisa, glad again that she could not see her friend's eyes. 'I don't remember much for two days except for the pain, and the smell. And the shame – that's the worst of it – lying in your own filth like an old woman. When they could see I'd recover, they told me how lucky I'd been.'

'You were,' said Raisa.

'Then they told me Milenochka had died. She'd been taken ill the same time as me, and I never even noticed. I wanted Vitya to come out for the funeral, but they said it had to be done quickly. They'd already buried Stasik – I never found out where. I searched and searched. At least I know where Milenochka is.' She knew, but she also knew that Milena was not alone. It had been a mass grave. Not a pauper's grave – it wasn't a question of money. She was always keen to point that out when she spoke of it, as though boasting of which school her children went to. It was simply that with such great numbers of dead, things had to be done quickly. Perhaps Stasik's body was at the bottom of that same grave pit – it was a strange thing to hope for.

'So it was just you and Luka?'

'For a while. In the autumn, Vitya wrote to say it was safe now. He tried to hide it, but even in his writing I could tell that he'd changed. It wasn't just Milenochka and Stasik – he must have seen so much death in the city.'

'So you went back to Petersburg?'

Tamara nodded. 'As fast as we could.'

'And how was Vitya?'

'He was dead.' For the first time in the conversation, Tamara allowed emotion to seep into her voice and her words sounded to her like a lament. She breathed deeply to regain control of herself. 'Not the cholera – not directly. Murder plain and simple. One of his patients – a peasant he was treating free of charge – thought Vitya must have money. Stabbed him a few days before we got back.' Freedom was the freedom to kill.

'Did they catch him?'

'God did. He was a genuine patient – died to prove it. Vitya might have saved him.'

'You had Luka,' said Raisa. There was nothing consoling in her voice.

'No, Luka died too.' It was a lie, pure and simple, but nobody ever questioned it. Sometimes Tamara almost believed it herself, or wished she could.

'My God!' muttered Raisa.

'There are thousands suffered the same – or worse,' said Tamara.

'Peasants,' said Raisa.

It was true; the serfs were always hit harder – by disease, by famine. Freedom wouldn't change that. Freedom was the freedom to die. Raisa expressed the common view that they were inured to it. If they were, so was Tamara.

They turned off Tverskaya Street into Degtyarny Lane. The

115

wind had eased and a little late snow had begun to fall gently, illuminated by the lamps at the windows. It wouldn't settle.

'Home at last,' muttered Tamara, and then paused to think about what she had said. She'd had many places to call home, all of which she'd had to leave, either through circumstance or of her own volition. She'd not been here ten weeks, and it surprised her that already she could think of it as such. She looked at Raisa and smiled. Raisa's face was quizzical, but she said nothing.

It was only as she approached the front door and noticed that it was wide open, with no one in attendance, that Tamara began to feel anything might be wrong.

Nadia Vitalyevna was on the verge of tears when they entered. She was at the top of the stairs, on the landing that accessed most of the girls' rooms. Within moments Tamara and Raisa had joined her, and the girl threw herself into Tamara's arms.

'It's Irina Karlovna,' she said, her voice fractured.

'What about her?' asked Tamara.

'Her door's locked. She won't answer.'

'You mean she's not there,' suggested Raisa.

'No,' said Nadia. 'I saw her go in.'

'Why didn't you use the spare keys?' asked Tamara.

Nadia sniffled, and glanced from Tamara to Raisa and back.

'We can get to her through mine,' said Raisa, exasperated at the girl's silence. Tamara had already considered using the connecting door between the two rooms, but even as she spoke, Raisa tried her own door handle and found it too did not yield.

Tamara turned back to Nadia. 'Where are the keys?' she insisted.

'Irina asked me for them,' sobbed Nadia. 'I knew I shouldn't. I've been running between her door and the front for the past half-hour, seeing if she'll answer and looking out for you.'

Tamara raced down the stairs to her own rooms. Inside, she retrieved her master set of keys and then hurried back up. Nadia and Raisa stood waiting.

'Did she have any customers?' Tamara asked.

'A captain came and asked to see her,' said Nadia. 'That's when she didn't answer the door.'

'Where is he now?'

'I don't know. I didn't recognize him. He didn't stay.'

'I bet,' muttered Raisa.

They had come to the door. Tamara inserted her key. Nadia was still right beside her, ready to go in, but Raisa, guessing wisely what they might find within, held back. Tamara glanced from her to Nadia and back, and Raisa took the girl's hand and led her a little way away. Tamara turned the key in the lock and opened the door.

The mirrors didn't help. Tamara could not immediately see the bed because of the door, and even when she stepped into the room it was visible only out of the corner of her eye. But reflected in Irina's many beloved mirrors, just as Irina had intended, she saw the image of what lay on the bed again and again and again.

It was as though an artist had made a series of preparatory sketches of his model, each from a different angle, unable to decide which point of view would show off her beauty at its fullest. But the mirrors had the advantage of showing the scene in its full, vivid colour.

From some angles, Irina appeared demure, her head tilted away in shyness. From others she was licentious, her legs lying open to reveal that part of her which had been her livelihood and, most likely, the reason for her death. But what predominated were those reflections which showed her face, still and pale with eyes that gazed into Tamara's and showed no recognition – and beneath that young, childlike face, visible wherever Tamara looked, was the wide, red gash between her chin and her collarbone where some monster in human form had torn away the flesh of her once elegant neck. There was no aspect to the bloody, mangled mess of tissue that, by looking somewhere in the room, Tamara could not see.

From outside she heard Raisa's voice shout, 'No!' and then felt Nadia at her side. The girl didn't even glance at the mirrors, but turned straight to the bed.

Her shrill, regular screams, filling the room, reminded Tamara of a locomotive's whistle.

CHAPTER VII

'AND SO TO OUR TOAST,' SAID VALENTIN VALENTINOVICH, 'IN an order which is intended to imply no preference. To our beloved daughter and to our city's beloved saint. To a slayer of dragons and a slayer of men's hearts.' He was a little drunk, even on a little wine, but Tamara did not mind. She had drunk more, but to no beneficial effect. 'To Tamara and to Saint George!'

'Tamara and Saint George.' Two voices echoed the sentiment – Yelena and young Vadim. Tamara was happy to be with just those three.

It was Saint George's day. He was the patron saint of Moscow, and revered throughout the country. On the table in front of them stood the remains of the traditional meal of roast lamb, enjoyed by all. But if it was Saint George's day then that meant, inescapably, that it was Tamara's birthday. It was also five days since Irina Karlovna had been murdered. Tamara was now thirty-four. Irina had been twenty-one.

There was no question of her telling them. They did not know where she worked or what she did. They might have heard something of the murder through gossip – from their servants if not from their friends – but Yudin had taken charge of affairs within hours of the discovery of Irina's body; and Yudin's instinct was for secrecy. It was simple for him to ensure that the regular police did not investigate the crime – they were answerable to the Ministry of the Interior. Instead he had called in the Corps of Gendarmes. Their ultimate commander was Count Orlov, who was also head of the Third Section. It was no coincidence. Although the two were officially separate institutions, the fact that they were led by the same man revealed the truth. The Corps of Gendarmes was the uniformed branch of the Third Section.

When Yudin had spoken to the gendarmes who came to Degtyarny Lane, it was clear who was in charge, regardless of the blue uniform and plumed helmet of their captain. Yudin's suggestion had been that Irina had killed herself. Tamara questioned her motive and her method, but Yudin had countered that those were vague doubts set in the face of a body found alone in a locked room, a room to which Irina herself had insisted on taking the keys. But then Tamara had pointed out that the keys were nowhere in the room – neither was anything that could be thought of as a weapon. Yudin conceded it was a puzzle, but asked why, if Irina had been with a man, no one had seen him leave.

In the end Tamara accepted that Yudin had his own reasons for letting the murder lie uninvestigated. It would be bad for business. A murder like this would discourage the clientele of any brothel. For one whose customers were of such high status – and thus had so much to lose – it could mean the flow of information dried up completely. Even if Yudin knew beyond peradventure who had killed Irina, he might keep it quiet just so as not to rock the boat. If that were so, Tamara doubted whether she would catch any hint of it.

She looked up at Valentin Valentinovich, and tried to conjure the image of her real father toasting her, standing at the end of the table, instead of him. Valentin so failed to come up to the mark. The dining room where they sat held no strong associations with her true father and only slight ones with her mother – it was the same in all the rooms downstairs. And yet the calm familiarity of the place was an incalculable blessing. She didn't partake much in the conversation, merely sat back and enjoyed it. Somewhere at the back of her mind she felt the urge to smoke, but she knew she could not here. It didn't bother her very much. Talk had turned to the war. Valentin was telling his grandson of affairs in the north – and therefore of the boy's father.

'The British, of course, have sent a second expeditionary force into the Baltic.'

'But Papa will stop them.'

'Absolutely. Before they can take Petersburg, they have to take Helsingfors. And to take Helsingfors they'll have to destroy Sveaborg – and that's where Rodion comes in.'

'You sound like *my* papa,' said Yelena, with an affectionate laugh. '"Before Bonaparte can take Moscow, he'll have to capture Smolensk. Before Smolensk, he'll have to take Vitebsk. Before Vitebsk, Vilna."'

A frown appeared on Valentin's face. His grandson had already spotted the flaw. 'But Bonaparte did capture Vilna,' he said earnestly, 'and Vitebsk and Smolensk and then Moscow.'

'And then Vadim Fyodorovich sent him packing,' said Tamara, grinning at her nephew, 'just like Rodion Valentinovich will.' Perhaps the tales of Vadim Fyodorovich, great-grandfather to Vadim Rodionovich, were where Tamara got her image of the gallant male that somehow transformed into her imagined father. He was the true hero of the family, naturally to Yelena, his daughter, but also to Valentin.

'Not just Vadim,' added Vadim Rodionovich. 'There were four of them: Vadim, Maks, Dmitry and Aleksei. They all did it together.' Clearly he knew the stories as well as Tamara did – perhaps better. She knew enough about the exploits of Vadim Fyodorovich, but the lives of Maks, Dmitry and Aleksei were less easy to remember. It was just Vadim and his comrades – the exploits and characters of the other three merging in her mind into one.

There was an awkward silence. Valentin glanced at Yelena, while the young Vadim remained happily unaware of it. The cause was obvious – the older Vadim might have got rid of Bonaparte, but he had died in the process. Rodion had been born within days of his grandfather's death – Tamara nine years later. But from what she had heard of him, it was Vadim more than anyone who made her wish she was truly part of this family.

'And now this second Napoleon is coming back for more,' exploded Valentin, breaking the uneasiness.

'Third,' said Vadim.

'He calls himself "the third",' said Valentin, with more than a hint of bile, 'but he's only the second one to claim to be emperor of France.'

'And the last,' added Tamara.

'Ha!' said Valentin, impressed by Tamara's unexpected patriotism. 'Yes.' He stood and raised his glass. 'A new toast. To Toma, to Saint George, and to Napoleon the Last.'

The other voices chimed in unison. 'Napoleon the Last!'

Saint George's day had not been widely noticed in Sevastopol. Those officers who came from Moscow joined together to celebrate as best they could, but any chance of an evening of enjoyment was marred by the fact that outside the city thousands of Frenchmen and Englishmen were planning to destroy them. True, the English revered George in much the same way Muscovites did, but it had caused no let-up in their determination. And as Dmitry more than once pointed out to his fellow officers, that was in no small part because the English had celebrated the feast of Saint George twelve days earlier, thanks to the absurdities of their calendar.

That evening Dmitry was blessed with Tyeplov's company, though the circumstances were hardly convivial. Again, Dmitry had been tasked with inspecting the state of Totleben's defences – and of the men's morale – this time in the fourth bastion, regarded as the foulest posting of the lot. When they'd spoken at the barracks, Tyeplov had seemed almost casual in suggesting he come along. The company of any man that night would have cheered Dmitry – that it was Tyeplov meant something more.

Winter had vanished completely and where once the streets had been hardened by frost, now they were a sea of mud. Embedded sporadically in the ground were cannonballs. It was unusual but not unheard of for them to reach into the heart of the city, though most arrived here accidentally. The Allies knew that it was Totleben's ramparts that stopped them from taking Sevastopol, not the buildings and people within, and so that was where they concentrated their fire. As Dmitry and Tyeplov walked along the bank of the Military Harbour and got closer to the bastion, the concentration of the discarded iron balls became more dense. Eventually they would be gathered up and reused by the Russians, only to be replenished in another bombardment. No guns were firing today – not yet, at least.

As they came out of the city, the road descended into a narrow trench, with wooden planks placed intermittently along the sides to prevent the earth from cascading back into what it regarded as its rightful territory. In construction, it was much like the tunnel beneath the Star Fort where Dmitry and Shulgin had made their gruesome discovery – with the exception that it had no roof. As long as Dmitry was free to stand upright, he felt none of the terror of entombment that would otherwise have descended upon him.

As they came closer to the bastion, the dug-out walls of the trench became augmented by gabions. They could absorb some of the blast from a shell and sometimes a direct hit from a cannonball. There had been times where they had proved dangerous in themselves, toppling over and crushing the soldiers they had been constructed to defend, but in most cases they were strapped securely in place.

The trench began to ascend and ended at the inner wall of the fourth bastion itself. There was little to distinguish it from any of the others. A few of the braver men peered out over the top towards the enemy lines. Most sat and hugged themselves to keep out the cold. At least there was no rain tonight, and the wind was not too severe. Dmitry spoke to the first soldier he saw.

'Where's your commanding officer?'

The man – a boy really – glanced up, but seemed unimpressed by Dmitry's seniority. 'In the naval casemate.' He jerked his thumb over his shoulder, pointing down another trench that ran parallel with the bastion wall. Dmitry felt no desire to reprimand him; instead he and Tyeplov followed the trench. At the end of it, a wooden door was visible, beside which sat a sailor smoking a pipe.

'Is it all right to go in?' asked Dmitry.

'Just a moment, sir.' The sailor, showing a better sense of rank than had his army comrade moments before, was on his feet in an instant. 'I'll tell them you're here.' He opened the door and stuck his head through it. Moments later he stood upright and pushed the door wide open, indicating that the two officers should enter.

Dmitry had never been inside this casemate before. All the bastions had them – some several. From outside there was no hint, apart from the door, that this part of the earthworks was not as solidly built as the rest of it, but inside was an entire room, a large one at that, acting as a shelter from the weather and a haven of relative safety. Compared with the others he had visited, Dmitry was struck by the degree of decoration inside. The floor was parqueted, no less; a little bumpy in places, but a leap forward compared with the raw earth or duckboards that he had seen elsewhere. Against the wall at either end stood two beds, with curtains that could provide a modicum of privacy. In the corner near one of them hung an icon of the Virgin, with a pink vigil lamp burning in front of it, resting on a stool. On one of the beds lay a naval officer, fully clothed in the uniform of a *michman* – apparently asleep. At a table in the middle of the casemate, one seated, the other standing, were two infantry officers, each at least ten years Dmitry's junior.

'Anatoliy!' exclaimed the standing officer, embracing Tyeplov as an old friend. Then he turned to Dmitry, offering his hand. 'I don't believe we've met.'

They had met, in the mess weeks before when Dmitry's conversation with Tyeplov had been interrupted. He chose not to mention it. Instead he dumped his knapsack beside the door before walking over to shake the officer's hand.

'I'm *Shtabs*-Captain Mihailov,' said the man, 'and this is Lieutenant Wieczorek.' Dmitry always found it difficult to trust Poles who fought for Russia. More than one senior Polish officer had switched sides to the Turks, taking on a Turkish name to hide his treachery. Dmitry knew for a fact the so-called Sadyk Pasha, a leading light of the 'Sultan's Cossacks', was none other than Micha Czaykowski, a Polish turncoat. But it was unfair to judge Wieczorek by the standards of his countrymen; he was, after all, still here. 'And that reprobate,' continued Mihailov, picking up a bread roll from the table and hurling it at the sailor on the bed, 'is *Michman* Ignatyev.' Ignatyev showed no reaction as the projectile bounced off his chest. 'Care for a glass of Bordeaux?' asked Mihailov, lifting a bottle from the table and jiggling it in their direction.

For a brief moment Dmitry hoped against hope that Mihailov had genuinely meant Bordeaux, but he only needed to glance at the bottle to realize that it contained just the local Crimean brew.

It was a joke he'd heard often enough now to forget its original humour. He accepted a glass anyway, as did Tyeplov.

'I don't think I've ever seen anything quite like this on the front before,' said Dmitry, glancing around him and taking in the room once more.

'One has to maintain one's standards,' replied Mihailov.

'It's like a country gentleman chose to transfer his home into a cave. Don't you think, Tolya?'

'Quite unique,' said Tyeplov, after a momentary pause and with an enigmatic smile.

'Much action out here?' asked Dmitry.

Mihailov glanced at Wieczorek, who answered, 'Nothing for two days.' Dmitry could detect no hint of a Polish accent in his speech.

'A blessing, I suppose,' said Tyeplov.

'Means it's due,' came Ignatyev's voice from the bed.

'It's been quiet over the winter,' said Dmitry.

'It's spring now,' said Ignatyev, using his fingers to tidy his moustache as he sat upright. 'They won't give up.'

Mihailov reached forward and refilled Dmitry's glass. Dmitry hadn't realized how quickly he had emptied it. If it was Bordeaux, then it hadn't travelled well. Even its short journey from the vineyards between here and Bakhchisaray had done it little good. Despite that, Dmitry enjoyed the sensation of it on his throat, if not the taste.

'Listen!' said Ignatyev suddenly. They all stopped talking. There was no sound to be heard. Dmitry took a breath to speak, but Ignatyev raised a finger to his lips to silence him. Then there was a thud, coming through the ceiling above them.

'Cannonball,' said Mihailov, confirming what Dmitry had guessed.

'You heard that coming?' Dmitry asked Ignatyev, the incredulity evident in his voice.

'You get attuned to it.'

They heard the sound of a second impact in the ground above the casemate. Ignatyev leapt off the bed, and Mihailov and Wieczorek were already pulling on their greatcoats and making for the door. Ignatyev wasn't far behind them. Dmitry didn't know many officers who would be so keen to get out into the battle. He followed, as eager as they for action. Tyeplov was close on his heels.

Outside the settled indolence that had been so evident when they arrived had vanished. The sailor who sat at the door had gone off in search of a more valiant post. Gunners who had been huddling to stave off the cold were now at their positions, looking to pick off the enemy if they tried to advance, hoping to have a lucky shot and disable one or more of the crew members of the big guns. Dmitry rushed to the nearest gap in the wall to see whether an advance was being attempted. Deep, regular blasts came from behind them and to the side, which he knew were their own cannon responding to the combined French and British assault.

Perhaps twice a minute he would hear somewhere near him the whistle and splat of a cannonball finding its way into the trenches. They were wasted shots. At best they would kill two or three men, or maim them – an awful lot of iron and powder for so little gain, doing nothing to damage the defences themselves. A moment later, Dmitry saw the effect of a cannonball on a man for himself. A *ryadovoy* had been running through the trenches towards the edge of the bastion, carrying bags of powder and shot to enable the musket men at the front to reload. Dmitry had not had a chance to see the ball as it swiftly sailed through the air, with almost the same speed as it had exited the muzzle of the cannon, and with an inexorable weight behind it.

It hit the *ryadovoy* square on the forehead and found little resistance. The man's skull cracked into a dozen fragments, which exploded through the flesh of his head as the cannonball tried to supplant the grey matter inside. The shot hit the mud behind him as his body fell forward, still clutching the ammunition he had been fetching. Dmitry felt something warm and moist splatter against his cheek. He wiped it away and flicked it from his fingers on to the ground without looking. He heard the whoosh of another shot coming in and then an explosion, throwing a cloud of smoke and mud into the air that obscured Dmitry's view of the headless, twitching body. He ran back to the trench, knowing that there would be others wounded, but perhaps some with hope of survival. Another blast shook the ground and he reached out to the wall to steady himself, scratching against the compressed earth and feeling a strange sensation of comfort as the dirt penetrated beneath his fingernails.

The haze thrown up by the explosion quickly began to settle, revealing along the trench the damage that it had caused. Dmitry stiffened as he saw Tyeplov leaning forward, a look of distress on his face, but his friend soon straightened up, and Dmitry felt sure that he was uninjured. The same could not be said of the slumped figure towards whom Tyeplov was directing his concern. Dmitry recognized it as the Pole, Wieczorek. His left arm was missing. Dmitry could see a tangled bloody stump where the ball had caught him, just above the elbow. Wieczorek's face showed the determined stoicism of a man who knew that such an injury almost certainly meant death. Tyeplov turned his head and looked into Dmitry's eyes.

The sound of the Russian guns was louder now – loud enough to drown out the firing of the Allied cannon, but not to stop the sound of their shot landing nearby. Dmitry glanced up at the sky. It seemed for a moment as though the stars were falling, but it was merely shells breaking up early, leaving their fiery traces across the heavens. Then he heard a new sound, a whistling from something large coming in to land, close enough to hint that he himself might be its hapless target. He threw himself face down on the ground and felt it shake as the projectile splashed into the mud.

Dmitry dragged himself to his feet and looked around. A shell had landed just a little way down the trench and was rolling feebly towards him, like a puppy slowly but eagerly coming to meet its master. He could see the fuse glowing red, but could not guess how long he had until it exploded. When it did it would wreak far more damage that any iron cannonball.

At that instant, Dmitry realized how little he wanted to die, but at the same time the power to move drained from him. He felt a terror that he had never experienced before. He was immobile, half standing, half crawling, staring at the scintillating fuse, counting the seconds until his death. Then his view was blocked, and he felt his body racked by a sudden collision which could only be the impact of the exploding shell. The blow picked him up and carried him down the trench and then, surprisingly, round the corner that led back to the casemate. He had not been thrown, but was being carried.

Inside the casemate he was shoved on to the parquet floor and felt a body hurl itself on top of his. He could not see, but he knew simply from the scent of the man – a scent that he had subconsciously absorbed over the past weeks – that it was Tyeplov. Moments later, the explosion shook them both. Dmitry heard a rattle as debris fell through the door and hit the hard wooden floor, but they were too far away for the shell to do them any serious damage.

Tyeplov stood almost immediately. 'I'll go take a look,' he said, his voice confirming, if Dmitry had held any doubt, who he was. Dmitry rolled on to his back and slid across the floor away from the doorway, pushing himself along with his hands. Eventually he felt the wall behind him and stopped, pulling his knees up to his chest and clutching them there. His whole body shook, not from any blast outside but of its own volition.

He breathed deeply and tried to let the music come to him, to be the secret friend and comforter that it had been ever since he was a child. He heard fragments of it, but each one was interrupted by an explosion from outside, be it the sound of a Russian cannon or a French shell. The more he tried to hear his music, the louder the detonations became. He rested his head against his knees, but found he could not even cry. He did not know where the fear had come from, nor why it had arrived so suddenly.

'It's hell out there,' said Tyeplov, coming back in. Dmitry did not look up. 'There's dozens dead and the whole side of the earth-work has slid into the trench. We're virtually buried. It'll be hours before they can get to us.'

Through the on-going barrage of gunfire, Dmitry heard foot-steps walking across the floor and sensed Tyeplov sitting down beside him. His very presence was calming. Dmitry felt an arm around his shoulders and he yielded to its pull, lying with his head on Tyeplov's chest and able to feel his heartbeat. Still the music would not play inside his head, but as Tyeplov's arms held him tightly, he knew that he could do without it.

It was approaching midnight when Tamara returned to Degtyarny Lane. Vadim was too young to stay up into the small hours, and her parents were too old. They had chatted for quite a while after dinner, but when Valentin had dozed off she had decided it was time to leave. She had lit a cigarette as soon as the front door closed behind her, and now she was on her second.

She had not raised the subject of her parentage with them, and doubted she ever would again. As Yelena had suggested, if they hadn't told her anything by now, then it was unlikely that they would in future. Even so, Tamara would have liked to simply talk about it. Aside from work, it had for the last few months been her main preoccupation. She had spent many hours in the archive, once Gribov had allowed her access to it, but to little avail. There had been letters and documents relating to Volkonsky, and even written by him, but they told her no more than she already knew. But she had not got far yet. She had begun with the stratum of papers that roughly corresponded to 1820, the year before her birth, and had so far reached only the autumn of 1825. Volkonsky had not even begun his payments then. She would continue looking.

She approached the door and threw her cigarette into the gutter before raising her hand to knock. It was still business hours and Saturday evening was always popular, so the place would be awake. Since Irina's murder, they had all become a little more cautious. They'd even acquired a man, Isaak, to stand at the door – Yudin had found him somewhere. She didn't see how he would have prevented Irina's death, but she supposed the sight of him might have scared her killer away before he even entered the building.

She heard a sound. Her hand froze, inches from the door. Footsteps approached her from behind, accompanied by hoarse, wheezing breath. She dropped her arm to her side, ready to reach down for the knife which, since Irina's death, she had carried hidden in her boot. Before she could turn, she felt a hand on her shoulder.

'I wouldn't go in there, my love.'

Tamara slapped at the hand, knocking it away from her, and

turned. It was an old woman; about the age of Tamara's mother – her adoptive mother – though she wore it less well. Her hair was long and grey, tied in a ponytail, most of which was hidden under her coat. She was stooped and had to tilt her head upwards to look into Tamara's face. There were more and more of these beggars on the streets now, as if they sensed Tsar Aleksandr had already lost some of the control his father had exercised.

'Piss off!' snapped Tamara.

The woman's eyes looked up at her calmly. Tamara detected a slight wince in reaction to her words, but she must have been used to that, and far worse.

'It's not a place for you,' said the woman. She lifted her hand and rested it on Tamara's arm, but Tamara again knocked it away.

'That's for me to decide.'

'What would your mother say, knowing you worked in a place like that?'

Tamara inhaled deeply through her nose and she felt tears rush to her eyes, though she denied them access. The question was not new to her. It was Larionov who had asked it first, during their third liaison – right in the middle of it, when she had believed that she could never feel more humiliated, and when he had known better. She'd avoided asking herself ever since. The very question gave the lie to everything she was doing. She was searching for her parents, but what would she do if she found them? They'd already had reason enough to give her up to the Lavrovs – what would they think of her now if they discovered what she did for a living? She could give excuses, but she had imagined her parents time and time again, and could guess their reactions; her father's anger, her mother's shame.

'Go to hell!' she spat, and turned back to the door.

It took her only an instant to regret it. It was not in her nature to be so unnecessarily rude. She looked over her shoulder, back towards the woman, who had not taken her eyes off Tamara. Her face was very still – knowing, like Yelena Vadimovna's used to be when she had caught Tamara out in a lie.

'She's not the first to die, you know,' the woman said.

Tamara turned slowly, still angry, but her curiosity now piqued. 'What do you mean?'

'The girl who was killed on Monday – it's happened before.'

'When?'

The woman nodded her head in the direction of the bench on the other side of the street. It seemed a natural enough place to sit and talk. They went over, Tamara walking slower than usual so that the woman's aged steps could keep up with her.

'When?' repeated Tamara once they had sat down.

'What's your name?' the woman countered.

Tamara pressed her lips together and tried to remain calm. The old thing probably just wanted conversation, or perhaps there would be an appeal for money at the end of it. But she just might have some information on Irina's death. Tamara couldn't ignore the chance. 'Tamara Valentinovna Komarova,' she said.

'Tamara? It'll be your name day soon.'

It was true enough – 1 May would be the feast of Saint Tamara, Georgia's first queen. They'd celebrated it when she was young, but not to any great extent now. 'It's my birthday today,' she volunteered, surprising herself with her desire to reveal the fact to a stranger.

The old woman paused, studying her before speaking. 'You'd have been called George if you'd been a boy – after the saint.'

'I suppose I would,' she said. It had never occurred to Tamara to ask – not that there would be any point. How could Valentin and Yelena answer a question as to what her parents might or might not have done? Even to raise the issue would only cause another argument. She reverted to the topic at hand. 'What do you know about the murder . . . ?' Her voice tailed off, unable to address the woman by name.

'Natalia.'

'Natalia.'

'Natalia Borisovna Papanova,' she clarified. 'Lived in Moscow all my life. Are you married? Children?'

Tamara failed to hide her irritation at the question. 'Please,' she said. 'The murder.'

Natalia continued to stare at her, her eyes scanning Tamara's face as if looking to discover the secrets that Tamara would not reveal in answer to her questions. She quickly gave up. 'I lived here all my life,' she repeated. 'And in all that time, that place' – she pointed – 'has been a bawdy house.'

'And there've been other murders there?'

'Just one. One here. One I know – knew.' She gazed into the distance, towards Tverskaya Street, and perhaps into the past. 'Margarita Kirillovna – that was her name.' She craned her head up at one of the windows. 'Had her throat cut; ripped out, they said.'

Images of Irina, reflected again and again in the mirrors, flashed into Tamara's mind, and she felt the strange hope that Natalia had never had to witness such a thing. 'It was the same on Monday,' she whispered.

'That's what I heard.'

'When was this?' Tamara was surprised she had heard nothing of the first murder.

'Just after the French left.'

'What?'

'We stayed right through the occupation, me and my dad. He was a cobbler – made shoes for the French, or for the Russians; whoever paid.'

'Occupation?' Tamara could guess what she meant, but the idea was absurd.

'The French. Bonaparte.'

Tamara was on her feet. 'You mean 1812? What the hell could that have to do with this?'

'It's the same. Just the same – then and now.'

Clearly the woman was mad – desperate to relive her past. Perhaps there had been a murder all those years ago – more than forty – perhaps not. It had nothing to do with Irina's death.

'You stupid old cow,' she shouted, angrier with herself for having been taken in than with Natalia. 'Who do you think cares about that?'

'They'll get you next,' said Natalia. 'Please, Toma, listen to me.'

It was obvious the woman was lonely, but Tamara had no time for her. She reached into her bag and pulled out a silver rouble. Handing it to Natalia, 'I can't talk to you,' she said. 'I'm sorry. Take this.'

The old woman put out her hand and took the money, almost

as if it were a reflex action rather than a matter of conscious thought. Tamara turned and went back to the house. She hammered on the door and Isaak's flat, broad, impassive face peeked at her through the grille before allowing her in. Just as the door closed behind her, Tamara heard a single word shouted across the street.

'Toma!'

She went to her office, but did not light a candle. She stood in the darkness beside the window, looking out at the bench. Natalia sat there in stillness, except for the movement of her head, which looked at each of the windows of the brothel in turn. After a few moments, a blue-uniformed gendarme ambled past. Despite Yudin's prohibition on their investigating, they did at least send the occasional patrol to keep an eye on the area. He scarcely glanced at the old woman, but she noticed him. She stood and walked away as briskly as her aged legs could manage, throwing something into the gutter as she left the street – something that glinted silver in the lamplight.

Dmitry stared at the casemate ceiling, lit now only by the flickering pink light of the vigil lamp, which had, by the grace of the Virgin whose duty it was to illuminate, managed to remain upright despite the bombardment. Tyeplov was fast asleep, an arm draped over Dmitry's stomach and the side of his face resting against Dmitry's bare chest. Dmitry could feel Tyeplov's dry lips lightly touching his skin. The guns outside were quiet now, and the music had returned, a strange music that Dmitry had never heard before, not inside his head. Joyful – that was the word for it.

He looked down, but the position in which they were lying meant that he couldn't see much of the other man. He dared not move, for fear of waking him. Dmitry's hand rested on the outside of Tyeplov's thigh, which in turn was stretched across Dmitry's midriff, his lower leg curling back underneath Dmitry's bottom. His body was as chiselled as Dmitry had imagined. Even as he slept, the tension in the muscle of his thigh could be felt through his skin. And yet with Dmitry he had been very gentle, coaxing and cajoling him and rarely taking his eyes from Dmitry's. This was clearly something he had done before – and understood well. It was an agreeable reversal of roles. In their discussion on music, Dmitry had had the pleasure of introducing Tyeplov to experiences with which he himself was long familiar, and to enjoy them anew for experiencing another's initiation. Now, Dmitry hoped, Tyeplov took the same pleasure in helping Dmitry to enjoy sensations which for him were entirely familiar.

Dmitry smiled to himself at the comparison – music and sex. For most people, the latter was easily understood, and it would be music that needed explanation and analogy. Dmitry understood sex well enough too, or thought he had, and by now had become bored with it, until today when it had been, it seemed, reinvented. He remembered the first occasion: 16 December 1825 – two days after his father had been arrested and Yudin had gone missing, believed drowned; two days after Dmitry himself had fled across the frozen river and gone into hiding for fear of meeting the same fate as one or the other of them. It had been in Petersburg, with a whore in a brothel overlooking the Kriukov Canal. She had been expensive, but at that time Dmitry had had little hope for the future – little need to save his pennies. He expected arrest at any moment and even if he remained free, he felt that the shame of what he'd allowed to happen, of what he had run away from, made his life valueless. But she had been worth the money. It had been the first and the best. The irony was that it had given Dmitry a touchstone against which all other encounters could be compared, against which all had come up wanting – until now.

The only other occasion that had come close had been the first time he had slept with his wife, Svetlana. It had been only two weeks before their marriage, but for both of them the illicit nature of it – even if illicit by only fourteen days – had been an added thrill. Then he had been the tutor, she a virgin, she who had been eager to learn everything, anything. She had been like Tyeplov discovering Chopin, like Dmitry just minutes before. But as their marriage had gone on, sex had become increasingly mundane, increasingly, for both of them, a matter merely of satisfaction. As for other men, Tyeplov was not the first fellow officer towards whom Dmitry had felt some degree of attraction, but he had never felt compelled to act upon it, or thought of it as something that required action. Even today, it was Tyeplov who had acted, not Dmitry.

The sound of creaking hinges cut through the silence. Dmitry had never moved so fast in his life. He was out of the bed and across the other side of the casemate before the door even opened. He had no idea how long he and Tyeplov had been together, but was surprised it was long enough for anyone to have dug their way through the collapsed trench. Dmitry couldn't guess precisely the consequences if they were found together, but they wouldn't be good. Even now, it wouldn't help to stand there, casually leaning against the far wall trying to look innocuous with Tyeplov lying asleep in bed and their clothes strewn across the floor. But there was little he could do.

The door blocked Dmitry's view of who had opened it, but a voice behind it hissed, 'Are you there?'

Dmitry said nothing, and Tyeplov was dead to the world. A figure emerged from behind the door. Even in the dim light, Dmitry recognized it as *Shtabs*-Captain Mihailov. He did not look in Dmitry's direction, but made for the bed. He was followed by another figure – Lieutenant Wieczorek, who quietly closed the door behind him.

There was something unearthly – almost animal – about the way the two of them approached the bed, as if they were stalking something. And then Dmitry remembered Wieczorek's arm. The last time Dmitry had seen him, he had had no left arm at all, or only the blasted vestiges of one. And now he seemed quite capable of using it, as he had just done to close the door. Dmitry's father had once told him of a *voordalak* called Andrei who'd had his entire arm cut off by a sword, only for it to grow back. Dmitry had himself witnessed the missing fingers of a vampire's mutilated hand restore themselves, inch by inch. It seemed the creatures that had buried their earlier victims beside the Star Fort had not moved on. Wieczorek was one of them. There was no reason to doubt Mihailov was another.

Dmitry moved silently to his knapsack, still slumped where he had left it beside the door. The two vampires continued to approach the bed. These creatures were supposed to have heightened senses, or was that a myth? They certainly didn't seem to notice Dmitry.

Maybe the continual gunfire had deadened their ears. Dmitry grabbed his bag and reached inside.

At the same moment Mihailov snatched aside the curtain which hung half covering the bed. On it lay Tyeplov, his naked back exposed to the two monsters, his neck – on which Dmitry had so recently laid passionate kisses – undefended against their foul hunger.

'Get away from him!' growled Dmitry.

Both the vampires turned, almost before the words left his mouth. Wieczorek looked the naked Dmitry up and down. A smile formed on his lips. 'Major Danilov, you surprise me.'

'I know what you are,' said Dmitry.

'Good,' said Mihailov. 'That saves explanation.'

'You don't deny it?'

'Deny what?'

'That you are . . .'

'Say it!' insisted Mihailov.

'*Voordalaki!*'

Dmitry had been clutching his knapsack to his chest, but as he spoke he let it drop, still hanging on to it with his left hand, but revealing what he held in his right: a small, sharp wooden sword, just like the one his father had whittled for him as a toy. Within hours of seeing the two mutilated victims in the tunnel beneath the Star Fort, Dmitry had made a new one, and had carried it with him wherever he went.

Mihailov and Wieczorek both stopped in their tracks, eyeing the weapon, which Dmitry couldn't help but notice was shaking, along with his whole arm.

'We don't deny it,' said Mihailov. 'And I don't need to ask how you understand so much about us.'

'He doesn't understand much,' added Wieczorek, 'for a soldier.'

Mihailov gave a curt laugh and Dmitry looked questioningly at Wieczorek.

'You're outnumbered, Danilov,' explained the Pole. 'Waving your little stick at us isn't going to help that.'

'Maybe not,' said Dmitry, 'but . . .'

He didn't have time to say anything more. At that moment Wieczorek made a lunge towards him, coming from his right, where he had the sword to defend him. Dmitry took a step backwards and tripped on something, falling to the ground and losing his grip on the bag. Its contents spewed out, including, nearest to him, his pistol. He grabbed it and held it out in front of him, vaguely towards Mihailov, although his left hand was even less steady than his right.

The two vampires stood still, exchanging glances, puzzled as to what to do. Dmitry could perceive little difficulty for them in overcoming him. He realized now how truly unprepared he had been, even on the assumption that there was only one of these monsters in the city. He felt the fear of his trembling hands and understood how difficult he would find it to use that wooden sword against them. Even so, he managed to get his legs back under him and began to rise to his feet. Mihailov was scarcely more than an arm's length away from him, and the barrel of the gun almost brushed his nose.

Dmitry heard a shout – 'Mitka!' – and realized Tyeplov had awoken. The urge to save his friend overwhelmed his concern for himself. He turned his head to look at Tyeplov, to beg him to take flight, and at the same moment Mihailov made his move. There was no conscious action from Dmitry to squeeze the trigger, but the pistol fired anyway. Its explosion drowned the yelp of fear that formed in Dmitry's throat. Mihailov's face vanished in the blast. He fell backwards towards Tyeplov and Dmitry saw Wieczorek's gaze follow him down.

Terror and hatred filled Dmitry, though which drove him more, he could not guess. The pistol fell from his hand as he stepped forward, grabbing Wieczorek's shoulder. His right hand thrust outwards and between the pull of his left and the push of his right, the sharp wooden point penetrated its target, and kept on going. Finally it came to a soft, uncertain halt as the guard came up against Wieczorek's belly. Dmitry felt warm blood oozing over his fingers and saw the vampire's eyes turn to meet his own. The blade had gone nowhere near the heart, and the wound was as a scratch would have been to Dmitry.

He withdrew and stabbed again, angling the blade upwards, but with little understanding of how precisely he would deliver the fatal blow. The shout of 'Die, damn you!' on his lips must have sounded as feeble to the monster as it did to him. Wieczorek's hands grasped at Dmitry, one clutching at his sleeve, the other gouging its nails across his chest. The lips drew back to reveal sharp, glistening fangs and the neck strained so that they might reach for Dmitry's throat.

Panic took hold of Dmitry and he began to stab wildly at the creature, still gripping its shoulder so that it could not escape, even though escape seemed the furthest thing from its mind. Sometimes the wooden blade did nothing, simply missing the vampire altogether, or bouncing off a rib. At others, Dmitry felt the resistance of flesh being penetrated, but he had lost all intent of aiming for the creature's heart, his actions simply the last thrashings of a man who knows that his life is close to its end. Again and again he thrust his arm forward, as though punching his opponent repeatedly in the stomach, but to no effect. Still Wieczorek's teeth descended towards him.

Then all was calm. Dmitry realized that the last few strokes of his sword, although they penetrated the vampire's torso, had been met with no sensation of resistance. He left the sword where it was, inside the creature's body, his hand grasping its hilt so tightly that his fingers felt numb. Wieczorek's arms fell to his sides and Dmitry's left hand, still clutching the shoulder, began to close as the resistance to his grip collapsed. It was as though a child were showing off his mighty strength by grabbing a handful of dried leaves and crushing them to fragments. The arms that had begun to fall away never made it to their normal resting place. The right, once Dmitry had destroyed the shoulder that had held it in place, slipped out of the sleeve of Wieczorek's tunic and fell to the floor where it shattered silently. The left made its way to earth more gradually, the hand disintegrating first and then a dry, grey dust continuing to pour from the sleeve for several seconds as decay worked its way through the limb.

It was Wieczorek's face that was most fascinating. The animal snarl that had so recently menaced Dmitry collapsed into an expression of utter misery as the sides of his head began to fall away. The mask of comedy became the mask of tragedy. Those great teeth fell back into the mouth and then dropped through the crumbling tongue before falling out beneath the chin. The desiccated remains of Wieczorek's face cascaded down off his shoulders as raindrops would have done if he had been caught in a thunderstorm. It was a slow process, delectable to watch, but no less terminal than the destruction Dmitry had seen meted out to that young *ryadovoy* by a French cannonball.

After a few long moments, Dmitry was left clutching merely a dark green tunic, while from the tip of his wooden sword dangled the linen shirt which it had pierced. Below sat a pile of Wieczorek's remaining clothes, as a thin layer of grey dust spread itself across the parquet tiles, secreting itself within the cracks between them.

Dmitry attempted to breathe, but could only manage a mournful exhalation. His arms dropped to his sides, much as Wieczorek's had, and the wooden sword hit the floor with a clatter. He turned towards where Mihailov lay, cradled by Tyeplov, who, Dmitry could only guess, understood neither why Dmitry had attacked so brutally, nor how Mihailov could possibly remain alive. At last Dmitry's lungs were restored to function, and he took in a long, whooping breath. He began to breathe more normally, and walked over to examine Mihailov's face.

There was no face. The lower lip was there, but above it a hole which might at first be mistaken for a mouth stretched up and up across the front of where his skull once had been, terminating finally with what remained of his forehead, topped with dark, short hair that might seem like a moustache. Of nose and eyes, there was no trace. Inside the void was a mess of blood that Dmitry chose not to try to interpret. What concerned him more was that, even in the time since he had first looked, eyebrows were beginning to re-form. As he had seen so many years before, the creature was healing itself.

Dmitry stepped backwards, desperately looking on either side for where he had dropped his sword, but it was too late. Mihailov threw himself forward, his hands, unaided by sight, searching Dmitry's body for something to grip on to, but finding only bare flesh. His empty face was up close to Dmitry's and Dmitry shut his eyes, turning away rather than see so intimately what he knew dwelt within his own skull, but unable to banish the strange, foul smell of it. It was sufficient distraction to allow Mihailov's escape. Some memory of the layout of the casemate allowed him to find his way to the door. His hands padded against it, searching for the handle. There was still time. Dmitry grabbed his sword.

'No, Mitka! No!' Tyeplov's hand restrained him as he spoke. Dmitry hesitated, turning to look into Tyeplov's face, relieved to see the eyes and nose and mouth which one would expect.

It was time enough for Mihailov. The door slammed, and Dmitry and Tyeplov were alone.

CHAPTER VIII

THEY CLUNG TO EACH OTHER. DMITRY WAS SHIVERING AND THE warmth of Tyeplov's body did nothing to alleviate it.

'Mitka. What have you done?' Tyeplov hissed.

'What did you see, Tolya?' asked Dmitry. It was an important question. The more that Tyeplov had observed for which there could be no sane explanation, the easier Dmitry would find it when unfolding his own, insane account of what had taken place.

'I saw you shoot Mihailov,' he stammered. 'I saw you stab Wieczorek. I saw . . . Where is Wieczorek?'

Dmitry stood and offered his hand to Tyeplov. He felt suddenly aware of their nakedness. Tyeplov rose to his feet and Dmitry led him to where Wieczorek's clothes lay. Dmitry saw his own trousers where he had discarded them earlier, protruding from beneath the pile of garments. He grabbed them, shaking them to get rid of as much of the dust as he could.

'That's Wieczorek?' asked Tyeplov, a look of wild horror crossing his face.

'You saw what happened, Tolya. Only one of them made it out the door.'

Tyeplov nodded, and considered for a few moments. Then he turned to Dmitry, calmer. 'How though?'

'*Voordalaki*,' said Dmitry, simply. He waited for the word to sink in, for all of those stories that Tyeplov must have heard as a child to come to the forefront of his mind, so that Dmitry could pounce on them and convince him that they were no more stories than were the tales of the horrors perpetrated by the French at Borodino. It was a conversation Dmitry had had before, with his father, but on that occasion it was Dmitry who had been the doubting ingénu, his father the proficient and experienced slayer of monsters. It was again a reversal of roles, though no longer Chopin with which he would delight and intrigue his companion. It wasn't a position he relished, not least because, unlike his father, Dmitry was *not* an experienced slayer of monsters. In his whole life he had disposed of just one *voordalak* – the creature over whose remains they now stood.

'You're mad,' Tyeplov gasped.

Dmitry began to dress, scouting around the casemate for his various items of clothing. It had occurred to him that if the two vampires had made their way through the trench then before long so might mortal men. They would not be so much of a threat to Tyeplov and Dmitry's lives, but they would still react to finding the two men together like this. Tyeplov followed Dmitry's lead.

'So what's your explanation?' asked Dmitry, pulling on his shirt.

'I . . . I don't have one.'

'But mine is mad?'

'It must be,' Tyeplov shouted, more to convince himself than to persuade Dmitry.

'Why do you think they came here?'

'They're in command here. This is their casemate.'

'They came,' said Dmitry, 'to feed.'

'To feed?'

'Tolya, listen to me.' Dmitry squatted down to be on a level with Tyeplov, who was pulling on his socks. 'At the beginning of this month, in the Severnaya, I was shown two bodies. Their throats had been ripped out. It was those two that must have done it. That's what they had in store for us.'

'You can't be sure.'

'You think I should have waited?'

'No, but . . .'

'You saw how Wieczorek died. You saw how Mihailov *failed* to die, for God's sake. What do you need them to do?'

Tyeplov seemed to accept Dmitry's argument. His next question was on a different tack. 'How do you know? I mean, I'm not questioning it, but how do you know so much?'

'I've met them before,' said Dmitry. 'Thirty years ago. And my father fought them a decade before that.' Dmitry felt a sudden new pride as he spoke the phrase 'my father'.

'Those creatures?'

'Not Wieczorek and Mihailov, but creatures like them.' Just one creature like them in Dmitry's case, but it would do no good to admit it.

'So what do we do?' asked Tyeplov.

'We find Mihailov and we kill him.' Again, Dmitry reminded himself of his father. Yudin would never have seen things in such simple black and white. In many situations it made him the better man, but not here.

'But he's mortally wounded. He'll be dead soon anyway.'

'He'll recover,' said Dmitry.

'And so you'll kill him, just like you killed Wieczorek?' Tyeplov's voice wavered with rising panic.

'There are other ways.' Tyeplov gave a look of naive enquiry which left Dmitry uncomfortable about being specific. 'Remember your folk tales,' he said. He watched Tyeplov's face as his mind wandered through each myth and legend that he had ever heard about the *voordalak*. Fear turned to horror when, as far as Dmitry could guess, he came to the various ways that the creatures could be dispatched: a wooden blade through the heart, decapitation, fire, exposure to sunlight.

'No!' shouted Tyeplov, with sudden vehemence.

For a moment, Dmitry despised him, but it was in Tyeplov's nature – in anyone's – to feel sympathy. Only someone like Dmitry – or his father – knew enough to be able to expunge such doubts. But it would do no good to attempt to persuade Tyeplov, not at that moment. Dmitry turned on his heel and marched out of the casemate, hoping that Mihailov hadn't gained too much of a head start.

It was nearly dawn. The sky was a deep, heavy blue in the east, but still black away from the sun. But there was enough light to see by. The bastion was half gone. The fortification bore a huge breach down the middle through which Dmitry glimpsed the enemy guns. An infantry captain stood alone among the scattered gabions, bewildered. Around him men worked haphazardly on rebuilding the defences, stepping through the bodies of dead and wounded comrades.

However much Dmitry might have wanted to pursue Mihailov, needs here were more pressing. He felt suddenly invigorated by the prospect of dealing with a human battle.

'Captain!' he barked. The officer snapped to attention. 'What's the situation?'

'God knows how many dead, sir. The wall's breached in three places. This one's the worst. I've sent for engineers.'

'Any sign of them advancing?'

'No, sir.'

Dmitry moved on down the line, scrambling over the tattered remains of the bastion, making sure that sharpshooters were in their places in case the French did attack, organizing the repair of the earthworks and seeing that injured men were carried to the field hospital, back in the city. As for the dead, there was nowhere for them to be buried. He didn't have to order it, but the men knew the procedure; most of the bodies were hauled over the side of the defences, for the French to crawl through when they eventually decided to advance.

It was several hours before Dmitry returned to the casemate. By then, Tyeplov was gone.

The old woman must have been mad. Tamara had told herself that again and again. It was over a week since they had spoken, but still Tamara could not dismiss the conversation from her mind. It was a bright, sunny day now – not yet summer, but definitely spring – and it seemed a shame to be hiding from it among the gloomy records of the Kremlin's secret library, deep beneath the ground, but it was her first opportunity for several weeks to do any research.

Gribov still appeared to revel in the futility of her task. The only reason that he was prepared, grudgingly, to bring her down here was to crow over her failure.

'Any progress with Prince Volkonsky?' he asked.

'Not a lot.'

'Do you even know what it is you're looking for?'

Until recently, Tamara's answer would have been simple, if

unspoken – her parents – but for the moment at least she had been distracted by a new quest.

'Do you keep police records down here?' she asked.

'We have records for the Third Section and the Gendarmerie, of course. As for the Ministry of the Interior . . . you might be lucky. As with everything else, it is sorted by the order in which it arrived.'

'Whereabouts are the records for 1812?' she asked, knowing full well the stupidity of her quest.

'1812?' There was an edge of sarcasm to his voice. 'You might find something.' He glanced at one of the shelves and then turned abruptly left. Tamara followed. They came to a table piled high with papers, some tied with ribbon, some with string; others were loose. He picked up one at random and looked at it. 'That's 1811,' he said. He went over to a shelf and pulled down a bound volume, examining its spine. 'And that's 1814. So it's all somewhere around here.'

'Thank you,' she said curtly. She pulled up a chair and sat at the table, clearing a space in front of her.

'Of course, you'll find nothing on the Volkonskys – neither of them. They were both fighting in the war.'

'I know,' said Tamara.

Gribov placed the lamp on the table beside her and walked away into the darkness. She began looking at the documents, quickly rejecting each one as she saw its date or got some idea of its contents. In the distance, she heard a pause in Gribov's footsteps. She looked and saw his silhouette in the doorway, before it disappeared. The sound of the door slamming shut reached her a fraction of a second later. She returned to her work.

Natalia had said it had happened just after the French had gone, and the victim's name had been Margarita. She searched her memory for more detail. Margarita Kirillovna – that had been it – a patronymic, but no surname. The date was helpful though. The French had left Moscow in October 1812. It was an unimaginable time. The idea of French soldiers – of any foreign power – marching through the streets of the city seemed like something from a fairy tale. Today Russia was again at war with France, but there was no sense of any risk to the homeland. That was why it was so easy to send the country's young men out to fight. War was an unreal thing – foreign. Those diminishing few who remembered 1812 would see things differently.

She leaned back in her chair and asked herself why she was doing this. Natalia was an old woman; she could have dreamed the whole thing up, or at the very least been confused over the dates. And even if she was right, what possible connection could the two murders have? Tamara was wasting her time. She should be down here looking for her parents, not chasing murderers, especially when Yudin seemed pretty keen that the murderer remained undiscovered.

Then she thought of Irina's face, and her stillness and her horrible wounds. That deserved some investigation, surely. And if neither Yudin nor the gendarmes were prepared to do it, then it was left to her. And Yudin could hardly object; he might want to play down the murder of Irina Karlovna, but Tamara was not investigating that. He could not censure her for looking into the death of Margarita Kirillovna.

She grabbed the paper nearest to her, a letter, and began to read.

'Why did you kill Irina Karlovna?'

Raisa stiffened as Yudin spoke the words. She continued to gaze into her unreflected face in the mirror against the wall of his office, but she was not stupid. She would know he had observed her reaction, would know that he had chosen the precise moment of his question so that he was best placed to evaluate her response.

'How did you know?' she asked. She did not attempt a denial.

He continued to watch her, and she continued to avoid looking back at him. 'I believe in simplicity,' he explained. 'A woman is killed, quite obviously by a vampire. A vampire is the occupant of the adjacent room, with a connecting door. One hardly has to be Dupin.'

'We're not the only ones.' She turned to him at last. 'Perhaps not the only ones in Moscow.'

'Have you heard something?' He tried, successfully, to sound uninterested.

'No. And even if I had, you're right. The simple explanation fits.'

'You still haven't explained why.'

'She found out – heard me going down to the cellar. She didn't know what, but she suspected something. Then she got me into her room. The mirrors told her everything.'

'You should have been more careful,' said Yudin.

'Where would be the fun in that?'

He could hardly fault her. They had survived together, on and off, for three decades. She knew how to be circumspect. 'You should have told me,' he muttered, grudgingly.

'I knew you'd work it out.'

'Is your grave there still safe?'

Raisa nodded. 'She didn't have time to tell anyone.'

Yudin looked at her. Her face had a yellow tinge to it and the skin around her eyes was lined. 'Are you hungry now?' he asked.

'Just tired.'

Picking up a lamp, he went to the door opposite the mirror and unlocked it. The stairs went down a little way and then split into two flights. 'To the left if you are hungry; to the right if you want to sleep,' he said. She hesitated, then turned right. Further down was another door. He unlocked it and they went through.

They were directly underneath his office now. The room was almost bare – too deeply buried to be lit by windows. On the far side there was another door, much like the one they had come in through. The smell of the river was stronger here, but it was of no concern to either of them. In the middle lay two coffins, expensive ones – ageing now. Quite unaccountably they had been built to last.

Raisa went over and climbed into the smaller of them, on the left. Even to one of Yudin's vast experience, it was a strange sight – perhaps even a little unnerving. No human would comfortably lie down inside a construction whose design so obviously indicated that they would never rise from it again. But it did not concern Raisa for a moment. She lay back and closed her eyes, not bothering to make use of the heavy lid that lay beside her. Yudin walked over and looked down at her. She was unconscious, not even breathing. He knew that if he were to place his hand to her chest he would feel no heartbeat.

He turned and left, locking the door behind him. It was a clever mechanism, of his own devising, which would allow her to leave when she awoke, but would prevent anyone else from entering. It meant that they could sleep in safety, but need never fear being entombed.

He glanced through the letters on his desk – all of them from the diminishing band of exiles who scratched a living out in Siberia. There was nothing ostensibly from Aleksei – he seemed to write to his son less and less these days, no doubt because his son never replied. Or at least, when he did, those letters were intercepted and destroyed by Yudin. But Aleksei was not stupid. He might easily have persuaded a fellow exile to slip something into one of his letters. They'd all need checking anyway, but not just yet. There was no hurry for them to be delivered.

Thoughts of Aleksei, along with those of the murder on Degtyarny Lane, began to intertwine in his mind. It was in that same house that Aleksei's mistress, the lovely – although nowadays probably not so lovely – Dominique, had lived and plied her trade. Yudin smiled at the memories of a time when he had so thoroughly duped Aleksei. It had been so simple; Yudin had enacted a little charade involving himself and a woman, knowing that Aleksei was watching. But what Aleksei had never been able to determine was whether that woman had been his lover, Dominique, or some other. It had been enough to convince him that Dominique had become a vampire, enough to persuade him to offer himself up to her as a willing victim. Yudin chuckled, imagining the scene in which Aleksei had awoken to discover that neither he nor his mistress had joined the undead. Yudin had not witnessed it, or heard tell of it in any detail. He knew simply that it must have taken place, because he had planned that it would. He had played Aleksei for such a *prostak* that even now Yudin could look back on it as his finest hour.

But the thought itself brought up another memory, a memory of thirteen years later – Yudin lying on the frozen Neva, cradled in Aleksei's arms, a bullet from Aleksei's gun nestling in his heart. Aleksei had used that same word – almost that same phrase.

'Oh, this is no simple checkmate, Iuda,' Aleksei had said. 'You've been fooled – played for a *prostak* – and now I'm going to tell you all about it.'

Aleksei had little known that, even in death, Yudin had chosen life, of a sort. He had grabbed the vial that hung around his neck and drunk it – a vial of vampire's blood that would ensure that, though he might die, yet would he live again as a *voordalak*. Even so he had been genuinely fascinated to learn how Aleksei might have tricked him.

'Do go on, Lyosha,' he had said, and then, after drinking the blood, 'Go on, Lyosha.' Suddenly, for the first time, he remembered every word.

'Iuda,' Aleksei had said, patting him on his chest so as to amplify the pain of the bullet that lay there, 'I have beaten you.' Even then, it had been obvious he meant a greater victory than merely to have killed him.

'Carry on, Lyosha,' he had persisted. 'Tell me what you were going to say.' And then, 'Please, Lyosha, grant a dying man his wish.'

And then Yudin had noticed a change in Aleksei, a stiffening of his body that he had always suspected, but never been sure, indicated that Aleksei had guessed what Yudin had done, guessed that though he would die there on the cold, flat, frozen river, he would be reborn. Still Yudin had persisted.

'Please, tell me. How did you fool me?'

And at that point, Aleksei had relented – changed his story. Yudin remembered his smile. 'I didn't, Iuda. I was pretending, but I won't lie to you. I could never devise a trick clever enough to fool you.'

In the past, Yudin's memories of the moment had been vague – it had been so close to his death. But now it all came back to him with utter clarity. And in that same moment Aleksei's words made sense of another conundrum that had been puzzling Yudin much more recently: that of the inert nature of Tsar Aleksandr's blood. How could Aleksei's pretended or perhaps real trickery be related to that? The answer lay in the date. That scene on the frozen Neva had been played out in December 1825, just a month after the death of Tsar Aleksandr I.

And that was what lay at the heart of it: the reason that Aleksandr II's blood was immune to Zmyeevich's; the deception that Aleksei had wanted to reveal, but had hidden on realizing that Yudin would not die; the deception that was to be maintained for almost thirty years.

But now that deception was over. Yudin understood all. It was a simple enough concept, but it explained everything. Tsar Nikolai I might have died in Petersburg in February 1855, but in terms of the Romanov blood, that meant nothing.

The truth was that his predecessor, Tsar Aleksandr I, supposed to have died in Taganrog in 1825, had not died then and indeed had not died at all. It was the only explanation – and it made perfect sense.

Aleksandr Pavlovich, Tsar of All the Russias, vanquisher of Napoleon Bonaparte, still lived.

'Madame Komarova.'

Tamara's body jerked upright, instantly awake, but her mind was still blurred by sleep. She looked around and saw the man who had spoken. She recognized him, but could not place him. He was small, almost as short as she was. His hair was grey and there wasn't much of it. His eyes had a yellow tint as they peered at her through his spectacles.

'Gribov,' she mumbled, not even realizing where in her memory the name had come from. She looked around her again. The room she was in was vast. Even in the dim light she could see it was full of books and documents. One of them, she knew without understanding why, was of inestimable importance to her.

'You fell asleep,' said Gribov. 'You must have been here all night.' He began to tidy up the books and papers on the desk where she had been sitting, straightening out the ones that had been crumpled by her lying on them.

'No!' she shouted, memory pouring back into her consciousness as though through a broken dam. 'I found something.'

'Concerning Prince Volkonsky?'

That much she still couldn't remember, but she suspected not. She had been looking through the documents for 1812 for almost a month; there were far more than Gribov had suggested, despite the French occupation. Last night, late last night, she had found something. She began searching, not knowing what she was looking for but recognizing those papers that she had already rejected and throwing them to the floor. Gribov diligently followed her around the table, picking them up.

'Got it!' she shouted at last.

She handed it to Gribov, who soon returned it to her, though she noted that he had allowed his eyes to scan twice across its contents.

'And how is this helpful?' he asked.

Tamara could not remember. She looked at the paper again, refreshing her knowledge of what she knew had been so exciting a discovery the previous night. 'You remember the murder last month, at Degtyarny Lane?' she asked.

'Sadly,' nodded Gribov.

'Well, this is the police report of another murder. It's dated 11 November 1812.'

'And?'

'And it's the same; exactly the same,' said Tamara, her eyes continuing to scan the document.

In truth, the similarity was not exact. The victim, Margarita Kirillovna, was found in an upstairs room at a bordello on Degtyarny Lane. It could only be the same building – it was impossible to tell which room. She had suffered severe lacerations to the neck – just like Irina Karlovna – which were believed to be the cause of death. But then came the difference. Margarita Kirillovna had suffered an additional wound to the chest – she had been stabbed in the heart. There had been no sign of that with Irina. The report also stated that this last wound was believed, due to the lack of bleeding from it, to have been inflicted some time after death. But only a fool would ignore the similarities on account of that one discrepancy.

'You suspect there might be a connection?' Many might have uttered the question with an air of disbelief, but from Gribov it came merely as an enquiry.

'I don't know,' she said, still reading. 'I don't know.'

But she knew how she was going to find out. At the bottom of the page was a list of witnesses – three of them. She opened her own notebook, ready to write the names down, but discovered that she had already done so, the previous night. She checked with the document, but she had made no mistakes. She had three witnesses to a crime of four decades earlier:

Pyetr Pyetrovich Polyakov.
Domnikiia Semyonovna Beketova.
Aleksei Ivanovich Danilov.

CHAPTER IX

TAMARA WAS RETRACING HER STEPS. SHE HAD MOVED AWAY from the tables and shelves that represented the time of the Patriotic War and returned to those for the 1820s, where she had found so little information concerning her own early life. But she had seen something among those records, something which she had dismissed as of no interest at the time. With regard to the discovery of her parentage it was irrelevant, but for the moment she was more interested in murder, both in 1812 and in 1855 – and perhaps also in 1825.

She couldn't remember what the file had looked like, but she had some idea of where she had found it. It had been on a bookcase, close to the left-hand end, on either the second or third shelf from the top. There were three bookcases for 1825, each looking very much the same as the next. The picture of her pulling out the file was clear in her memory and she could isolate its position down to four or five documents, but still she could only guess at the correct set of shelves.

It was in the third bookcase that she found it.

Murders. Moscow. 1825. Unsolved.

There were twenty-two separate cases listed, mostly of women, mostly where a husband – in a legal or, often, less formal capacity – was the obvious suspect. That these deaths were listed as unsolved was more a reflection of the innate, unspoken freemasonry of the male sex than of any lack of evidence. But it was not these that had caught her attention. They might have involved the deaths of

152

young women, but the precise mechanisms of those deaths did not correspond with what she had read about Margarita Kirillovna, or seen first-hand with Irina Karlovna.

Then she found the document that she had remembered so clearly, after only a glance at it months before. It was dated Tuesday, 29 September 1825 and concerned the discovery of the body of a Kremlin guard in Red Square. To be precise, the body had been inside the Lobnoye Mesto, the circular enclosure to the north of Saint Vasiliy's from where, years ago, imperial decrees had been read out. In that case the victim was a man, whose body had been found in the open air. There was little to connect it with either of the two deaths in which Tamara was interested, but one thing was unmistakably familiar: the manner of his death.

His throat had been cut, cut deeply with a jagged knife so that a handful of the flesh was missing. And the wound was only to the left-hand side of the neck. The report on Margarita Kirillovna had not been clear on that last point, but Tamara could certainly remember it as being true of Irina.

Continuing through the file she found a cluster of similar murders; not clustered around a single location – they were spread all over Moscow – but clustered in time. There had been five other deaths, all in the space of a week at the end of September and beginning of October 1825. All but one of the victims were men. The first was a footman. His body was found on Great Bronnaya Street. That wasn't so very far from Degtyarny Lane, but it meant little. The second had perhaps the most detail, probably on account of the status of the victim. He was a prince – Prince Victor Markovich Kavyerin. The body had been found to the east of the city in Kitay Gorod. There was even a sketch of the wounds – again they matched what Tamara had witnessed for herself. There was also a brief description of what was known of the prince's lifestyle. The word 'homosexual' had been underlined three times.

The one female victim had been found floating in the river. There was not even a name for her and the description of her wounds was minimal, but enough to convince Tamara. It had been enough to arouse the interest of someone else too. A note had been scrawled on the paper, reading 'compare V. M. K.' The similarity to Prince Kavyerin's wounds had been noted, but beyond that, no one seemed to have made any effort to connect the five deaths.

The last murder had occurred on 3 October. The body of a cavalry captain named Obukhov had been found in the street running alongside the Maly Theatre, lying in a pool of blood. The wound to the neck was described in scant detail, but Tamara had little doubt that a more thorough investigation would have revealed all the hallmarks with which she was becoming familiar. She scanned through the report and noticed the names of two witnesses were listed – also both cavalry officers. The first – a Lieutenant Batenkov – meant nothing to her, but at the sight of the second name she clicked her tongue with excitement.

Colonel Aleksei Ivanovich Danilov (O.K.)

Whatever coincidence there might be in the similarities of the deaths of Margarita Kirillovna and Irina Karlovna, spaced forty-three years apart, was as nothing compared to the fact the same Aleksei Ivanovich Danilov was listed as a witness to both the 1812 murder and to one of those of 1825. Furthermore, the reasons that neither of those two crimes had been subject to anything like a full investigation now also became clear, based simply on those two letters that the investigating officer had so diligently noted after Danilov's name.

O.K. stood for *Osobennaya Kantselyariya* – the Special Chancellery. It was the predecessor to her own organization, the Third Section, which had replaced it only months after that last murder took place. It would have been as easy for Danilov to shoo away the regular police before they could reveal anything too damaging as it had been for Yudin to orchestrate the investigation into the murder of Irina, and thereby ensure that nothing came of it.

It did not mean that Danilov was the murderer – any more than Yudin was – but his presence in both 1812 and 1825 required explanation, and beyond that demanded an answer to the simple question, where was Danilov now?

The document in her hands had one last piece of information

which went some way to answering that. A huge arrow pointed at Danilov's name and at its end a single word, in a different hand from the rest of the report.

Декабрист

It seemed that Colonel Aleksei Ivanovich Danilov had not been quite as loyal to the tsar as might be expected from a man of his position. As had evidently been discovered – probably only months after the original report was written – Danilov had been a Decembrist.

Yudin fumed. He had been made a fool of. Aleksei didn't have the brains for it – didn't have the imagination – and yet for thirty years he'd been able to convince Yudin that Tsar Aleksandr I had died in Taganrog; convince the whole of Russia. The whole of the world.

It was unthinkable, and yet it was the one, simple conclusion that made sense of all that Yudin had observed in the new tsar's blood. If Aleksandr I were alive somewhere, then any power that Zmyeevich might be able to exert over the Romanovs could be focused only on him. He wondered if Zmyeevich had worked that much out. It didn't matter. Even if Zmyeevich were to track Aleksandr down and complete the process of making him a *voordalak*, it would be of little benefit. Power in Russia had passed to his brother Nikolai and now to his nephew Aleksandr II. Aleksandr I had made himself invincible by becoming inconsequential. Yudin laughed out loud at the genius of it.

Gribov turned and glanced at him, but said nothing. They were walking along the deep, dark corridor that led to the Kremlin's archives. It was a convenience that had played no small part in Yudin's choice of office – the fact that it gave him access to a network of tunnels and passages beneath the citadel that would have made Daedalus himself proud. He could find his way almost anywhere – and never have to venture into the daylight. It would have tested even his patience to await the safety of darkness before making that short journey, but he would have managed it. What was a few hours compared to the years during which Aleksei and Aleksandr and God knew who else had been laughing at him?

And it was the 'who else' that mattered most. If others were in on the subterfuge – and they must have been – then they might still know where Aleksandr was. He would be seventy-seven now. He could die at any moment, or live for another decade or more. It was a margin of uncertainty that Yudin could not endure.

They had arrived at the entrance to the library. Gribov opened the door and stepped inside. In the distance, through the forest of shelves, he glimpsed a single, glowing lamp. He'd also noted that Gribov did not need to unlock the door.

'There's someone in here?' he asked.

'Madame Komarova,' replied Gribov.

Yudin grunted. He would be interested to learn what she was up to, but it wasn't the matter that most demanded his attention. 'I want everything on the last days of Aleksandr Pavlovich,' he said.

Gribov led him over to the right of the cavernous chamber, through the mess of papers and books to an area that appeared much tidier than the rest.

'Papers relating to the imperial household are better organized than most,' Gribov explained. 'Even so . . .'

Yudin followed the direction that Gribov's hand indicated and found himself facing a huge bookcase, taller than either of them and three times as wide as it was tall. Books, papers and files lay in disorganized heaps.

'Is this all?' he asked.

Gribov didn't catch his sarcasm. 'These shelves cover his reign. There's more on his youth, if you're interested.'

'This will do.'

'I could stay and assist.'

That was the last thing Yudin wanted. 'No,' he replied. 'I'll manage. But stay down here. I'll call if I need you.'

Gribov departed, and within seconds had vanished into the shadows. Aleksandr had become tsar at the age of twenty-three. The shelves in front of Yudin represented his entire adult life – at least in the eyes of those who had fallen for Aleksei's trickery. Thankfully, Yudin needed only to concern himself with the final weeks of that life; somewhere, he presumed, around the right-hand end of the bottom shelf. He got down on his hands and knees and looked, pulling out several volumes, pamphlets and files and placing them on the floor beside him. When he was done, he carried them to a table and read them in the glowing lamplight.

There were a number of letters from Aleksandr himself, and from his wife, Yelizaveta Alekseevna, but they were lacking in the sort of detail that Yudin required. There was a copy of an account published only the previous year by a Scottish doctor named Robert Lee – a Fellow of the Royal Society, just as Yudin had once been, under the name Cain. They had not met. Nor did it appear that Lee had met Aleksandr for more than one short encounter, weeks before his death. Everything else in his journal was second-hand gossip; enough to please a British audience.

Baron Korff's official rendering of events was far more detailed, but again written long after they had taken place. Its purpose was clear: to remove any lingering doubt as to whether Nikolai had had the right to succeed his brother. To that end, it did not dwell too much on the details of Aleksandr's passing.

The most useful items were two diaries, written by Aleksandr's two personal physicians, Doctors Wylie and Tarasov. How the documents had found their way here was hard to guess, but they provided much detail of the tsar's final hours, in little of which Yudin placed any trust. That they had been rewritten to fit the official story of events was obvious, not least because both clearly asserted that His Majesty had died on 19 November 1825, which Yudin knew to be untrue. It was conceivable that the two doctors were themselves victims of the charade, but Yudin felt it unlikely.

He had never expected to find anything so direct as an account of how Aleksandr had cheated death, but after a few hours he had pieced together all he needed – a list of those present at Aleksandr's passing, at least some of whom would have been required to assist in the deception: the tsaritsa, Baron Diebich, Dr Wylie, Dr Tarasov and Prince Volkonsky. And, of course, Aleksei. And therein lay another reason to doubt the journals of Wylie and Tarasov – neither of them made any mention of Aleksei's presence in the tsar's retinue during the entire length of the stay in Taganrog, or during their excursions to the Crimea. If they had managed to expurgate that from their memoirs, what else might they have missed out?

Yudin looked at the list again. It was disappointing. The tsaritsa had died within a year of her husband. That was suspicious in itself. Might her death too have been a pretence, so that she could rejoin the man she loved? Yudin doubted it, but whether she was with Aleksandr or rotting in her grave, she would be of no help with the current problem. Volkonsky was also dead – since 1852. As far as Yudin could recall, Diebich was dead too. As to the doctors, he didn't know.

It took him only a little more searching to find the information he needed – he was, in this library, surrounded by information. He'd been correct – Diebich had succumbed to cholera in 1831. Wylie had lasted longer, dying only the previous year at the age of eighty-five. That left only Tarasov and Danilov still around to reveal to Yudin the secrets of so many years before. They were both old men now. Yudin knew Aleksei's location; four thousand versts away in Siberia. He had no idea where Tarasov was, though it was unlikely to be as remote.

But before Yudin could act, a little more research into both men was required.

Tamara saw a figure flitting among the shadows. She had heard voices earlier, but now there was silence. She looked at her pocket watch. It was heavy and would be considered ungainly for a woman. It had been Vitya's, and one of only two possessions that never left her. The other was a small, oval icon of Christ which hung around her neck on a silver chain. She'd had it since before she could remember. When she looked into the Saviour's kind eyes, it made her think of her real father, but she could not recall why. Vitya's watch told her it was almost midnight. She should have been at Degtyarny Lane keeping an eye on things, but they could manage without her. She was far happier here.

She saw the movement again and realized it could only be Gribov. He was here late too, but she was pleased he was. She rose and went over to him. By the time he had reached the point at which she had seen him, he had moved on. A moment later, she caught sight of him again. It seemed wrong to shout in the dark, studious library, and so it took her several minutes to finally catch up with him.

'Arkadiy Osipovich,' she said softly.

He turned and his face broke into a slight smile. 'Still here?' he asked. 'I take it your studies are bearing fruit.'

She smiled back. 'To a degree,' she said cautiously. 'They've led me on to another matter.'

'Indeed?'

'I take it we have records on all those involved in the Decembrist Uprising.'

'Naturally. To gather and collate information on men of their kind is the raison d'être of this department. Such documents receive the utmost attention.'

'Can you show me?'

He led the way, holding his lantern out in front of him, but moving with a swiftness that suggested he could have found his way about the place even if blindfolded.

'Here we are,' he said.

Tamara peered at the shelves as Gribov held up the light for her. They seemed to be well ordered, with the name of each man written on the spine of his file. She flicked through them, softly reading the names out loud. 'Grigoriev, Gusev, Demidov, Dmitriev. Oh!'

'A problem?' asked Gribov.

'It seems to be missing.' The shelf was not tightly packed, so there was no obvious gap where the file should have been. Tamara began scanning around, almost at random.

'Which name were you looking for?'

'Danilov,' she said.

Gribov went to the end of the bookcase and examined the manifest that was pinned there. 'We certainly have a Danilov listed.'

'Then where is it?' snapped Tamara, regretting that her irritation was being vented on Gribov.

'I have it.' The voice was not Gribov's – it was deep and slow and calm, but still familiar. Both Tamara and Gribov turned to where the voice had come from. There was another block of

159

shelves directly beside them, but the flicker of lamplight spilled from behind. Tamara peered round and caught sight of the man who had spoken, sitting at a table with the file in front of him.

It was Yudin.

'Who's for a game of noses?'

Dmitry turned his head. It was Volgin, a naval *podporuchik*. He had just come into the mess and was waving a pack of cards.

'I'm up for it,' said Dmitry quickly. Anything to distract him from his thoughts. It had been over a month since his encounter with Wieczorek and Mihailov in the casemate – and his earlier and quite different encounter with Tyeplov. Wieczorek was dead, and Dmitry had not seen Mihailov, or heard of any death that might be attributed to him. He had not seen Tyeplov either, and that was the concern that filled his mind.

'Kids' game,' said another voice.

Volgin slapped the deck lightly against the man's nose, imitating the game itself. 'What do you want to play then?'

'Preferans,' came the definite reply.

'Count me in,' said a captain, strolling over from the bar.

'Major Danilov?' asked Volgin.

'Why not?' said Dmitry. Preferans would be far less of a distraction, but he had no desire to make an issue of it. He pulled his chair up to the table. The other two players introduced themselves – Ilyin and Manin.

Volgin dealt, while Ilyin found a piece of paper and scribbled a *puljka* on it for them to score with. He laid it on the table so that each triangle aligned neatly with the corresponding player. Dmitry won the bidding with seven in clubs and stuck with clubs as trumps. All three of his opponents opted to defend. He picked up the two cards of the talon; ten of clubs and ace of diamonds – the latter bearing the duty stamp, showing a pelican with its wings spread over its nest, a reminder that the tax went to fund the imperial orphanages. He discarded two low spades.

Just as he was picking up the cards of his first trick, the table shook as a shell came in somewhere close.

'That one was from the ships,' said Volgin. The others nodded.

The sound of cannon continued. Dmitry played his hand, but couldn't concentrate. He made the contract, but it was obvious to everyone that he should have got overtricks. Ilyin noted down his score on the *puljka*. Next it was Dmitry's deal. No one chose to bid, and so the hand was played as a pass-out, with each player trying to win the fewest tricks.

'I was talking to a chap the other day,' said Volgin as they played, 'who thinks we should all go home.'

'Good idea,' said Manin. Dmitry felt the table shake, and thought another shell had exploded, but looked up to see it was only that Manin was banging his hand upon it, to emphasize his agreement. Dmitry threw a card almost at random, and won a trick that he hadn't intended.

'Says each side should send a man home,' continued Volgin, 'then another and another, till there's only two left – one of them, one of us.'

'Single combat,' said Ilyin.

'That's how wars start,' said Manin, 'not how they end.'

'It'd save lives,' suggested Volgin.

'They'd cheat,' said Dmitry.

'Not if they won,' replied Ilyin.

'Then we'd cheat.' Dmitry's final comment seemed to settle it. They finished the hand. Dmitry was happy to have taken only one trick, though he knew he'd been lucky. Ilyin had taken none, with the remainder split between the other two. Ilyin dealt.

'Six diamonds,' was Manin's opening bid.

Volgin followed with 'Seven spades.'

Dmitry considered his hand. The sound of a large, distant explosion filled the room, but this time the floor did not shake. Dmitry felt reckless. 'Eight no trump.'

He heard a sharp intake of breath from behind him. He hadn't seen who had entered the room, but it was the height of rudeness to comment on a player's hand, even in a non-verbal form such as that.

'Fifth player!' said Manin, looking at the newcomer behind Dmitry.

'Under the table!' said the other two in unison, pointing there as they spoke. It was a common enough response to unwanted advice. Dmitry felt the man move away and head over to the bar. Manin bid nine diamonds and nobody countered. Only then did Dmitry glance at the newcomer. He immediately turned back, fixing his gaze on his cards, his blood suddenly cold.

It was Ignatyev, the *michman* he'd met briefly in the casemate in the fourth bastion. At the time he'd seemed pretty chummy with Mihailov and Wieczorek, though he hadn't returned with them later. Even so, Dmitry could not ignore the possibility that Ignatyev might, like them, be a *voordalak*.

For his part, Ignatyev did not even look in Dmitry's direction. Since he had come into the room, he had been behind Dmitry, with no opportunity to see his face except in the brief moment when Dmitry had glanced over at him, and then he had been turned away. If he had seen and recognized Dmitry, surely he would have reacted. Dmitry missed two possible tricks, but Manin had overbid horribly. He finished two under. Just as Ilyin was tallying the scores, Ignatyev walked briskly out of the room.

Dmitry was on his feet in an instant. 'That's it for me,' he announced.

'But you're ahead,' complained Manin.

'Give us a chance to win it back,' added Volgin.

'Keep it,' said Dmitry, striding to the door and grabbing his knapsack from beside the chair where he had left it.

He heard muttered comments of '*Choodak!*' and 'Better with three, anyway,' but then he was outside.

It was a warm night, the sort of night that made you want to do nothing. Despite the proximity of the sea, the air was thick and humid; it reminded him of Moscow. Outside, the noise of the guns was louder. Dmitry could clearly distinguish the direction that the explosions came from, either from the land to the south and east, or from the sea. The glare that lit the sky preceded their accompanying blasts by seconds, and they were frequent enough to make it impossible to connect a particular report with a particular flash.

Ignatyev was nowhere to be seen. Dmitry had come out of the mess on to the bank of the Military Harbour. Almost immediately opposite, a boat bridge stretched across it, connecting the

162

eastern and western halves of the city. The harbour was calm, but the boats bobbed up and down in the water. Someone had just run across. Dmitry followed.

The west was a mass of small streets. Dmitry chose the one nearest to the end of the bridge and walked briskly down it. Above him, a shell sailed through the sky like a meteor, launched from one of the ships and aimed not into the city itself but at the bastions beyond. He heard the blast of its impact and tried not to imagine the carnage it must have caused.

He carried on down the street, glancing left and right at each side road that branched off. The entire area was all but deserted – those who were not on duty at the fortifications remained indoors for safety. Occasionally Dmitry saw someone, but not Ignatyev. Half the buildings he passed had been boarded up, some in hasty repair of damage caused by stray cannonballs, others simply because their owners had fled.

At last his eyes fell upon the figure he had been seeking. Ignatyev was no longer alone. Another man was walking beside him – this one in civilian clothes. Had Ignatyev found a victim, or a comrade? Dmitry scurried along the short distance to the next block of buildings, then turned into the road that ran parallel to where he had seen Ignatyev. He ran down that and then cut back to the right so that he would be ahead of them when they reached the next junction. He ducked into the doorway of one of the abandoned houses and waited. He could hear low voices approaching.

As they passed, Dmitry saw that there were now three of them. There probably had been before, but the third man had been obscured by the shadows. Like Ignatyev, he was in a naval uniform, and taller than the other two. He walked between them, as if they were leading him somewhere. Dmitry could not see his face.

The three men did not have much further to go. They stopped at the door of one of the houses, just beyond where Dmitry stood, hidden in the darkness. Compared with its neighbours, this building was in a decent state of repair – probably still lived in. Ignatyev unlocked the door and opened it, indicating that the other two should enter. At the same moment, a shell whistled low overhead, clearly off target. It landed a few streets away, shaking the ground and illuminating the sky. The three men turned to look, their faces momentarily lit by the blast, and Dmitry saw what he had already suspected.

The man in the middle was Tyeplov.

'Aleksei Ivanovich Danilov.'

Yudin eyed Tamara as he spoke. He tried to gauge her reaction, but could infer nothing. The name sounded unusual on his lips, at least in that form. In his mind the man would always be 'Lyosha', but to refer to him so familiarly would reveal too much. It was suspicious enough that she should be showing an interest in him. It could be quite innocent – but Yudin would not have lived to anything like his great age if he believed in innocence.

Tamara's response was simply to bat the question back. 'Yes, Vasiliy Innokyentievich?'

Yudin knew that he did not have to play games. 'Why the interest?' he asked.

'He's a witness to murder,' she said simply.

Yudin almost laughed. The idea that Lyosha could have anything to do with the death of Irina Karlovna was beyond ridiculous. But that was not the primary issue. 'I don't recall authorizing you to investigate the death of your colleague.'

'Not that murder. A murder in 1812. And another in 1825.'

Yudin considered her. She was sitting in his office, lit as usual by lamplight, and it was night outside. She was closer to the door than he, but even if she ran for it he could easily catch her. Gribov had shown her in, and might hear her scream, but he could be dealt with too, if necessary. None of it was necessary – yet. The very fact that she had come down here and was telling him indicated how little she must know. He felt safe – but also fascinated.

'Explain,' he said.

'There was a murder in 1812, just after the French pulled out. A prostitute. In Degtyarny Lane. Her name was Margarita Kirillovna.'

She gave out each fact separately, as if feeding a line out to Yudin so that he could become well and truly hooked. He knew full well that Margarita Kirillovna had been killed in 1812 – it was he who had killed her, and made it look like the work of a vampire. He had used a weapon he'd constructed himself, formed from two knives, virtually identical, bound together at the handles with leather strapping so the two blades lay parallel. Their upper edges were a jagged sawtooth, and the lower keen as razors. Each ended in a neat, sharp point. He'd made it specifically to imitate the wounds of a vampire's teeth, and now, even though he was a vampire, he still sometimes preferred to use the knife, and always carried it with him. It allowed him to look into his victim's eyes as he worked. He could recall the thrill as he had turned it on Margarita, her expression of surprise and terror. He felt an excitement inside him as he considered telling Tamara the truth and seeing that same look on *her* face, but he restrained himself. 'Prostitutes get murdered all the time,' he responded.

'Her injuries were almost identical to those of Irina Karlovna.'

'Almost?' He refrained from adding, 'That's not how I remember it,' but he was curious to know what differences there were.

'She'd also been stabbed in the chest.'

That, Yudin presumed, would be Aleksei's handiwork. Yudin had clearly done a good job of making it look like the work of a *voordalak* – good enough for Aleksei to take precautions. 'And how was Danilov involved?' he asked.

'He found the body.'

'Did they catch the killer?' It was a delightfully unnecessary question.

She shook her head. 'No, but that's not it. In 1825 there were five more murders.'

'In 1825 there were dozens of murders,' he snapped.

'In five the cause of death was a similar throat wound. In one, the man who found the body was Aleksei Ivanovich Danilov.'

Yudin raised an eyebrow, hoping it would disguise the true nature of his surprise. Aleksei had clearly been a busy man in 1825. He had come to Chufut Kalye and helped to destroy all Yudin's work there, he had saved Aleksandr I from a fate worse than death in Taganrog and he had taken part in the Decembrist Uprising in Petersburg. All this Yudin knew because he had been

165

present. He had not been in Moscow at all, but it seemed that there too Aleksei had not been idle.

'When in 1825?' he asked.

'Early October.'

That was before the events in the south of the country. It must have been what brought Aleksei down there. 'I see,' said Yudin. 'And now you think he might have come back and killed Irina Karlovna – for old times' sake.'

'I think it unlikely.'

'Because?'

'Because he's in Siberia.'

'You're sure of that?'

'That's what I was coming to check.'

Yudin thought for a moment. He doubted that she knew any more than she was telling, but even so, it was an impressive piece of investigation. And the fact that they were both now interested in Aleksei could be of use. Her investigations could provide a cover for Yudin's own – though he still had other lines of enquiry that might allow him to leave Aleksei to his fate.

'He's still there – in Irkutsk.'

'Any family?'

'His wife died. He has a son, Dmitry.' Yudin paused, trying to judge if she knew already. She said nothing, but she would soon find out. 'Whom I know personally.'

Tamara tilted her head a little to one side. Now she was trying to assess Yudin, but she would discover nothing. 'And where is he?'

'Sevastopol. He's in the army. Is that a good enough alibi?'

'Not as good as Irkutsk.' Yudin could not tell if she was being serious. 'How old is he?' she asked.

'Nearly fifty.' Yudin understood where she was leading. 'Which would have made him around five years old at the time of your first murder.' He was amused to find himself defending the man.

She smiled, and he was now fairly certain that she had been teasing him. 'What was your interest, by the way?' she asked.

Yudin had anticipated the question. 'As you might expect, I read all the mail to and from the exiles, including Danilov's.'

'And?'

'He mentioned a name – a possible co-conspirator; another Decembrist.'

'One that got away?'

'Not for very much longer.'

She seemed satisfied. She did not ask the name of the other man, and Yudin would simply have refused to tell her if she had.

'You think you can put together a case against him?'

'He'll confess.'

'Simple as that?'

Yudin smiled. Could she really be that naive? Her work had, so far, only introduced her to one side of the Third Section's activities, but she must surely guess what happened to the men she informed upon, once they were in custody. It was time to see what the woman was really made of.

'Let me show you something,' he said. She looked puzzled, but he said no more. He took out his key and went over to the door to unlock it. 'This way.'

She stood and followed him. He stepped back and let her go first. He heard her feet on the stone steps coming to a halt. She had reached the point where the stairs divided. He had no plans to let her see the coffins. What she would see would be enough – enough for him to enjoy that first hint of apprehension on her face. It would be their opening step on a journey together that would end in her understanding everything, and being horrified by it, and dying with only fear in her mind. With luck it would be a long journey, of which he at least would relish every moment.

'Down to the left,' he called lightly.

Tamara's steps resumed and Yudin followed her down, closing the door behind him.

CHAPTER X

'TOLYA!' DMITRY BANGED HIS FIST AGAINST THE WOODEN door and shouted again. 'Tolya!' He waited only seconds for a response, but knew this was no question of politely listening for the sound of footsteps and waiting for the butler to open the door and enquire into the nature of his visit.

He had hesitated just a moment in shouting from across the street and when he had called out his voice had been drowned by another exploding shell. Then Tyeplov and the other two had vanished inside. Tyeplov was forewarned of the existence of vampires and was a strong man, but if it turned out that both Ignatyev and the other figure Dmitry had seen were *voordalaki* then he would be in no position to defend himself.

Dmitry stepped back a few paces and then charged at the door, aiming his shoulder at its centre. It did not yield. He tried again, but the only damage he succeeded in inflicting was upon himself. He stood in front of it and kicked, but with the same lack of effect. He stepped back out into the street. It was a large building. All the houses in the block stretched back a long way, and this one had windows on either side of the front door. None of them was showing any light. Dmitry went back up to the door and then stepped out on to the window ledge to the right. He turned away from the building and pressed his back against the glass, finding what little grip he could on the window frame, and then raised his foot.

Dmitry paused. He did not even know for sure that Ignatyev was a vampire; there might be some entirely different explanation. He might break into the building and chase through the rooms, searching in one after another, only to find the three men quietly playing cards. Tyeplov would regard him as obsessed – a jealous lover who could not stand for a moment to see the object of his affection happy in the company of others. Worse still, Dmitry might find the three men in a situation that genuinely could be a cause for jealousy. He would rather live in ignorance.

But none of that would serve as an excuse. Were Tyeplov to die, he would be unable to listen to Dmitry's reasons for not coming to his aid, but Dmitry would hear them all, over and over again, becoming less convincing with each repetition. He could not live with it. He thrust his heel backwards and heard the glass shatter. He turned and slipped through the broken window into the house.

The room was unremarkable – a study of some kind, but Dmitry did not linger to examine it. His only useful observation was that it was empty. There was a door in the far left-hand corner. Dmitry reached into his knapsack and drew out his wooden sword and his pistol. He knew that a bullet could not kill a vampire, but he had witnessed how effective it could be in disabling one, if only temporarily.

The door led back to the hallway. It was darker here. Dmitry glanced and saw the locked front door. More doors led off the hall as it disappeared into the gloom at the back of the house. A flight of stairs ascended just opposite the point where Dmitry had entered.

'Tolya!' he shouted again, and then listened. There was no response. He proceeded along the hall, glancing at the bottom of each door he passed, but seeing no sign of light. The sound of cannon firing and shells landing was quieter in here, but still the building shook every minute or so as another explosion brought the fall of the city a step closer. Soon the corridor ended in a door from beneath which shone the faintest glimmer. Dmitry stood and listened, his hand resting on the doorknob.

'Tolya!' Still silence. He opened the door swiftly. It was a kitchen. On a shelf stood a candle, burned almost to nothing. He was at the back of the house now. The windows looked on to a small yard and beyond it other houses, some with lights in their windows.

There was a sound – muffled as it penetrated from a different room. It could have been a scream; it could have been a cat. Immediately following came a heavy thud, directly above. Dmitry turned and dashed to the stairs, climbing them three at a time, his arms, still clutching sword and pistol, swinging wildly to speed his ascent. The stairway turned twice and at the top he momentarily lost his bearings. The landing was long and narrow, matching the hall below. Dmitry ran along it, but soon found himself at a window. He looked out and saw the street by which he had come. He turned and ran back down the corridor, ignoring the doors on either side, imagining the layout of the rooms below so that he could place himself directly above the kitchen.

At the far end he came to a door, in exactly the position he had expected. There was light coming from this one – not just from beneath it, but along one side and through the keyhole. Dmitry scarcely broke his run as he opened it and burst into the room beyond. Then he froze.

The scene was composed like a painting – a crystallization of domestic ennui as if captured by de Hooch. All three men were in the room. Tyeplov was at the washstand, his wet hands half covering his face as he gazed between his fingers at himself in the mirror on the wall. On the other side of the room, on the floor, on a striped rug just beside the bed though not quite parallel to it, lay the body of the unknown civilian. His head was closer to Dmitry than his feet and it lolled backwards, so that the man's eyes stared upwards, as if pleading with Dmitry to help him.

He was beyond help. The gash to his neck was vivid and red. A streak of blood across the carpet revealed the exact spot at which his throat had been severed, where it continued to ooze from the man's veins, not smoothly but in pulses, as his fading heart struggled foolishly to do its duty to the last. It was a moot point whether the man could yet be regarded as dead.

Between the body and Tyeplov, still seemingly frozen in the moment of Dmitry's arrival, was Ignatyev. He was on one knee, halfway through the process of moving on from the first victim of the night to the second. Moments before he must have been kneeling over the dying man, inflicting that fatal wound and enjoying the flavour of the blood that spilled from it. Now he had turned. His left leg was bent, its foot tensed against the floor, ready to launch him across the room at the ingenuous, unseeing Tyeplov. It meant that Ignatyev's face was turned directly towards Dmitry, and Dmitry could see in every detail the residue of the abomination he had just committed. His chin was red with blood. His mouth – half open – showed tendrils of ruddy saliva that clung and stretched between his teeth. His moustache, normally blond, was fringed by a dark band where blood had soaked into it. Other matter was caught up among the bushy whiskers, whose exact nature Dmitry didn't care to consider.

'Tolya!' Dmitry hissed.

Tyeplov stood upright and turned, looking first at Dmitry and then at Ignatyev. His face was the epitome of consternation. Ignatyev was on his feet now, changing his direction to move towards Dmitry. Dmitry's pistol fired, this time with none of the chance and indecision of the fight in the casemate. The bullet went into Ignatyev's neck and emerged the other side. Behind him, on the mantelpiece, a vase shattered and its fragments fell to the floor. Dmitry could see the wound, just below Ignatyev's Adam's apple.

The vampire took a step backwards, but the effect was nothing like as devastating as when Wieczorek's face had been just inches from the muzzle. Dmitry held his wooden sword tightly, low and out to his right, ready to stab upwards into the creature's chest, but still he noticed how his hand shook. He tried to speak – to warn Tyeplov – but found that his throat could produce no sound. He sidestepped into the room, placing himself between Ignatyev and his unarmed friend. Ignatyev turned, always keeping his face towards Dmitry. His mouth was closed now, but the blood on his moustache and chin was a constant reminder of the vile entity that he was. It hardened Dmitry's resolve as he readied himself for a fight to the death.

But Ignatyev did not attack. He raised his hands, open-palmed in a gesture of pacification. The expression on his face was one of confusion, as if he was asking Dmitry what it was that he should do next. Dmitry did not care to fathom the *voordalak*'s motivations. It might be a ruse or it might be a sign of weakness. Dmitry guessed it was the latter and took a step forward.

The room vanished in an instant. The rear and side walls were gone, along with the bed, the mantelpiece, the fireplace and half of the floor. Ignatyev was gone too. Dmitry felt the floorboards beneath his feet shifting, and suddenly he was falling, only to be saved by firm hands that he knew to be Tyeplov's grabbing him under the arms and pulling him back.

The shell had exploded just outside, its noise filling the air, but insignificant compared with its more concrete effects. Dmitry gazed out into the starry night and saw in front of him the rooms of other houses, much like this one, their walls ripped away to reveal what lay within. The gun had been way off target for it to have hit here, and in at least one of the buildings the occupants had been taken completely by surprise: a woman stood in her nightdress, her back against her bedroom wall with only just enough floor remaining for her to stand on. She was looking down, looking to where her husband – so Dmitry presumed – lay in the remains of the room beneath. He reached up towards her with his hand, then fell back and moved no more.

Dmitry looked down into the crater beneath him. Two bodies lay there, in the rubble that was the amalgamation of a bedroom and a kitchen. One had been dead even before the shell hit. It lay on a wooden table, standing strangely undamaged in the chaos around it, partly shrouded by the striped rug. Ignatyev was almost directly beneath Dmitry, writhing as if he were a pinned insect. The floor beneath him had opened like a trapdoor, the end closest to Dmitry remaining in situ as though hinged there. Ignatyev had slid down until his leg penetrated a gap in the surface. At that point he must have swung round, for now he hung almost upside down, his leg still trapped against the floorboard, the femur clearly shattered. His fingers clawed upwards, though they could do nothing to free him.

Dmitry knew that he would escape in time. He must finish the monster now, while it was vulnerable. He looked for a way down into the shattered kitchen and realized the fastest, or at least the safest, would be the most traditional. He half turned and gave a shout of 'Stay there!' though Tyeplov displayed no intention of doing otherwise, remaining frozen – pressed up against the wall. Dmitry raced out of the room back to the stairs and was down them in a moment. Soon he was in the kitchen, face to face with

Ignatyev, except that from the view of each of them, the other's face was upside down.

Dmitry considered what to do. Ignatyev lay back on the sloping floor, watching him, waiting. There were two options. He could stab the creature with his wooden sword, or attempt to behead it with his steel one. The former seemed the more reliable option, except that Ignatyev's chest was too high for Dmitry to reach, certainly not with the ability to apply any force. Dmitry looked around him. Nearby stood the kitchen table, the body of Ignatyev's last – and thankfully final – victim still sprawled on it. If Dmitry could pull it just a little way across the room, then he could climb on it and plunge his wooden blade into the monstrous heart.

He grabbed the table with his left hand and gave it a heave. It wouldn't budge. He glanced over at Ignatyev again and saw that he was still unable to move. He put the wooden sword on the table within easy reach, and then tugged at it again, this time with both hands. He pulled again, and again.

On the third attempt, it yielded, as did the remainder of the ceiling above. Somehow the table had been supporting the fragile remnants of the wall, but with Dmitry's help that support had gone, and the collapse of that part of the building was complete. Dmitry was thrown backwards, but managed to roll under the table itself, which saved him from being hit by any of the debris.

It was quiet again within seconds, and Dmitry slid himself out of his protective refuge. He regained his feet as quickly as he could and looked around the room. The sloping floor had fallen in completely, and Ignatyev was no longer trapped. He was standing upright, his weight clearly on only one leg – his broken bones causing the other to bend at an impossible and unusable angle. In his hand, he held Dmitry's wooden sword. He approached, hopping at first, but even as Dmitry watched, his left leg began to straighten and he dared to place increasing amounts of weight on it. He looked down at the wooden sword in his hand and then grinned, snapping it in two like a twig and casting it aside into the rubble. His grin became broader, so that Dmitry could see his still-bloody fangs. Whatever indecision might have come upon him in the room above had been forgotten in the fall. Now he approached Dmitry with only hunger and hatred in his eyes. Dmitry drew his sabre and prepared to defend himself, but he knew he could do little to stave off what fate had decreed for him.

'No!'

The voice came from above. Both Dmitry and Ignatyev looked up and saw that it was Tyeplov, still managing to find some small patch of solid floor in the ruined bedroom. Ignatyev looked at him for a few seconds, then turned his attention back to Dmitry. His leg seemed fully healed now, and his gait was quite normal.

'No!' came Tyeplov's voice again.

Ignatyev gave one last contemptuous look at Dmitry and turned away. He scrambled over the collapsed masonry of the walls and was soon out in the yard at the back of the house. The wall that divided it from the next property had vanished, and soon so had Ignatyev. Dmitry felt no urge to pursue him. Instead he looked up to see Tyeplov's face just disappearing behind the edge of the jagged hole in the ceiling above. He heard footsteps going across the landing and raced to catch him, clambering over the table and the body that still lay upon it and making his way out into the hall.

He was halfway up the stairs when he heard the sound of breaking glass, and at the top he quickly saw that the window overlooking the street had been shattered – not simply broken, as Dmitry had the window below, but utterly smashed. Tyeplov had thrown himself through it. Dmitry stood and looked out of its splintered remains, just able to catch a glimpse of a tall figure sprinting away down the street.

'You will have heard of Sheshkovsky's Room.'

Yudin asked the question as they reached the bottom of the stone staircase. They were in a short cramped corridor. The brick walls curled over to form an arched roof which only just failed to brush the top of Yudin's head. The walls themselves were only a little wider than his shoulders. If they wanted to pass each other they would have had to turn sideways, and it would even then have been an intimate operation. The only light came from the lamp in his hand, which made the damp walls glisten. The floor, again brick, was dotted with shallow puddles. Along each side of the passageway were three small wooden doors, with another one at the far end.

'A myth,' Tamara replied dismissively.

'Possibly – but a useful one. Some say that the room still exists, in the building beside the chain bridge.'

'Unlikely,' she replied, forcing herself to appear at her most rational.

She could not see Yudin smile, but she heard it in his voice. 'A fascinating approach to torture, nonetheless. The suspect would be placed in a chair and Chief Secretary Sheshkovsky would engage him in quite friendly conversation. And then at the pull of some unseen lever, the floor of the room would drop away, along with the seat of the chair, and a team of experts would use knouts to beat at the man's nether regions until they bled.' He took out a key and unlocked the nearest door, inviting Tamara to enter with an opened hand. 'And then Sheshkovsky would resume his questioning.'

Inside, the room – cell would perhaps be a better description – was quite large, certainly in comparison with the corridor they had come from. It contained a single piece of furniture: a solitary chair. Tamara walked cautiously towards it, eyeing the floor as she went, but it seemed solid enough. When she reached the centre of the cell she saw that the chair was not entire – simply a wooden frame from which the seat had been cut out.

'My rc-creation,' said Yudin. 'Far simpler – with none of the unwieldy engineering.'

She turned and looked at him. In his hand he held a knout; behind him, on the wall, hung several others. He caressed its three leather strands, each of them tipped with a small lead ball. Tamara knew that he wanted her to show fear, but she did not feel it.

'They call this a *plyet*,' he said. 'His Majesty – His *late* Majesty – changed the law to make this form of lash the only one we're allowed to use.'

'And you wouldn't disobey His Majesty,' said Tamara, eyeing the plethora of different whips on the wall behind him that belied his words.

'We serve His Majesty.'

175

'And I'm sure he approved of everything you have down here.'

'He didn't disapprove.'

'His successor might.' Tamara glanced at Yudin as she spoke. He seemed to take what she had said in his stride.

Yudin stepped outside again, taking the lamp with him, and the cell was plunged into darkness. By the time Tamara had followed him, he had opened up the door opposite and gone inside. The cell was the same size and shape as the last, but even more sparse – empty at first glance.

'These chambers go back to Ivan the Third,' explained Yudin. 'The features are not entirely original – though the idea dates back even further.' He glanced upwards and towards the centre of the room. At first, Tamara saw nothing, but then the lamplight caught metalwork and she saw, suspended from eyelets in the ceiling, two sets of iron manacles. Yudin walked towards them and put his hand in the air. He pressed his palm flat against the brickwork above him without even having to fully straighten his elbow. 'Unfortunately, people are so much taller these days,' he said.

As they left, Tamara noticed two dark stains in the floor, neatly positioned beneath each set of metallic cuffs. Still she did not experience the fear or nausea that Yudin was clearly anticipating – that would be the reaction of most women. She thought of the train to Pavlovsk, and of Stasik's little body cradled in her arms, and of the stench that came from his clothes. Yudin had not yet shown her anything to compete with the Lord above.

'Of course,' he continued, 'these things have their advantages too.' He opened the middle door in one of the walls. The space behind was tiny. Only a child could have stood up in there. 'In olden days, these would have been quite spacious.' Yudin's tone was deliberately light. 'Now, they can break a man in hours.' He closed the door. 'The one opposite is just the same.'

They moved on. They were at the end of the passageway, faced with doors, one on either side, another at the very end. Yudin unlocked the one on the left, but did not open it. 'We won't step inside here,' he said. He pushed the door ajar and thrust the lamp inside. A thousand tiny voices squealed together, punctuated by the sound of sharply pointed claws scrabbling over the stonework and the slither of scaly tails. He swung the lamp back and forth and a hundred pairs of black, gleaming eyes sparkled back at them.

Yudin closed the door quickly. 'They soon learn to lose their fear,' he said. 'Particularly when they're hungry. Man's fear lasts longer.'

Still Tamara failed to feel the terror that Yudin so evidently wanted to induce in her. She had seen rats before – in the streets, beside the river, even running along the railway tracks, to hide under the platform when a train came in. They survived, like any other creature, and their greatest threat to man was that they stole his food – just as man stole theirs. A room full of wolves would seem a better way to make a person afraid. But Tamara was being rational – and she knew that that was a state of mind that Yudin would have eradicated long before he brought his captive to this room.

'Why are you showing me this, Vasiliy Innokyentievich?' she asked.

'Because you expressed an interest.'

Tamara searched her memory, but could not think of anything she might have said to give that impression. 'I did?' she asked.

'When you began to investigate a crime. An investigation leads to an arrest, an arrest to an interrogation, an interrogation to a confession.'

'If the man is guilty.'

'Or the denunciation of a friend if he is not. Either way, your investigation will come to an end down here. Are you prepared for that?' As he asked the question, he moved to the door across the passageway and began to unlock it.

'What about this one?' asked Tamara, indicating the door at the very end of the corridor. It was different from the others: more sturdily built, with iron bands across acting as braces. In addition to the lock, there were three heavy bolts at different levels sealing it tight. And unlike the other six doors it had no grille in it at eye level to allow the activities within to be observed.

Yudin glanced at the door and then at her, silent in thought. His face seemed to smile, although his lips never moved, and a look of excitement, exhilaration even, came into his eyes. Then, in an instant, the expression faded, and he turned back to unlock the other door. 'Perhaps another day,' he said quickly, and then disappeared into the room that he was happier to show her. She was reminded of the story of Bluebeard.

Even before following him in, Tamara could hear the trickle of water. Inside, her first impression was that the room contained a coffin. It abutted the side wall and was made of stone – more a sarcophagus than a coffin. Above it a lead pipe protruded from the wall, pouring water into it, filling it almost to the brim. Not a coffin, or even a sarcophagus, she thought, but a bathtub. A small notch in the side allowed the water to flow out again without the tub brimming over completely. It ran along a gutter and then disappeared through another hole in the wall. The water stank with the familiar reek of the sewer.

'Are you prepared to do it?' repeated Yudin. 'To do whatever it takes to extract the information you need?'

She considered, but not the prospect of bringing a man down here to discover his secrets. She considered the image of Irina Karlovna, lying on the bed, the description of Margarita Kirillovna in much the same circumstances, along with those of the others who had died. If whoever had killed them had the stomach to do what he had done, then was it fair that she lacked the stomach to discover the truth?

'If it becomes necessary.'

The smell from the water seemed to become stronger, filling the room.

'Many fear drowning more than anything,' said Yudin wistfully, staring down into the rippling water. Then he looked up, straight into Tamara's eyes. 'Danilov is seventy-four years old. Could you bring an old man down here?'

'He's not the murderer – not of Irina.'

'But he may know who is.'

'Then he'll tell me.'

'He's kept his secret for thirty years,' Yudin persisted.

Tamara corrected him. 'Forty-three years.' She was finding it hard to breathe. The stench reminded her of Petersburg and of 1848.

He smiled, almost imperceptibly, then turned to look back into

178

the water, its odour seeming not to affect him. 'The water comes from the Neglinnaya, as far as I can make out, and must drain into the Moskva. Filthy these days, of course, but that only adds to the effect.'

Tamara tried to breathe through her mouth, but the stench had already filled her nostrils and she could not escape it. She felt bile rising in her gullet and closed her mouth tightly to restrain it, which forced her once again to inhale the foetid air through her nose until she could stand it no more. She turned and fled, at last, she knew, giving Yudin the response he was hoping for, though not for any reason he would predict. It was simply the smell – the miasma that had filled Petersburg in 1848 and had brought with it cholera. It had spread from the rivers and canals and through the streets and into the houses and taken her children from her. Half of her wanted to stay there, to breathe deeply of the foulness and be taken by the disease that had taken her family, and it was not fear of the disease that made her run, but fear of the memories that the stench brought with it.

Once out of the cell and away from Yudin's lamp, she found herself in darkness. She turned the wrong way and felt the wood of the door that was forbidden to her against her hands. From the other side she thought she heard a sound – a voice pleading for help – but she realized it was only an echo of the cries she had heard from Stasik as he lay in agony, years before. She turned and went the other way, not quite running, trailing her fingers along the enclosing walls, counting the doorways that she passed. She tripped as her toe caught the first of the stone steps, but was able to push out with her arms and brace herself on the walls on either side before falling.

She climbed the stairs in the way she had done as a child, leaning forward and half crawling so that her hands touched the steps in front of her, ignoring the filth and grime that they picked up, almost pleased that in the darkness she could not see it. The steps flattened out and she thought she must be in Yudin's office, but she remembered the small landing where the stairway had branched into two. She turned right, and soon felt the steps rising again.

At last she came up against another door. She pushed at it, but it would not open. Her hands fumbled around, searching for a handle or latch. Eventually she gripped something metallic. She pulled on it and the door opened. Now, finally, in Yudin's office, there was some little illumination, but it did not stop her flight. She crossed the room and carried on upwards on the stairs that she knew led to the surface. Soon another door was in front of her, but this one opened easily. She spilled outside and took in great gasps of the cool, clean night air. Eventually her breathing slowed.

She waited for Yudin to join her, but he did not. She knew she should go back down – only to his office – and speak to him, but she was unable. Instead she headed home. The taste of the foul air below was still on her tongue, its scent still in her nostrils. She lit a cigarette and drove the stench – and the memories – away.

It was the small hours before Dmitry made it back to his lodgings and went to bed, but he did not sleep. The enemy bombardment had begun to subside, but still the occasional blast could be heard, which was enough to keep him awake – as was his state of mind.

It should have all been quite inexplicable. Dmitry had been at the mercy of Ignatyev and yet the creature had not killed him. More than that, Ignatyev had desisted at Tyeplov's instruction. Why should Tyeplov command him? Why should he obey? And yet the explanation came in the image that filled Dmitry's mind as he lay in the darkness and gazed at the ceiling.

It was the scene in the bedroom, before the explosion – the dead man on the floor, Ignatyev turning away, blood streaming from his lips, and Tyeplov, his face in his hands at the washstand. Dmitry let his mind create music to accompany his recollection, but the tunes that came were strangely light-hearted; clarinets and piccolos danced over the melody, laughing at Dmitry. And there was good reason for it, for there was one aspect of the tableau that proved Dmitry to have been an utter fool.

In the mirror on the bedroom wall, above the washstand, Tyeplov had shown no reflection.

Dmitry had never seen him in daylight. He had seen him consort with men who had later proved to be vampires – Mihailov, Wieczorek and now Ignatyev. When Mihailov and Wieczorek had come to them in the casemate, it was not as two vampires come to feast on two men. They were merely rejoining their comrade in the hope of sharing at least a taste of the blood that Tyeplov had so cunningly taken into his possession.

And that was another way in which Dmitry felt a fool. It was so absurd he even chuckled at it – thinking of himself as some deluded young virgin, tricked by an old letch. Tyeplov had wanted him only for his body. If that were true in the normal sense, then Dmitry would not have minded; he was not a romantic who needed to be flattered to be seduced. He had enjoyed Tyeplov's body just as much as he had believed Tyeplov enjoyed his. But for Tyeplov, the night they had spent together had not been the goal of his seduction, but merely a phase of it, a way to weaken Dmitry's resistance when the moment came for the final consummation of the flesh, which Dmitry would have found impossible to enjoy.

The same thing must have happened that night. Whoever their poor victim had been, Dmitry could only suspect that Tyeplov and Ignatyev had lured him with promises of much the same enjoyments as Dmitry had experienced. Clearly Tyeplov had learned from his mistakes with Dmitry, and had allowed Ignatyev to strike swiftly.

The bed suddenly shook. Someone had sat down on it, beside Dmitry. In the darkness, Dmitry could see only a silhouette, but he knew Tyeplov's scent intimately. He felt a finger placed on his lips.

'Have you guessed?' said Tyeplov softly. He held his finger there for a few moments more and then pulled it away so that Dmitry could speak. Dmitry lay still, terrified by the simplicity of the situation. There was no need for conversation or seduction or for leading men away down a quiet city street. Tyeplov had come to his room, and would kill him and devour him, all in the space of one night, and Dmitry would be able to do nothing about it. Even if he could fight off one vampire, Ignatyev would be somewhere near.

'Where's your friend?' he asked, his voice hushed and bitter.

'I'm alone.'

'Why should I believe you?'

'Why should I lie?'

'You've lied to me before.'

Dmitry felt Tyeplov lie down beside him and rest his arm across his chest. His face was now close and Dmitry could feel breath on his cheek. The smell was repellent, like rotting meat. Dmitry wondered that he had never noticed it before, but then realized: in their previous encounters, Tyeplov had not recently eaten.

'Have I?' said Tyeplov.

Dmitry thought back. Perhaps he hadn't. 'You deceived me.'

'I had to. Look at what you did to Wieczorek.'

'And look at what you did to that poor fellow tonight. Why do you need to pretend with me?'

'You're different.'

For a ghastly moment, Dmitry feared that Tyeplov was about to tell him that he genuinely loved him, that, though he lusted after human blood, in Dmitry's case a deeper emotion meant that he would resist his basest urges, and hoped that Dmitry could overcome his natural revulsion at such a creature and reciprocate his affection. It was a revolting concept. Unholy. A union between man and beast, fouler even than the beast itself.

'Different?' he asked.

'"For the sins of your fathers you, though guiltless, must suffer."'

'So it's about Papa?' Dmitry had suspected something from the moment Tyeplov had shown such interest in Aleksei. 'He's too far away for you to take your vengeance on him, so you plan to take it out on me?'

'Quite the opposite. It was the three-fingered man who saved us. His son will be the instrument of our vengeance.'

'Papa saved you?'

'We were imprisoned – tortured by a man called Cain. Your father freed us – or at least attempted to.'

'Where?'

'Near here – a place known as Chufut Kalye.'

'When?'

'In 1825.'

As with any deceit, it was founded upon truth. In 1825 Aleksei had travelled to the Crimea, in pursuit of a vampire, Kyesha. On his return, he had told little of what had happened, and the death of Aleksandr I had begun a sequence of events that seemed far more pressing. But before then, Dmitry had heard his father speak of vampires with nothing but loathing; that he would side with them, and against a human, was absurd.

'And only now you seek your revenge?'

'Cain tricked us – we were entombed. We were freed only recently.'

'He must be getting on a bit now,' said Dmitry. 'He may be dead.'

'He has become like us.'

'A *voordalak*?'

Tyeplov nodded, his face scarcely visible in the darkness. 'Will you help us?'

It was absurd. Dmitry was being asked to take sides in a battle, not between Russian and Frenchman, or even between man and monster, but between *voordalak* and *voordalak*. Even if it were true that Aleksei had sided with them in the past, it did not mean that Dmitry should do so now. Fundamentally, all of these creatures merited but one fate – death. But Dmitry's concerns were far more immediate.

'I thought I was your friend,' he said.

'You are,' Tyeplov insisted. 'To the extent that I can have a friend.'

'You made me your friend, to get what you wanted.'

'I sensed what *you* wanted,' said Tyeplov.

Dmitry could not deny the truth of what Tyeplov said, but it only went to show that Tyeplov had been accurate in detecting Dmitry's weakness. It had all been a matter of seduction, though it seemed he had guessed wrongly again as to the ultimate goal. If Tyeplov had wanted his body – in any sense – he could have taken it. Dmitry would have succumbed willingly to one expression of his lust, and was in no position to resist the other. But Tyeplov had found a third way to exploit him.

'I won't help you,' Dmitry said quietly.

'What?'

'You're a vampire,' said Dmitry. He meant it figuratively as well as literally. 'If you want revenge on another vampire, what should I care? How can one of you be right and one of you be wrong, when you're both spawned from Hell? I hope you all die – and if

183

I see you again, it will be me that kills you.' The calm of his voice belied a strength of passion that surprised him, but he knew that it came not from his hatred of all vampires. That existed, though it was of little relevance. At that moment it was the depth of his emotions towards one *voordalak* in particular that drove him.

Tyeplov stood. Dmitry could see his body, dimly silhouetted against the curtains. 'Your father thought differently,' he said.

'Then my father was a fool.' Dmitry believed his own words and, for some reason, believed Tyeplov's too. The whole story about Aleksei could be a fantasy, but it fitted with the fact that Tyeplov had come to him. Over his life, his view of his father had fluctuated through every conceivable sentiment, but at that moment Dmitry hated him – hated him for his weakness in once siding with this creature, and for his short-sightedness in not seeing that one day that weakness would come to haunt his child.

'You should talk to your father,' said Tyeplov. 'Write to him.'

'When I get round to it, I'll be sure to mention your name.'

Tyeplov paused. His head tilted to one side. 'He won't know me by this name,' he said. Perhaps it was the nature of the vampire, or perhaps it was just him, not to recognize sarcasm.

'What did he call you then?' Dmitry's voice was laden with disdain, but still Tyeplov failed to recognize it.

'We never spoke, but there is a name by which he might know me.'

'And what's that?'

'Prometheus.'

CHAPTER XI

TYEPLOV WAS GONE. HE HAD WALKED OUT OF DMITRY'S ROOM and Dmitry had not seen him again, neither had anyone he spoke to. Neither had anyone seen anything of Ignatyev or Mihailov. Neither had he heard stories of any more dead found with their throats ripped out – though there had certainly been many more dead. It was over two months since he had spoken to Tyeplov – Prometheus – in his room. He had not said any more and had not attempted to harm Dmitry in any way and Dmitry had not attempted to harm him. He possessed no weapon with which he might achieve it, but even if he had done, he would not have tried.

He thought of writing to his father, but what would be the point? He could not conceive of how to discuss matters in a way that would not alert the suspicions of the censor. And if Aleksei had not deigned to reply to him before, then why now?

Over the intervening weeks the sound of the roaring guns had stopped, recommenced and stopped again. Today the guns had once more begun to fire. Official reports back to Petersburg described this as the sixth bombardment, but Dmitry could find few in Sevastopol, other than the most senior officers, who had wasted a moment on counting. The shells of the latest bombardment were very much the same as those of the first except that – at least for Dmitry – they were louder.

Yet still the city had not fallen. Things had quietened down a little in the summer, when cholera and dysentery had taken their toll on the men of every nation's army, reducing both their ability and their need to kill one another. But Generals *Juillet* and *Août* were less partisan than their hibernal brothers, and their departure would leave both sides equally weakened. And since the enemy had begun the summer stronger than Russia, they would leave it stronger. Dmitry doubted that the siege would hold beyond September. September? They still had to survive another week of August.

He was out in the third bastion now, as he had been, when on duty, for the last few weeks. As the supply of able-bodied men dwindled postings became fluid, with officers assigned to tasks purely on the basis of numerical necessity, without any regard to their background or skills. It was the cavalry that tended to be moved around the most – a joke at the expense of their renowned manoeuvrability. At least they got to withdraw back to the city when off duty.

The third bastion wasn't getting the worst of it. To the left, the French were concentrating their fire on the Malakhov Tower. Since the fall of the Kamchatka Lunette and the White Works, this was the main defensive position in the east. Each night, Russian soldiers would work furiously to repair the damage that had been done by day, but would not quite have time to do enough, and at dawn the barrage would begin again. And so the decline of the Malakhov, like every other defence around the city, was slow enough that it could be watched day by day.

To the right, the British were attacking the fourth bastion. It was holding out better than the tower, but even so it was decrepit compared with earlier in the year. If it did not eventually fall, it would only be because the defences elsewhere failed sooner. Thoughts of the fourth bastion brought Tyeplov to Dmitry's mind once again. Had he really left the city, intent on taking his revenge on this man Cain without Dmitry's help, or had he merely gone into hiding, forgetting his personal vendetta and realizing that the day would soon come when the city fell and there would be fresh livestock – French, British, Turkish and Sardinian – swarming in, on which he and his kind could feed?

The guns boomed and the shells exploded and Dmitry gazed out over the enemy lines to the south, and he knew that that day would not be long in coming.

*   *   *

It was over six months since Tamara had been in Petersburg. When she left she had made no vows never to return, but she had not anticipated that she would be travelling back quite so soon, or that her purpose would be to carry out research. She thought she had exhausted the capital of all the information it could give her concerning her parentage. But now she was interested in a new topic. She had only one clue regarding the murders in Moscow – the name Aleksei Ivanovich Danilov. And with regard to Danilov she had only one useful fact – an address in Petersburg. Yudin had not returned the file on the Decembrist exile, and there might be far more there to be discovered.

But Gribov's library was, to say the least, imperfectly sorted. Although the vast majority of the papers regarding Danilov might have been collated into that one file that Yudin held, a few had slipped through the net. Tamara had found a report from the Manège – the riding school in Moscow – dating back to 1827 and describing the success of a cadet named Dmitry Alekseevich Danilov. Yudin had already revealed that Aleksei's son was named Dmitry, and now this document provided an address for him and his mother in Petersburg. They might have moved on years ago, but it was still somewhere to start.

The train whistle sounded three times, signalling the conductors in each carriage to apply the brakes, and they began to slow. The stop at one of the many intermediate stations along the route was not primarily for the sake of passengers, but because the locomotive itself needed to be replenished, taking on wood and water. Over a journey of twenty-two hours, it was not possible for the engine to carry all its provisions.

They were coming into Bologoye, close to the halfway mark of the journey and one of the three big stations between Moscow and Petersburg. Tamara looked at her husband's watch. It was almost ten o'clock at night. The wait here would be around half an hour and many of the passengers would alight to get something to eat, but Tamara didn't feel hungry.

She felt the train lurch to the left and the station buildings began to skip past, splitting the two tracks apart like the prow of a boat. The train came to a halt, then moved forward a little then forward again. Finally it seemed to have come to a position where the driver was happy. Once they got going again Tamara, like most passengers, would try to sleep, but since that wouldn't be for a while yet, she decided to get out and stretch her legs. The line of bodies moved slowly down the second-class carriage towards the exit. Ahead of her, as people emerged from the carriage and stepped on to the platform, Tamara sensed a certain buzz among the crowd, as each of them encountered something that she could not yet see.

Once outside she understood. The imperial train was already in the station, on the other side of the platform. She looked along its length and saw that the locomotive was at the northern end, so it too was heading to Petersburg. It was allowed to travel much faster than the regular passenger services. It would leave first and would be in the capital hours before her own train.

The crowds headed somewhat reluctantly for the Kartsov Restaurant, situated at the opposite end of the platform from the exclusive royal quarters. Stomachs conflicted with the desire to catch the slightest glimpse of some grand duke, grand duchess or perhaps even His Majesty, and for the most part the more visceral hunger won out. A few, like Tamara, remained in the middle of the platform, but soon became discomforted by the cool night air and either went to the restaurant or got back on the train.

Tamara lit a cigarette and inhaled deeply, holding the smoke in her lungs until the sensation of its presence had dimmed to nothing, then blew it out through her nostrils, watching the billowing fumes caught in the station lamps and quickly absorbed into the smoky atmosphere that hung over the station whenever a train was in.

'You can't do that here,' said a voice. Tamara turned to see a blue-uniformed gendarme, performing the mundane duty of maintaining order on the railways which, by some quirk of bureaucracy, was tasked to the same organization that acted as the public face of the Third Section.

As Tamara turned the man's face fell. His voice dropped to a mumble. 'Oh, I'm sorry,' he said, and hurried off. Tamara hadn't known him personally, but it seemed he had recognized her and feared what might happen to his career if she chose to take offence at his enforcement of petty rules.

'It's silly, isn't it?' said a voice close to her. She hadn't even noticed the man standing there. 'Here we are in this temple of Russian modernity, and we're still beholden to an Oprichnik like that, telling us what to do.'

She tried not to react to the word 'Oprichnik'. It was a common enough term of abuse for any police officer or government agent whose job it was to protect the nation's interests – a reminder of the hated secret police force of Ivan the Terrible. It was a word from three centuries before, but under Tsar Nikolai the people's resentment of the power of the state had risen, as had the use of the word. It was a term that had been directed at Tamara only occasionally in her career. But it was a sign of the times, of the weakening of imperial authority that was already taking place under Aleksandr II, that a man on a railway platform would use the word in front of a complete stranger, who could easily be – and in Tamara's case was – a government informer.

She turned and looked at him. He was a short man – scarcely taller than herself – of about twenty-five, with a slightly wedge-shaped face. His moustache and sideburns revealed him to be a military man, though he was not in uniform. The spectacles perched on his nose gave him an air of intellectualism – which made his comment all the more predictable. He held between his fingers a cigarette, burned down to almost nothing.

'He's doing his job,' said Tamara.

'Ah! So you're saying it's not the fault of the man who enforces the law, but of the men who make it?'

Tamara paused, considering carefully what to say. Perhaps it was she who was about to be trapped into producing some innocent phrase that would be twisted and then reported to her superiors.

'The law is made for the good of us all,' she said.

He took one final draw from his cigarette and dropped it on to the platform, extinguishing it with the sole of an elegant, imported leather boot. 'And what good does it do you or me to be told where and when we can smoke?' he asked.

'Some laws are meant to be honoured more in the breach than the observance,' she replied.

'Ah! Shakespeare!'

Tamara gave a smile of acknowledgement, but she had not known where the phrase came from. The man spoke a sentence in what sounded like English, and she guessed he was merely translating her words. 'I prefer Gogol,' she said.

He seemed enthused. 'Really? Really?' In truth she knew only a little of the author. She admired his skill with words, but sensed that, like all writers, he used them to hide views that did not make sense in a country such as Russia. 'My father was a great admirer of *The Government Inspector*,' the man continued, 'which I suppose shows just how little he understood it.' A look of distant remembrance came into his eyes. Tamara noted it, and his use of the past tense. He was young to have lost his father.

She smiled at him warmly and genuinely, liking his vivacity and deciding that his seditious comments were a result merely of stupidity, the stupidity to be found in many intelligent men, who simply could not believe that what they said could really have an impact on the world. It was a trait that was both likeable and dangerous. He smiled back and flushed very slightly.

'I think I'm happier not to understand it,' she said, discarding her own cigarette.

He tapped his nose and nodded his head towards the gendarme who had now moved well down the platform. 'Very wise,' he said. He slipped his hand into his pocket and brought out a gold cigarette case, which he flipped open, offering it to her with the words, 'These are French.'

She took one and thanked him. He selected another for himself and returned the case to his pocket, bringing out a small glass tube with a metal top. He held it up towards her and she realized it was some sort of device for lighting tobacco. She put the cigarette to her lips and he pressed a small switch in the metal top. The apparatus hissed, but no flame was evident. He tried again, and this time the hiss was quieter, and tailed off. Tamara reached into her reticule and produced a box of matches. She struck one and used it to light her cigarette, before offering it to him. His gloved hand took hers and guided it towards the tip, which soon began to glow orange.

'Much more suited to this temple of Russian modernity,' she said.

He laughed briefly but loudly. 'I hear that *The Gamblers* is playing in Petersburg,' he said. 'Have you seen it?'

'I'm afraid not.'

The sound of a train whistle cut through their conversation, causing him to look round. He threw his cigarette, barely started, to the ground. 'You must join me in my box,' he said. 'Where are you staying?'

'Dussot's Hotel,' she said without even thinking.

'Under what name?'

'My own.'

'Don't tease me, mademoiselle.'

She didn't correct him. 'Tamara Valentinovna Komarova,' she said.

'I will call on you, Tamara Valentinovna,' he said, and with that he ran across the platform – an ungainly activity for one so short – and jumped aboard the train. Tamara noticed a few of the people nearby staring, both at her and at him, but her eyes could only follow in the direction he had gone, as the train he had boarded began slowly to pull out of the station. There was no need for her to worry that she herself had missed it, for the young man had not been travelling on the same train as her. Its carriages were not the dark green of the passenger service, but a vibrant ultramarine. It was the imperial train.

The train began to move again, pulling out of the station. Yudin could not be sure which one, but his best guess was that it was Bologoye. It was night now, he could tell, even if he couldn't see it. During the day he had slept and his journey had been comfortable, but once darkness had fallen, then a *voordalak* became restless. Even though he could go for many days without feeding, he still felt the urge to walk the earth at night.

It was approaching autumn now, and so the nights were getting longer, but still Yudin could not have travelled the whole journey from Moscow to Petersburg sitting in a carriage like any other passenger. He travelled as baggage, in a separate wagon at the end of the train, without even the comfort of a roof to give protection from the elements. That meant the wooden box enshrouding him had to be particularly well made. One ray of sunlight finding its way through a crack in the crate would mean the end for him. It was not a true coffin, and was not listed on the train's inventory as such. There was no danger that any inquisitive employee of the railway would look inside – the stamp of the Third Section on the documentation saw to that. Once they arrived in Petersburg in the morning, the crate would be unloaded and left in the depot for collection. When night fell, the mechanism to open it from the inside was simple to use.

Yudin could easily release that catch now and, for the hours of darkness, sit like any other passenger in the first-class compartment. But what would be the point? A small but unnecessary risk in order to emulate the members of a species to which he no longer belonged. Both he and Raisa Styepanovna had made this journey many times before, and always they had remained in the safety of the baggage wagon. Now was not a time to change things.

For some months Yudin had desired to travel to Petersburg, but in summer it was a risk. At the sun's zenith, the night was scarcely five hours long. At least in Moscow he could rely on six and a half hours – and there he had sufficient boltholes about the city that he was never in too much danger of being caught out.

But the journey had to be made, and time was not an inexhaustible commodity. Only two men still living knew – or had any chance of knowing – how the trickery over the death of Tsar Aleksandr I had been perpetrated and where Aleksandr had hidden himself for the last thirty years. And both of those men were old and might soon die.

And one of them lived in Saint Petersburg.

It was all very familiar. Tamara's home, where she had lived with Vitya and Milenochka and Stasik and Luka, was not very far from here, but she had no desire to visit it. She continued along Nevsky Prospekt, the tower of the Admiralty far ahead acting as a beacon. She passed the Yeliseyev Brothers' store and thought of all the times they had gone there to buy wine – the New Year of 1847 when Vitya had come back with two bottles of champagne because the manager remembered Vitya's treating his wife's cousin the previous summer. She passed the Armenian Church, which she had never been inside. She had once promised to take the children in there, if they were very good. They hadn't been good and they hadn't been taken on a visit and now Tamara dearly wished she'd not been so strict in sticking to her word.

She crossed the Kazansky Bridge, as indistinguishable as ever from the rest of the road – so wide that it might be mistaken more for a square than a bridge. Only the Yekaterininsky Canal, emerging from beneath it at either side, gave away its construction. Tamara began to look around her more alertly. She knew that the street she was after – Great Konyushennaya Street, the last address she had for the Danilovs – would be coming up soon on the right. She passed Little Konyushennaya Street, and the Lutheran Church, and then there it was.

It was typical of that district; the ground-floor properties were all shops, with apartments above them. Number 7 was only a little way down. She knocked, using the heavy iron ring that hung from the door. She waited. There was no response. She knocked again and listened, but there was no sound of anyone coming to answer the door. She tried a third time, but finally gave up. In her bag she had a letter that she had written for such a case as this, asking the present owners to get in touch with her. It seemed so little to achieve for so long a journey – but there were other options.

The shop beneath was a bookseller's. By the look of the stock, it had been there for many years. There was every chance that they might know more than the residents of the apartment itself. Tamara went through the door. The interior was filled with books, some on shelves, some on tables, some in precarious piles that reached almost to the ceiling. The whole place smelt of old paper. Being on ground level, it would be liable to flooding. The books at the bottom of some of the piles would probably have been soaked and then dried a dozen times. It reminded her of the Kremlin archive. She expected to see Gribov's bushy eyebrows poking from around a set of shelves at any moment.

When the proprietor did appear, he was nothing like Gribov. He was tall and gaunt, with a full head of white hair that had a slight curl to it. He spoke good Russian, but with a strong German accent, and seemed very aloof.

'May I be of some help?'

'I do hope so,' said Tamara, looking up at him. He was behind a desk so that she could not see his feet, but he towered so far above her that she wondered whether he might be standing on a box. 'I'm looking for information on Aleksei Ivanovich Danilov.'

The shopkeeper's eyebrows rose together in the middle as he considered her question. 'Danilov. Danilov.' Then his eyes, and his mouth, widened. 'We have, of course, the *Byliny*, compiled by Kirsha Danilov – at least so they say. Personally, I have my doubts.' He frowned again. 'But I don't recall any Aleksei Ivanovich.'

'He's not a writer. He used to live in the apartments above you.'

'When?'

'Until 1825,' said Tamara, hoping the date wouldn't reveal too much of Aleksei's history. 'But his wife would have remained for some time after. And his son – Dmitry Alekseevich.'

'Ah!' said the man, somewhat theatrically. 'I remember. I remember. I remember. It was she who was resident in the property when I first arrived here. M . . . M . . .' He tried to produce a name from his memory, but could not. 'She said she was a widow.' A charming way to keep alive the memory of her exiled husband, thought Tamara, though she heartily approved of the shame the woman felt at her husband's treason. 'I was only here for a year before she died.' He looked at her gravely over his spectacles. '1848, you know.'

'I know,' said Tamara quietly. 'So who inherited the place?'

'Well, no one really. I had very little dealings with her.' His voice suddenly rose in excitement. 'Marfa Mihailovna, that was it. Marfa Mihailovna Danilova.'

Tamara felt the tiniest thrill – just as when she had read Volkonsky's letter mentioning the child he was paying for in Moscow. She realized that the exhilaration then was not purely down to its being a step closer to her parents – it was simply that, like today, it was a step forward. The thrill was in the chase as much as the prize. A moment later, the idea filled her with melancholy. In either pursuit, was the prize going to prove a disappointment?

'What do you mean, no one inherited it?' she asked.

'She was a tenant, just as I am. I still pay the rent to the same man. Never met him. He's called Makarov; Vasiliy Denisovich.'

Another step forward. 'His address?'

'I'm afraid I've no idea. I merely make payments to his bank – on Great Meshchanskaya Street.'

'I see,' she said. It wasn't far from here, but she'd never get them to reveal information on their customers without a letter of authority from Yudin at the very least. 'Who lives in the apartment now?'

The bookseller lowered his voice and glanced from side to side before speaking. 'A young woman,' he said. 'She's visited regularly by a major general. We exchange "good mornings", but I don't know her name. Not at all appropriate for the neighbourhood, but what can one do?'

Tamara took her leave.

'I hope I haven't shocked you,' said the man in a raised voice as she departed, making Tamara suspect that he hoped he had. She went back to the door of the apartment and delivered her letter. The new tenant might have her reasons not to make any reply, but if they could get in touch, their shared profession might allow Tamara to elicit a little more from her than otherwise.

She turned back towards Nevsky Prospekt, but before she could move very far she heard a shout. She turned and saw the bookseller, his upper body protruding from the shop door and his hand waving a small piece of paper. She walked back over to him.

'I remembered that I had this.' He handed her the paper. 'It was in case there was any mail, but there's been nothing for years now.'

She reached into her bag and took out her notebook, jotting down the details. She thanked the man again and went on her way. This was a big step. The address the man had given her was less than half an hour's walk away, and the name was one she already knew.

Dmitry Alekseevich Danilov.

'Oh!' said Tamara.

It was a large apartment, occupying the first and second storeys of a building overlooking the Fontanka. Tamara had asked whether Dmitry Alekseevich was at home. Given Yudin's assertion that Dmitry was in Sevastopol, she did not expect a positive response, but her hopes were raised by the fact that the footman, without any real response, had led her straight through to a drawing room. After announcing her, he had shown her in, and Tamara had felt a sense of disappointment to discover only a woman of about forty seated on a divan.

'Can I help you?' said the woman. She was thin, to a degree that indicated she tried very hard so to be. Her hair was blonde, but almost certainly it was not her natural colour. Her eyes seemed instantly resentful of her visitor.

'I was hoping to find Dmitry Alekseevich,' said Tamara.

'Major Danilov is fighting for his country.'

'Of course. You must be very proud.'

'Is your husband in the military?'

'My husband is dead.' Tamara immediately regretted saying it – not because the woman's supercilious pride did not need deflating, but because it was an insult to Vitya to use his death as a pawn in a social encounter. Even so, it had the desired effect.

'I'm sorry,' said the woman, dropping her eyes to the floor. 'Do please sit down.' She offered her hand. 'I'm Svetlana Nikitichna.'

Tamara took her hand briefly and then sat. 'An unusual name,' she said.

Svetlana smiled. Tamara guessed she had heard the comment before. 'My parents were lovers of Zhukovsky.' Four decades earlier Zhukovsky's poem had begun to popularize the name; it fitted with Tamara's estimation of the woman's age.

'I was actually here to enquire about your husband's family,' said Tamara, deciding that directness was the best approach.

The response was almost too quick. 'My husband has no family – other than myself.'

'His father is still alive.'

Svetlana's eyes flared. 'But he has the propriety to pretend otherwise. We've heard nothing from him for years.'

'He never writes?'

'In my opinion, it is his only expression of decency.'

'You knew him?' asked Tamara.

Svetlana shook her head. 'We weren't married until 1840.' The same year as Tamara.

'So you knew Marfa Mihailovna?'

'Oh yes.' Svetlana did not smile at the memory. 'You know men and their mothers. We should have lived further away. Fortunately Mitka's service took us abroad for much of the time.'

'He must have been devastated when she died.' Tamara had already gathered enough not to imply that Svetlana might also have been.

Svetlana's eyes glared at the suggestion that Tamara might know her husband's mind, but she controlled herself. 'We were in Bessarabia,' she explained. 'Mitka was putting down the revolution.'

'It was cholera?' Tamara hated saying the word.

Svetlana nodded. 'We couldn't even get back for the funeral. It had to be done . . . quickly.'

'Did you inform Aleksei Ivanovich?'

'Of course – but he maintained his silence. If it hadn't been for Vasya, I don't know how Mitka would have managed.'

'Vasya?' Tamara already had an inkling of who it might be.

'Actual State Councillor Yudin – he's an old family friend.'

Tamara already knew of the connection with Dmitry, but perhaps it went further. 'He knew Aleksei?'

Svetlana suddenly became annoyed. 'I've really no idea – and why should I tell you if I did?'

'I just want to find out about Aleksei Ivanovich.'

'Well, he's Mitka's father, not mine.'

Tamara rose. She would get no more from Svetlana. 'Perhaps I should call when he returns.'

'You could try. I don't imagine he'll be leaving Sevastopol soon though.'

Tamara offered her hand and tried to smile in a way that wouldn't further anger Svetlana. It seemed to work. Svetlana took it and managed a brief smile in return.

'I'm sorry to have been so intrusive, Svetlana Nikitichna. But the Decembrists are still important.'

'Not to me – but Mitka's father is certainly important to him. I'm sure he'll speak to you on his return, though as I say, that may not be for a very long time.'

Tamara left and headed back to her hotel. It had not been a hugely productive day, but she had learned one more name –

Vasiliy Denisovich Makarov. And she held a much greater hope of Dmitry returning soon than his wife seemed to – but then she probably wasn't as au fait with the military situation as Tamara. From what Tamara had heard, Sevastopol would fall within days.

Even from the grave, Bonaparte had reached out and taken his revenge on Russia. All the pieces were in place: a French army led – however remotely – by a new Napoleon; a desperate retreat by a broken army; a rickety bridge which men, horses and civilians must cross in order to escape. Admittedly the weather was different – late summer rather than the depths of a freezing winter – but other than that it was the Berezina reborn. And there was one other difference: today it was Russia, not France, who retreated.

Defeat, when it came, had come quickly. It was only the previous day that Dmitry had shouted orders for his men to fire on the French infantry as they advanced remorselessly towards the third bastion. They'd been lucky. The attack had been repelled. In a moment of calmness Dmitry had looked to his right, towards the fourth bastion, and seen that there too Totleben's defences had held against the British onslaught. But then he had looked to his left. He saw no soldiers advancing, no barrage of artillery, no collapsing battlements. What he did see told him, without room for debate, that Sevastopol was defeated.

Atop the Malakhov Tower, red, white and blue, the French tricolour fluttered in the breeze.

He had paced back through the deserted streets of the city towards the naval barracks, where he knew other officers would be assembling, a dark anger descending upon him. For the first time in the whole war, he hated the French and hated the British and hated all of them who had come to deprive Russia of her rightful access to the Black Sea. He had suffered the war, with its disease and death, but in the end it was defeat that he could not stomach. He felt, for once, like a patriot.

At headquarters there was no dissent over the conclusion that the loss of the Malakhov would mean the loss of the city within days – perhaps hours. The eventuality had been planned for. Work on the pontoon bridge stretching north from Fort Nikolai had begun in the summer. Everyone knew its purpose, but few dared to speak of it. The pretence of hope was a greater comfort. Details of how to phase the evacuation were carefully drawn up. No one spoke of comparisons with the Berezina.

Dmitry felt his movement come to a halt. He opened his eyes and gazed upwards. It was dark now – he could see the stars and the looming figures of the three men who carried him, using his greatcoat as a stretcher. Although they were no longer moving, he still felt a gentle sensation of rocking from side to side, as though he were on a boat. He could only guess that they were dead centre of the bridge by now. Most of the city had already escaped across it – escaped north across the Sea Harbour to the Severnaya where they might retrench; or at least where their further retreat was not blocked by so immovable a geographical feature.

The previous evening it had all seemed so straightforward – as if to plan was the same as to act. Dmitry remembered that no man had looked into another's eyes as they spoke, as if it might allow them to forget what was to become of the city once they departed.

Then someone had muttered the name of Rostopchin.

All understood the implication. Again it went back to 1812, but this time not to Napoleon's retreat but, just months earlier, to his occupation of Moscow. Dmitry had heard the story countless times from his father. Moscow's governor, Fyodor Vasilievich Rostopchin, had given orders, before his departure, that fires should be set throughout the city. The inferno had raged for five days, razing two thirds of the buildings. Some now doubted whether it had actually been Rostopchin who gave the order, but it made no difference to the outcome. Moscow had become untenable; Napoleon had been forced to retreat, and therein had lain his downfall. Whoever had issued the command, they had shown the truest love for the city – preferring to see it destroyed over falling into the hands of another.

Dmitry did not know how deeply he loved Sevastopol, but he had been one of the first to volunteer to lead a party of fire-starters. As the multitude had moved north, towards Fort Nikolai and the bridge that would lead them to safety, Dmitry and teams like his had spread out through the city. They set the first fires in the south, in areas that had already been evacuated. Even there they found some who continued to hope; to believe that the city

199

could be saved. They were sailors mostly, for whom Sevastopol had been the only home they had ever really known; the only home that didn't rock from side to side with the motion of the sea. A blow from the stock of a musket or a poke from its bayonet moved them on and Dmitry hoped they would have the sense to leave with the rest of the evacuees – or at least not to come back here.

Each time he thrust a flaming torch into the piles of tinder and paraffin that he and his men had laid he almost laughed at the futility of it. Enemy cannon had already flattened more than half of the city's buildings – and there had been no let-up in the shelling even today. Who could it benefit to see the other half reduced to ashes? And yet Dmitry was beyond rationality. The sense of purposelessness that had held him when he arrived in Sevastopol was now doubled. Briefly he had thought that Tyeplov had given him a reason to carry on, but Tyeplov had betrayed him. Now, all Dmitry had to fulfil him was his duty. And if duty meant to destroy what the French wanted to take, then that was all the better.

'Time to go, sir,' his sergeant had shouted as dusk began to fall. Dmitry, the sergeant and three *ryadovye* had been out there for hours. They'd started a dozen conflagrations, but had not stayed to see the outcome of any. Already they'd heard the shouts of advancing troops, just streets away from them.

'Just one more,' Dmitry replied, looking up at the edifice in front of him. They were in the east of the city, on the other side of the Sea Harbour from the naval barracks. Dmitry knew the house well enough. It was to there that he had followed Ignatyev and Tyeplov and their unwitting victim, so many weeks before; there that he had seen Ignatyev feeding; there that he had seen Tyeplov gazing into a mirror – and understood what he truly was. It would make a fitting farewell to the city, and to his memories of it.

They set the fire quickly. The sergeant had pointed out that the back of the house was bombed out anyway, but by then they'd done most of the work. Dmitry stood and watched as the flames took hold – despite his men's pleas that they should get away. It was an ending for him. Tyeplov might be anywhere, but for

Dmitry he was nothing any more. Dmitry truly believed it.

Then the gunfire had begun. The redcoats were on them in seconds – ten of them; more likely a reconnaissance party than an occupying force. One of the *ryadovye* dropped to the ground in the first volley, but Dmitry knew their only hope was to counterattack before the British could reload. They raced down the street, sabres raised. Dmitry heard a yell form in his throat that was taken up by his comrades. Almost as they fell upon the enemy, Dmitry dispatched two of them with swift strokes of his blade. His pistol dealt with another. Then the butt of a gun caught him under the chin and he fell backwards. Around him he could see his comrades continue to fight, but they were outnumbered. The Englishman who had knocked him down stood over him, his *shtutser* reloaded with the same speed that Tyeplov had displayed months before. Dmitry could see straight down the length of the rifled barrel, and beneath it a finger coiling around the trigger. He tried to raise himself up, but his head still swam from the blow. He began a prayer that he knew he would not have time to complete.

It was then that his memories became vague. At the same moment that he heard the report of the gun and saw the flash of powder in the lock, one of his men had charged into the redcoat, knocking him and his rifle off target. Dmitry had felt a searing pain as the bullet shattered his right ankle. He'd attempted to lift himself up again, but the pain was unendurable. He passed out.

His next memory was of lying on his back, moving through the city at tremendous pace, and yet without the constant jolting and bumping that he would have felt on a wagon. Around him he could hear the sound of tired, laboured breathing, and beyond that, the ever-present noise of cannon fire.

'Don't worry, sir,' he heard his sergeant say. 'We'll get you out.' He was lucky not to have been abandoned. He tried to speak, but didn't have the strength. He'd swum between consciousness and oblivion several times, and wondered why God had chosen to save him when he'd had so little desire to save himself, but he could find no answer.

And now they were on the pontoon bridge, and at a standstill – so close to safety and yet still prone to the shellfire that could so easily be heaped upon them. The pain shot upwards through his leg in regular pulses. He dared not look at the wound, but he doubted he would walk again. He turned his head to the right and saw the crowds surrounding him. Beyond, the harbour opened into the Black Sea itself, where the British and French fleets waited. His hand dropped off the side of the makeshift stretcher, and he felt water. He looked and saw that the men around him were in it up to their thighs. He could feel it soaking his back, despite his bearers' efforts to raise him out of it. The pontoons were sinking under the weight of the men crossing them, but still they managed to bear the load. Dmitry remembered his father describing how, at the Berezina, one of the two French bridges had collapsed completely, sending men, horses and carts into the icy waters. Here the water was not so cold as to kill, but Dmitry doubted he would be able to swim very far.

The face of his sergeant – he had never bothered to ask the man's name – peered over him. 'We'll be moving again in a moment, sir. Just getting a bit clogged up ahead.'

Dmitry tried to speak, but he had nothing to say. He laid his head back and gazed at the low clouds as their folds and billows flashed with the light of shells exploding in the city below them. It was as though they were being illuminated by the lightning of some great storm that raged within, though the splashes of water that fell upon his face were not rain but from the foaming harbour.

And then all turned to chaos. Dmitry heard the whistling of a shell, followed by a splash somewhere close by on the left. He felt the rumble of an explosion beneath the water, but noticed that the whistling did not stop. The second impact was closer still, and the third, immediately following, felt as though it had detonated beneath the bridge itself. It was not enough to cause much damage directly, but from the little that Dmitry could see, it looked like over two dozen men instinctively threw themselves away from the explosion and into the water. His stretcher bearers stood firm, but while they might be able to resist their urges to panic, the forces of nature were a different matter.

With so much weight released, the pontoons beneath them erupted from the water, sending a wave of disruption along the bridge in both directions. The two *ryadovye* on Dmitry's left lost their grip and were flung into the water. It would have been better if, on the other side, the sergeant had done the same. Instead he clung on, spilling Dmitry out to the left as surely as if he had pushed him. Dmitry hit the wooden struts of the bridge first and felt bolts of pain through his leg, but he could do nothing to help himself.

A moment later all was silent, as the cool water of the harbour embraced him.

CHAPTER XII

THE DOOR CLOSED BEHIND TAMARA AND SHE HEARD A KEY TURN in the lock. She looked back at it. It was an unassuming door, like any of those that punctuated the walls of the Marble Palace. When wandering past the building in times gone by she, like many, would have glanced at those doors and wondered just what it was that lay behind. Did such a door open into some dark corridor, guarded by one of the empire's most trusted men, or into a kitchen, providing easy access for grocery deliveries? Or did the door perhaps open on to one of the imperial family's personal apartments? Was it merely a few inches of solid wood that separated the humble passer-by from the greatest and most powerful men in Russia?

Now Tamara knew. For her it was now a surprise to be returned to the familiar reality of Saint Petersburg, after the wonders of the palace in which she had spent the evening. She quickly glanced around her and regained her bearings. She was on the embankment, overlooking the Neva. Behind her was the Marble Palace and ahead, across the river, the Peter and Paul Fortress. She turned left and began to walk.

Behind the door from which she had just emerged there was indeed a corridor, but there had been no guard when she entered or when she left. The corridor had been accessed by a short flight of steps, which in turn she had reached through a small door halfway up one of the grander staircases in the northern wing of the palace. The contrast between the two flights of stairs – one of stone, the other of wood – had been striking. Clearly the former was intended to be used by the residents and their guests, the latter by the staff. Tamara evidently fell somewhere between the two categories. She had come down that greater staircase, escorted by a silent footman, after crossing a huge, marble-floored landing which she had walked out on to through the most beautiful pair of doors that had ever been opened for her.

In the room behind those doors, the grandest room in which she had ever sat down, she had spent three hours of the evening eating the most delectable food she had ever tasted. Her dinner companion had been of some note as well – he was the Grand Duke Konstantin Nikolayevich Romanov, second son of the late Tsar Nikolai and brother to Tsar Aleksandr II. More than that, he was the new tsar's closest confidant.

It had begun in her hotel when, the previous evening, she had returned from her visit to Svetlana Nikitichna. There was a note waiting for her. It had been brief.

My dear Tamara Valentinovna,
    I was so pleased to make your acquaintance today. I'm afraid that, as you might guess, a visit to the theatre will prove difficult to arrange. Instead, may I suggest dinner tomorrow at seven? I will send a carriage for you.
    K.N.R.

Having seen him board the imperial train at Bologoye it had taken only a little thought on her part to realize who the man must be. She had never seen a portrait of him, but for a Romanov he was marked out by his short stature and the need to wear spectacles – or perhaps a sufficient lack of vanity to wear them when he did need them. The initials on the card served only to confirm what she had guessed, but the fact that their encounter on the platform had been, on his part, more than a passing flirtation astounded her.

She was not a woman so blinded by the stature of the tsar and his family as to be unaware of the stories of their almost insatiable sexual appetites, and though she did not believe all she heard, it would be foolish not to credit some of it. If a man had the power to take to his bed any woman he chose, then he would be inhuman not to exploit that power to some degree. But if he

205

had that power then why, Tamara wondered, choose her? The old generals and *chinovniki* who paid for her services at Degtyarny Lane might, from their own perspective, see her as young and voluptuous. They might even have acquired the wisdom to understand that a twenty-year-old did not know all of the secrets of how to make a man happy. But Konstantin was only twenty-seven. To him Tamara's thirty-four years must make her seem ancient. And yet he had sent her the note.

But even if it seemed the stuff of fairy tales, she knew that it was her duty to comply with his request. It was the duty of every Russian to obey the tsar's will, of course, and it seemed not unreasonable to extend that fealty to his brother. But Tamara had a duty to her job as well. As Yudin had explained to her, this new generation of Romanovs had come into contact with ideas that might ultimately prove dangerous to their dynasty. It was the task of the Third Section to protect that dynasty, even from itself. When the carriage arrived, she found it hard to believe that the horses had not once been mice and the coachman a rat, but still she had happily climbed aboard.

It had taken her to that same side door in the Marble Palace by which she had just now departed and she had been escorted, by a footman who might well have led a previous life as a lizard, up to where her host awaited her. Konstantin introduced himself formally and apologized for leaving her so abruptly at the railway station. He also apologized for entertaining her here, not at his more usual home in Strelna, but explained that he felt it would be far more convenient for her to come here, since she was staying in the city. Convenient also, she thought, to avoid encounters with his wife and children.

Konstantin talked more than Tamara, which suited them both. They began where they had left off, discussing theatre. Tamara had been out early and purchased a couple of plays by Gogol, so was able to keep up with the conversation to some degree. But then Konstantin turned to his true love – music. Here Tamara was on even less steady ground, but the grand duke was more than happy to talk. He was something of a namedropper, mentioning musical evenings when he had been personally entertained by Johann Strauss and Hector Berlioz, but the effect would have been greater if the names had meant anything like as much to her as they did to him.

He asked her nothing about herself, and while she was thankful not to have to reveal to him any more than was necessary, it struck her that most would regard it as rude not to make a few enquiries into the life and interests of the woman he had chosen to treat to such an elegant evening and whom he planned, as the finale of that evening, to bed. The answer came as they drank coffee and stood beside the tall windows, looking out over the Neva.

'I must confess, Tamara Valentinovna,' he had said, deliberately avoiding her eye, 'that I have made enquiries about you. I know the nature of your profession.'

She stiffened and looked at him, feeling her face flush. It was an odd reaction. She could hardly object to the fact that a potential customer – and that was all that Konstantin was – knew perfectly well that it was all he was. But she realized she had succumbed, if only slightly, to the illusion that she had professionally been trying to instil into him – that this evening had been about a man and a woman getting to know each other.

'If you know my profession, then why waste all of that time and effort over dinner?' she said icily.

He turned and looked at her, uncomprehending. 'I was told that you work for General Dubyelt at the Third Section,' he said. Then the implication of what he had learned of her and what they both had said dawned on him. He blushed a deeper shade of crimson than Tamara suspected showed in her own face, and his mouth began to open and close like a fish's. Tamara scarcely managed to suppress her amusement.

Konstantin beamed and then burst into a laugh. He went over to the table, where he poured two glasses of brandy and proffered one to her. She joined him and took it.

'I'm sorry,' she said.

'Think nothing of it.' He smiled. 'Though I'm glad you appreciate the dinner.' He caught her eye as he spoke, and she laughed again. Now though, his reasons for bringing her here were even more puzzling.

'Would it be wise for you to consort with someone who spies for your own brother?'

'"For"? I would have thought that "on" would be a more apposite preposition.'

'I've never even met His Majesty.'

'I didn't mean you personally. You, I'm sure, are a loyal subject of the tsar.' They looked at each other for a moment, and then Konstantin threw himself back in his chair. 'I'm sorry, Tamara Valentinovna, I meant that genuinely – about you – but say it of half your colleagues and the irony would not be misplaced.'

Tamara said nothing. She understood the distinction Konstantin was making, but she had never heard it from the point of view of one so close to the seat of power.

'Things are changing.' He leaned forward as he spoke and clasped his hands together on the table. 'My brother belongs to a new generation. That's not happened in half a century. We're going to make a difference.'

'Didn't Aleksandr I say that?'

'He did! He did! He wanted to free the serfs too.'

'Really?'

'He wanted it. But he never achieved it. The war saw an end to that.'

'We're at war now,' Tamara pointed out.

Konstantin shook his head. 'Not for long. That was our father's war. There'll be peace by the New Year. And then we can begin. Sasha – His Majesty – has appointed me head of a secret committee to put an end to serfdom.'

'Secret?'

'Absolutely.'

'And you're telling me?'

'And you'll tell your masters within the Third Section – I know. And they'll think that they've got their eye on us.'

'Because they will have.'

'To the extent that you tell them what you know. And you'll tell us how they react.'

'I might lie.'

'You won't.'

He seemed very sure of her – more so than she was of herself. As far as she could judge, that was where they left it. Konstantin had mentioned a few of their other plans for reform and then the conversation had turned back to music. Konstantin had promised that next time they met he would play the cello for her, at which she had smiled politely. And then he had said that she should leave. He appeared to have forgotten the other aspect of her profession, and she chose not to remind him, but the way he had said they would meet again told her he had not abandoned the idea.

Minutes later she was out on the embankment, beside the Neva. There was no carriage waiting for her – not even a pumpkin. She began the short walk back to her hotel.

At least this rail journey was short enough that Yudin could enjoy the comforts of a first-class carriage. It was the first ever railway route in the country – fourteen years older than the second, the more prestigious line from Petersburg to Moscow. This line covered a mere thirty versts from Petersburg to Pavlovsk, and Yudin would alight before that, at Tsarskoye Selo.

He glanced around the carriage at his fellow passengers. There was only a scattering of them. This was the last train of the day, and so these would be residents returning home from the capital, not visitors on a day trip to glimpse the majesty of the imperial palaces. It was a very royal location – the name literally meaning 'the Tsar's Village'. Yudin could sense the looks of disdain that he received from a number of those around the carriage. He was, he thought, pretty well turned out, but breeding would always show. He doubted if any of them could guess at his particular breeding.

The train drew into the station and Yudin climbed down on to the platform. He pulled a piece of paper from his pocket and glanced at the map he had scribbled there, based on what he had found in the archive in Moscow. The resident he would be visiting was not perhaps quite as high born as most of those who lived in the area, but he had achieved high rank by dint of study and hard work – much like Yudin himself. And all his neighbours would be well aware of the fact that the old man in their midst had once, many years before, been personal physician to His Majesty Tsar Aleksandr I.

It was a small house – small for the town – some way from the centre. Yudin had to pass both the Yekaterininsky and Aleksandrovsky palaces before he found it. He slithered over the wall – a far easier climb than had been required to get into the Peter and Paul Fortress – and dropped into the garden on the other side. He could see light at only three windows; two on the ground floor and one on the first, at a window that was accompanied by a balcony. That would be his best bet. He scuttled across the lawn, unseen in the darkness, and in moments had ascended one of the stone pillars, finding himself on a small terrace on which sat a wrought-iron table and two chairs. Behind them, a French window stood open. Yudin slipped through.

The decor inside was a strange combination. In part it reminded Yudin of what he had heard about the room of the woman Raisa had killed in Degtyarny Lane – all those mirrors. Today Yudin did not mind the fact that anyone attempting to observe him in one of the dozens of looking glasses that bedecked the walls would be able to see nothing. Today anything that might help to instil fear in the man he had come to talk to would be of assistance. The preponderance of mirrors suggested that such fear already existed, and had done for many years.

What lay between the mirrors, filling every other available patch of wall, indicated that same fear – a plethora of icons and crucifixes. These would feel less at home on the walls of a Moscow brothel, and yet Yudin knew full well that many of the women had at least one religious symbol in their rooms, unaware of the ironic contrast it made with their profession, or perhaps able to reconcile it in some way that was beyond Yudin's imagination.

Despite widespread superstition, religious imagery had no influence on a *voordalak*, beyond the fear that might be lurking within him on the basis of his own irrational imaginings. Yudin had no such apprehensions, and yet the dozens of pairs of the Saviour's eyes staring at him from the walls did make him feel uneasy. As with the mirrors, they indicated that he was expected.

'You must be Cain.'

Yudin turned. The old man was sitting in an armchair, beside his bed. The one lamp that lit the room stood on a table beside him. Next to it was a book – it looked like a Bible.

'You must be Tarasov,' said Yudin.

Dr Tarasov nodded. The two of them had never met, not even

in 1825 as they stood on separate sides in the battle for the tsar's soul. 'It seems Danilov was right about you.'

'In what way?' asked Yudin.

'He said you had become like your master.' Tarasov glanced around at the mirrors, in which Yudin knew he would see no reflection of the figure that stood so obviously in the middle of his room.

'I have no master.'

'Then why have you come here?'

'You know why,' said Yudin. 'To meet a man who would dare counterfeit the death of his own emperor.'

Tarasov paused. His eye twinkled. 'So you finally worked it out then, did you? Danilov said you would. And that you'd come here.'

'Why did he think I'd come here?' Yudin asked.

'Because I'm the only one left.'

Yudin postponed the most obvious question. Instead he stuck to the purpose of his visit. 'Where is he?'

'Danilov? In Siberia by all accounts.'

'Romanov.'

'Aleksandr Pavlovich? I've no idea.' Tarasov smiled as he spoke. 'What was it that persuaded you at last, I wonder?' It was a rhetorical question – one he had clearly thought through long in advance. 'His Majesty's death, I suppose – Nikolai Pavlovich, I mean. You and your master decided that now was the time to make a move against his son, only to discover that you could not.'

'I have no master.' Apart from that one detail, it seemed that Tarasov – or somebody – had worked it all out.

'He's well prepared, you know – Aleksandr Nikolayevich – he knows you will come.'

'Perhaps he will welcome it.'

Tarasov's smile broadened, with what appeared to be genuine pleasure. He seemed confident that the new tsar would not easily be persuaded of his destiny.

'Where is Aleksandr Pavlovich?' Yudin asked.

'I've no idea.'

'What name does he go by?'

'They never told me.'

'They?'

'Volkonsky and Aleksandr himself; they were the only ones who knew.'

Yudin took off his jacket and hung it over the back of a chair. He took a step towards Tarasov, hoping that the man would see the danger he was in. 'You *will* tell me,' he said.

'I'm sure I'll tell you everything I know,' Tarasov agreed. 'But I can't enlighten you over matters of which I have no knowledge.'

That remained to be seen. For now Yudin would discover just how much Tarasov would tell of what he did know. 'Who was in on it?' he asked.

'Just the four of us – plus His Majesty.'

'Four of you? You, Danilov, Volkonsky and . . . Diebich?'

'Wylie.'

'Another doctor. What fools people are to trust the members of your profession.'

'Aleksandr didn't trust us – that's why he only told Volkonsky.'

'And not Aleksei?'

Tarasov didn't answer. Yudin smiled, revealing his teeth, and took a step closer. The doctor was fast – and prepared. Before Yudin had even moved, he had grabbed the Bible from the table beside him and was holding it out in front of him. Yudin could see his knuckles whiten as he tightly gripped the book. Behind it his eyes flared with hatred for the creature from which he thought the holy words protected him. Yudin reached out and plucked it from him, then threw it aside. Already Tarasov had moved to his next line of defence. Now, clasped between his two hands, he held a silver crucifix, thrusting it forward into Yudin's face. It was large enough that Tarasov's clenched fist only came up to Christ's knees; every expression of agony that the silversmith had so lovingly worked into the Lord's face was plain for Yudin to observe.

'I've been preparing for this day for some time,' said Tarasov.

Yudin threw his hands up as though to protect himself, and cowered, if only slightly. He peered over his arm at Tarasov, hoping to see some glimpse of victory in the doctor's eyes. When it came, Yudin moved quickly. He reached out and snatched away the crucifix. It had no more effect on him than did the icons or

212

the Bible. He put the silver figure to his lips and kissed it tenderly on the loincloth, then, taking one end of the object in each hand, he bent the soft metal so that Christ's eyes could witness close up the nails that penetrated his own feet. He cast it aside, as he had the Bible.

Tarasov's third line of defence was more original, but only marginally. Garlic – half a dozen bulbs, their stalks woven into a ring. Yudin stood and watched, unmoved, as the doctor pulled off a large clove and then crushed it between his bony fingers. The smell assailed Yudin's nostrils and he breathed deeply, enjoying the aroma. Then he reached forward and plucked the crushed garlic from Tarasov's fingertips and popped it into his mouth. He chewed it to a pulp and again savoured the assault of its flavour. When he could taste it no more, he leaned forward so that their faces were close. He breathed out deliberately, his mouth wide, but Tarasov did not flinch at the smell. Yudin spat out the white paste and watched it slither down the old man's cheeks and on to his chin. He leaned in even closer.

'You believe in myths,' he whispered.

'I've been preparing for this day for some time,' repeated Tarasov. His eyes were not on Yudin, but looking beyond him. Yudin stood upright. In the mirrors on the wall behind Tarasov he could see the whole room and everything in it, with the exception of himself.

They were no longer alone.

Yudin turned. There were four of them. They were not uniformed, but they had a military bearing – and they were armed. Three of them carried in their left hands solid stakes of wood; hawthorn, Yudin guessed, in keeping with Tarasov's predilection for folklore. But in this case the adherence to it was overkill – any wood would do – and those stakes could swiftly be driven home by the mallets that each man bore in his right hand. The fourth man was armed only with an axe. His fingers caressed its blade as if verifying in it the same keenness that he himself had for the task at hand. A blow from it correctly aimed at Yudin's neck would be as effective as a stake through his heart.

He had no idea how Tarasov had summoned the men, but it was easy to suppose that wherever it was he had hidden his garlic and his crucifix also had some bell pull which had served to rally these killers. No doubt the scenario had been rehearsed many times. Two of the men stood by the door; two covered the windows out on to the balcony by which Yudin had entered. There was no other exit that he could see.

'Danilov said you would come,' explained Tarasov from behind him. 'And he suggested I should protect myself. You'd be surprised how easily men can be persuaded to believe in the existence of your kind – as long as they're paid enough.'

Yudin turned. Tarasov was standing now, although it was clearly a strain for a man of his age. He too had a wooden stake in his hand, but shaped more like a sword so that he could drive it home without the help of the hammer.

'How did Aleksei contact you?' Yudin asked. Time was short, and suddenly the question of how, from the depths of Siberia, his old enemy had managed to warn Tarasov of what would unfold seemed more pressing than the reason he'd originally come here.

'By letter,' replied Tarasov.

Yudin laughed curtly. 'Impossible. It wouldn't have got past the censor.' There was no need to reveal that he himself was that censor.

'He had an envoy. Someone he could trust.'

As Tarasov spoke he nodded towards his four bodyguards. In the mirrors, Yudin saw them begin to close in. With them behind him and only Tarasov in front, there was little question over where to go. And therein lay the flaw in Tarasov's long-nurtured plan – he had nothing like the physical strength of any of his four guardians. A single blow from Yudin's clenched fist knocked the weapon to the floor and in a moment Yudin was behind him, his double-bladed knife to the doctor's throat.

'Dr Tarasov and I are going to be walking out of here,' he said, pressing the tips of the knife into the old man's wrinkled skin. None of the men moved.

'You think I wouldn't exchange the few remaining years of my life for yours, Cain?' asked Tarasov. 'You think any of them would dare to disobey the orders that have been drummed into them for so long? Their instructions are not to save me; merely to kill you.'

Yudin looked at the men and decided that Tarasov was telling the truth. He could kill the doctor easily, and then there would be only four of them to deal with. The chances of his defeating them were good, but not so good as to make him leap at the opportunity – and they understood enough not to attempt to fight him like a man. They would know what he feared.

But they would also have discounted what he feared as a weapon that he might use against them. Something that could be a danger to both man and vampire could swing the odds in his favour.

He grabbed the lamp from the table and hurled it at one of the men by the window. It was a modern device, fuelled by paraffin rather than oil, and so when it shattered against the man's shoulder he was quickly enveloped in the liquid, which in an instant was aflame. The curtains behind him caught alight too and soon the whole of the window was framed with lashing orange and yellow tongues.

Yudin tightened his grip on Tarasov and began to shuffle towards the door, navigating his way around the bed and not needing to fabricate the terror that the fire held for him. The two men at the door stood their ground, as did the one who remained at the window. Clearly they had been trained well. They watched unmoved as their burning comrade rolled around on the floor, his agonized screams filling the room. The scent of his roasting flesh reached Yudin's nostrils.

At last the other man beside the window could bear it no longer. He had been forced to take a few steps from it, because of the intense heat, but now he abandoned his post altogether and threw himself towards his fallen colleague, attempting to smother the flames by covering him with a rug. Yudin did not wait to see the result of this act of humanity. He released his grip on Tarasov and flung himself across the room towards the window. Tarasov shouted, but it was too late. All that Yudin could see was the fire, but he overcame his every instinct to cower from it and instead plunged through and out into the night. His feet scarcely touched the balcony beyond before he was over it and falling on to the lawn below.

He was up again in an instant. The arm of his shirt was ablaze, but he knew he could not waste time there trying to put it out. He raced over to the bushes at the side of the garden and disappeared within them. With a few pats of his hand, ignoring the pain which he knew would be only temporary, he put out the flames on his arm. He looked at the blackened, blistered flesh beneath, but it didn't concern him. Fire might kill a vampire, but only if it consumed his body totally. Otherwise, as with every injury, he would soon recover. He climbed the wall and glanced briefly over his shoulder. The fire was still blazing, but wasn't so large that it would not soon be put out. Tarasov would almost certainly survive, and that was all to the good. Yudin might soon have need to question him again, though on such an occasion he would be more circumspect.

But that occasion would not be soon. Yudin dropped from the top of the wall on to the street below and ran.

CHAPTER XIII

DMITRY STEPPED DOWN FROM THE SLEIGH, MAKING SURE HIS left leg touched the ground first and then putting down his right, taking most of the weight on his stick. Moscow looked beautiful – matching the picture in his memory that could only be true for half the year. The whole city was covered in snow. The people took it in their stride. All wore heavy coats and hats and mittens, and travelled in sleds rather than carriages, but other than that, life in the city continued.

It was late November now – almost three months since Sevastopol had been evacuated. Dmitry had been in the water only moments, unable to hear the shouts of the men above him but still perceiving the low rumble of explosions. Then his sergeant on the bridge and the two *ryadovye* in the water had managed to heave him out. The remainder of his short journey north had been on foot – on one foot – rather than lying in a makeshift stretcher, but his brief immersion had invigorated him. He had recuperated for a few days in the Severnaya, where the great surgeon Nikolai Ivanovich Pirogov himself had treated him. He'd told Dmitry to sniff a liquid called ether, which made him light-headed, and had then stretched his ankle back into something like its correct shape. The effect of the ether had been to dim the agony, and also to make Dmitry care less about the not insubstantial degree of pain that remained. It hurt more to recall it than it had to experience it. Then Pirogov wrapped Dmitry's foot, ankle and calf in wet bandages, which after a few hours miraculously stiffened and became hard as stone, allowing Dmitry no movement of his foot.

After that he was moved north, to Simferopol, away from the

heart of the action, and after several weeks the hardened bandages had been cut away. Beneath them, his leg was withered, and the skin was dry and scaly, but he was able to move his foot very slightly and even put a little weight on it, though not without pain. They said that that would improve and had given him the stick. Then had begun his slow journey home. He'd travelled only short distances each day, at least at first, which resulted in many of the hostelries he slept in being of the lowest order he had ever experienced. But who was he to complain? He'd cheated death – he could suffer a few flea bites. He spent over a week in Kharkov, the largest city en route, and after that had felt sufficiently well to travel faster.

He'd finally arrived in Moscow late the previous afternoon. He slept in his hotel for almost twelve hours and the following morning his first port of call was the office of his oldest friend – the man he must nowadays remember to call Vasiliy Innokyentievich Yudin.

The sleigh had dropped him right beside the Armoury. He had never seen the building completed, though they had been constructing it when he was last in Moscow. That was over five years ago – longer than he would have guessed.

He was about to knock on the door when it opened and a small, bespectacled, balding man with bushy grey eyebrows appeared from behind it.

'Major Danilov?'

'Yes.'

'I'm Titular Councillor Gribov. Actual State Councillor Yudin is expecting you.'

Gribov led him down a flight of stone steps which Dmitry found difficult to navigate. There was no banister rail and little room for Dmitry to place the tip of his cane. Gribov seemed concerned at Dmitry's injury, but hesitated to offer any direct assistance, guessing perhaps how much Dmitry would have loathed it if he had. Dmitry lost his footing only once, but slipped down just one step and easily took his weight on his left leg. Soon he was in Yudin's office.

It was a grim place, but much like the rooms which had served Yudin the last time Dmitry had seen him. That had been in 1849, still in the Kremlin but further to the south. Yudin was on his feet the moment Dmitry entered and walked swiftly over to embrace him.

'Mitka!' he said, warmly.

'Vasya! It's good to see you.'

Yudin stepped away. 'You're doing better than I had dared hope,' he said. 'You'll soon be throwing that cane away.'

'I'm not sure. I think it's beginning to suit me,' said Dmitry. 'But you're looking wonderful. You never seem to age.' It was a lie, and they both knew it. Dmitry had never been sure just how old Yudin actually was. They had first met in 1812 when Aleksei had been away fighting the French and Yudin had introduced himself to Dmitry's mother as a friend of Aleksei's. Dmitry had been only five at the time, so it was hard for him to recall how old Yudin was, but he must have been a young man. Generally, Yudin was vain about his appearance. His obviously dyed hair was testimony to that. Dmitry remembered how in younger days he had possessed a striking blond mane. But Yudin's face – his skin – had always remained young. Today it did not seem so. Even the backs of his hands showed wrinkles. He must have been at least in his sixties, perhaps even his seventies. For the first time it showed.

Yudin pulled back a chair at his desk and Dmitry sat down. Yudin returned to his own seat, speaking as he went. 'I've heard all about what happened. Not just in your letters, but in dispatches too.'

'It's nothing heroic,' said Dmitry. He meant it. However necessary it might have been, burning down a Russian city was not a noble act.

'You were wounded in the service of the tsar – that's what matters. Your mother would be very proud.' A slight pause. 'I'm sure your father is.'

'You've not heard from him?' Dmitry tried to disguise his eagerness.

Yudin shook his head. 'I'm afraid not.'

'You're sure he's alive?'

'I would have been informed,' explained Yudin. 'I've written to the governor of Irkutsk, to see if he can speak to Aleksei and explain his silence, but as yet I have heard nothing.'

'He's ashamed of me,' said Dmitry.

'It's not that. It couldn't be. But Lyosha can be a difficult man. He may just think it's for the best.'

'For the best?' said Dmitry angrily.

Yudin shrugged, but could explain no more. He changed the subject, if only slightly. 'As it happens, you're not the only person who's interested to know what's become of Aleksei.' Dmitry raised a questioning eyebrow and Yudin continued. 'A colleague of mine is very keen to hear about him.'

'Raking up dirt on the last few Decembrists?' Dmitry did not know exactly what Yudin's role within the government was, but doubted it was anything underhand. The same generosity could not be extended to his colleagues.

'No – this goes back before the revolt. It's about murder; two sets of murders, here in Moscow – one in 1812, the others in 1825.'

Dmitry stiffened. He knew a great deal about deaths in Moscow in those two years. His father had told him about the former, and to those of 1825 he had been a witness. 'So what does he want to know – your colleague?'

'She.'

'She?'

'Her name's Tamara Valentinovna Komarova – née Lavrova.'

'Lavrova?' It was a name that Dmitry knew well.

Yudin nodded. 'The same family of Lavrovs that took in your father's mistress for a time.'

'Does she know?' asked Dmitry.

'That she's investigating her nanny's lover? I don't think so. And I wouldn't tell her. Be careful of her – she's a shrewd woman.'

'Why don't I just refuse to speak to her?'

'Because *I* need to find out how much she knows.'

'About Papa?'

'No – I'm sure that's nothing. But Tamara Valentinovna belongs to a strand of the civil service that is somewhat less in favour of the new regime than you and I. I need to find out how far they're prepared to go.'

Dmitry nodded. Yudin had never been as radical as him or Aleksei, but he had grown to share their distaste for despots, especially Nikolai. Yudin would never have conspired against the old tsar, but Dmitry guessed he would do anything to protect the new one.

'When shall I see her?' asked Dmitry.

'There's no rush. I'll arrange something. You still need to recover.'

'Lana is expecting me in Petersburg.' Yudin said nothing, and Dmitry was glad to put off his return home. 'But if I'm needed here, she'll understand.'

'Good. Good. Now, you be on your way, and enjoy the city. And make sure everyone knows you're a hero.' Yudin rose and indicated the stairs up to the Kremlin. Dmitry stood and slowly made his way across the room, the tapping of his stick sounding louder in the enclosed space. 'And we must have dinner one evening,' Yudin added, 'so you can tell me all about Sevastopol.'

Ascent of the steps proved to be easier than coming down had been. At the top he looked down and saw Yudin staring back up at him. He waved, and his friend waved back, then Dmitry turned and walked outside, pausing only to glance into the office where he saw Gribov diligently working.

The sleigh was waiting for him, as instructed, but he dismissed it. Just to see Yudin's familiar face once again had made him feel stronger and he decided to walk. A hero of Sevastopol could not disdain a little snow on his boots.

'He lied,' said Raisa. 'You *are* looking old.'

She had emerged almost as soon as Dmitry left, from the door that led down to the dungeons.

'I know,' replied Yudin.

'How can you know? A mirror won't tell you, and everyone else will flatter you, just like he did.'

'I know I look old because I intended to look old,' he said. 'I don't need to see it to be sure.'

She held out her hand. 'Come with me. Let's drink. It will make you young again.' She smirked. 'As young as you can be.'

Yudin contemplated. He was thirsty – more thirsty than he could ever recall. It had not yet affected his strength, or his mind, but the skin was always the thing that changed the soonest. He had seen it first in Zmyeevich. When they had met, the old vampire had appeared to be just that – an old man, weak and decrepit. On the next occasion, Yudin had hardly recognized him. He was young – or at least vibrantly middle-aged – restored to the state he had been in when first he had become a *voordalak*, centuries before. It hadn't taken Yudin long to guess that the rejuvenation was the effect of feeding. A few experiments had proved it beyond doubt.

'I can't,' he said to Raisa. 'Dmitry has known me longer than anyone. He'd suspect.'

'So you starve yourself for him?'

'What did you make of him?'

'He's diffident – a typical soldier – but he can't hide his sadness. He can't hear his father's name without pausing to imagine what might have been.'

'He's his father's son,' said Yudin. 'That makes him as dangerous as he is useful. I'll have to deal with them both soon enough.'

'You sound disappointed.'

'It's taken me a long time,' Yudin sighed. He was always melancholy as the final moves of the game approached.

'So what will you do with him?'

'I don't know yet. It depends on Dmitry. I'd like you to be there when he meets Tamara.'

'Why?'

'To tell me what they say.'

'I thought the idea was that they would both relay it straight back to you.'

'They will,' said Yudin, 'and both will lie.'

'So you need me to tell you the truth?'

Yudin smiled. 'No, I just need there to be an odd number of participants, so that I can take the majority view.' He doubted she would lie to him, but it was better to treat everyone with equal mistrust, and, certainly in the case of Raisa, to make her aware of how little faith he put in her.

'You really do look terrible,' she said.

'If you want to drink, go. Your beauty matters.'

Raisa did not wait to be told twice. She turned and set off down the stairs. Yudin's eyes followed her until she had gone.

It was a difficult balance for him to maintain. To Dmitry, who had known him longest, he must appear old, but different people knew him at different ages, and he could not satisfy them all. He could not even know with any certainty how they perceived him.

He opened the drawer at the side of his desk and pulled out the heavy package, unwrapping the brown paper to reveal the block of polished crystal. Iceland Spar, they called it, and as the name suggested, it could only be found in one place on the planet. Having it shipped through the naval blockade in the Baltic had been tricky, but Yudin had friends among the British. He held up the crystal and inspected one of the documents on his desk through it, smiling at what he saw.

There were two images; two sets of lettering separated by about the width of a single character. It was like the double vision of a drunk, but this was reality, not a failing of the senses. The phenomenon was well enough understood. An ordinary block of glass affected what was seen through it – diffracted the light – so that the image observed was slightly displaced. But light, it seemed, was made of two different types – two polarities – and travelling through Iceland Spar, each was diffracted to a differing degree; hence the two images.

But what, Yudin wondered, if the material could be used in place of the glass of a mirror? The light would be split as it entered the mirror and then those split images would be further separated as the light departed. Might one of those reflections make it through the defences of the observer's mind and reveal the *voordalak*'s true self? Might Raisa at last be able to gaze upon her own beauty? All of his experiments suggested it, and now there was just a little more work to be done before he would know for sure.

He licked his lips at the prospect, and realized in an instant that Raisa had been right. He was thirsty. He only needed a little blood – not enough to rejuvenate him, but sufficient to sustain him. He put the crystal lovingly back into the drawer and went over to the stairs that Raisa had descended, following the path down and closing the door behind him. At the junction that led to their coffins, he turned left and was soon in the short low corridor lined with six doors, leading to the cells he had shown Tamara.

The seventh door, at the end, was open, its heavy bolts drawn back. Raisa had already gone in. As he approached, he heard a voice. It was not Raisa's; this was weaker, older, and utterly terrified. And the words it spoke would not have come from Raisa's lips.

'No more. Please, God. No more.'

The cold did nothing to help the pain in Dmitry's ankle. He had soon given up walking and travelled everywhere in the city by sleigh. He had been in Moscow for over a week, and already it had lost its charm for him, though he knew that the city itself was unchanged. It could only be something in him that made this once vibrant town seem dull and mundane. If he had thought the fault lay in Moscow itself he wouldn't have bothered to stay, instead making straight for Petersburg, but he knew he would find it even worse there.

Was it war that had changed him? He doubted it. Sevastopol was not the only action he had been engaged in, though it was certainly the bloodiest. This was the first major wound he had received, but, to be honest, he was rather enjoying that side of things. The combination of a military uniform, a stick and a pronounced limp had an effect on all those he encountered that was entirely favourable to him.

But the thing that had affected Dmitry's whole outlook on life was not that he had come through the war with a limp, but that he had come through it at all. He had survived. When he had arrived in the Crimea he had not been afraid to die but he had, he knew, been afraid to live. Tyeplov had changed all that. Thanks to him, Dmitry had done things he would never have dreamed himself capable of. He had slept with a man. He had slept with a vampire! He had little desire to repeat either experience, certainly not the latter, but the fact that he had dared to made him feel he might dare do anything. It was Tyeplov who had taught him that. His motivation? If Tyeplov was to be believed it was for the sake of Aleksei, but if Tyeplov thought that Dmitry would now feel somehow indebted to him, he was a fool. It didn't matter.

Tyeplov was thousands of versts away, feeding on the invaders of Sevastopol, who little knew what awaited them within the city.

And there was someone else who wanted to know about Dmitry's father – this Tamara Valentinovna. That was who he had now come to meet, at Yegorov's restaurant. Yudin had told him they would be joined by a friend of Tamara's, so he knew to look out for two women. He saw them as soon as he handed over his coat and hat at the door – one with her back to him, the other facing.

Even if Dmitry had not been looking out for them, his eyes would have fixed on this woman as he entered the room – more of a girl than a woman. She could not have been much over twenty. Her natural blonde hair was coiled into tight, artificial curls which bounced as she spoke. Her blue eyes blazed, and yet behind them Dmitry sensed there was very little – or very little that she cared to give to the world. He stood still and watched her for a moment. He was sure she was aware of him, but she did not once look in his direction.

She was not Tamara. The woman she was speaking to, whose back was turned to Dmitry, was Tamara. She had been about five years old when he had last seen her, the child of Yelena and Valentin Lavrov, through the window of their house, but her red hair was unmistakable. It had perhaps darkened slightly, but that could easily be a trick of his memory. There was a lot of it, but it was tied back in a ponytail – more a matter of practicality than aesthetics.

He walked over to the table, noticing that his limp had become more pronounced, though not out of any conscious effort. The blonde girl looked up as he approached, as did the redhead a moment later.

'Tamara Valentinovna Komarova?' he asked.

'Indeed,' she said, rising and offering her hand. 'You must be Major Danilov. This is my friend, Raisa Styepanovna Tokoryeva.'

Dmitry sat at the end of the table so that he could easily see them both.

'You're recently returned from Sevastopol, I hear,' said Tamara.

'Yes. Stuck it out to the very last, but they got me in the end.' He lifted his cane briefly, to make it clear what he meant.

'What happened?' asked Raisa, bluntly. Tamara flashed her a look to say that she shouldn't ask such things, but Dmitry didn't mind.

The story he told was close to the truth, except that he didn't mention precisely why he had been in the city so long after the rest of the army had evacuated. But the attack by the redcoats was there, his men's brave battle, their loyal rescue of their commanding officer both from the enemy and from the water, and the final, sodden trudge across the harbour to safety.

It all sounded as though it had been such fun. In the past, Dmitry had despised the way that soldiers failed to describe the hell that war really was. It seemed a greater cowardice than any displayed on the battlefield; to come and say to those back home that one would gladly go out and do it again instead of admitting that the sound of the guns just made you want to run away and hide and that there were times when you'd trample over the backs of your comrades just to make it to some dark, damp hole where you could press your hands over your ears and pretend it was all far away. The worst was when they told the stories to young men, knowing it would only encourage them. But he knew the ladies loved it, and he felt Raisa's eyes on his cheek as he spoke, almost as though she were touching him.

They were interrupted by a waiter, who delivered a bottle of vodka and took their orders. Blini were the speciality of Yegorov's and that was what each of them chose. When the waiter had gone, Tamara took the opportunity to turn the conversation on to the subject that interested her.

'I'm trying to find out about your father,' she said.

'So Vasiliy Innokyentievich tells me,' said Dmitry, pouring vodka into their glasses. He let the sound of his ramming the cork back into the bottle punctuate his final word. 'Why?'

'He was witness to at least two murders.'

'What makes you think that?'

'I've seen the police records. The first was in 1812, in a house just off Tverskaya Street.'

'I don't see how I can help. I was only five then.'

'Four or five,' said Tamara. Yudin had said she was shrewd. He should have asked her the precise date, or kept quiet. 'And you'd have turned eighteen in 1825. That's when the second one took place. Right outside the Maly Theatre.'

Dmitry forced his face to remain relaxed, hoping it revealed nothing. He felt the urge to glance over at Raisa, just to avoid Tamara's eyes, but he knew it would hint that he was lying.

He could remember it all so clearly. He'd been there. The dead man's name was Obukhov. Dmitry could even recall his rank – a captain. There'd been a group of them, led by Aleksei and – Dmitry liked to think – himself. He'd only been a lieutenant then. They'd set out to trap a *voordalak*, though only he and Aleksei had known it to be such. That had been unfair on the men. Obukhov had died for it. Aleksei had sent most of them away, including Dmitry, and dealt with the police himself. None of it was for Tamara to know.

'Two murders, thirteen years apart. Hardly related,' he said.

'There were five murders in 1825.'

'Yes, I remember that much.' Dmitry had thought and spoken quickly. At the time the deaths had caused something of a stir even among those who sought a more natural explanation. If he denied remembering the events at all, Tamara might easily catch him out.

'You were in Moscow?'

To Dmitry's relief, the waiter arrived with the blini. Tamara had chosen to have hers with red caviar, while Dmitry and Raisa each had cherries and cream. As soon as they were alone, Tamara repeated her question. 'You were in Moscow?'

He nodded, without breaking eye contact. She wasn't as pretty as Raisa, but no one would deny that she was attractive. Her face was quite square, perhaps a little masculine, and her eyes were of a dark brown that seemed unusual in contrast with the colour of her hair. She was not petite, like Raisa, but well proportioned. She looked as though she was probably quite strong. There was something familiar about her face, particularly the nose and the jawline.

'But your father didn't speak of it to you?'

'Why should he? Papa reported lots of crimes. It was part of his job.'

'Are you still in touch with him?'

Dmitry felt a bitter taste in his mouth. It wasn't her fault – it was a perfectly natural question – but he didn't need to be reminded of his father's recent silence. It was time to turn the tables on her.

'He was a friend of your parents, you know,' he said.

If she had been walking she would have tripped. Her confidence vanished into the air.

'My parents? Your father?'

Dmitry tried to press his advantage. 'That's right. Well, it was Vadim Fyodorovich that he knew really – that would be your grandfather.'

This seemed like more comfortable ground for her. 'He was,' she said, with infectious enthusiasm. 'They fought together in the war. I've heard all about him – but I'd never have guessed. Aleksei was Aleksei Ivanovich – your father?'

Dmitry nodded. 'That's right. I was too young to really remember Vadim, but Papa told me so much, just like your mama must have.'

'She always speaks of Grandpapa in the war, and his comrades: Vadim, Dmitry, Maks and Aleksei. But Aleksei was never more than a name.'

'He was the only one of the four to survive. Maks was Maksim Sergeivich Lukin and Dmitry was Dmitry Fetyukovich Petrenko. I was named after him when he saved Papa's life at Austerlitz.' A thousand stories bombarded Dmitry's mind, and he wondered which he should tell her first. Then he paused as suddenly a realization hit him. He looked at Tamara's smiling face, but said no more. He turned instead to Raisa. 'We must be boring you horribly.'

She smiled broadly. 'Not at all,' she said. 'Your father must have been quite a man in his day. I can see you're proud to take after him.'

'He was,' said Dmitry, then he turned and looked into Tamara's dark eyes. 'He was.'

'I'm sure he was,' she said. 'I was just hoping he might have said something about these murders.'

'Not a thing,' he lied. Now more than ever, he would not expose Tamara to the knowledge that Aleksei had shared with him. The *voordalak* could be consigned to the memories of the past. Even Tyeplov and the Crimea seemed distant now. 'Why are you so keen to find out?' he added.

'Murder is murder,' said Tamara, 'however long ago it happened.' She glanced over at Raisa as she spoke and then unaccountably laughed. Dmitry turned back to Raisa and saw why. A large blob of whipped cream adorned the tip of her nose. Dmitry tried not to laugh but smiled broadly as Raisa looked from one to the other, unaware of the cause of their amusement. Tamara rubbed her nose to mimic how Raisa should remove the unwanted item, but still she didn't catch on. Eventually, Dmitry picked up his napkin and leaned over towards her to wipe the cream away. He was almost touching her face when she took the napkin from him. He felt her fingers briefly come into contact with his.

'Dmitry Alekseevich,' she said jokingly, smiling into his eyes, 'you presume too much.' She began to clean the cream away for herself, but her voice and her eyes had suggested to Dmitry that there might be far more he could presume, given the chance.

They left soon after. Dmitry paid for the meal and outside hailed a sled and saw them on their way. Moments later he too was snuggled under the furs in the back of a sleigh and was heading for his hotel. He smiled to himself, feeling happier than he had for many years. Raisa's flirtation was pleasant, if meaningless, but it was nothing to do with how he felt. That was down to something quite different.

Tamara had no idea. Neither had he until that evening. It should have been obvious, but his father was a clever liar. And when both he and Domnikiia had gone to Siberia and left Tamara in Moscow, they had put everyone off the scent, including Tamara herself, the poor little girl. He laughed. Not a girl any more. It was her face that had given it away. He was surprised no one else had noticed, but who knew Aleksei's face better than he did? He even remembered Domnikiia's, just as he had last seen it, on a cold winter's evening much like this, outside the Lavrovs' house, as little Tamara waited inside.

Tamara's nose was Domnikiia's; her jaw Aleksei's. It was strong for a woman, but it suited her. The Lavrovs must know, of course, and they would probably see it in her, even while they raised her as their own. But Tamara had never been their natural child. Her mother had been the woman who had posed merely as her nanny – Domnikiia Semyonovna. Once that fact was established, then, even without other evidence, her father became obvious: Domnikiia's lover, Aleksei Ivanovich. They had taken their secret with them into exile, and not even told their daughter. Nor had Aleksei told his son, and Dmitry could well understand why. At the time, Dmitry, with a priggishness that can only be found in the young, had been outraged at his father's betrayal of his wife, Dmitry's mother, Marfa. To reveal that there was a child would have been foolhardy. But now Marfa was dead and Aleksei was as good as, and until today Dmitry had believed that with regard to family he was alone in the world.

But now that had changed. Dmitry smiled even more broadly and wrapped himself tighter in the furs, relishing the concept. He even said it out loud, though not so as the driver would be able to hear him. The words sounded wondrous on his lips.

'She's my sister.'

CHAPTER XIV

IT WAS THE MOST WONDERFUL NIGHT OF THE YEAR, AT LEAST TO
Yudin's mind; the winter solstice – the longest night. The night
he felt most free. If vampires were not such solitary creatures,
then today they would throw a party; they would join their
brethren on city streets across the world – across the northern
hemisphere – and feast on the living, secure in the knowledge
that dawn was as far distant as it could ever be. The humans
celebrated their festivals, be they pagan or Christian, a few days
later, when they first noticed that the days were getting longer
and the sun was beginning to rise from its nadir. In Russia, where
the misunderstanding of priests was favoured over the calculation
of scientists, Christmas followed the solstice by an even greater
gap, but no amount of prayer could change the path of the Earth
around the Sun and so the shortest day fell, as Yudin could easily
predict, just when it should.

It was a little after four in the afternoon now, and the sky was
dark. It would not be light again until past eight the following
morning. And Dmitry was in Petersburg, so Yudin had no immediate concern about appearing too young to his friend. Tonight
he deserved to indulge himself. Tonight was Yudin's Christmas.

He had only just left the Kremlin. He wore a coat and hat, not
for warmth – simply to fit in. In his hand he grasped a small black-
leather case, in which he carried a selection of instruments that
might bring greater enjoyment to the evening. Red Square was
full of people, some up to their knees in the snow, but still happy
to be in Moscow in the heart of winter. The lamps had been lit so
that all could see where they were going as they travelled home

231

from work, or out to visit the shops, or to take tea with friends. Yudin looked to the south and saw Saint Vasiliy's, and before it the Lobnoye Mesto. That was where one of those deaths had occurred in 1825. Yudin could not guess what had happened back then, but he had no doubt that a *voordalak* had been involved, and so too had Aleksei.

It would be tempting to re-create that night's events, but also foolish. It would quieten down here later, but so close to where he worked there was always the chance that someone glimpsing his face would begin a trail of discovery that would eventually unveil the truth about him. He had been cautious for almost thirty years, and was not going to be stupid now.

He turned left and passed under the Resurrection Gate, glancing up, but not pausing, to note the mosaic of George slaying the dragon that had been cemented above the archway. Everywhere, there were reminders for Zmyeevich, should he choose to return.

He made for the station – a good place for anyone in search of the innocent and naive. It was where Raisa had found a new girl to replace Irina Karlovna at the brothel, fresh off the train from Petersburg and looking to start a new life. It served also as a reminder of England; not the station itself – Yudin had left the country of his birth long before Stephenson had come up with his first locomotive. It was the Russian word for it – *vokzal* – not too dissimilar from 'Vauxhall' in south London, an easy ride from his family home in Surrey. Some said there was a connection between the two words. The story relied, as so often, on the assumed stupidity of Tsar Nikolai. He had been in London in the 1840s and seen Vauxhall railway station and – ignorant buffoon that he was renowned to be – assumed that the word meant 'railway station'. And none of his entourage was brave enough to contradict him. In truth, Nikolai was a long way from being a buffoon, but there were always those, even within Yudin's own department, who liked to portray him as such.

They should read their Pushkin. 'At fêtes and in *vokzals*, I've been flitting like a gentle Zephyrus.' He wrote that in 1813 and meant by it a sort of public park. And there was one such park at Tsarskoye Selo, which was the destination of Russia's first ever railway, back in the 1830s. Hence the name. But Yudin remembered the beautiful public gardens in Vauxhall that he'd visited as a boy, so maybe there was a connection. He smiled to himself. He remembered them as being beautiful – he did not remember them and judge them as beautiful; he was no longer capable of that.

It was then that he saw them – the ideal victims: a man and a woman walking through the snow, and between them, clasping each of their hands, a child, certainly no more than ten years old. The child was so well wrapped up that he couldn't guess its sex, but that did not matter – it would not be the focus of events. It was the emotions that would be roused in its parents on seeing it suffer as Yudin slowly fed upon it that would most thrill him; would make their blood all the richer when he got to them, the woman first, and then the man. He smiled to himself – that was fanciful. Their blood would not be transformed in any way by their terror, but Yudin's appreciation of it would be.

From their dress and the district they were travelling through, Yudin guessed they were not poor. That could mean they had servants – easy enough to deal with. He followed at a safe distance and within a few minutes the family arrived at their house. They went inside. Yudin saw no sign of anyone receiving them at the door, but that was not enough to be certain. Even if there were no staff, there could be other family members in there. But there was a long night ahead and Yudin could afford to wait and watch. He glanced up and down the street, but there was no suitable place to hide. His mind stepped back to 1812 when, though he had not then been a vampire, he had stalked men through these same city streets. Back then, with Moscow deserted, it had been easy to simply hide in a doorway and wait, but today anyone passing would think it suspicious. The best thing to do was to patrol.

He walked down the street, turning right at the end, circling his prey, looking for any other entrance through which he might get at them or by which they might escape. There was nothing; the block was a single edifice of houses, built side by side and back to back. He would enter through the front door, and they would be trapped. He imagined them, sitting happily now beside a warming fire, and then later cowering, pleading. What would they offer him to spare their child? What would he take? How long would he let them believe that he had shown compassion before they witnessed its little body being desecrated and destroyed? He had the whole long night.

Within minutes he was at the front of the house again, eager now to get in there, to begin turning his imaginings into reality. But he was not so overwhelmed by his desires to forget to take one final circumspect glance up and down the street. It was then that he realized he was not the only hunter abroad in Moscow that night. On the corner at the end of the block stood a figure. It was too far to make out the face, but he was tall and his stature was recognizable enough for Yudin to remember seeing him before, at the other end of this same street and earlier in the evening as well. He couldn't be sure, but he could soon find out.

He turned and went back the way he had come till he reached the next junction. Now he was at the opposite corner of the block from where he had last seen the figure. He crossed so as to get a better view of both streets, along one of which he expected to see that same man approaching. He did not have to wait. The figure came into view and then instantly stepped back, catching sight of Yudin.

Now Yudin began to walk swiftly, but not too swiftly – he did not want to lose the man completely. As prey he needed somewhere crowded, just as when he had been predator he had sought isolation. He turned south-west and headed back towards Lubyanka Square. As he walked, he listened, but the snow dampened the sound of any footsteps. Even so, he felt confident his pursuer would not have given up.

Despite the snow and the darkness, there was a cheerful mood to the crowds of people who crossed the square from all directions. A number of stalls selling food and drinks were doing a reasonable trade. Yudin made a sharp sidestep behind one of them and waited. It was not long before a tall figure walked past that could only be the man who had been following him. It would be easy to lose him now and resume his planned activities for the evening, but Yudin was not so short-sighted. If this man – or whatever manner of creature it might be – had found him tonight, he could find him again. And even tonight, he might not be alone. Yudin needed to discover more.

Moments later, the figure walked past the gap between the two stalls, his long legs moving him swiftly forward and his head scanning from side to side in search of Yudin. There was no chance to see his face. Yudin stepped back out into the square and watched his pursuer walk on a little further and then stop opposite a stand selling *pelmeni*. Yudin ducked away again and ran along behind the little wooden stalls, counting them off as he passed. The one belonging to the *pelmeni* vendor had no back to it, but was hung with various vegetables and preserved meats, there to act as decoration as much as ingredients. Yudin stood a little way back, hoping that the darkness would hide him.

The man remained, still looking south across the square, still trying to discover where Yudin might have gone, little knowing how close he was. Finally he turned and stared towards the stall, gazing almost directly at Yudin. Whether he saw anything, Yudin couldn't tell, and for the moment didn't much care. More important was what Yudin himself had seen: a face from the past, and with it a dozen memories, memories of an ingenious torture, of a *voordalak* chained to a wall, of the sun rising and falling as the Earth spun. But what came back to him most clearly of all was a name. It had been a joke at the time, but now there was little for Yudin to laugh at.

The name was Prometheus.

Even after arriving in Petersburg, Dmitry had hesitated to go home. He'd had a slow, lonely lunch at a restaurant near the station, and then hired a sled to take him to Senate Square. He stood now where he had stood then, thirty years ago – or it would be in five days' time. He smiled. Tsar Nikolai had not made it; he had not even managed thirty years of power. Dmitry had survived him, as had Yudin. Even Aleksei had lived longer, if the fate that Nikolai had condemned him to could be called a life. A man on the train had said he reckoned that the new tsar would pardon all those who had plotted against his father – those who were left. Tsar Aleksandr II had been lucky enough to know his father – to be there at his deathbed. Would he grant Dmitry the same privilege with Aleksei? There was always hope.

And that would mean that Tamara would also have a chance

to meet her father. There was nothing to suggest she knew the truth. Should he tell her? It surprised him that he felt no resentment towards her. Thirty years ago he would have. Thirty years ago he had hit Tamara's mother across the face out of frustration when he saw that he could never tear his father away from her. It was laughable – childish. He understood Aleksei better now, as with each year the son became more like the father. How could Dmitry pass judgement on a man's infidelities? And even if some vestige of hatred remained for the way that Aleksei had betrayed his mother, he could not see how that should be passed on to the daughter. None of it was her fault. And however much he tried to rouse his feelings of antipathy, he couldn't escape the warm sensation of brotherly affection that he had felt since the moment he had realized who she was.

But the question remained: should he tell her? Would she be pleased to learn the truth; that her apparent parents were no such thing, that they had lied to her throughout her life, that she was the bastard offspring of a whore and an exiled traitor? But would that not be compensated by gaining a new-found brother, by the lost time they could make up together? He shook his head. That would be a boon for him, but not her. She did not yearn for a brother, just as he had not yearned for a sister until he knew that he had one. On this issue at least, he would not be so self-indulgent. He would stick with his father's wishes, as best he could perceive them. Aleksei had clearly gone to great efforts to hide himself from Tamara – Dmitry would not act against him. Perhaps, if the rumours of the amnesty were true, Aleksei would return home with a changed mind. Time would tell, but until then, Tamara would not hear the truth – not from Dmitry's lips.

He looked out across Senate Square, then turned to face the Admiralty. He shifted a few paces to the left and leaned on his cane. Now he was at the exact spot where he had been standing back then. He could clearly see the Bronze Horseman, and just a little way in front and to the left had been Yudin and his father. There was one major difference – there was no bridge there any more. The Isaakievsky Bridge was in the process of being reconstructed upstream, away from Senate Square. It had been a floating bridge of pontoons – somewhat grander than the one in Sevastopol, but on the same principle. Now there was a new bridge, originally the Annunciation Bridge, but quickly renamed in honour of the dead Tsar Nikolai – the first real, solid bridge ever to be built over the Neva. It stood opposite the Church of the Annunciation, a little way downstream, so the pontoon bridge had been moved to keep a distance between them.

Today, as in 1825, there was little need for bridges. The surface of the river was frozen solid, though it still flowed swiftly beneath. It was across the ice that Aleksei and Yudin had fled, there that Yudin had been shot, there that Aleksei had comforted him and there that Aleksei had been arrested. Dmitry could see their figures as he had seen them for the last time, minutes before that – Aleksei desperately signalling that he should get away, Yudin calmer, but with the same intent.

Dmitry turned now as he had turned then and left the square. His destination was as it had been then, but his route was less circuitous. There were no troops out today searching for straggling revolutionaries. He walked past the Admiralty and turned down Nevsky Prospekt and soon he was outside his home – not the home that he shared with Svetlana on the other side of town, but the home in which he had grown up with Marfa and Aleksei – where Marfa had died. Underneath was a bookshop. That hadn't been there when he was young. He remembered Marfa writing to him about it when the old man had moved in. She had never seen so many books in one place. It was soon after that that she had stopped writing, and instead Yudin had sent a letter to explain that she had died.

Dmitry looked up at the windows of the apartment, remembering which room was which. The one in the centre of the first floor was the salon. That's where his harpsichord had been, and after it his piano – a gift from Aleksei. It had arrived only a day or so before the revolt, and so his father had never heard him play it. Now it was across town, in the home that Dmitry shared with Svetlana. He knew he should go there.

But he didn't go immediately. Instead he stood in the snow and looked up at his former home, and let the music fill his head.

*　　　*　　　*

237

Tyeplov. That was his real name, as best as Yudin could remember. It would be in his notes. Prometheus the Titan. It had seemed fitting when Yudin had scrawled the word on the cave wall at Chufut Kalye, all those years ago.

But whatever he was called, Prometheus should not have been in Moscow. He should not have been anywhere on the surface of the Earth, but deep beneath it. Yudin and Raisa had left them all entombed beneath Chufut Kalye. Prometheus himself had been shackled to a wall, but had evidently escaped his chains. And then, somehow, he had dug his way to freedom. And now he had come for Yudin.

Of that there was little doubt. Prometheus had been following him, and there could be no question as to his motivation – revenge. For such antisocial creatures, vengeance was an unusual passion in vampires. Yudin had more than once turned the trait against them, or at least used it to his own advantage. Aleksei's friend Maks had killed three *voordalaki* back in 1812. With a little direction from Yudin, the retribution that the others had meted out to him had been quite wonderful to behold. But Yudin had no desire to become the victim of a similar vendetta – and what he had done to those *voordalaki* he held captive beneath Chufut Kalye was far worse than anything achieved by Maks.

He left Lubyanka Square and walked north-east, away from the centre of the city and the Kremlin. He knew full well he would not be going there, or to his house in Zamoskvorechye, while Prometheus was following him – and for the moment it seemed that the easiest way to be certain of where Prometheus was, was to have him always just a few paces behind. Yudin had no direct reason to suppose that his pursuer was there, but he had been so indiscreet about his movements that only a fool would have lost track of him. From the little he could remember, Prometheus was no fool.

He turned on to Rozhdestvensky Boulevard, heading west, deciding that it was best to take a path tangential to the one that would lead him home while he pondered what to do. As he turned, he glanced over his shoulder, but did not see the tall figure of Prometheus. He had no doubt that he was out there, somewhere. And perhaps not just he alone. A dozen or more had

238

been buried there at Chufut Kalye. How many had escaped? Had they all come to Moscow and was Prometheus merely the one that Yudin had recognized? Anybody he passed in the street might be one of them. Or perhaps they were keeping back, encircling him, preparing to close in.

And there was another consideration. It was not just Yudin against whom the vampires of Chufut Kalye would seek vengeance – there was also Raisa. She had been one of them, ostensibly. Yudin had experimented on her. Most of his discoveries about reflection were based on observations of her. And yet he had always avoided being cruel to her, at least so cruel that she would notice. He had never been quite sure why but, as with his friendship with Dmitry, it was down to a feeling that one day it would prove useful.

With Raisa, even when that day had come, he had not been sure of her till the last. It was Aleksei who had ruined everything – released all of Yudin's prisoners and turned them against their master. Even without Raisa's help Yudin would probably have escaped, but it would have been much tougher. She had helped him to entomb the others. Still he had not delivered to her the reward he had promised – the mirror she so craved. But it meant that the other vampires would hate her as much as they did Yudin – perhaps more. Would they accept her as a sacrificial offering to appease their wrath, and so allow him to live? If it came to it, he would certainly make the offer.

Yudin turned right down a narrow alleyway and immediately broke into a run, making sure that his feet came down with an audible stomp, stomp, stomp, despite the attempts of the snow to muffle them. After a few seconds he swiftly turned and came to a halt. In the mouth of the alley, caught in the moonlight, stood his pursuer.

It was not Prometheus. The fact that he was following Yudin became clear as he first froze for a moment, then fled back out into the street. So now it seemed there were at least two of them – two who had escaped the caves. And while Prometheus had seemed a very able huntsman in the city streets, this new arrival was an outright amateur.

Yudin ran back up the alleyway after him.

239

The sleigh moved slowly along Nevsky Prospekt. There was traffic ahead, but Tamara was in no hurry. It was Konstantin who had invited her here to Petersburg and he who had sent the sled – if she was late, he could hardly blame her. The Kazansky Bridge was chaotic, as some sleighs turned down to ride alongside the canal and others turned out on to the Prospekt. There was even a wheeled carriage ahead, but it was hopelessly stuck in the snow. Tamara's driver flicked his whip at his horse and steered them around the obstruction. They passed Great Konyushennaya Street and Tamara glanced over towards Aleksei Ivanovich's former apartments, but she knew that there was nothing more for her to learn there. She had received a reply to her brief note to the new tenant, who signed herself simply as Mademoiselle Nevant. It was clear she had something to hide, but it was nothing that would help in Tamara's quest.

The bridge over the Moika was less congested. The sleigh would have glided over easily had it not been for Tamara's sudden scream of 'Stop!'

The driver pulled up almost immediately, and Tamara leaned out of the carriage. She pulled her scarf tighter round her face, so that she would not be recognized. On the left-hand side of the street was a row of shops. Most sold food and drink, but some sold other goods such as furnishings. One of them sold toys.

The window of the store was decorated for Christmas in the Germanic style that was becoming ever more popular in Russia. At it stood a little boy, his hand clasped in his mother's. He was nine years old – Tamara knew that precisely. She could not see the boy's face, but she could see the mother's clearly as she attempted to press on through the snow. And in recognizing the mother, she knew the child.

Soon, the boy was pulled away from the window and mother and child continued along the street. Tamara told the driver to carry on, slowly, and they kept pace with the pair, allowing Tamara to keep her eyes on the boy for a little longer, before he and his mother turned left towards Saint Isaac's, disappearing from view as Tamara's coach travelled on. At the end of Nevsky Prospekt they turned right, passing in front of the Winter Palace. In Palace

Square, dwarfed by the column commemorating Aleksandr's victory over Bonaparte, stood a decorated spruce tree. Again it was an import from the Germanic traditions of celebrating Christmas. The imperial family, with so much German blood in it, had erected such a tree at home for many years. This was only the fourth year that one had been placed here for public display, much to the disgust of the metropolitan.

They drove across the square and out into Millionaire's Street. It led straight to the Marble Palace, and to the same door she had used on her last visit. She knocked sharply and the door was opened by the footman she had seen before. Her suspicions of his dark past in the form of a lizard were now forgotten. Now, it all seemed very real – almost familiar. He led her along the corridor to the flight of wooden steps, then up them and out on to the stone staircase. At the top of it, he took her across the marble landing and then paused at the high doors to knock. From within he heard a response that Tamara didn't catch and he opened the door. Tamara stepped inside.

Konstantin came over to her, his arms outstretched. He took her hands and kissed them both through her gloves. Then, still holding them, he leaned back slightly and looked into her face. Straight away he frowned. She could well understand why. Despite the effort she had made with her make-up, she knew that it must now look awful. She could feel the tracks that her tears had cut through the powder on her cheeks and could taste their salt at the corner of her lips.

'My dear Tamara,' asked Konstantin, 'what has happened to make you cry so?'

She could not think of any lie with which to appease him, and she doubted whether she wanted to. More than anything, she had the overarching desire to explain to somebody how she felt and tell them what had happened. And so she told him.

'I've just seen my son.'

Once back on the main street Yudin's pursuer soon caught up with him again. He was more stealthy now, or thought he was, but it was very easy for Yudin to ensure that this new *voordalak* was never too far behind him. Yudin let him follow as far as the Vysokopetrovsky Monastery before deciding to turn the tables.

He ducked inside the monastery. It was a sprawling collection of buildings, and a place wherein a man could be lost from view simply by turning two corners. That was easily achieved. Now Yudin stepped back into the shadows. He saw the *voordalak* walk past quickly, looking from side to side, trying to pick up a trace of Yudin. Once he had gone, all was quiet and the monastery seemed deserted, but from within the pale blue walls of St Sergius's Church came the sound of chanting. It became momentarily louder and a patch of yellow light told Yudin that a door had been opened.

The light vanished and the sound dimmed and from the side of the church emerged a priest. He was perfect for Yudin's needs. Yudin waited a moment until he had almost disappeared from view and then scuttled silently after him, hiding again as he got close. He made an easy quarry – his head too full of thoughts of his Saviour for him to have any awareness of what was going on around him on Earth. Soon he wouldn't need to worry about either. His final destination appeared to be the monastery cathedral, an unusual brick rotunda whose tower seemed to dwarf its body.

Yudin caught up with the priest just inside the doorway. His teeth sank quickly into the aged neck and he felt a gush of warmth as blood spilled over his lips. The priest died without uttering a sound. Yudin held him for a few moments and drank, but there was little pleasure in it. Once the prey was dead, the blood began to stale quickly – and without experiencing the suffering of his victim, what real enjoyment could Yudin draw from any of it? This was nothing like the hours of self-indulgence that Yudin had been planning for the evening – a night of hedonism of the sort that he rarely allowed himself – but it would have to do. Besides, there were many hours until dawn and perhaps still the prospect of spoiling himself.

He dragged the priest's body into the cathedral and moments later emerged wearing his vestments. He still clutched the little leather bag that he had brought with him from the Kremlin. It didn't look quite as ecclesiastical as the rest of him, but he knew he might be needing it. The bottom of his overcoat peeped out from under his *ryasa*, but he did not want to leave it with the body, and later on he might need to abandon this disguise. The next step was to become reacquainted with his erstwhile pursuer. He positioned himself on the corner of Petrovsky Boulevard and Petrovka Street, where he could keep an eye on two of the three sides of the monastery, knowing that eventually the *voordalak* would emerge.

He didn't have to wait for long. The figure was easily recognizable as it came back out on to Petrovsky Boulevard. Knowing he would look conspicuous if he remained still, Yudin began walking straight towards him. He was tempted to pass right by him, but it would be a foolish risk. The *voordalak*'s face might have made little impression on Yudin, but the reverse was unlikely to be true. Before Yudin reached him, he planned to cross over the road and watch from one of the side streets to the north.

In the end, it was unnecessary. The vampire looked briefly in either direction, without even registering the approaching figure of a priest. He hung around for a few moments more and then headed off cast, evidently concluding that Yudin had escaped him. Perhaps tonight his attention was more easily held by ideas of hunger than of vengeance. Yudin let him get a little way ahead and then followed, always one bend in the road behind, always just out of sight.

The *voordalak* kept to the road for a little way, then turned left, cutting through one side street after another as he wended his way broadly northwards. They were well outside the centre of the city when the vampire, entirely as though this was the route he had planned, turned into a lane heading east. Yudin quickly ran up to the corner and looked round, but the street was empty. On the left-hand side there was a tavern. It seemed the likely destination, but Yudin couldn't be sure – and wasn't going to wait.

The sight of a priest in a tavern wouldn't be too unusual, and so Yudin chose not to change his disguise. He wrapped his scarf around the bottom half of his face, for fear of being recognized close to. At the tavern door, he paused. It could be a trap. He could have been led here deliberately. But to a tavern? He could hear the hubbub of many voices within. It was too crowded for them to act against him – unless all of them in there were *voordalaki*, expectant of his arrival. Just how many of them could have escaped Chufut Kalye?

He went inside. It was as busy as any hostelry in the city at that time of night and at that time of year. A quick glance around identified the figure who had been following him, standing beside a table at the far end of the bar. He seemed to be introducing himself to the three men sitting there, and holding out a bottle of vodka, which he could only just have purchased, in the hope of gaining admittance to the group. His overtures were accepted and he sat down, filling the others' glasses.

Yudin went to the bar and ordered wine, and then sat in the furthest corner from the four of them, watching. He sipped his drink without enthusiasm, keeping his eyes on the table across the room, trying to fathom what the plan was. Those other three were humans, Yudin was sure of that; not comrades that the *voordalak* had arranged to meet, but potential victims that he had happened upon by chance. As far as Yudin could tell, they were drunks, like most Russians. The *voordalak* went back to the bar and ordered another bottle, drinking as freely as the others, and by the end of it they were all 'mates'. Yudin could not have managed the deception, not even when he had been human. In his life he'd had few friends and no 'mates'.

Then the *voordalak* sprang his trap. Yudin could not hear a word of what was said, but he could guess every meaning. The vampire stood and signalled towards the door. He knew a great place where they could go. Maybe he was offering women; maybe more, cheaper vodka. Whatever the bait, one of the men bit. That it was only one would make it easier. The man stood and, arms round each other's shoulders, he and the *voordalak* headed for the door, each using the other for support. A vampire couldn't get drunk, however much he consumed, and it was clearly all for show. But it would make them easier to follow.

Yudin let the door swing closed behind them and then got to his feet. As he exited, he saw the two figures, carrying on along the road in which the tavern stood. They were singing – the *voordalak* better than the man. He followed them, remaining stealthy, not letting the appearance of inebriation fool him into thinking that the vampire was not still on guard.

The road they followed ran alongside the railway track, at the very beginning of the long route to the capital, high on an embankment so that the gradient would never be too steep. On that side of the street there were no houses, those that had once stood there wiped away and the occupants made homeless in the name of progress. Yudin smiled at the thought. At last they came to a church. It was a small, unimpressive place, in a sorry state of repair. Away from the road, the cemetery was quite extensive, but the line of the railway had cut it neatly in half. The vampire signalled to his new friend that this was where they had been headed, but the man appeared reluctant. The vampire went over and unlocked the main door in the side of the squat red-brick nave, then staggered back out to the street. He said a few more words to the man and then started singing again. The aria immediately became a duet, and the two figures, arms once again around shoulders, tottered inside. The door closed behind them and Yudin raced up and put his ear to it.

The building screamed of being a vampires' nest. It would have a crypt in which they could sleep during the day, comfortably, as undead among the dead. It was a little way from any other buildings, but not too far so that they wouldn't be able to go out and find fresh meat. And the whole place smelled of *voordalaki* – or smelled of their victims. The one scent was never far from the other.

From inside the sound of two voices in perfect discord reduced to one – the man, Yudin guessed. Then there was a thud and a shriek and another, louder thud, and all was silence. Next would come the feeding. That was good; it would make the *voordalak* unwary. Even so, Yudin would not enter by the door. He began to circle the church, looking for an alternative way in.

They hadn't sat at the dinner table. As soon as Konstantin had seen Tamara's tears he had taken her over to a divan. He brought her a glass of wine and then sat beside her. Occasionally, he would go to the table and bring her something from the banquet that had been laid out for them, or bring something for himself, but then he seemed reluctant to eat in front of her. He appeared entirely discomforted by the whole situation, but never once annoyed by it.

She had told him the story of her marriage and her time in Petersburg. Not the whole of it – she had missed off any mention of Prince Larionov or any of the other men she had met through him. But she told him of how she believed she was not the Lavrovs' child, and of her search for her true parents. She had explained that she had been married to Vitya and had borne Milenochka, Stasik and Luka. She had told him about the epidemic of 1848, of her flight to Pavlovsk, of the deaths of Milena and Stanislav, and of the murder of Vitya. She told it all as she had previously told those few friends in whom she felt she could confide.

But when it came to Luka, her youngest boy, for once she told the truth.

'After I came back to Petersburg with Luka, and found that Vitya was dead, I fell ill again.'

'Another attack of cholera?' asked Konstantin.

'No. Melancholia, some doctors said – others, hysteria. They say I screamed whenever they tried to bring Luka into the room, and hid my face in the pillows.'

'"They say"?'

'I don't remember very much, but I do remember hating Luka. I can't understand it now, but I hated him in the same way I hated myself – we'd both survived.'

'Something to praise God for.'

'For killing three and sparing two?' she snapped. Konstantin did not try to defend the idea. 'But in the end, I did learn to be thankful. Not to God, not to anyone, but I was overjoyed that Luka was alive, and that I was there to be with him.'

'So why does seeing him make you cry?'

'Because by that time they'd decided I wasn't fit to keep him. How could they trust me, after the way I'd been?'

'A mother can always be trusted.'

'You wouldn't say that if you'd seen me. And in the end, they persuaded me they were right.'

'Who did?'

'Two doctors. They'd been friends of Vitya's, so they understood what he would say.'

'From what you've said, it doesn't sound as though they did,' said Konstantin.

'Perhaps not, but I believed them. They even let me meet the couple who were going to take Luka. Fine people. That's how I recognized the mother today.'

'The mother?'

'When I saw her with Luka, on Nevsky Prospekt.'

She felt him place his hand on top of hers between them on the divan. She looked up at him for the first time in several minutes. Konstantin gazed up at her over his spectacles, looking small and not at all regal.

'Was that the first time?'

'No. They live in Petersburg, so I've seen him three or four times.'

'Have you *tried* to see him?'

Tamara smiled sadly. Konstantin was very astute. 'Only once,' she said, 'on the spur of the moment. It was in the Summer Garden. I was sitting outside the coffee house and I saw them. All three of them. I don't even know if I was going to approach them, or just walk past as close to Luka as I could. But she saw me and said something to her husband, and he bundled Luka away, and she stood and blocked my path. She didn't say much. She had a strange look of confusion on her face. I don't know which I hated more – the anger or the pity.'

'It must be very difficult for them,' he said. She looked at him almost as if he had betrayed her. She felt him squeeze her hand. 'I'm sorry,' he said gently, 'but it must. Nothing like what it must be for you though.'

She smiled and squeezed his hand back.

'You know their names? Where they live?' he asked.

'Oh, yes.' That had been easy to find out. 'But there's nothing I can do.' She lapsed into silence for a few moments, before adding, 'They still call him Luka.'

'Good,' he said, then a little more brightly, 'Do you think that's why you're so keen to find your parents?'

'What?'

247

'In the hope that one day Luka will do the same and look for you?'

It had never occurred to her as plainly as that, but it could well be true. She allowed the scene of an adult Luka, having searched as she had searched, finally being reunited with her to play itself out in her mind, and felt her eyes well with tears. Then she felt Konstantin's arm around her.

'I'm sorry,' he muttered. 'I shouldn't have said that.'

'No. It was very perceptive.'

'It's not for me to tell you what you think,' said Konstantin. 'Not for anyone.' He stood up and walked across the room, his hands clasped behind his back. Her eyes followed him. He kept his back to her as he spoke.

'I lost someone very dear to me,' he told her. 'My favourite sister, Adini. She was only nineteen. Consumption.'

Tamara thought to say the words 'I'm sorry,' but decided they were inadequate.

'And then when I married Aleksandra, everyone said it was because she reminded me of Adini.'

'Do you love her?' asked Tamara. 'Your wife?'

'Of course,' he said. Then he turned and Tamara could see that he was smiling. He came back and sat beside her. 'I mean really. Yes.'

'Then why am I here?'

'You're nothing like my wife – or like Adini.'

He suddenly looked very young and very innocent, though Tamara knew full well that he was nothing of the sort. She leaned forward and kissed his lips. He seemed for a moment surprised, but then his mouth opened and he pushed his body forward, as if to take charge. When they separated, she was reclining on the divan and he was above her.

'Why did you do that?' he asked. He sounded genuinely curious.

'You deserved it; for being happy to sit here and listen.'

'I'd have done that for nothing,' he replied.

She believed him – that was why she was still here. 'I deserve it,' she said, and she meant that too. A little forgetful abandon would take her away from her troubles, if only for a while. It had been a long time since she had had the chance to sleep with a man for her own pleasure. She felt a warmth inside her at the prospect.

'People don't always get what they deserve,' said Konstantin.

'I think I will,' she replied.

Konstantin stood and took her hand and led her to a door at the side of the room.

'I expected you earlier.'

Dmitry felt as though he were a guest in his own house. The footman, Konyev, had only been employed a few months before his last departure, so although they recognized one another, Dmitry felt immediately that Konyev was more at home in the apartment than he was. He was shown to the drawing room, where Svetlana was sitting, waiting for him. She had scarcely looked up as she spoke.

He stood still, like a child being upbraided by its mother. 'I'm sorry,' he said. 'I . . . I . . . I didn't know what you'd make of me.' Was that the reason? He doubted that was the whole thing, but it was in there somewhere.

She raised her head sharply. 'Make of you?'

He held his stick a little towards her to make it clear, and with his left hand indicated his ankle. Then he walked across the room with, he knew, exaggerated fortitude and dropped himself into the armchair beside her with a loud sigh of relief. She leaned forward and clasped his hand in hers.

'Oh Mitka, I'm sorry. I never thought. I've been so worried, wondering how bad it was for you. It never occurred to me that you'd be thinking of how it affected me.'

'Do you mind?'

'Mind? How could I mind? It makes you look quite distinguished. Everyone will know I'm married to a hero now.'

'You used to think you were married to a god.' He suddenly feared that she would give him the honest answer, and say how she gave up on that long ago, but, as ever, she would make no admission that anything was wrong.

'You still are a god, Mitka. One with feet of clay.' He didn't smile, so she tried another approach. 'It's only a limp.'

'Only!' His outrage was affected, but he knew she would be expecting it.

'From the outside, I mean,' she pleaded. 'I know it must hurt you terribly, but it's not like some horrible scar or as if you've lost an arm or even . . .'

Dmitry knew why she had stopped. She was about to mention his father's missing fingers. Svetlana had never met Aleksei, but Dmitry had told her about the disfigurement, and she had been unable to hide her disgust. If his ankle was causing her disgust now, she hid it better. And perhaps she was right – a wounded soldier could seem all the more valiant, but as the scars grew deeper and more obvious, he would become in the eyes of the world a monster.

He stood and walked over to the piano, now doing his best not to limp, but that made it hurt more. He sat down, resting his cane at the top end of the keyboard, and considered what to play.

'You said in your letters that you managed to play down there,' said Svetlana.

'There was a piano in the mess, but I had to wait my turn. And it wasn't in tune.' His mind drifted to the memory of his playing for Tyeplov, and he forced it out. 'I didn't get a chance on the journey home.'

He began to play the fast triplets of Chopin's nineteenth prelude. It was a moderately easy work, suitable for fingers that had not been stretched for many weeks. They moved swiftly and nimbly, as though they had been playing the piece only yesterday. The piano was out of tune – Svetlana didn't understand these things, however much he explained them – but that could be remedied in a few days, and he could hear enough through the slight clashes between strings of the same note, especially on the high $E^\flat$, to know that he was playing well. Then, after about four bars, he suddenly stopped, snatching up his leg and rubbing his ankle.

'What's wrong?' asked Svetlana.

'I can't bloody pedal!' he shouted, slamming his hand on the keys to produce a raucous crash of notes. Although his ankle could take most of his weight now, it had very little movement. He'd not even thought about it, and gone at the piece pressing the pedal on almost every beat. The pain had been sudden and searing, forcing him to stop.

'You could play something else.' She meant it sincerely – she had no idea. He put his hands back on the keyboard and played a Bach invention, going as fast as he was capable. It was written for harpsichord, before the concept of controlling the sustain of a note after the key had been released, and of letting the other strings resonate with it, had ever been thought of. It led to music that was complex, but had no soul. He could learn to pedal with his left foot, but it would take months, and it would never feel natural.

He stood up and walked back to his seat beside Svetlana. 'You just need to exercise it,' she said. 'It took you long enough to be able to walk.' She leaned forward and lifted up his foot. He was wearing a laced boot, which he found unfashionable and effeminate, but his ankle was still too stiff to pull in and out of a normal riding boot. She untied the laces and took it off, placing his foot in her lap. She put one hand under his heel and gripped the foot with the other, just below his toes. Then she began to rock it backwards and forwards, with very slight movements, stopping and reversing direction as soon as she hit resistance.

'Ow!' he said petulantly, although it didn't really hurt very much, and felt as though it would do him good.

'A woman came to see you,' she said after a few minutes.

'A woman?'

'She was asking about your father.'

'Ah! Tamara Valentinovna. I saw her in Moscow.'

'What does she want to know?'

'Some historical case that Papa was investigating – before . . .'

'You make him sound like more of a policeman than a soldier.'

'He was a bit of both,' said Dmitry.

'She's pretty.'

'Who?' Dmitry felt pain in his foot as Svetlana bent it a little further forward than it wanted to go. It had been a mistake for him to play dumb.

'Tamara. Wonderful hair.'

'I suppose,' he said. Like everyone else, Svetlana did not seem to notice the similarities between them that Dmitry had found so obvious. It was the hair that was the most striking thing about her. Neither Aleksei nor Domnikiia had had red hair but that didn't lead Dmitry to doubt for a moment that they were her parents.

'She's a little plump,' said Svetlana. It might be true, but it suited her. It would suit Svetlana to be a little less skinny, but she seemed proud of it so he never told her. Women – men too, he supposed – had a natural shape and did well to conform to it. Raisa was slim and was meant to be. He smiled to himself. It was odd that she should pop into his mind, but not unpleasant.

Svetlana had stopped massaging his ankle. Now she was gently tickling the skin just behind it, on both sides. 'Have you eaten?' she asked.

'Yes,' he said. 'I'm sorry. I should have waited until we were together.'

'I'm not hungry.'

A silence descended. Dmitry laid his head back and prepared to hear music. It came, but not as quickly as usual, and as a distant memory he could still hear the boom of French and British cannon, spoiling his enjoyment of the melody and harmony. But it was better than nothing.

'It's been two years, Mitka,' said Svetlana softly. 'Since we were together.'

'A long time,' he said.

'A long time to be alone.' She stood and took his hand. He wasn't sure whether she had meant that he, she or both of them had been alone. He had felt no more alone in Sevastopol than he did here. But for her, the solitude must have been agonizing – and he knew she would not have taken a lover. He rose to his feet, finding it harder than ever to walk with only one boot, and followed her into the bedroom.

CHAPTER XV

INSIDE THE CHURCH ALL WAS QUIET, BUT FOR THE SOUND OF THREE pairs of lungs breathing – each reflecting a different state of mind in its owner.

The drunk from the tavern was drifting between consciousness and unconsciousness, breaths rasping and interrupted. When Yudin had entered the church, the *voordalak* who had brought the man had already put him to one side, to deal with later. Both the man's legs were broken just below the knee and were splaying out as though he were a frog freshly jumped from a pond. Yudin had not seen how it had been done, but it would not have been difficult with a *voordalak*'s strength. It was easier than tying him up, and ensured he would not escape. Occasionally, when the man's desire for life overcame the pain, he dragged himself across the mosaic floor using only his hands, but like a fool he headed not for the door and possible freedom but towards the iconostasis and the Beautiful Gate, in the hope of unlikely salvation. It didn't matter. Even if he had made it halfway to the door, his captor could easily have strode across the nave and dragged him back to begin his journey again.

At least his captor might have been able to do that, until Yudin had arrived.

Yudin's breathing was slow and calm, belying the excitement he felt. He needed to be lucid, and to keep a steady hand, so that what he was doing could be achieved swiftly. He did not know when Prometheus – perhaps others too – would return, but it would most certainly be before dawn. Even so, Yudin knew that the anticipation he had felt when setting out earlier that evening

253

would not go unfulfilled, though his victim was utterly different from what he had expected.

It was the breath of the *voordalak* that came in the loudest, shortest, most unsteady bursts. It was the breath of the terrified, the breath that prepares the body for action and yet which the body chokes off before it is complete. Yudin pondered why a vampire should breathe like that. A vampire could be terrified, he had verified that many times, but it had so little need for air that a change in breathing was quite unnecessary. Perhaps it was merely a memory of being human, the body reacting to events in a way that would once have been helpful but was now merely for show – like a dog half-heartedly kicking the earth over its faeces as a memory of the wolf that it once was.

'So, you're Mihailov,' said Yudin. 'I'll have to take your word for it. I don't remember the name, but I never forget a face.'

'I'll never forget yours,' Mihailov replied. Yudin glanced up and saw the hatred in his eyes. He had been easy to capture, and easy to persuade to talk, at least to reveal his name, but the rest would come. Mihailov's goal was vengeance, and vengeance was a meagre feast if its victim was not fully aware of the reasons for it.

Yudin tugged at Mihailov's feet. All seemed secure. He had only used rope to bind him. Normally he would have used thick chains on a creature with the strength of a *voordalak*, but when packing his little black-leather bag he had been intending only to deal with humans. Fortunately, most of what he had brought would still prove useful. To compensate, Yudin had found a way to ensure that Mihailov could apply no leverage to his bonds – and the Saviour had assisted. To one side of the iconostasis, a little way back into the nave, a stone statue of Christ, life-sized, stood with His arms open in a sign of welcome. Yudin had hooked the rope that bound Mihailov's wrists together over Christ's right arm and let it nestle in the crook of His elbow. He had been worried for a moment, but it seemed the Lord was able to bear the weight even of this most abominable of sinners.

Mihailov's arms were stretched above his head and his feet dangled at about the level of Yudin's knees. His shoulders would have been dislocated by his own weight, but his torn ligaments and tendons would be healing now, leaving his shoulders permanently misshapen. It would make it even less likely that he could free himself. Yudin had held captives in this sort of pose many times before, enjoying the air of helplessness that it lent them. The manacles in the cell back at the Kremlin achieved much the same. It was a long time, though, since he had enjoyed the scene with a fellow *voordalak* as the centre of attention.

'You remember me from Chufut Kalye, I take it?' said Yudin, going back over to his bag.

'We all remember you.'

'All? How many is all?'

'How many of us were there?'

Yudin began to rummage through his possessions, but then realized he would probably need everything. He picked up the bag and brought it back over. 'Oh, dozens, I should say. But I can't believe that all of you escaped.' He put the bag down close to Mihailov's feet. 'I've only seen the two of you in Moscow.'

'Then at least two of us escaped.'

'How?'

'Some soldiers fought. One of them bled heavily. It seeped down and revived us.'

'Even so,' said Yudin, laying out his paraphernalia on the step in front of the iconostasis, 'you were still trapped.'

'We had almost dug our way free soon after you left us. And over the years the earth had shifted. It was easy enough.'

'On a dead man's blood?' Yudin knew that both the flavour and the nourishment of blood died quickly.

'Once we had escaped, we drank from his foe. Then we had the strength to move on.'

'The one who bled,' asked Yudin, 'where did he bleed from?'

'Where?' Mihailov seemed confused, as well he might be.

'Where on his body?'

It took a moment's thought. 'His thigh.'

'Good,' said Yudin. 'A good place for it.' He looked up. 'So then you came here, in pursuit of me?'

'We went to Sevastopol.'

'A bucket,' said Yudin, as though talking to himself, but knowing he would be heard. Mihailov's face showed the puzzlement he had hoped for. 'I need a bucket.' He cast his eyes around, searching. 'Go on,' he said more loudly. 'Why did you go to Sevastopol?'

'His son was there.'

Yudin saw what he was after in a dark corner. He hurried over. For all his bravura, he was afraid that Mihailov's comrades might return at any minute. He needed to be swift. 'Whose son?' he called over his shoulder.

'The three-fingered man's.'

'Aha!' said Yudin, as much at what he saw as what he had heard. It was a pewter font, quite a large one – big enough to drown the baby if the priest so desired. The semicircular handle, lying on one side and aligning perfectly with the rim, reminded Yudin of a witch's cauldron. The entire font rested on a wooden stand, but he didn't need that. He lifted it off and placed it on the floor, then began to drag it by the handle back over to Mihailov. 'You thought he'd help you? Like father like son?'

Mihailov waited until the scrape, scrape, scrape of the font against the mosaic tiles had stopped before replying. 'We thought he might.'

'But he didn't.' Yudin's voice remained calm, but his mind quickly analysed the possibility that Dmitry had sided with them. It seemed preposterous. Dmitry was devoted to those he regarded as his friends. Even if they'd told him every detail of Yudin's past, even if he'd believed it, he'd have come to Yudin and offered him a chance to explain. But when they'd met, Yudin had noticed no trace of change in Dmitry's attitude towards him. Even so, it was not a possibility entirely to be ignored.

'He didn't,' confirmed Mihailov, but on a matter such as that, he was not to be trusted.

Yudin began to pull off Mihailov's boots, making sure that as he did so he exerted maximum force on the creature's shoulders. 'I take it Prometheus is your leader.'

'Prometheus?'

'Tyeplov,' Yudin clarified, moving on to the second boot.

'He's the one who hates you most.'

'I'm glad to hear it.' Yudin stood upright. 'Now,' he said, 'this is where it all gets a bit friendly.' He reached up and took hold of Mihailov's belt in his left hand, pulling it away from his body. In his right hand he held his knife, which he used to saw through the belt and then to continue to cut through the breeches right down to the crotch. With a quick pull, Yudin had removed them. He threw them into a corner. The *voordalak* was naked from the waist down. His genitalia hung limp and ugly, distracting Yudin and making him regret having exposed them. But it was too late.

'He'll be here soon,' said Mihailov.

'Good,' replied Yudin. 'And I take it you all bear the same loathing for Raisa Styepanovna that you do for me.'

'She's a fool, but she must still be punished. What we do will act as a warning to others.'

'As will this,' replied Yudin. He selected a couple of items of equipment and then stepped close to Mihailov's leg, holding it behind the knee. With the scalpel he made a small, precise cut on the inside of the thigh. Blood flowed quickly from it, sticking to the skin of his leg as it ran down towards the ground. Yudin pressed the catheter into the wound, but before he could get it in place, the bleeding stopped as the cut began to seal itself. Within seconds it was as though the damage had never been done. 'Damn!' said Yudin. 'You're healthy.'

'We have eaten well here.'

Yudin glanced over at the man who would have been Mihailov's next meal. He had abandoned his attempts at the Beautiful Gate and had turned his attention at last towards the narthex and the door beyond. He had not got very far, and now lay still. But he was not unconscious. His head was on its side and his eyes were fixed on the two vampires.

'And you've been here since – what – September?' It was only a guess that they had stayed in Sevastopol until it had fallen. He cut again into Mihailov's skin. The *voordalak* did not flinch. He could have little idea what Yudin planned. This time he made the incision wider, to give himself more time. It was untidy, but that didn't matter.

'We've been here long enough.'

Now the glass tube slipped in before the wound could heal. Even so, the *voordalak*'s flesh did its best, reducing the lesion to a tiny hole, which would itself have vanished had not the catheter prevented it. The glass became red in a moment as it filled with blood. Yudin stepped back so as not to spill any upon himself. The blood shot from the end of the tube and splashed on to the tiles of the church floor. Yudin watched for a moment, enjoying the desecration, even though he knew there was no one present to be offended by it. Then he pushed the font over a little with his foot until it was directly beneath Mihailov and able to catch his blood. At first it made a tinny rattle as it hit the metal, but once the bottom was covered with the liquid the remaining blood made a light splashing sound as it fell. If it weren't for the colour of the fluid, anyone would think that Mihailov was taking a piss.

'You came straight to Moscow?' asked Yudin.

'What are you doing?' asked Mihailov.

'I'm killing you. Slowly. Now answer my question.'

The *voordalak* remained impassive at the announcement of his imminent death, perhaps doubting Yudin's ability to fulfil his promise. 'That's right. We had to travel slowly, but we ate well along the way.'

'And tonight you decided to act?'

'No – we were still formulating our plans.'

That was good news, if it were true. If tonight they had been planning on making a move against Yudin, then this all might be part of a trap. As it was, it seemed that Yudin was in charge of the situation. Mihailov could, of course, be lying, but with each drop of blood that drained from him, his will would weaken. That meant that now was the time to ask the more important questions.

'How did you know where to find me?'

'Tyeplov knew.'

Not a very satisfactory answer, but then another, similar question occurred to him. 'How did you know that Dmitry Alekseevich was in Sevastopol?'

'Tyeplov knew.'

'How did he know?'

There was no answer. Yudin grabbed the catheter and pushed it a little further into the artery, taking care not to break it. Mihailov winced. He was weary now. Yudin knew he must not drain too much blood, or Mihailov would lose consciousness altogether. His body would manage to regenerate the vital fluid, just as it could restore any other part of itself that was lost or injured, but that would take time. With some effort, a perfect balance could be achieved, with blood flowing out at the same rate it was created. But even that would not last long. The effort of producing blood would further weaken the creature, in much the same way as if it were starved.

Yudin put his thumb over the tip of the catheter and stopped the flow. He counted a minute and then released it. The trickling and splashing of the draining blood began anew, pulsing in time with the beat of Mihailov's faltering heart. Yudin looked at the blood on his hand. If he hadn't been aware of its origin he would have been more than tempted to lick it up, but he knew that vampire blood tasted foul – it had already been consumed once. It would be like offering urine to a human in place of wine. He wiped his hand clean on Mihailov's discarded breeches.

'How did Tyeplov know?' he asked again.

'Zmyeevich told him.'

Yudin's blood ran cold. This was no act of petty vengeance by a group of inconsequential *voordalaki* who had escaped the laboratory. It was vengeance to be sure, but of a far more awful nature. Zmyeevich was the most powerful vampire there had ever been, and Yudin had deceived him, and used him, and caused him pain. He suddenly felt far less sure that it was he who was in charge of events.

'Zmyeevich was with you? In the Crimea?' He asked that question out of fear of the answer to a slightly different question: whether Zmyeevich was still with them, in Moscow.

'No.' Mihailov tried to shake his head, but didn't have the strength.

'How did he tell Tyeplov then?'

'Zmyeevich created Tyeplov – created him as a vampire. Their minds are together.'

Yudin felt relief. It was merely the mental bond between vampire parent and vampire child. That Zmyeevich was involved still caused him a deep, unyielding terror, but the fact that the great vampire was not physically present gave him some hope.

'And Zmyeevich conveyed to him where I was, and where Raisa was, and where Dmitry was?'

'He did.'

Yudin could think of little more to ask, so he tried a question that had failed previously. 'How many of you are there?'

'Three. There were four, but one died in Sevastopol.' Mihailov's voice was singsong – almost as if he were happy.

'What happened to him?'

'The three-fingered man.'

'His son, you mean?'

'Yeah.' It was casual, half-asleep.

That it was Aleksei himself had momentarily raised a fear in Yudin – not as great as his fear of Zmyeevich, but approaching it. But Aleksei was an old man now, even if he ever managed to leave Siberia. It was pleasing – yes, genuinely pleasing to know that the son took after the father. It would make Yudin's revenge upon the father all the greater.

'Who's the other one?' he asked. He was running out of questions, but any information could be useful.

'Ignatyev. It's just him, me and Tyeplov now. Wieczorek was the one that died.'

Both names stirred vague recognition in Yudin. He would find the details in his notebooks.

'You all sleep here?' he asked.

'Yes.'

'Where?'

'In the crypt.'

Yudin checked the ropes that bound Mihailov's hands, and the statue of Christ that supported him. There was no prospect of escape. He looked around and saw the stairs leading down to the crypt, to the left of the iconostasis. He also noticed that the drunk had managed to haul himself halfway across the floor. Yudin strode over and gripped his ankle, dragging him away from freedom. The man screamed as his weight was transferred through his mangled shin, but a swift kick to the stomach silenced him.

Yudin took a candle from the many that adorned the walls. He had watched Mihailov go through the building and light them all – as though he were the church's *dyachok* – before climbing through the window and pouncing on him. One would do to see in the crypt.

It wasn't very deep, but it was sufficient. There were three coffins there, which tied with what Mihailov had said. It could have been a clever lie, revealing what Yudin could easily discover by other means, but Mihailov was at present not in the best condition to be clever. Still Yudin had to consider the possibility that more of this group lived elsewhere in the city. Even if there were only three, they would have another nest somewhere, just in case.

But the crypt was not only a dark vault where the undead rested. The *voordalaki* had also used it as a place to store their dead. There were about twenty bodies in all, each drained of its blood, in various stages of decay. It was a repellent idea – like a human sleeping beside a latrine. Yudin paused. How often he made comparisons between that which was vampire and that which was human. He had been thirty years a vampire. How much longer until it stopped? He chuckled to himself and dismissed the question from his mind.

The fact that there were twenty bodies was of little help in telling him how long the *voordalaki* had been here. If necessary, three vampires could have eked out that supply of food for over a year. If they were greedy, it might be less than a week. He remembered the vampires he had come to Moscow with in 1812. They had usually each consumed one soul every night, sometimes two. But times had been different then. The war had meant there was little chance of them being discovered. That was why they had been so eager to come.

The degree of decay of the oldest body, however, could give some clue as to when it had been brought here. It was cold down there, and that acted to preserve what remained of the flesh, but Yudin's guess was that this one had died two or three months before. Again it fitted with what Mihailov had said. He returned up the stairs to the nave.

Little had changed. The drunk had given up any hope of escape, and lay where Yudin had left him. Mihailov still hung from the arm of the Saviour. It was in the sound that Yudin first noticed a difference. The pitter-patter of drizzling blood had transformed into a slower drip, drip, drip. Yudin looked at the catheter protruding from Mihailov's thigh and confirmed what he had heard. The *voordalak*'s body was now scarcely capable of manufacturing any more of the vital fluid. That didn't matter for now, but it would spoil a little of the fun later. There was time to deal with it though.

Yudin went to the door and stepped outside. The moon was still bright, but low in the sky now. It was still several hours until dawn, although the city would be awake well before then. Would the other *voordalaki* return sooner? He hoped not. They would not want to waste the darkness of the solstice any more than he had. He skirted round the church and into the graveyard. High in the side of the building he could see the broken window by which he had gained entry.

The cemetery was old – Yudin could see no signs of new burials. Some of the graves were simple, some ornate mausolea. It was these latter that were of interest to him. He soon found the perfect refuge, comfortably distant from the church, which he could easily break into and therein hide from daylight. He went back into the church.

As he had noted earlier, the huge, richly decorated circle of a horos was suspended from the vaults of the church roof like a great crown bedecked with icons. The rope that supported it stretched across the ceiling and down the wall, where it was tied off on a cleat, almost directly below the window he had come in by. He unhitched it and took it over to the blood-filled font that still stood beneath Mihailov's hanging body. He threaded the rope under the handle and tied it off.

The horos was heavier than the font, even with its cargo of blood. If he let go, the font would shoot into the air and spill. He didn't want that. He carried it back over to the wall and began to climb, using his feet and one hand to grip the brickwork, and his other hand to hold the font, letting the weight of the horos gradually raise it up.

Inch by inch, they approached the open window.

Tamara opened her eyes. It was still dark, but in Petersburg in winter that did not mean it was early. Konstantin lay beside her – Kostya, as he had, at some point during the evening, insisted she call him. In turn he had called her Tamarushka. She was normally called Toma by those close to her, but it was nice to have something to distinguish their relationship – both in allowing her to forget her family and in having something that only she and Kostya shared.

He was breathing deeply, but not snoring. She turned to look at him, but it was too dark to see anything more than the lump of his body in the bed. She reached out and touched his cheek. He didn't react. She ran her finger down to his moustache and stroked it. He emitted a single snort and turned on to his side. Tamara giggled to herself silently. Suddenly, she felt very guilty. He was six years her junior, but in terms of his understanding of sex, many years behind that. He'd had lovers before his marriage, he'd told her, but she was the first since – and with all of those, and his wife, the women had been too much in awe of him to venture far beyond the limits of *his* imagination. She had corrupted him.

She liked the feeling of guilt – so different from what she had felt after almost every other sexual encounter of her life, except those with Vitya. With Vitya it had always been sublime – as if ordained. She smiled – that was a rose-tinted memory. Sometimes it had been a duty, either on her part or, less often, on his. But even then, it had been right and good. With the men since, she had felt guilty, but it was a different guilt from now. Before it had come from deep within her, a knowledge that, by her own standards, what she did was wrong – it was shame. Now it was a guilt that asked merely: what if someone knew? A breach of morality that she could suffer, even if others could not. It was a child's guilt, born out of external fear and before conscience had developed. She had not been bad, she had been naughty. She looked over at Kostya again. They had both been naughty.

She turned on to her back and gazed up towards the ceiling, but still she could see nothing. She knew she would have to leave before dawn – Kostya had told her he had appointments. Normally she wouldn't regret so speedy a parting of the ways. They'd meet again, she had no doubt, but it would end eventually. Of course, she'd heard that grand dukes and even tsars often openly kept mistresses and set them up in lavish homes. But that was decades ago. Nikolai had frowned upon it and it had fallen out of favour. There were still mistresses, but their existence was kept secret. And none would ever be as lowly as Tamara.

Not for the first time, she wondered where she was going. Most women widowed at her age would have remarried – and it was by no means too late for that. But there had been no proposals, not least because she had never put herself in a situation where a man might think such an offer would be welcome. What had driven her, ever since 1848, was the search for her parents, but she had never clearly considered what she would do when that search came to an end. If she found them, would she suddenly become part of a happy, welcoming family? It was a dream, though not an impossible one, but achieving it would not be an ending. To be an adult child within a family was a beginning; a point of departure. It would be then she would have to decide on how the remainder of her life would play out. The search for her parents was merely a deferral.

Her profession – lying here now, beside a grand duke – was also a deferral. How many more years did she have? That a man like Konstantin should find her attractive was something that became less and less likely – and men like him were a rarity anyway. She had money saved, and Konstantin had hinted that he could give her more. She did not know whether she would take it. Having wealth meant merely that she would not starve, but not to die was one thing; to live was another. To live was to have a reason to live.

She had had a reason, and it had fulfilled her utterly – to be a mother. To be a wife had been a joy, but to be a mother was a purpose. She felt a sudden urge to go there now, march across Petersburg to their home and grab Luka and run away with him, to raise him as she should have been doing all these years – as they should have raised her. Kostya would help her; he had power – the power of the entire nation, almost. He knew how much she loved her son, and he'd let nothing come between them.

She let out an audible sigh – a mournful sound. It was all a rambling dream, like finding her parents, like finding the killer of Irina Karlovna – a way of escaping from the life that she had made for herself. She looked over again at Konstantin. Many women would think of this as a dream, and one to be welcomed, and for Tamara it was – now – a reality. She had been right last night to give herself to him, to yield to the moment. A momentary escape was better than none.

She sat up and slid her feet on to the floor. It was cold. She felt around the room for her clothes and began to dress. She knew that outside the door a servant would be waiting for her, just as Konstantin had ordered him. Once she was dressed, Tamara had merely to step outside and summon his attention and he would lead her across the landing, down the stone steps, down the wooden steps, along the corridor and back out into the real world.

Dmitry had not slept. Perhaps he had. It was hard to believe that he could have lain here for so many hours without drifting into unconsciousness, but he could recall no moment of waking, and he was awake now. What he could recall were the same thoughts, echoing through his mind in a weary, predictable procession.

Svetlana lay beside him. She wasn't sleeping peacefully, but at least she slept. He'd noticed her turn many times, and occasionally heard her mutter some incoherent phrase. Once or twice his own name had emerged from somewhere in the babble that fell from her lips. He could have blamed her for keeping him awake, but it had nothing to do with that.

Even a separation of two years had not been enough to arouse his passion for her. At the first touch of her body against his, he had been reminded of Tyeplov and experienced a sense of guilt. He considered what Svetlana would think of it – a matter of such greater substance now that she lay beside him. He knew for certain that she would be horrified. Had he been unfaithful to her with another woman, she would have been upset, but she would have blamed herself.

He knew it for sure because it had happened in Warsaw. Then it had only been a kiss that Dmitry had stolen from the daughter of a brigadier. Someone had seen, and the story had got back to Svetlana. Dmitry was lucky it wasn't the girl's father who had been the recipient of the gossip. Svetlana had been angry, for sure, but in the end had said she understood. She was getting older, and though she tried her best, she knew she was not the woman she once had been. It was soon after that that she had returned to Petersburg. Dmitry suspected that she hoped he would insist on her staying, but he had been happy to see her go; not because he wanted to be free to consort with the daughters of brigadiers, but simply because he wanted to be free.

And so today he felt confident that, if he told her he had slept with another woman, she would react in a similar way. But that it had been a man – she would be disgusted. There would be no prospect of her competing, no way that she could blame it on her age and argue that once, in her youth, she could have been that muscular figure whom Dmitry had clasped to his chest. She had made her attitude plain enough, in conversations with friends about the supposed predilections of other friends. Dmitry had always been relaxed about it but he had been happy to let Svetlana have her views. She was only a woman.

Of course, even if Dmitry had told her that he had slept with a man, it would have been a lie. He had slept with a *voordalak*, although he'd had no idea of it at the time. How long would that have taken to explain to her? By the time he had told her all he knew, what had been told him by his father and what he had witnessed for himself, would she have forgotten the actual transgression? And, in the end, did it make any difference? Dmitry had not been attracted to Tyeplov as a vampire, but as a man. At least he hoped so. The idea that there was something in Tyeplov as an undead creature that had entranced Dmitry was as revolting to him as the concept of one man's attraction to another was to Svetlana. Dmitry felt a momentary impulse to go out and find another man – a verifiable human man – to sleep with, just to prove the point.

From somewhere the image of Raisa had again forced its way into his mind. In many ways she was like Svetlana; a similar figure, similar hair. Their faces were not unalike, though Raisa was prettier than Svetlana had ever been. And yet in Dmitry's mind, Raisa did not supplant Svetlana, but Tyeplov. There were no comparisons to be made between them that Dmitry could see – not of themselves – but the thrill that each had caused in him on their first meeting was similar, as was his desire for them to meet a second time. With Raisa, it would come to nothing, but at least it was a more healthy predilection.

And at that moment, Dmitry had turned away from his wife

and told her to go to sleep and that they would try again later. He'd complained that his ankle was hurting, and she'd not been so ingenuous as to ask how an ailment in that extremity could spread to the rest of his body. She had gone to sleep quickly. The problem was that thoughts of Raisa had aroused him, and he had suddenly felt that he could not betray Svetlana by using the image of another woman to hide her face from him as they made love. Now, as he lay there in the dark, he wondered if the reverse might not be true – that it was better for him to deceive her, and thereby to flatter her, by reacting to her ageing body as he would do to the younger, lither one that he pictured in his mind, and fooling her into believing it was all down to her. He knew that he would not get much pleasure from the deception, but it wasn't only about him.

Yet it should be about him. How quickly he had forgotten his new-found zest for life after escaping Sevastopol. He knew that during the siege he had been foolhardy in so many ways, trying to make his existence more exciting by toying with its abrupt ending. Now as he began to glimpse the earliest, pre-dawn light peeping through a tiny gap in the curtains, he understood. If Raisa Styepanovna found her way into his dreams, why should he reject her? If chance dictated that they met again, why should he avoid it? And if not Raisa, then why not some other beauty who was happy to offer herself to a wounded hero? Why not a dozen?

He closed his eyes and imagined the future.

Yudin loved the twilight – in the morning, before dawn, even more than in the evening. In five days' time, as dawn broke, it would mark thirty years since he had last been able to enjoy the sensation of the sun's rays upon his flesh. He had gone out that morning with no knowledge of what would befall him, but with the certainty that, whatever came his way, he could control it. The dark blue-black of the sky now was the closest he could ever again come to the sun, but his sense of mastery over events was absolute.

He sat in the arch of the window, high in the wall of the church; behind him, the snow-covered cemetery and the grave in which he would sleep. Immediately beneath him, close to

267

the outer wall of the church, lay the font, just where he had dropped it. It was empty now, but Yudin had made good use of its contents.

Ahead he looked down on the interior of the church. The candles that Mihailov had lit were burning low, but still they illuminated the nave, and caused the gilt of the iconostasis to glitter. Soon, the light of the rising sun would make them redundant, but Yudin would not be able to stay and witness it.

The drunken man from the tavern had once again crawled a little closer to the door. Viewing from high above, Yudin found his gait fascinating. Obviously most of the effort went through his arms, but even with his legs broken he had found some way to at least make use of their upper part. Where his feet could not be lifted to find purchase on the floor, somehow he achieved some little amount of grip with his inner thighs. He had struggled on like that for over a minute, before collapsing, exhausted. Yudin had watched as a pool of his own urine had spread around him. That would make it harder for him to find purchase again, once he had recovered his strength.

He was sober now, and with his wits recovered had tried calling out for help. Yudin had let him holler until he was exhausted, and now he was quiet again. There was the risk that the sound of his voice might alert the others, as they returned, that something was amiss. More likely it would whet their appetites for the meal that Mihailov had provided for them to share. They couldn't be long now. The sun would be up in twenty minutes. But the closer they left it, the better.

Yudin clutched Mihailov's body close to him. The catheter still dangled from his thigh and an occasional drop of blood would slowly form at its tip, swelling until it became too heavy to support its own weight and so breaking free to fall gracefully to the black and white tiles of the floor below. There was quite a puddle gathering there. With luck they would notice it before understanding its source. Mihailov's hands were still tied, and he had no strength to try and break his bonds. His feet were tied now too, to the end of the rope that had supported the horos. The tangle of the iron framework and the icons it supported now sat in the middle of the nave, the rope stretching up and, ultimately, leading to Mihailov's ankles. They would certainly notice that before they saw him.

It was a disappointment that Mihailov would perceive so little of what was going on. Dmitry had described in a letter how the doctors had used ether to reduce the pain as they set his ankle. In a human, Yudin supposed, there was some sense in it. Too much pain could kill a man, however strong or brave. The same was not true of a *voordalak*, and so Yudin found that, though he enjoyed their suffering less than that of a human, he could indulge himself in the infliction of it with less need for restraint. But it was time for Mihailov to recover a little. Yudin plucked the catheter from his thigh and threw it over his shoulder into the churchyard. The wound healed slowly, and blood still dripped for a few moments, but at last the tiny puncture sealed itself. Now, as Mihailov's body continued to manufacture blood, it would at least be of benefit to him. But he would not grow strong enough to be a danger to Yudin – not before dawn.

The building began to shake, not violently, but enough to make Yudin tighten his grip on Mihailov. It was only a train passing on the track nearby, something that Russians – the whole world – would have to get accustomed to. Again it reminded him that the city outside was awakening.

'I take it they'll be coming here,' he whispered in Mihailov's ear.

'They'll come,' said Mihailov sleepily. 'They like to leave it late.'

'Proving to each other how brave they are.'

'I suppose,' said Mihailov. Yudin put a hand to his cheek. Already it was a little warmer, and the colour was returning. Yudin would have to be careful. He glanced sideways and verified that his knife was to hand.

They certainly did leave it late. It was only a few minutes before sunrise when Yudin heard a key rattle in the door and the two other vampires entered. Between them they carried a bundle that might be mistaken for many things, but that Yudin could easily guess was a body – unconscious, but not dead. Tyeplov was instantly recognizable by his height, even before Yudin could clearly see his face, and so by elimination the other creature was Ignatyev.

'Take that down, quickly,' said Tyeplov, dropping his end of the body. Ignatyev began to drag the load towards the stairs of the crypt. Only then did Tyeplov turn and see the state of the church.

He surveyed the scene for a moment, not looking up towards where Yudin was perched, and then shouted.

'Mihailov!'

Mihailov stirred in Yudin's arms, but did not respond. Tyeplov approached the body of the drunk, still close to the iconostasis. The man's face was to the floor. Tyeplov prodded it with the toe of his boot. The man awoke suddenly and tried to stand; only as he felt the pain shooting through his legs did he remember that he could not. He wailed incoherently and pointed upwards, straight towards where Yudin and Mihailov were perched, where he had earlier watched Yudin make his preparations.

Fortunately Tyeplov's wrath denied him the chance of learning anything that might be useful. He kicked the drunk hard in the temple and the man's head flipped in an instant to one side. Yudin fancied he heard the click of his neck breaking. He certainly remained quite still after that. It was a pity to see him put out of his misery so swiftly.

'Put that down,' said Tyeplov. Ignatyev dropped the bundle he had been dragging and came over. The two of them stared at what was the most obvious incongruity in the church: the fallen horos. As though they were marionettes, controlled by the same set of strings, their heads rose in unison to follow the rope that still stretched upwards from the horos and towards the ceiling. Yudin had little time now. He reached for his knife and, holding Mihailov's head with a hand across his mouth, used the sharp, parallel blades to cut into his throat. Normally with a vampire it was an insipid form of torture; either the wound would heal or the head would be severed and the creature would die. But with Mihailov weakened as he was, although the wound would heal, it would heal slowly. Yudin cut right back until he felt bone. It was all quite unnecessary, but it added piquancy. For the others to see one of their own kind unable to repair such a horrible wound would introduce one more stratum of fear.

Throughout, Yudin kept his eyes on the two vampires below. In the time it had taken him to cut Mihailov's throat they had traced the rope to an anchor at the apex of the church's ceiling, then followed it down, across the emptiness beneath the vault to where Yudin sat.

As their eyes fell upon him Yudin pushed Mihailov away. The body swung in a slight ellipse, going out just to the right of its pivot in the ceiling and coming back an equal distance to the left. The head, inverted, was almost exactly at the level of the *voordalaki* standing beneath. All the way, it spewed out blood from the gaping wound to its throat, not a huge amount, for it could not manufacture very much, but sufficient for both to be splattered with a little of it as it passed. As they watched its graceful orbit, they didn't appear to notice Yudin, still at the window. That would come.

'Don't just stand there; get him down!' shouted Tyeplov. Ignatyev raced over to where the rope was fastened to the horos and started to chew at it with his fangs. Tyeplov grabbed at Mihailov to try and stop his motion, and perhaps bring him down. The only effect this had was to tear open the wound at Mihailov's neck, and Tyeplov let go, as if stung. Mihailov began a new orbit, a different ellipse, but around the same centre.

Yudin could sense now that sunrise was very close. Those below would know it too, distracted though they were, but would not fear it too much inside the building, with the crypt so close. Yudin pictured the Earth turning in space and remembered a recent experiment he had read of, conducted by a Frenchman named Foucault who had used the movement of the plane of a pendulum as the day passed to demonstrate the Earth's rotation. It would have appealed to both sides of Yudin's character to stay and watch Mihailov's body precess around the nave of the church, but there were other laws of nature that prevented it.

'Prometheus!' he shouted. The vampire turned and looked straight at him. There was recognition in his eyes, not just of Yudin's face but also of his handiwork. Their stares locked for only a moment, but it was all that Yudin required.

He dropped down into the churchyard, his feet kicking occasionally against the wall to slow his descent. As soon as he hit the ground he began to run. He only needed to go a little way before he reached the vault. Where he had earlier dug at the earth, a brick arch was revealed, like the upper part of the eye of a toad, peering out of a bog. He slipped inside and peeped through the opening, back in the direction he had come. He had chosen this tomb in particular because it was due east of the church. Thus when the sun rose, it would be behind him. He would be protected from it by the back wall of the vault, but would still be able to see its effects before him.

Seconds later, the sun did rise. Yudin could see the shadows of the graves as it cast them against the side of the church. Higher up the wall, free of shadow, the sun's illumination was clear, as it was upon the church's wooden roof.

It was Mihailov's screams that Yudin heard first, if only by a fraction of a second. His throat must have healed well for him to be able to make such a noise. He wondered if they had managed to get him down. If so, his sudden agony would be even more bewildering to them.

It was only a moment later that the roof erupted in flame. It was soaked in Mihailov's blood. Yudin had dragged the font right to the very top and emptied it down the slope. The snow had soaked it up, red streaks running through it like a raspberry sauce on an iced dessert. It was all to the good, holding the blood in place. Some made it down to the gutters, but at this time of year the drains were blocked with ice, so it could not escape. The blood itself would have frozen quickly, but that would make no difference to the sun's effect on it.

As the blood began to boil and combust, Mihailov would feel the pain as though it were still running in his own veins. It was a trick Yudin had employed more than once before, but in those cases the amount of blood involved had been just a smear. Here, with the entire body's blood supply exposed to the sunlight in a single instant, the pain would be unimaginable. Yudin could only guess that it would be the equivalent of walking into the daylight and exposing one's body. Except that in that case pain would end in moments with death. Here it would last, until all the blood had burned.

Only then would follow the full exposure to the sun's rays.

That stage was almost upon them. Yudin could see from the colour and height of the flames on the church roof that it was now mostly wood that was burning, rather than blood. From within, Mihailov's screams had subsided. When, Yudin wondered, would they realize? They must be aware by now that the roof was ablaze. They wouldn't dare leave – it was far too light outside. They would make for the crypt, hoping that the flames would not penetrate so far down. Only then would they discover the door blocked. Perhaps they would break through, perhaps not. Yudin cared little.

With a huge crunch, part of the roof caved in. Yudin heard a scream, loud but suddenly curtailed. It could have been any of them. Then another segment collapsed. Now the whole of the nave would be filled with light. He imagined them in there, scrabbling for any bit of shadow, fighting among themselves for a dark corner where the sun did not penetrate. They might find something, but it would not stay safe. The sun would move throughout the day, and what had been in shadow would be restored to light and what had lurked therein would be no more. It was just a shame that the sun was so low in the sky at this time of year.

Yudin stood and watched until almost midday, when the sun at last became a danger to him. The hue and cry was soon raised, and groups of men came and threw water on the fire. They managed to put it out, but it would have consumed itself eventually. None of the men went inside – they would be afraid of the walls collapsing. It happened a little later; the eastern wall fell inwards, no longer able to lean against the roof. Yudin slunk back into the tomb. There were two coffins in there, and he lay between them to sleep.

It had been fun – much better than anything he had planned at the beginning of the night. That couple with their little child would have come nowhere near it. But there had been a purpose to it as well. It was a warning. Why warn creatures that would minutes later be dead? Why not kill them more simply and more certainly? The answer was straightforward. It was none of the three *voordalaki* who had perished in that church that he was attempting to warn, but a fourth such creature, many versts away.

Zmyeevich could see through Tyeplov's eyes, and Tyeplov through his. That was how Tyeplov had known where to locate Yudin – and Raisa and Dmitry. And that meant that Zmyeevich

273

would have seen all of this, and heard it, and hopefully felt it. He needed reminding of just how resourceful an opponent Yudin could be. It would be no more than a bee sting to him; but it might make him keep away from bees.

But as Yudin fell into slumber, there was one question that still puzzled him. Tyeplov had brought the others to Moscow because he had known that Yudin was there. Tyeplov had known because, through their joined minds, Zmyeevich had told him. But that was not the end of the chain, only a link in it.

Zmyeevich might have informed Tyeplov, but how did Zmyeevich know?

1856

CHAPTER XVI

DMITRY REMINDED HIMSELF OF HIS FATHER. HE ITCHED TO BE in Moscow again. He yearned for it. And soon he would be there. Aleksei had been just the same, although at first Dmitry had been too young to realize it. As a boy, he'd been sad whenever his father had left their home in Petersburg, but he'd understood that it was necessary. Aleksei had hugged him, and kissed Marfa, and promised to write and promised to be home as soon as he could possibly manage, and to a growing boy it had all appeared genuine.

It was only on that last trip, in 1825, when Dmitry had been eighteen and off to join the cavalry and he and his father had travelled down together, that he understood the truth. Although Aleksei had displayed the same emotions as ever to Marfa when they left – and she had been sadder still for also losing a son – once they were en route, Aleksei had cheered up no end. As they arrived in the city, Aleksei had been scarcely able to contain his enthusiasm. Then, of course, his father had had to put up with a journey of four days on the stagecoach, whereas Dmitry could achieve it in less than one. There was something to be said for the old ways, though. He remembered the coach taking them right into the heart of the city and how Aleksei had chattered incessantly, pointing out every sight. The train's approach, though faster, came through the dreary outskirts, and would deposit its passengers on the very rim of civilization. There was nothing to tantalize Dmitry, except in his own mind.

Even back then, in 1825, Dmitry had known the primary reason for Aleksei's zeal. He had a mistress in the city, a former prostitute by the name of Domnikiia. It was Yudin who had warned Dmitry of her existence. At the time, he despised his father for it, and hated the woman more. Eventually – thankfully before he and Aleksei had parted for ever – he had grown to see that his father's weaknesses vanished to nothing when set beside his strengths. And as Dmitry had grown older he had learned that few men were in a position to judge their fellows. Dmitry was not one of the few.

The train was slowing now. Dmitry looked out of the window at the buildings rolling past. Some were familiar, others less so. They passed the remains of a church – no more than a burnt-out ruin – and Dmitry tried to remember whether it had been like that when he left, at the end of the previous year. Whatever the changes, this was Moscow. He didn't stand yet, but sat up a little straighter, his cane pressed between his knees. His ankle was almost healed now, but he kept the stick as an affectation. He could even pedal at the piano, though it would ache if he forgot himself and played for too long. That would pass.

But whatever reasons Dmitry might personally have to embrace the future with excited anticipation, he was not alone in his optimism. It was mid-March now and spring was here – not just as a season of the year, but for the whole of Europe; the whole of the world.

The war was over. Many – himself included – had said it was over on that terrible day in August when the French had taken the Malakhov, but it had gone on a little longer in the eyes of the leaders of Russia, Britain and France. The last major action, an attempt by the Russians to retake southern Sevastopol, had failed in January. February had seen an armistice and a peace conference opening in Paris. The latest news was that a treaty would be signed within days. The terms were intended more to humiliate Russia than to enfeeble her. The loss of southern Bessarabia was a petty territorial adjustment. The destruction of the Black Sea fleet was an unprecedented act of vindictiveness. But neither of them justified a war so long, so bloody and so brutal. At least the French emperor had what he wanted: revenge for Russia's humiliation of his uncle, four decades before. But in the end, for all sides, peace was a greater booty than any territorial gain. Peace was what Russia needed; what Europe needed.

But in that regard, there was one new cloud on the horizon. Napoleon III, warmonger and self-appointed emperor of the French, now had a son to continue his dynasty. He had, of course, been named Napoleon. One day, just like his father and his great-uncle before him, he would grow up to plunge the whole of Europe into a pointless war. Dmitry felt sure of it. He wondered if he would live to see the day.

He was old already; older than he had been three days ago. That had been his birthday; his forty-ninth. He'd stayed in Petersburg just long enough to celebrate it with Svetlana. Then he had been off to Moscow, feeling as though he were nothing like that old, and with a wealth of ideas for how to prove it – ideas and an enthusiasm that he wished he had possessed as a younger man. He'd landed a convenient posting – a place on a committee to organize the cavalry parades for His Majesty's forthcoming coronation. It was the best he could hope for with his injury, but it meant he would be in Moscow. Just as his father had been drawn to the old capital, so now was he.

And, of course, back in 1825 there had been one other reason that Aleksei was so thrilled to return to Moscow – one of which, at the time, Dmitry had been totally unaware. If he had, back then, known of that reason – that person – he would have despised her perhaps more than he did her mother. Thankfully, Dmitry had changed. Aleksei had travelled to the old capital to visit his daughter, and now Dmitry would be able to visit his sister. In each case, it was the same individual: Tamara Valentinovna.

The year so far had been busy. The end of the war, though not yet formalized, allowed the passions of the soldier to be directed more towards his fellow woman than against his fellow man. For the most part, Tamara had managed to avoid being the object of that passion herself, but had still found her time fully occupied organizing the other girls, buying wine, vodka and food for the clients, stocking up on willow leaves as a prevention and penny-royal as a cure. Over the whole year she had been at Degtyarny Lane, there had been only three suspected pregnancies. Most of the girls used a pessary soaked in vinegar in addition to the willow leaves. Some of them had their own methods, but where possible, Tamara ensured that those were additional to what she told them to use. She'd learned it herself from Vitya – a doctor naturally knew these things – when they'd decided that with three children their family was perfect and complete.

Of the three girls who had fallen pregnant, one had proved to have been imagining it, and one had been dealt with successfully using pennyroyal. The third had gone back to her family to bear the child, and had returned to work within two months, explaining that she had left the little boy in the care of her sister. Tamara hoped she could believe it.

It was only Raisa who made no specific efforts at all towards avoiding the risk that came with her profession. Tamara had asked her about it.

'I can't,' Raisa said.

'Can't take willow leaf?' Tamara replied.

'Can't have children.'

'You're sure?'

Raisa had nodded sadly. Tamara grasped her hand. 'I became pregnant when I was very young,' Raisa continued. 'My father was horrified. He sent a woman to me. She removed the baby – and more besides.' Raisa had looked up at Tamara and blinked, but no tears formed in her eyes. 'It's a blessing in this job,' she concluded. Tamara couldn't imagine anything more awful.

Today though, for the first time in many months, Tamara had managed to go back to the archives and continue her research. There was a specific reason for it – a note from Gribov telling her he had discovered something. It seemed he had taken pity on her, watching her plough through the reams of paper with little success, and had asked her who and what most interested her. She had drawn a blank on Aleksei, but her visit to Petersburg had brought up the name of Vasiliy Denisovich Makarov, so she'd asked Gribov if he could follow that up. Then, for want of any other names, she had mentioned to him Natalia Borisovna Papanova, the old woman who had first set Tamara down the path of investigating the original murder at Degtyarny Lane – the one in 1812.

It was a fine afternoon when Gribov met her beside the tapestry behind which the stairs to the archives descended. A little snow remained, scattered in a few patches around the Kremlin, but it seemed that spring was truly upon them. He picked up a lamp and led her down the steps, along the dark, low corridor and, once they had entered the library, to a table where several papers had been laid out.

'You don't come up with easy requests, Madame Komarova.'

'You wouldn't have it any other way,' she teased.

'I do enjoy a challenge,' he said, allowing a rare hint of emotion to creep into his voice. 'Let us deal first with Vasiliy Denisovich Makarov.'

'Yes?'

'A difficult man to find. We have no official record of him. That is to say "we" as the Third Section or any of its predecessors.'

'So he's never been political.'

'Not that we suspected. I can find no record of his birth, and only a few mentions of him on a number of commercial invoices and legal documents. The earliest is in Petersburg,' he said, handing her a rental agreement for a building.

'When?' she asked, without really looking at it.

'1812.'

She bit her bottom lip and considered. 'He must have been an adult then. That would make him in his sixties now – at least.'

'Had he lived,' said Gribov. Tamara felt deflated. Gribov replaced the document in her hand with another. 'I say he had not been suspected of political activity, but I did find this. It's from an interview with a Decembrist rebel.' He pointed to about halfway down the page of small, tight handwriting. Tamara read:

The prisoner was asked to comment on reports of him being seen on the Great Neva, comforting a man who appeared to have been shot. The prisoner replied that the man had been shot, but had not died, and that his name was Vasiliy Denisovich Makarov. The prisoner was asked if Makarov had been with the rebels and responded that he had been, adding that he had been one of those keenest to bring about the death of Nikolai Pavlovich. The prisoner's claim of Makarov's survival contradicts other witness testimony which states he fell beneath the ice. No trace of Makarov, alive or dead, has been found.

'The witnesses were wrong,' said Tamara. 'He's still collecting rent for properties in Saint Petersburg.'

'Interesting,' said Gribov, at his most non-committal.

'Who was the prisoner being interviewed?' asked Tamara.

'I'm glad you asked that.' Gribov flicked back through the document and showed her the cover.

Tamara clicked her tongue in wonder at what she saw.

15 February 1826
Commandant's Office
Peter and Paul Fortress
Interview with Colonel Aleksei Ivanovich Danilov

'I never saw this,' she said.

'It was misfiled,' he explained.

'I have to read it all.'

'Now?'

Tamara said nothing. She had already sat down and pulled the lamp towards her. Her eyes began scanning back and forth across the pages.

'I'll leave you to it.'

Tamara scarcely noticed him depart. It took her only ten minutes to read the short document, but she read it through again immediately. There was no mention of any of the murders – not even the one that Aleksei had witnessed outside the Maly Theatre, but that would have been more than she could hope for. There was only one further mention of Makarov, when the interrogator asked how Aleksei knew him. Aleksei said that he had only encountered him a few times, at meetings of the Northern Society. It seemed to Tamara like a lie, but the interrogator chose to accept it.

Aleksei was also asked about his son, Dmitry. Tamara thought back. Dmitry would have been just eighteen then. Aleksei denied that his son had anything to do with the uprising, even though the boy had been in Petersburg at the time. Again the interrogator accepted this. Here there was a note added in the margin: *P. M. V. confirms.*

There was no mistaking the initials: Pyetr Mihailovich Volkonsky, the man who had watched over her and paid for her upkeep until his death four years before. For whatever reason, it seemed he had been watching over Dmitry too.

Overall though, despite there being little useful information in the interview, Tamara sensed that she was beginning to get a feeling for the sort of man Danilov was. She pictured him as looking like Dmitry. He came across as very brave, very clever, and an out-and-out liar. He'd clearly been tortured. She already knew what the Decembrists had suffered, and although the document was not specific, it made a few mentions of pauses in the interview, after which it was hoped Aleksei would be a little more willing to talk. He told them nothing that they couldn't easily discover by other means. Only that one assertion – that Makarov was not dead – stepped outside of what he could be sure was already known.

He refused to denounce any of the other rebels, except one, Kakhovsky, who he said had shot Governor Miloradovich. Tamara remembered that Kakhovsky was one of only five Decembrists sentenced to death for their crimes. Aleksei was even asked about the poet Pushkin, but denied his involvement, though with none of the condemnation he had expressed when saying the same thing about his own son.

She wished she had been there. She'd have done a better job than whoever it was had actually spoken to Aleksei; the rumour was that Tsar Nikolai himself had carried out all the interrogations. She'd have followed up on so many of the answers that just didn't seem to make sense. Even so, she couldn't be sure she'd have been smart enough to catch Aleksei out, certainly not on this new question: had Dmitry in fact been a Decembrist, just like his father? She was surprised how little she cared about the answer.

She left the document on the table from where Gribov had fetched it and went back along the winding, dark route to the surface and to Gribov's office.

'Thank you very much, Arkadiy Osipovich,' she said. 'That was very interesting.'

'I thought you'd like it. But I don't suppose it helps in the main line of your research.'

'No.'

'There was one other name you were interested in.'

'Yes?'

'Natalia Borisovna Papanova – the daughter of a cobbler, you said, I think.'

'That's right.'

'I found a record of her marriage, in 1816, to a man named Bazhenov – Ilya Vladimirovich, also a cobbler. There's an address.'

'Show me,' said Tamara, holding out her hand.

'It's forty years out of date.'

'These people don't move,' she said, though she knew less of the life of a cobbler than she did of . . . a grand duke. Gribov handed over the paper. 'Thank you again,' she said.

Could he have betrayed me? It was the first thought on Yudin's mind as Dmitry sat down opposite him. They were at Testov's, where Yudin was finally making good his promise to take Dmitry out to dinner. It was always a useful ruse, as Yudin had discovered over the years – no one expected to see a *voordalak* in a crowded public place, nobody expected to see one eating fish or drinking wine. He doubted the possibility had ventured into the furthest extremity of Dmitry's mind, but it was ploys like this that stopped it from getting even that far. But Dmitry might have other, more concrete reasons to suspect Yudin; that was what this dinner was all about. As for the wine, that would pass through Yudin's body easily enough. The food he would throw up later, when he was alone.

They had not met since Yudin's encounter at the church with his former captives. That was the cause of his suspicion of Dmitry. There were two reasons behind it. The first was obvious; that the vampires had gone to seek out Aleksei's son in Sevastopol. Mihailov said they had been rebuffed, but it could easily have been a lie. The second reason was more subtle: somehow, Zmyeevich had known of Yudin's whereabouts – his new identity. Not many people could associate Yudin with any of his former aliases. Only two, in fact: Raisa and Dmitry. Raisa was not beyond suspicion – Yudin was no fool – but today it was Dmitry who sat before him.

'I must say, you're looking very healthy,' said Dmitry, interrupting his thoughts. It was an accurate observation. Yudin had not starved himself in preparation for this meeting as much as he should. He looked younger than when the two of them had last met. But it was the least of his concerns.

'As do you,' he replied. 'Your ankle must be almost healed now.'

'I still feel the occasional twinge. Hence the stick.'

'I'm sure you'll soon be your old self.'

'Old indeed,' laughed Dmitry. 'I'll be fifty next year.'

'Fifty? Really? Lyosha's little boy that I dandled on my knee.' Dmitry grinned, but Yudin instantly regretted saying it. It was not wise to remind Dmitry of just how old he really was. But it did allow him to turn the conversation down his chosen path. 'By the way, Mitka, there's something I meant to ask you. Nothing important, just a little strange.'

'Fire away.'

Yudin did his best to sound hesitant. 'I came across a letter – in the course of my work – from years ago. Ancient history now, but it referred to someone by a sort of nickname, and I'm trying to find out who the man was, and I'm wondering if it might possibly have been your father.'

'What was the nickname?'

'It's silly . . . and a little offensive, to be honest.' Dmitry looked at him with his head on one side, telling him not to be so delicate. 'Did you ever hear of anyone,' continued Yudin, 'calling him the three-fingered man?'

Dmitry hesitated for just a moment before replying, but it was enough for Yudin to know that the phrase meant something. 'Odd you should say that,' was his reply.

'Odd?' asked Yudin. 'Why?'

'Someone used that exact phrase in Sevastopol. An old friend of Papa's.'

'An old friend?'

'Well, the son of an old friend. What was this letter about?'

The phrase had come from Mihailov's lips, not from a letter, but it was easy for Yudin to extemporize. He lowered his voice. 'The Decembrists.'

Dmitry nodded sombrely. 'We were both lucky – luckier than Papa.'

'Lucky thanks to him. Anyway, what was your friend's name – in Sevastopol?'

'Tyeplov,' said Dmitry without hesitation.

So it was true that Tyeplov had spoken to Dmitry – though that much had never been in doubt. The real question was what, if anything, he had told Dmitry about Yudin – whether he had even identified him as the object of their vengeance. He tried a different tack.

'How is Svetlana Nikitichna?' he asked.

'She's fine. She's fine. She asked after you.'

Now to dangle the bait. 'You know who she reminds me of?'

'Who?'

'Raisa Styepanovna.' There was some superficial resemblance – it was enough to bring her into the conversation; to bring her into Dmitry's life.

'Really?'

Yudin nodded. '*She* asked after *you*, by the way.' It was almost true. She had told Yudin how she had flirted with Dmitry – how he had, however subtly, responded.

'I only met her once.'

'You made quite an impression.'

'Really?' asked Dmitry.

Raisa had evidently judged his reaction well; she knew her business. But Dmitry still had to be played. Yudin laughed a little. 'I shouldn't have said anything.'

'Why not?'

'My dear Mitka – you're a happily married man.'

'And why shouldn't I be even happier?' It was meant as a joke, or at least disguised as one.

'Mitka!' Yudin's tone was meant to scold – he'd spent years building up his image with Dmitry as a surrogate father; he could not drop that too willingly.

'I'm sorry, Vasya. I shouldn't tease you,' said Dmitry before changing the subject. 'I still can't fathom why you never married.'

'I think we both know the answer to that,' said Yudin softly.

'Because of Mama?' Dmitry's response was in the same tone.

Yudin sighed. 'It could never be.' It was astonishing that Dmitry had not the slightest inkling that Yudin had been screwing his mother since her son had been – what? – eleven years old. He thought too much of her to think her capable of it. And that high opinion rubbed off on Yudin.

'Not even after Papa went into exile?'

'They were still married.'

'He took his lover with him.'

'That would not have made it right. We saw things differently, your father and I. As do you and I.'

'Would you despise me, if I were unfaithful to Svetlana?' asked Dmitry earnestly.

Yudin gave the appearance of thinking for a moment, but in truth every move was planned in advance. 'I would forgive you,' he said. Dmitry smiled. Yudin sat back upright in his chair, his mood now lighter. 'But anyway,' he said, 'I don't quite think that it would be Raisa Styepanovna who would steal a man like you away from his wife.'

Dmitry was disappointed. 'Really? Not that kind of girl, I suppose.'

Yudin laughed loudly. 'Oh, quite that kind of girl, I assure you, Mitka. But I don't think *that* kind of girl is *your* kind of girl.'

'I don't get you.'

Yudin lowered his voice. 'Mitka – to call her a courtesan would be to pay her a lavish compliment. For a small fee she will go with any man and let him do whatever he wishes to her.'

'You're joking!' Dmitry flushed as he spoke.

It was hard to discern whether it was out of embarrassment or excitement. Yudin guessed a mixture of the two.

'She works in a house up on Degtyarny Lane.'

Dmitry looked at him slyly. 'How do you know all this, Vasya?'

Yudin made an effort to seem flustered. 'Let me assure you, Mitka – I have never, *would* never . . .' He petered out, pleased with his understated performance.

'God, no. I know. I'm sorry. I was just teasing.'

'As you know, I work for the government. Since we have these establishments, they must be regulated; yellow tickets to be issued and so forth. But whenever I can, I try to persuade these girls to leave such places – and I pray for their souls every night.'

'I wouldn't expect any less, Vasya. And thank you – for the warning.'

Yudin smiled warmly. Dmitry was much like his father, and it was in that very establishment that Aleksei had first met his paramour, Domnikiia. Dmitry would be no different. He would be ashamed for fear that Yudin found out, but he would go there all the same. And Raisa would be ready for him. Dmitry would lay his tortured soul at her feet and, when morning came, Raisa would gather it up and bring it to Yudin to examine.

They were entering the endgame, the culmination of a plan – not even that, merely a conceit – that had formed in Yudin's mind long ago as he had gazed for the first time upon the innocent face of a five-year-old boy. Now all that mattered was to ensure that Aleksei found out.

CHAPTER XVII

TAMARA HAD ONCE AGAIN BEEN SUMMONED TO PETERSBURG, once again at the behest of Grand Duke Konstantin, but she had a few days to prepare for her trip and there was one particular visit she wanted to make before leaving. The address Gribov had given her for Natalia Borisovna was in Zamoskvorechye, at the southern end of Little Ordynka Street. There were half a dozen cobblers' shops, all huddled together on the eastern side of the road. The address that Gribov had given her was one of them, but the shopkeeper had not heard of Natalia Borisovna, not by her maiden name or her married name; neither had he heard of her husband.

Tamara tried the other shops without success, but just as she left the final one and was about to give up, a woman came out of the first and ran up to her.

'Is it you that's looking for Ilya Vladimirovich Bazhenov?'

'That's right,' said Tamara.

'My husband's an idiot.'

'You do know him, then?'

'No, but we know Oleg Ilyich Bazhenov.'

'His son?' asked Tamara. The woman shrugged. 'Where is he?'

'He has a shop in Ordynsky Lane, just there.' She pointed up the street to where another road cut across it. 'Number four.'

Tamara thanked her and walked up in the direction she had been shown. She found number four easily. It was a locksmith's.

'Oleg Ilyich?' she enquired of the man who stood behind the counter with a welcoming smile and a dirty leather apron.

'Indeed I am. How may I be of service?'

'I'm looking for your mother. At least, I think I am.' He was in his late thirties, which would fit with his mother having married in 1816.

'My . . . mother?'

'Natalia Borisovna Bazhenova – Papanova before she was married.'

'That's certainly my mother,' he replied. 'What about her?'

'I wanted to talk to her; about 1812.'

'1812?'

'Yes – do you think she'd talk to me about it?'

'You mean about the occupation?'

'Around then.'

He smiled wistfully, pausing in happy recollection before speaking. 'We could never get her to stop. I remember all her stories. She used to go on and on when we were children. About the French. About the fires. She and her father lost their home. They had to live in a churchyard.'

'It must have been dreadful.'

'They managed. Anything to beat the French – not like these days. She had a brother who died at Borodino – Fyodor.' He smiled again. 'And then there were her two captains.'

'Captains?'

'She rescued them from a fire. One of them was quite badly injured, but she nursed him back to health. I think she was quite taken by him, but she never admitted it – not to him or to us. Petrenko – that was his name.'

'Petrenko.' It was a name she had heard, not so long ago, on Dmitry's lips. It was too ridiculous for there to be a connection – and yet she felt certain there was.

'That's right. Can't remember the other fellow's name. She didn't mention him half as much. Began with a D.'

Tamara almost hoped she would be wrong, but had to offer the suggestion. 'Danilov?'

'Danilov!' He pointed to her as he acknowledged the suggestion, and didn't notice the shiver that ran down her spine. 'Captain Petrenko and Captain Danilov. She helped them to get out of town – give the French the slip so they could come back fighting all the stronger. And they did.'

'Did she ever mention a murder around then?'

'Murder? There was a bloody war on.'

'This was after the French left. In Degtyarny Lane.'

'Where's that then?' he asked.

'Up north. Off Tverskaya Street.'

He shook his head. 'She never mentioned anything like that.'

Tamara had come to speak to Natalia Borisovna in person, and was still tempted to ask if she was there, but it was easy to guess the truth from the way her son spoke of her. 'When did she die?' Tamara asked instead.

Oleg gave her half a glance and half a smile, acknowledging that she had deduced what he had never stated. 'You ever meet her?'

Tamara nodded and smiled broadly, she hoped convincingly, though she'd felt no affection for the woman during their brief encounter. 'She was quite a character.'

He nodded. 'It's been a long time. 1846 she died. Can't complain. She's up at St Clement's if you want to pay your respects.'

'Thank you,' said Tamara. 'I will.'

She didn't. What would be the point? There was no reason to doubt Oleg's word that his mother lay there, nor to doubt his assertion that she had died ten years before. And so unless she had somehow risen from the grave, the woman that Tamara had met just one year ago was not Natalia Borisovna Bazhenova.

'In a way, I'm sorry you've come.'

Raisa sat on her bed, wearing now only her undergarments – linen pantalettes that went down to her ankles, and a tight corset that was the secret behind both her waistline and her bust. She gazed at the floor as she spoke, her voice meek and contemplative.

Dmitry sat on the bed beside her and placed his hand on her thigh, but immediately withdrew, feeling he was being too forward.

'I'll go, if you like,' he said.

She turned to him and clasped his hand, staring into his eyes. 'No. I didn't mean that. Please. It's just that . . .'

'What?' He almost laughed at her discomfort, but restrained himself.

'I'd been looking forward to it.'

Dmitry had been looking forward to it too, and still was, but he suspected that so flippant an answer would not be welcomed. She was not referring to quite the same thing. 'To what?' he asked.

'To being wooed by you.'

He smiled – partly in amusement at her romantic simplicity, partly flattered by the fact she had hoped for more from him than from her other clients. He wished now that he had been more patient, more trusting of what he had seen in her when they first met than what he had heard of her since.

'I think it's too late for that now,' she added.

'Why?'

'Because the thrill of the chase is lost if you know that conquest is already assured.'

'I can't change that,' he said.

'It's not your fault. It was impossible from the moment you found out about me. Who was it told you? Tamara?'

'Goodness no!' exclaimed Dmitry. 'I hardly think she'd approve.'

'Tamara?' Raisa laughed delightfully. 'You do know she works here too?'

Dmitry felt himself redden. His stomach knotted. 'Tamara?' His sister? And yet how like her mother. It was a strange consolation.

'Oh, not like I do. Tamara's the boss. What she says goes.'

'I never guessed.' Then an entirely different horror filled him. 'You won't tell her I came, will you?'

'Why on earth should that matter?'

It was a question that Dmitry could not answer even to himself. He had taken this revelation of his sister's profession in his stride, so why should he fear her opprobrium at his coming here? He said nothing. It was farcical. One day, perhaps, he could see them together laughing at it.

'She's away just now, but she'll find out,' continued Raisa. 'Even if I don't tell her, some of the other girls have seen you.'

'They don't know my name.'

'They'll describe you. You're quite . . . distinctive.' She leaned forward and kissed his lips lightly, but pulled back before he could respond. 'So it was Vasiliy Innokyentievich who told you?'

Dmitry nodded.

'He probably thinks you'll charge in here and rescue me from all this.'

'I could,' said Dmitry.

'I don't want rescuing.'

'Why not?'

She smiled salaciously. 'Guess,' she replied. Dmitry felt the desire for her beginning to fill his body. He leaned forward to kiss her, but she had already turned her back to him. 'Would you like to untie me?' she asked.

Her corset was neatly fastened at the back with laces of brightly coloured blue silk, contrasting with the creamy white linen. A double bow tied at the top kept it secure, pressed hard against her back. He had to pull it away from her body to get at the knot, tightening the lacing even more as he did so.

'Ow!' she giggled. 'Aren't I thin enough for you?'

'Sorry,' said Dmitry. He finally got the knot loose and began to unlace the garment all the way down. When it was entirely undone, Raisa pulled it off and threw it on to the floor. Viewed from behind, her figure seemed as perfect in its natural condition as it had been when shaped by the stiff bones of the corset. He slid his arms around her waist and pulled her close to him, pressing his face into her neck and smelling her – though detecting only the scent of her *eau de toilette*. He raised his hands and cupped them around her breasts, noting the slight shiver of her body as he touched them. There too, it seemed, her underclothing had needed to do little to improve upon nature.

They remained like that for a few moments before she pulled away from him and stood up, still with her back to him. She quickly stepped out of her pantalettes, revealing a delightful posterior perched atop her long, tapering legs. Finally she raised her hand to her head and, removing a number of clips and hairpins, allowed her hair to cascade in golden waves down her back, threatening, but never quite managing, to hide her charming bottom.

She turned and smiled at him. She looked angelic, almost to the degree that it would be a sin to even touch her. But sin was the entire purpose of Dmitry's visit. He sat and gazed for an eternity.

He felt sure his mouth had dropped open, but he had no strength to close it.

'Don't you feel overdressed?' she asked.

Dmitry was stung into action, and quickly remedied the situation. Soon he was out of his overcoat and jacket and shirt and sitting topless on the bed, reaching forward towards his boot. She squatted down in front of him.

'Let me,' she said.

He sat up and extended his left leg. Raisa grasped the boot and pulled it off smoothly – his ankle was healed enough that he didn't need laces now. She moved on to his right foot, and as she tugged at it she twisted slightly, sending a shot of pain through his injured ankle, from which Dmitry drew a perverse enjoyment. He suspected she had done it deliberately, and the look in her eye, fixed on his as she did it, gave him no reason to change his opinion.

Once Dmitry's boots were off, Raisa climbed on to the bed, lying on her side with her head resting in her hand, displaying the full beauty of her body. Her eyes never left Dmitry as he removed the remainder of his clothing. When he was as naked as she was, he lay down on the bed beside her, mirroring her pose.

She moved her leg towards him and ran her instep down his calf, pressing a little harder as she came to his ankle. Dmitry winced, but again saw the fire in her eyes as she caused him pain.

'That must hurt,' she said, giggling at the same time.

'Not when you do it.'

'Oh?' she said disappointedly. 'What about that?' As she spoke, she stamped her foot against his, just below where the bullet had hit. Pain shot up Dmitry's calf and thigh and mingled with the more predictable sensations they found there, amplifying both. For a moment he was reminded of Tyeplov, and the pleasure they had shared taking potshots at the French infantry with a stolen rifle from the White Works. He dismissed the thought from his mind.

He grinned and pushed her back on to the bed, climbing on top of her. Her smile suddenly faded to a look of concern.

'I'm sorry,' she said. 'I shouldn't make light of it like that. It must have been terrible in Sevastopol.'

Again, he rejected the obvious memory. 'I made it out of there,' he said. 'That's better than many.'

'Do you want to tell me?'

It seemed like a bizarre question from a woman to a man who was poised above her, his mind intent on one thing only, almost as if it was meant to distract him. But he was surprised to realize just how much he did want to talk about it, and to talk to her about it. She understood him better than he did himself – but she must have been with many soldiers.

'Later,' he said.

She nodded and blinked, then reached out and put her arms around his back and pulled him down towards her.

It was spectacular.

'For your birthday,' said Konstantin. He crawled across the bed and kissed the back of her shoulder.

Tamara looked at the necklace. There were five large stones, pink with a hint of blue, each surrounded by clusters of what she could only guess were diamonds. The settings were silver, as was the chain.

'That's not till Wednesday,' she replied.

'I won't be able to see you on Wednesday.'

She was surprised how sad the thought of not being with him made her. 'Where will you be?'

He chuckled, and she took it to be a reprimand, but a gentle one. 'Put it on,' he said.

'I'm hardly dressed for it.' She wasn't dressed at all; neither was Konstantin, but the palace was not cold.

'It doesn't matter. If it can compete with your beauty now, it will be fit to be seen with whatever you choose to wear.'

She giggled, but enjoyed the flattery. She felt his hands at the nape of her neck, unfastening the one item that she had not removed from her body before making love to him.

'No,' she said, putting her hand on his. It was sentimental of her – and so rude. She sensed his fingers draw back, and felt suddenly lonely. It would do no harm to take it off. The gold watch, a reminder of her husband, lay in her bag, somewhere in the adjoining dressing room. She'd had no qualms about being separated from that as she had climbed into Konstantin's bed. Why then should she be so precious about an icon of Christ that, somehow, reminded her of her father? 'I'll do it,' she said, and reached up to unfasten it.

She put the icon on the table beside the bed, glancing at the delicate little knot in its silver chain – a hasty repair from some occasion when it had been broken. It had been like that as long as she could remember. Perhaps it had been she who had broken it – her father who had repaired it. If so, the recollection was lost in her childhood.

She picked up Konstantin's gift and raised it to her chest. It was heavy. She felt his hands take it and bring its ends together. She clasped her hands behind her neck to lift her hair out of the way. It was loose now, out of its ponytail, and wild. Konstantin liked it like that. Most men did.

'Stand up,' he said when he had finished. 'Show me.'

She stood and turned to face him, feeling the weight of the necklace on her neck and chest. The lowest stone nestled comfortably at the top of the cleft between her breasts. It would require a low décolletage to show it off to full advantage – that was the idea. His eyes didn't rest for long on the ornament, but began to wander down her body, lingering nowhere for too long, but marvelling at all that he saw. His gaze caressed her, down to the tips of her toes, and then moved back up her body, pausing a little more now in the expected places, until his eyes met hers.

He giggled. 'You look like an African princess,' he said.

'African!' She threw herself on the bed beside him, her face close to his for a moment, the gemstones banging against her chest as she landed. Then she rolled on to her back, and he knelt up to lean over her.

'You know,' he said. 'You've seen pictures; too primitive to display any modesty, but adorned with jewels to show off her husband's wealth.'

'So I'm primitive, am I?'

'You can hardly claim to be modest.'

She stuck out her bottom lip, unable to deny it. 'But African?' she complained.

'True. A bad comparison. When it comes to your complexion you are' – he kissed her on the shoulder – 'snow white.'

She giggled. 'And are you my handsome prince – or one of the dwarfs?' For a moment she regretted saying it – Konstantin was not the tallest of men – but he laughed with her.

'And around the world, how many wicked queens look into their mirrors, only to be told that you are more beautiful than they?'

'Not many, I'd think.'

'Mirrors are liars,' said Konstantin. 'You can never trust them.'

Tamara fell silent, scenes from the story of Snow White beginning to play through her mind. She saw the wicked queen, disguised as an old woman, approaching the innocent princess, offering her laces for her corset, and then a poisoned comb, and then the apple. Tamara's mind went back to another old woman in disguise, who had called herself Natalia Borisovna, but could not be her. Who was that old woman? It was her words that had set Tamara on her whole journey of investigation. And even though she wasn't who she claimed, there was still some connection between the true Natalia and Aleksei, going back to 1812; her son had revealed as much. Above all, Tamara still did not know whether the old woman meant good or ill in what she claimed.

'Still with us?' Konstantin's voice broke her reverie.

'Yes,' she said. 'I was just thinking.'

'What?'

'How much I love the necklace. The amethysts are beautiful.'

His face contracted around his nose and eyebrows, then broke into a smile. 'I'm afraid they're not amethysts,' he said gently. 'They're pink sapphires. Your birthstone.'

Tamara's skin was suddenly no longer white as snow. She felt herself flushing a deep red which covered more than just her face. She had insulted his generosity. A necklace of amethysts of that size would have been valuable, but with sapphires, it must be worth more than Tamara had ever dreamed of possessing.

She raised herself up off the bed and kissed him fiercely. He swung his leg across her so that he was now crouched over her on all fours. She dropped her head back on the pillow and gazed up at him.

'But when shall I ever wear it?' she asked him softly.

'Wear it for me.'

She ran her eyes up and down the lengths of their naked bodies, huddled so close to each other.

'That's hardly practical,' she said, raising an eyebrow.

'Just this once,' he replied.

'*Spieglein, Spieglein,*' Yudin muttered to himself, then smiled, adding, '*in meiner Hand.*' He could feel the mirror's handle, ornate and gilded, pressing into his tightly clutched fingers. He examined it – its reverse at least. It was beautiful – more so than it could ever have been if Yudin had constructed it himself. But he had not dared to. How could he risk what a single glimpse into the glass he had created might reveal to him? Instead he had sent the block of Iceland Spar, along with precise instructions, to an expert – a Venetian émigré in the east of the city. The carving and the gilt went beyond those instructions, but there had been no extra charge. Yudin could remember more than one occasion when he had gone beyond what had been requested – what had been paid for – simply because of the pride he took in his work.

It would be so easy to turn the mirror round and stare into its glass. Surely he, if anyone, would be able to cope with whatever was reflected. It might even, as with any other mirror gazed upon by a *voordalak*, be nothing. It was a disappointment he would be able to cope with, though it would defy every investigation he had so far conducted.

But a further experiment was what was needed. Not on himself, not even on Raisa – not yet. He searched through his desk drawers and found an old shawl which he wrapped around the mirror, for safety's sake. Then, still clutching his newest treasure, he descended the steps to the dungeons beneath his office. He would begin with the lowliest of God's creatures. He went to the third door on the left and opened the little wooden hatch that covered the inspection grille; for this cell, metal bars alone were not enough to prevent the escape of those held within. He pressed his face against the iron, knowing the smell of him, of his breath, would attract them. Soon he heard the scratching of their tiny claws as they raced hungrily towards him. How they could find purchase to climb the smooth, vertical wood of the door, he could not imagine, but he knew that many would marvel just as much at the abilities of his own species to scale an apparently unassailable precipice.

He felt a tiny, cold, fleshy paw against his cheek and pulled away. The rat behind continued to claw at him, desperate in its hunger, but unable to reach and too big, despite its emaciation, to slip through the bars. The first to arrive were, inescapably, the best fed. More of the animal's brethren joined it at the grille, reaching out like a starving mob, hungry for bread. Yudin could almost hear the sound of their begging.

Then one of the smaller ones found its way out, wriggling through the tiny gap between the bars. Before it was free, Yudin grabbed it, slamming the door back over the grille at the same time. The creature writhed and attempted to scratch, but Yudin gripped it tightly around its chest, squeezing enough of the breath out of it so that its resistance faded. He shook the shawl off the mirror and held it up, not to see himself in it but to see the rat.

Four black eyes gazed back at him, four ears pricked to hear what danger might approach. A dozen whiskers twitched and, separated by only the tiniest fraction, another dozen echoed the first exactly. Yudin could see the rat as well as if he had looked at it directly, except that looking at it through the Iceland Spar that formed the mirror, he saw it twice.

And if Yudin could see the rat, then the rat could see Yudin.

It stared at him blankly. Its eyes, entirely pupil, gave no clue as to where it was looking. It had been a long shot. Yudin had done a hundred times more experiments on humans and on *voordalaki* than he had ever attempted on rats, but his guess was that these creatures relied little on their eyesight, and understood less of what they saw. If the sight of Yudin's reflection had set the rodent squealing with fear it would have told him something. That it did not told him nothing.

He held the rat against the grille again and it happily scrambled back inside the cell, more comfortable with its own kind than with a human – or indeed a vampire. Yudin closed the door. He should have brought his notebook with him, but the results of this first experiment would be easy to remember. Now he would move on to a second.

He began to unbolt the door at the very end of the corridor and considered which of his human menagerie would make the most suitable specimen.

CHAPTER XVIII

A KNOCK AT THE DOOR ROUSED TAMARA FROM HER REVERIE. She had been back in Moscow for several weeks now, after spending most of March and the whole of April in Petersburg, awaiting the irregular but not infrequent summons of her lover, the grand duke. It had been a dereliction of her duties back here, but Yudin could not complain. He was desperate to learn what Konstantin might whisper in his lover's ear – as desperate as Konstantin was that Yudin, and others like him, should hear it. Two items had been of particular interest. The first was that Tsar Aleksandr was determined that it would be he who went down in history as the liberator of the serfs. Yudin had raised the usual objections, and observed that Aleksandr I had once held an identical ambition. Tamara could only convey to him the determination of this new Aleksandr, as conveyed to her by his brother. Yudin had accepted her conviction that they were in earnest, even while doubting that they would carry their intentions through.

The second matter was more modest in its scope – and therefore more likely to come to fruition. The Decembrists would be pardoned. The announcement would be made at the coronation – just three months hence. For both Tamara and Yudin it meant the same thing: that Aleksei Ivanovich Danilov would return to the west. Each had questions to ask him.

Finally, Konstantin had sent her home. He had had to leave Petersburg on the instructions of his brother, as an envoy to Europe. They had not even had the chance of a final meeting, which was probably for the best. In his letter he had promised they would meet again. She did not doubt his sincerity, but she knew how fate could conspire against a man of even his status, to say nothing of a woman of hers.

The knock came again. It was easy to recognize Isaak's heavy fist, but the increased urgency of this new assault was inescapable.

'Yes?' she bellowed.

The door opened and, as she had predicted, Isaak's broad, stupid, sincere face peeped around it. He said nothing, as was his wont, but his pinched eyebrows were enough to tell Tamara that she was needed. She pushed herself out of her favourite chair, downed the vodka which she had been attempting to savour, and followed him into the salon.

She immediately recognized the tall, uneasy, somehow slightly childlike figure that stood glancing around the salon, impatiently tapping his walking stick against his boot. It was Dmitry Alekseevich. They had met on several occasions since their first encounter at Yegorov's the previous autumn, generally at the beginning or end of one of his frequent visits to Raisa. At those times, he had always appeared a little embarrassed to see her. It wasn't unusual among the clientele, but it was odd that Dmitry's diffidence showed itself only in his dealings with her. She had heard enough about him from Raisa to get a clearer idea as to his character. That the major was genuinely taken with Tamara's colleague seemed beyond doubt. Raisa's attitude – as ever – was harder to deduce.

Dmitry bowed briefly and attempted to smile at Tamara. 'Good evening, Tamara Valentinovna.'

'Good evening, Major Danilov,' she replied, glancing over to Isaak to see if he could offer further explanation to why he had called her out. Dmitry took half a step towards her.

'I'm sorry,' he said. 'I'm being impatient. But Raisa *was* expecting me.'

'I'm sure she'll be here soon.' Of all the girls, Raisa was the least likely to be governed by the regulation of a clock.

'She is here' – Dmitry's voice was the model of self-control – 'but I'm told she's busy.' Tamara tried to picture his father in him. Was it that same self-control that had kept Aleksei going through the months of interrogation and torture after his arrest? Tamara had read only a fraction of the full story, but she knew it would take a little more than that. Aleksei's motivation was one with which she could easily empathize: to save his son. Tamara was still convinced that Aleksei had lied in insisting Dmitry was not a Decembrist. Would he be proud of the man Dmitry had become, standing here, waiting his turn with a cheap whore? Perhaps not about that, but Tamara knew that all in all he would be proud of his child – she could conceive of no other possibility.

As to the more immediate question, regardless of who Dmitry was, it was bad business for Raisa to ignore a prior booking. 'I'll go and see,' Tamara said. 'I can't promise anything.'

As she began to ascend the stairs she saw Nadia Vitalyevna coming down them. They met halfway. Tamara glanced back at Dmitry and spoke in a low voice, ensuring he did not hear them.

'Who's in with Raisa?' she asked.

'There's two of them,' Nadia whispered back.

'Two?' It wasn't the strangest or the least common request to come from the clientele. 'Do we know them?'

Nadia shook her head. 'They're navy officers.'

'Couldn't they have gone with someone else?'

'They asked for her specifically. She didn't seem keen when I told her, but as soon as she set eyes on them she said it would be fine.'

Tamara continued up to the landing and walked along to Raisa's room. She raised her hand, but before knocking paused to listen. There was no sound. She rapped gently and then waited a moment before knocking louder. Still there was no response. She shouted Raisa's name and at the same time placed her hand on the doorknob.

The door was locked.

Memories of the discovery of Irina Karlovna's body – over a year ago and in the room adjacent to this one – flooded into Tamara's mind. She could not face it happening again. She fished out her keys, flicking through them to find the right one. She shoved it into the lock, but it would not go. Another key on the inside prevented it. It was not the only way in. Tamara carried on down the corridor to what had been Irina's room – now it belonged to Sofia Semyonovna, her young replacement. She was downstairs, waiting for custom. Tamara unlocked the door and went in.

They'd never bothered to take down the mirrors – Sofia seemed as enamoured of them as Irina had been. Whenever Tamara went in there, regardless of how she looked away to avoid it, the multiple reflections still directed her gaze to the bed, teasing her with the memory of the horror that had once lain there. But today she had no time to linger. She went straight to the far corner of the room, to the door that connected it to Raisa's. Another key, another lock, but soon she was through and faced, as she had known she would, a third door.

The wall was thick here, and the space between the two rooms might almost have been thought of as a corridor, except that it was not even as long as it was wide. There was just space for one person to stand, with the doors at either side closed. It took Tamara only a moment to unlock this final door. She reached down to her boot and drew her knife, holding her breath in trepidation at what she was about to discover. Then she was in Raisa's room.

Three pairs of eyes fell on her. Raisa was seated on the bed, with her back to the wall, hugging her knees close to her chest. Only the look of fear in her eyes gave a hint that something was amiss. Her two clients appeared nonchalant. As Nadia had said, they were both in naval uniform. The taller of them, a lieutenant, was seated in a chair, his long legs stretched out and resting on the bed. The other was closer to Tamara, leaning on the mirror-less dressing table. He was a *michman*.

'What's going on?' asked Tamara, hoping they would not notice how the knife she was holding out in front of her shook.

'Two men in the bedchamber of a woman of Raisa Styepanovna's reputation?' asked the seated man. 'I think even the most genteel of imaginations can draw the correct conclusion.' He turned his head to glance for a moment at Raisa, allowing Tamara a glimpse of the taut muscles of his neck. Raisa's expression of terror and loathing did not change. The man turned back to Tamara. 'Unless you'd like to join us and even up the numbers,' he added.

Tamara didn't move, knowing that staying close to the open door behind her might be her only chance of flight. 'Why don't you both just leave now?' she said. Still there was nothing concrete to suggest that they were anything other than what they claimed to be, but Tamara knew in her gut that something was wrong. The lieutenant looked at his comrade and gave half a shrug, then both began to move, as if to leave.

The next seconds were difficult for Tamara to perceive. The speed at which the *michman* travelled from his place beside the dressing table and got behind her was phenomenal. She heard the door slam almost before she realized he had moved at all. Then his hand was at her neck. For a moment she couldn't breathe as he carried her across the room, her legs kicking, throttled by the force of her own weight pressing down on to his hand. Then he threw her on to the bed beside Raisa and began to crawl towards her, his lips forming a twisted leer. It seemed he was a man who preferred to take what he could so easily purchase. In moments he was above her and she felt his warm breath on her cheek and smelled its foulness. She clutched tighter on the knife in her hand, which neither man seemed to have noticed.

'Wait!' The order came from the lieutenant, who now stood at the foot of the bed. It had an immediate effect on his comrade, who paused, his face just inches from Tamara's.

'Who is she?' asked the lieutenant, addressing Raisa.

'No one,' she said.

He looked at her, trying to judge her words. For Tamara it was an odd question and an odd answer, making her doubt whether she had really understood what was happening here. The lieutenant soon made up his mind.

'She's yours then,' he said to the other man.

The *michman* turned his head back towards Tamara, his lips parting as he prepared to press them against her skin. Their eyes met. She knew that hers were filled with hatred, but suspected it would be interpreted as fear. The man's expressed a lust that she had seen many times before, but also a sense of victory. It was not the desire for her flesh that drove him so much as the fact that she could do nothing about it. It reminded her of the look in Prince Larionov's eyes that first time, so many years before.

Larionov had eventually learned he was mistaken. Today, the lesson would be dealt out sooner.

The blade hit him in the left cheek as Tamara stabbed downwards with all her strength. It carried on through the base of his tongue and deep into his throat, behind his Adam's apple. He jerked upright, but she knew enough to hold on tight to the knife and as he pulled away, it continued to cut through his cheek, eventually emerging via the corner of his lips, just below his moustache. He knelt astride her, his hand held to the wound, failing to hinder the flow of blood that oozed between his fingers and trickled down his forearm. Tamara pushed herself up the bed, wriggling her legs to get them out from under him, and in a moment she was standing on the floor. The lieutenant had not moved, and seemed unimpressed by the horrible wound she had inflicted on his friend. She held the knife in front of her.

'Go and get help, Raisa,' she said. 'Get Isaak. Dmitry's down there too.' Raisa did not move. 'Quickly,' urged Tamara.

'I think Raisa Styepanovna understands the futility of such an action,' said the lieutenant.

'Your friend didn't find it so futile,' said Tamara, edging towards the main door, the knife always towards the lieutenant.

'I'll admit you took him by surprise, but he won't be so foolish next time.'

'I don't think there's going to be a next time for him.'

'Really?' As he spoke, the lieutenant turned his eyes towards his friend, inviting Tamara to do the same. She glanced left, guessing that it was a trick to distract her, but once she began to understand what she was seeing it became impossible for her to turn her gaze anywhere else.

The *michman*'s hand was still bloody, but it had dropped to his side, allowing a clear view of his mutilated face. And therein lay the fascination. Already, the injury was far less severe than what Tamara was certain she had inflicted. Where half the man's face should have been hanging away from his jaw, now his lips were once again complete. Yet still the hole in his cheek bore testament to what had happened. Through it Tamara could see his tongue running along his teeth. Occasionally he poked it out through the bloody gap; yet even that quickly became difficult and then impossible as, in a matter of seconds, the tear receded and shrank until it was no more than the dark circle where her knife had first penetrated. At last, it was gone.

Tamara opened her mouth to scream. It was a gut reaction, but also a plea for help from whoever in the house might hear her. Even as her throat tensed, she remembered what the lieutenant had said about how little help anyone could be, and began to understand what he meant.

Before she could make a sound, a hand clamped itself over her mouth and another knocked her dagger to the ground. It seemed that the lieutenant did not have complete faith in his own invincibility. He whispered in Tamara's ear, 'No surprises this time.' Then he held her tight to him, one arm across her chest and the other hand under her chin, pulling it upwards so that her neck was stretched tight, but not so that she couldn't see the *michman* as he began to advance once again, his lips parted in that same libidinous grin.

'Have your fill.' Tamara knew the lieutenant was not speaking to her.

Then the door exploded in upon them.

Dmitry had hoped he was mistaken, but now there was no doubt. Ever since he had spoken to Nadia Vitalyevna, just minutes after he had seen Tamara do the same, and heard of the two naval officers who had gone up to Raisa's room, he had feared the worst. There were enough sailors in Moscow now that the war was over for an innocent explanation to be entirely possible, but somehow Dmitry knew. And then Nadia had mentioned how tall one of them was – as tall as Dmitry himself.

His shoulder ached from where he had charged the door. He had thought it might take more than one go, but some passion had driven him to exert all his strength. He'd managed to keep a firm grip on his cane. He would need it – though not to help him stand.

'Let her go, Tolya,' he said.

Tyeplov, like the others in the room, was frozen in the pose of the moment of Dmitry's raucous entry, his hands sullying Tamara's body and offering her up to Ignatyev. Dmitry was reminded of when he had come upon the two of them – along with their victim

– in the abandoned house in Sevastopol. Then he had completely failed to understand what his eyes were telling him. Now, at least, it was all plain to see. They had come after him, followed him to Moscow and, realizing that they would get no more from him here than they had there, had turned on Raisa, hoping the threat to her would change his mind. Tamara was just an innocent who had got in the way – they could little guess what she meant to him. At least Raisa was safe on the bed, for the moment. He gave her the briefest glance, but knew he must not drop his guard for a second.

Tyeplov released his grip on Tamara and took a step away from her. Ignatyev remained where he was, ready to pounce. Tamara stood between them, still easy prey for either. Dmitry silently cursed his father for bringing the *voordalak* into the life first of his son and now of his daughter. But it was not Aleksei's fault – not this part of it at least. For the danger now brought to Tamara and Raisa there was only one man to blame – one human – and that was Dmitry himself.

'Come over here, Tamara,' he said.

She obeyed, walking backwards and never taking her eyes off the two monsters. Moments later she was beside him. He swapped his cane to his left hand and reached out with his right towards Raisa, feeling a thrill as her flesh touched his. He guided her to her feet.

'This has nothing to do with them, Tolya,' he said quietly. 'It's about you and me. Let them go, and we can talk.'

Tyeplov said nothing.

In truth, Dmitry had little intention of talking. If he could achieve it, both vampires would die here tonight by his hand. He'd given them the chance to leave him alone, and they'd ignored it. He knew that he could never be free until they were no more.

'Get out of here,' said Dmitry, nodding at the two women and towards the door.

'I'll get Isaak,' said Tamara.

'No!' snapped Dmitry. 'Keep him away. I'll be with you in a few minutes, believe me.' Raisa and Tamara glanced at one another, but said nothing. They began to move towards the door.

'She stays,' growled Ignatyev. Tyeplov shot him an angry look, but it was too late. Ignatyev strode across the room in a few paces, repeating the phrase more loudly. He reached out his hand to make a grab for one of them – whether Tamara or Raisa, Dmitry could not guess. His reaction was instinctive. In a single motion he drew his sabre and brought it down on Ignatyev's wrist. Ignatyev stepped back and raised his arm. His hand hung limply, attached by only a few tendons and a little skin. At the same moment, Tyeplov came to life, pacing towards them. Dmitry knew he must act quickly.

He threw his sabre aside and transferred the cane back to his right hand, still holding on to its tip with his left and giving it a slight twist. The cap came away easily to reveal the sharp, wooden point that he had whittled during his slow journey back from the Crimea, knowing – while praying against it – that this day would come.

Ignatyev was taken quite off guard. Dmitry's attack was nothing like the one against Wieczorek in the casemate, when he had stabbed blindly and repeatedly with little understanding of what he was doing. His lunge was swift and precise, straight from the textbook of Sainct-Didier. The thin wooden blade penetrated at a slightly upward angle between the fifth and sixth ribs, just as Dmitry had planned and envisaged so many times, spreading them apart and allowing access to the heart behind.

Ignatyev's face froze as all integrity was lost from the flesh of his body – he did not even have time to adopt a look of surprise. Dmitry did not wait to watch the slow collapse of his remains, but pulled the stick straight back out of him and turned towards Tyeplov.

'I told you that if I saw you again, I would kill you,' said Dmitry. When he had said it, he hadn't known for sure whether he meant it. Now there was no doubt. If Tyeplov had left well alone, then some of the friendship – some of the love – that Dmitry had held for him might have lingered. But to come here in pursuit of him, and then to try to use Raisa as a bargaining chip, was too much.

'This isn't about you, Mitka,' Tyeplov replied.

Dmitry gave a curt laugh. He knew he would be a fool to allow anything to distract him from what he must do, but still there was something deep inside that forced him to engage with this creature.

'It never was,' he said. 'You're using Raisa to get to me now, but you only wanted me so you could take revenge on a monster as foul as yourself.'

'Are we so wrong to seek vengeance?'

Dmitry laughed again. '"We"?' he sneered, glancing from side to side to emphasize the point. 'There's no "we" any more, Tolya. Wieczorek's long dead. And now so's Ignatyev.' Even as he spoke, Dmitry realized that there was one name unaccounted for. He paused, hoping that Tyeplov might volunteer the information, but the vampire remained silent, accepting what Dmitry had said. Dmitry was forced to ask the question directly. 'What happened to Mihailov?'

At the words Dmitry noticed the tiniest change in Tyeplov's demeanour – imperceptible to anyone who knew him less well. 'Mihailov?' the *voordalak* asked.

'That's right. Is he dead, or has he simply abandoned you?'

'Neither.' The curl of a smile appeared on Tyeplov's lips.

'So where is he?'

'He's . . .' – the smile broadened and Tyeplov's eyes moved from Dmitry's face to over his shoulder – 'behind you.'

As Tyeplov spoke, Dmitry heard the sound of heavy footsteps snapping the shards of the broken door. He spun round, his sharpened cane outstretched, ready to kill again, but found himself facing only Isaak, finally arrived to do his job of protecting the ladies who worked in the house.

At the same time the clatter of breaking glass and splintering wood assaulted Dmitry's ears. He turned again, but Tyeplov had needed only a moment to flee, throwing himself out through the window and landing in the street below. It took Dmitry only two paces to reach the shattered frame and, just as he had done that awful night in Sevastopol, watch Tyeplov flee into the darkness.

'*Voordalaki!*'

Tamara laughed briefly, but it was an instinctive reaction – a defence against superstition. She saw a similar response in Raisa. The *voordalak* came from stories she'd heard as a child, heard from Yelena Vadimovna and Valentin Valentinovich, but neither had given her the slightest reason to think of them as real. They went with Grimm and Perrault and all those other tales that children loved to believe, but knew to be untrue.

But she couldn't deny what she had seen. She had cut through what she had thought to be human flesh and seen it heal before her eyes. She'd seen the same thing when Dmitry had slashed at the creature's hand. Most convincing of all, she had seen the monster die, and watched its body crumble to nothing.

She could not deny that what she had witnessed defied everything that rational understanding of the world insisted to be true. But it was still a step too far to go from that to *voordalaki*.

'Why do you say that?' she asked. Both Dmitry and Raisa looked at her askance. They were sitting in her office, each, like her, clutching a glass of vodka that had already been refilled more than once. 'I mean why *that* word? They weren't human, I'll grant you that, but we can't jump to conclusions. I mean, I didn't see them drinking anybody's blood.' Even as she spoke she wondered if the *michman* might have been lusting after her body in a way that was quite different from what she had imagined. She shuddered.

'I've got good reason to say it. This wasn't some chance encounter. Why do you think they were after Raisa?'

Tamara hadn't had a moment to consider it.

'They wanted her so they could get to me,' continued Dmitry. He rose and took a step towards Raisa, taking her hands in his. 'And I'm so sorry, my darling, that I ever brought you into such danger.' She said nothing – she was even more stunned than Tamara. Dmitry kissed her on the lips and she responded. He had the romantic streak of a man half his age.

'Why you?' asked Tamara.

'Because of Father – my father.' He paused. 'You asked me, Toma, to tell you about Aleksei Ivanovich. I'll tell you now. It began in 1812, when Bonaparte was marching on Moscow, and nothing seemed like it could stop him.'

Dmitry then told a fantastical story, of how his father had recruited a group of vampires to help save Moscow from the French, and how, once the French had left, they'd turned on the

Russians, and begun to feast on them. He told of how, one by one, the monsters had murdered Aleksei's comrades. They were names Tamara knew well – Maksim Sergeivich, Dmitry Fetyukovich – names that her mother had often spoken while recalling the exploits of her grandfather.

One thing Dmitry recounted would stay with Tamara for ever.

'Your grandfather, Vadim Fyodorovich, was killed by a *voordalak*. They hung his body from a nail on the wall and left him to rot.'

Tamara felt her stomach tighten, but Dmitry was right not to spare them any detail.

'But Aleksei dealt with them all, in the end?' asked Raisa when Dmitry had finished.

'All of the twelve, but there were other vampires – there still are.'

'And the woman who was murdered here in 1812 – Margarita Kirillovna – she was killed by a vampire too?' asked Tamara.

'Papa never mentioned it, but it would make sense – especially if it was he who found the body.'

'The way she died would make sense too,' said Tamara. Then she remembered that additional wound; not to Margarita's neck, but to her chest. 'I think your father may have attempted to save her soul.'

Dmitry looked at her, but didn't ask her to explain.

'And you were how old then?' asked Raisa. 'Five?'

Dmitry nodded. 'Neither of you was even born.'

'And then it happened again in 1825,' said Tamara. 'Five deaths then.'

'There were far more in 1812 – they just went unrecorded,' said Dmitry.

'And in 1825 your father was witness to one of them – outside the Maly Theatre.'

'I was a witness to that too.' Both women looked up at Dmitry as he spoke. 'Papa thought it best to keep my name out of it.'

'So what happened?' asked Tamara.

'A *voordalak* named Kyesha. He came to find Papa – to lure him south. Papa followed – I presume he dealt with him.'

'You don't know?' asked Raisa.

'When he came back he didn't have time to tell me much. The revolt put a stop to that. Do you remember nothing of it?'

Tamara looked up, and saw that Dmitry was addressing her, though why she should remember it, she couldn't guess.

'Me?' said Tamara. 'I was in Moscow, certainly. But I was only four.'

'But your connections with Aleksei . . .'

'Grandpapa was long dead by then.'

'No, I meant through . . . your nanny.'

Dmitry seemed flustered. It mirrored Tamara's own confusion. 'Nanny?'

He paused, looking at her thoughtfully, then spoke. 'She and Aleksei – they . . . knew each other. Don't you remember?'

Tamara laughed. 'I don't even remember having a nanny. What was her name?'

Dmitry paused again. 'I . . . I'm not sure. It doesn't matter.'

'What about what happened tonight?' asked Raisa. 'Why have they come back?'

'They found me in Sevastopol; the two we met tonight – Tyeplov and Ignatyev – but there were others too.'

'What did they want of you?' asked Raisa.

'They wanted Aleksei's son,' said Tamara. It was guesswork, but it made sense. 'They wanted vengeance, even on the next generation.'

'That's right,' said Dmitry, 'but not for that reason. They wanted revenge, but not on me, on a man called Cain. They said Aleksei had helped them defeat him once – when Kyesha had led him to the Crimea.'

'You believed them?' asked Raisa.

'Perhaps I did then, but not now. Papa knew right from wrong.'

'So you refused them?' asked Tamara.

Dmitry nodded. 'I killed one of them.'

'But they didn't kill you.'

'What good would it do them?'

'It'd fill their bellies,' said Tamara, surprised how quickly she had grown to despise these creatures.

'There was plenty for them to eat in Sevastopol,' said Dmitry.

'So why have they come here?' asked Tamara. 'What did they want with Raisa?'

'I can only guess it was to get at me through her – either they were making one last attempt to get me to help them, or they finally decided they wanted me dead.'

Before Tamara could say anything, Raisa spoke up with a sudden firmness. 'That's right. That's what they were saying. And they don't want your help – not any more. They're just after revenge.'

'Really?' Dmitry sounded sad. 'Even Tyeplov?'

'Especially Tyeplov.'

'There's only him left,' observed Tamara.

'Perhaps,' said Dmitry. 'But there was one more of them in Sevastopol – Mihailov. God knows where *he* is.'

'Did they say anything?' Tamara addressed her question to Raisa, who shook her head. 'So what now?' Tamara continued. 'Will they come for Raisa again? Or you?'

'I don't know. Now that Ignatyev is dead, Tyeplov may give up.'

'He didn't seem the type,' said Raisa.

'We'll worry about it tomorrow,' announced Dmitry. 'Is it all right if I stay here tonight?'

There was a pause and Tamara looked up to realize that Dmitry was addressing her. Although it was Raisa's bed that he would be sleeping in, it was, in some sense at least, Tamara's house. She glanced at Raisa, but saw no hint of objection from her. 'Of course,' said Tamara. 'I'll check the room.'

She left Raisa and Dmitry together and went back upstairs, back to the room in which it had all happened. Isaak was just finishing off his makeshift repairs; planks across the shattered window frame. It wasn't a great job, but at this time of year the wind did not blow too coldly, and with the curtains closed it would be difficult to tell the difference. Isaak himself had seen nothing other than Tyeplov's hurried exit – nothing that required a supernatural explanation. The pile of men's clothes on the floor, marking all that remained of Ignatyev, was not an incongruous sight in a house such as theirs.

Tamara went back downstairs and told Raisa and Dmitry that the room was ready for them. Those few clients who had called that night were long gone now – and they'd admitted no newcomers after the events in Raisa's room. All was quiet. Tamara poured herself another vodka and lit a cigarette. She knew she would not sleep. Her mind spun. She had solved them – the murders from 1812 and 1825. And it even seemed clear that one of these monsters had killed Irina Karlovna – either Tyeplov or Ignatyev or one of the others. They had come here before and . . . Tamara could not bring herself to think of it. It was what would have happened to Raisa if she had not intervened; what would have happened to Tamara herself if Dmitry had not saved them both. There were still questions to be answered, but the main problem had been solved. It was not a matter of who had killed Irina Karlovna, but what. And the answer to that question was a *voordalak*. The very idea was more than she could cope with. To even concede that such creatures might exist went against every rational instinct she possessed. The idea that they might directly threaten her and those around her was beyond terror.

And despite the horror that she felt at the concept, and at the knowledge that Tyeplov and maybe another were still out there, she felt disappointed, as though her quest were over. But her discoveries that evening did not simply relate to the undead. Dmitry had given her one vital piece of information that might help with that other quest; the search for her parents. In 1825, when she was four, she had had a nanny. She searched her dim, early memories, but could find no trace of the woman. Her parents – the Lavrovs – had certainly never mentioned any such person.

Then a terrible thought struck her. She *did* have memories of a woman who had looked after her when about that age, who had loved her and cared for her. But she'd always taken it that those recollections were of her mother. Was it possible that all along they had been images of some nanny who had left the Lavrovs' employ when Tamara was but a tiny child? Could the whole foundation of Tamara's understanding of her place in the world be based on so trivial a mistake?

Tamara shook her head. There was more evidence than her own remembrances. There was the money from Volkonsky, and his letters that she had read in the archive in Petersburg, and a host of other clues. Perhaps in Tamara's mind there had been some confusion over the images of her nanny and her mother, but she had no doubt that both existed. And though the trail might have gone cold on her parents, there was still hope of finding the nanny. And if Tamara could find that woman – if she was still alive – perhaps *she* would be able to unlock the secrets of Tamara's childhood.

CHAPTER XIX

WHEN DMITRY AWOKE, RAISA WAS GONE. SHE HAD LEFT A note, but it didn't say much – just that she had things to do. It was daylight now, so she wasn't in danger; he'd explained all that to her. As they'd lain beside each other, he'd asked her to recount everything that Tyeplov and Ignatyev had said. It fitted completely with his suspicions. Their plan had been to get her out of the building and away to wherever it was in the city they were holed up. Thence they could summon Dmitry and once he came – and they knew, as he did, that he would have gladly thrown away his life to save her – both he and Raisa would die.

He was genuinely surprised that they had followed him to Moscow – surprised too that they should tell Raisa the same story they had told him: that they wanted his help in taking vengeance upon Cain. Perhaps it was true. If their desire was merely to feast, then they would have done far better staying in the south. Clearly they had some particular need to pursue Dmitry across the country, and all of his encounters with them demonstrated that their motivation was not a desire to taste his blood. There was a certain nobility to it which went beyond the simple carnal lusts which Dmitry had once imagined to be all that drove the *voordalak*. To seek revenge required a sense of being wronged, and that required an understanding of right and wrong. And could it be true what they said, that in 1825 Dmitry's father had been forced to make a choice, not between right and wrong, but between the lesser of two evils, and had chosen to help Tyeplov and the others to escape Cain?

But it was too late for that. If Tyeplov had come to Moscow and again begged Dmitry's aid, it might have worked. But they had threatened Raisa, and Tamara too, though they as little realized Dmitry's relationship to her as she did herself. That would, to some degree, keep her safe. She had stumbled on the scene in Raisa's room, but there was no reason that the *voordalaki* would come after her. Raisa was the connection to Dmitry and so it was she they would pursue, once night fell; she that Dmitry must protect. He could not do it alone, but he knew the one man in Moscow who might be able to help him – if anyone could.

And yet what if they did learn that Tamara was Dmitry's sister? The full horror of it suddenly hit him. It wouldn't be a question of them using her to get to him. That she was his sister was linked inescapably to the fact that she was Aleksei's daughter – the daughter of the three-fingered man. However Dmitry might have helped with their plan of revenge, might they not think that she could also? And if she refused to help – as Dmitry could not doubt she would – what more use would they have for her?

Dmitry sat bolt upright, remembering his conversation with Tamara and Raisa the previous night. He had told Tamara about Domnikiia, or at least told her that she had a nanny – he had never mentioned his father's mistress's name. He had been a fool to do it, but it had been so tempting to utter even the mildest suggestion of the relationship between them; like the thrill of mentioning a lover's name in conversation with mutual friends who know nothing of the truth.

She would go to her adoptive parents, the Lavrovs, and ask them, and then the truth might be revealed. And once Tamara's parentage was out in the open, how long would it take for Tyeplov to discover it? Dmitry hadn't seen the Lavrovs for many years, but he knew that his father had sworn them to secrecy over this. Now he must go and stand in the place of his father and tell them again, warn them that however much Tamara might plead with them, they should tell her nothing.

But first he would ensure Raisa's safety.

He began to dress.

*   *   *

Dmitry tumbled down the stairs to Yudin's office, ignoring the now slight pain in his right ankle each time it hit one of the steps. He stood still at the bottom, breathing heavily. Yudin looked up from his paperwork.

'Mitka, what an unexpected pleasure. Shall I ask Gribov to bring us some tea?'

Dmitry raised a hand to turn down the offer. Instead he slumped into the seat opposite his old friend.

'Perhaps something stronger?' suggested Yudin.

'All right.' They would both need a drink after what Dmitry had to tell him. Yudin walked over to the cabinet and poured a glass of brandy, bringing it over. He had nothing himself. When he had sat down again, Dmitry began to speak.

'Vasya,' he said. 'You and I have been friends for many years.'

Yudin nodded.

'You've always known me to be rational – level-headed.'

'You take after your father in that respect.'

Dmitry smiled to himself. It was appropriate that Yudin should raise the similarity. He took a deep breath and then spoke. 'Vasya, do you know what a *voordalak* is?'

Yudin looked at him in surprise. He pressed his lips tightly together, but could not restrain himself. He laughed loudly and broadly.

'This is no joke, Vasiliy,' said Dmitry firmly. 'I'm not some mad old starets. These things are real. I know it. I've met them – so did my father.'

Yudin calmed himself. He reached forward with his hand and laid it on Dmitry's. 'Forgive me.' He laughed again – unable to help himself. 'I'm not doubting you. If anything, I'm laughing because I'm relieved.'

'Relieved?' Dmitry was aghast.

'Mitka – I know. I've known for years. I know about vampires. I know that your father fought them – defeated them.' He went back over to the cabinet and fetched the brandy, refilling Dmitry's glass and this time pouring himself one.

'How long have you known?' asked Dmitry.

'Since the war – since 1812.'

'You fought them, alongside Papa?'

'I'd hardly say that. I certainly didn't manage to kill any – that was all down to Lyosha.' His voice became more subdued. 'But I saw what they were; what they could do.'

'Why did you never say? Why didn't Papa?'

'You were very young then, Mitka. Lyosha made me promise. He said he didn't want you ever to have to share in what we'd been through. Then, of course, we fell out, and in those few minutes we had together in Senate Square to make our peace – well, there were more pressing matters to consider.'

'I suppose so,' said Dmitry. It sounded like Aleksei.

'But when did Lyosha change his mind?' Yudin showed genuine curiosity. 'He was so adamant when we spoke of it.'

'He didn't change his mind – not until it was forced upon him.'

'Forced?'

'In 1825, only months before the revolt, we encountered one of them, here in Moscow.'

'My God. What happened?'

'Papa dealt with it, eventually, but it meant he had to tell me all he knew.'

'But he never told you about me?'

Dmitry shook his head.

'Just like him,' said Yudin, with a chuckle of nostalgic laughter. 'Wants to protect you. Wants to protect me.'

Dmitry couldn't disagree, but there was no time to dwell upon memories of Aleksei. His face became grim. He looked Yudin straight in the eye. 'This isn't just history though. They're here. Here in Moscow.'

'My God!' Yudin leaned forward, running his hand across his mouth as he considered the enormity of what Dmitry had said.

'They came after me,' Dmitry explained.

'After you?'

'From Sevastopol. They found me there. They were looking for me – for the son of the three-fingered man.'

'Why?' asked Yudin.

'To help them. They want revenge against a vampire called Cain.'

'Cain? Ha! A myth.'

'What?'

'He's the vampire's equivalent of Baba Yaga.'

'How do you know?'

Yudin stood and walked around the desk. He leaned forward towards Dmitry, one hand on the desktop, the other on the back of the chair. He spoke swiftly and quietly, as if afraid of being overheard. 'Mitka, you know the kind of man I am – a man of thought rather than action. Your father was happy to kill these monsters, but my approach was to study them. Ever since I first met them, I have studied them. I know their strengths. I know their weaknesses. I know their customs.'

'So even vampires have folklore?' asked Dmitry. It had never occurred to him – and yet it made perfect sense. 'And Cain is part of it?'

Yudin nodded.

'But why did they tell me?'

'To trick you. To make it all the easier for them to drink your blood.' Yudin turned away, his hands clasped behind his back.

Dmitry needed to think about it for only a moment. 'No,' he said firmly.

Yudin spun on his heel. 'What?'

'Believe me, if all they wanted was my blood, they had ample opportunities to get it.'

'Are you sure?'

Dmitry felt suddenly sick. The prospect of telling Yudin, a man he so respected, of his encounter with Tyeplov revolted him. He would avoid it at any cost. 'Believe me,' he said simply.

'Then perhaps it's something worse,' said Yudin.

'How could it be worse?'

Yudin squatted down, his face level with Dmitry's. 'Blood is not the only thing that a *voordalak* craves. Sometimes they desire . . . companionship.'

'Companionship?'

'To turn a human into one of their kind, to be with them throughout eternity. Surely you've heard legends of these things?'

'I'd never heard it put quite like that.'

'It hardly matters how it's put – it's a repugnant idea,' said Yudin with force. 'That's why it can only happen if the victim is willing to go along with it.'

'Well, I certainly wouldn't have been.'

'No.' Yudin stood and patted him on the shoulder. 'You're too good a man for that, Mitka. Perhaps they sensed that. Perhaps they'll move on.'

It took Dmitry only a moment to see the inevitable consequence of his friend's words. His head swam and a starry pattern began to creep into his vision. He downed the brandy in his hand with a single gulp.

'Raisa,' he murmured.

'Raisa?'

'They paid her a visit last night – at Degtyarny Lane. I thought they just wanted to use her to get to me, but . . .' Tyeplov's words burned in his mind: 'This isn't about you, Mitka.'

'Is she . . . ?'

'She's fine. I killed one of them, but the other escaped. But they'll come after her again. I'm more certain of it now than ever.'

'They?'

'The one who survived was Tyeplov – I told you about him, asking about Papa. And I think there's another, Mihailov. They were both in Sevastopol.'

Yudin returned to his seat. He took a deep breath. 'Mitka, this is very important. How much did Lyosha tell you of the mechanism by which a man can become a vampire?'

'Not much.' It was true – there had been so little time, Aleksei had not really told him anything beyond his own exploits.

'Then listen. The process is simple. First the vampire drinks the human blood – from the neck, just as it would when feeding. It takes enough to kill, but not immediately. Then comes the difference. The vampire will deliberately wound itself – often in the chest, but in truth it doesn't matter where. The creature has to exert great willpower to prevent the wound from healing until the human has time to drink its blood in return for what was taken. The victim will still die, but he will become undead. He will become a *voordalak*.'

Dmitry listened in horror. 'Why are you telling me?' he asked once Yudin had finished.

'That is what they would have tried to do to you.'

'But they won't now?'

'Not if you've proved to them that you cannot be swayed from the path of righteousness. But who knows what Raisa might do?'

'Never,' growled Dmitry. 'She'd never do that – not willingly.'

Yudin nodded thoughtfully before speaking. 'I think you're right,' he said slowly, 'but I also think we'd both be happier if she was never put to the test.'

Dmitry looked across the desk with half a smile, acknowledging Yudin's subtlety. It would be abhorrent for Dmitry to concede that there was any real prospect of Raisa succumbing to Tyeplov, but Yudin had avoided that discussion altogether.

'Of course,' he muttered.

Yudin considered for a moment, his eyes flicking across the room before settling on Dmitry. 'Mitka, could you stand to be parted from her?'

'To save her? Of course.'

'Good. Good. Look, I have a friend in Klin. She'd take Raisa in, for a price. It's far enough from Moscow. She'd be safe.'

'I'll pay whatever's necessary.'

Yudin nodded, thoughtfully. 'Don't worry about that now. We'll share the costs, but only once it's over.'

'When will it be over?'

'I don't know, but once Raisa is safe, you and I will work out a way to solve the problem for good.'

'Can't I go with her?'

'No. With the two of you together, it would be much easier for them to find you. And you need to be here, in Moscow, to hunt down and destroy these monsters.'

Another problem occurred to Dmitry. 'Do you think Raisa will be happy to go?'

'You'll have to persuade her. You *must*.'

Dmitry nodded.

'I'll write to Madame Zhiglova in Klin, and tell her Raisa is coming. Then you and I will talk to Raisa herself – and may God help us to convince her.' He reached for pen and paper and began to write.

Dmitry sat and watched him, trying to force from his mind any consideration of what might happen if their plan failed. Even so, he could not help but let his thoughts wander.

'Vasya,' he said at length. 'You know her. You don't think she would . . .'

'Would what?'

'You said she would have to be willing . . . to become a vampire. That's not her, is it?'

'My dear friend, no. Of course not. Not when she has you.' He paused. 'But if they find her, and find her unwilling, then the outcome will be almost as foul.'

Dmitry didn't speak. He understood what Yudin meant, but still his friend spelled it out.

'They will still get their pleasure from her. And if she will not drink their blood, then have no doubt: they will not hesitate to consume every drop of hers.'

'Toma. How lovely to see you again.'

It had been only a few days since Tamara's last visit to the Lavrovs. Yelena Vadimovna's voice showed an appropriate mix of surprise and delight.

'I'm afraid your father's not at home at the moment, but . . .'

'I have a question, Mama,' interrupted Tamara, 'about when I was young.'

She watched as her mother's face fell. More and more, Tamara hated the pain she brought to her parents by bringing up the subject of her . . . other parents. But on this occasion that wasn't really what she was asking about. Her mother's reaction was the sign of a guilty conscience. But Tamara was interrupted before she could explain.

'I rather hoped you'd come to see *me*,' said a voice from behind her. She recognized it in an instant. She turned and ran over to him.

'Rodion,' she yelled, and threw herself into her brother's arms. He was not her brother, of course, but she could not imagine loving a true brother better. Unlike his parents, he did not usurp anyone by taking the role he assumed. There was room in the world for dozens of brothers, but only one father and one mother.

After a long embrace, she stepped back and looked at him. In her eyes, he looked just the same as he had always done – apart from the full beard that he now sported. He was perhaps a little fatter than when they had last seen each other, three years before, but he had always had a big, strong frame, so it hung well on him. He was forty-three now, and Tamara noticed a little greying at his temples. He looked resplendent in his captain's uniform. Ultimately, he was commanded by Grand Duke Konstantin, as head of the navy. Tamara hid a smirk, and decided not to reveal her own connection to the tsar's brother.

'He's the image of his grandfather,' said Yelena.

The mention of Vadim Fyodorovich brought back to Tamara the conversation of the previous night, when Dmitry had told her of how he died. She saw Rodion in the same pose, hanging from a nail, his throat bearing the teeth marks of a *voordalak*, his body slowly decaying. She tried to force the image away, but it began to fill her mind; when she looked at her brother she could see the maggots crawling among the hairs of his newly grown beard. Try as she might to ignore it, it lingered at the back of her mind, waiting to find readmittance.

They sat and talked for some time – mostly Tamara and Rodion, with their mother smiling happily on them. The vision of Vadim returned to her again and again, Rodion's words emitted from his grandfather's dead, caked lips. Of all she had learned from Dmitry the previous night, that was the thing that most personally affected her. That and one other: throughout she was itching to ask the question that had been the whole reason for her visit. She marvelled at her own priorities. Last night she had seen first-hand creatures she had never dreamed existed, heard stories of horror that she had no reason to doubt were true, and yet her obsession was with the one tiny clue that Dmitry had given her that might lead to the truth about her parents.

Rodion sensed her impatience.

'Weren't you about to ask Mama something?' he said at length.

Yelena scowled, but with Rodion there she could do little to avoid the issue. Tamara posed her question.

'Mama, when I was young, did I ever have a nanny?'

Yelena hid her reaction well, but it was plain to see that the question meant more to her than Tamara might have expected. Her mother's eyes narrowed, trying to fathom what was behind it. Even Rodion seemed taken aback. His eyes shot over to his mother to watch how she dealt with it.

'You had several,' said Yelena calmly.

'Really? I can scarcely remember.'

'Only when you were very young. Once you started growing up, there was less need for one.'

'Do you remember any of their names?'

Yelena made a show of thinking about it, but Tamara knew at once that she wasn't going to get an answer. Clearly this nanny did know something – something that Yelena wanted to remain a secret.

'It was so long ago,' Yelena said at last. 'None of them comes to mind. I'll ask Valentin, but I doubt he'll do any better.'

I bet he won't, thought Tamara.

The door burst open and a voice shouted across the room. 'Come on, Papa, we'll be late.'

'Vadim!' said Yelena sternly. 'Don't be so rude. Say hello to your aunt Tamara.'

Vadim bowed and kissed Tamara's hand. She beamed back at him, but again visions of his great-grandfather and namesake haunted her. He turned to his father. 'Now can we go?' he asked.

'Let me go and get ready,' said Rodion, rising to his feet. He bid farewell to Tamara and Yelena and followed his son out of the room.

There were a few moments of silence, broken by Tamara. 'Do you mind if I go and look at my old bedroom?' she asked.

'Your bedroom?' Yelena was still suspicious, even of so innocent an enquiry.

'Fond memories.'

'This is still your home. It always will be.'

Tamara went out to the hall and up the stairs. Her old room was at the front of the house. She hesitated as she put her hand to the door. She had slept here until she was nineteen, when Vitya had taken her away to Petersburg. The ghosts of the past still resided in there, somewhere. She hoped that just one of them would give her some clue to this mysterious nanny.

The door creaked as she pushed it – it always had. The large double bed, in which she had spent so many nights, was still there, and beyond it the window. The bed was made up – ready for whenever Tamara chose to come home, but she'd never once stayed there since her marriage. To the left, there was another room, which could also be accessed straight from the landing. Tamara always thought of it as the study, but she never recalled it being used as such. She looked inside, but it was just boxes, as it had always been. Valentin had his own study, downstairs, so why should he need to use this as one?

She went back into the bedroom. To the right, near to the bed, a smaller room led off. She went into it. Here there was another bed – a child's bed. She had slept in here too, when she was small enough to fit in the bed; she had almost forgotten. And her nanny had slept in the main room then.

Tamara felt a shiver. She tried to hold on to the thought – the memory. She was sure of it. As a little girl, she had slept in the small bed and a woman – such a beautiful woman – had slept in the bed in the other room. It could only have been her nanny. She remembered being put to bed and having lullabies sung to her. She tried to picture the woman, but could not see her face. Then that sweet, soft voice came flooding into her mind.

> *Bayoo, babshkee, bayoo,*
> *Zheevyet myelneek na krayoo,*
> *On nye byedyen, nye bogat,*
> *Polna gorneetsa rebyat.*
> *Vsye po lavochkam seedyat,*
> *Kashoo maslyenoo yedyat.*
> *Kasha maslenaya,*
> *Lozhka krashenaya,*
> *Lozhka gnyetsa,*
> *Rot smyeyetsya,*
> *Doosha radooyetsya.*
> *Bayoo, babshkee, bayoo.*
> *Bayoo, babshkee, bayoo.*

Tamara went back to the main room and another image came: her nanny standing at the window looking out. She could only picture her from behind, but she was as real as had been her grandfather's ghastly, dead face minutes before. A long plait of dark hair ran straight down her back. It was a strange image to have of the woman just standing there – watching and waiting. But it was how she most remembered her.

And then Tamara recalled that she herself had done the same – stood in that same pose, sometimes beside her nanny, sometimes alone. She went over to the window and put her hand down to touch the ledge. It scarcely reached her waist, and yet she remembered a time when she had only just been able to peek over it. Outside in the snow, a man had stood watching, always watching. He had been tall – and young – but Tamara could remember his face no more than she could her nanny's. And just as the face would not come to her, neither would the name. She stared down into the street below.

'Domnikiia Semyonovna.' The two words cut through the room and through her recollections, shattering the images that played in her mind and dragging her, unwillingly, to the present. Before she could turn to look, the door had closed, but she knew well enough who had spoken.

Rodion had been there, all those years ago when Tamara was a child, though he would have been in his teens. He would have known about everything. And then later, the first time Tamara had asked the Lavrovs about her true parents, he'd witnessed that too. Their reaction then would have been enough for him – as a loyal son – to keep whatever he knew to himself, and Tamara had never spoken to him on the subject. She had no idea what he knew, but now he had given her something – a name; the name of a nanny who until yesterday she had not known existed. And it was a name with which she was already familiar. There had been several names on that list of witnesses to the first murder, in Degtyarny Lane, in 1812. Aleksei's had been one. Another was Domnikiia Semyonovna Beketova.

Again she let the image of the woman standing, waiting, staring out of the window come to her. But what was it that Domnikiia Semyonovna had been waiting for? Tamara remembered herself, standing beside her nanny, just where she stood now, also waiting; waiting for her parents, she felt sure of that. She glanced down into the street again and felt her blood chill at what she saw. Her memories had come to life. There stood that same tall, brooding figure in silent vigil, just as he had done when Tamara was a child. Another memory came. The man had made Domnikiia cry. He had hit her. As a child it had made her sad, but now she felt only anger towards the man who had done it. Could it be that same man who stood there now, or was it mere coincidence?

She studied the figure. His back was turned and she could not see his face. He was unusually tall. Could it be Tyeplov? It made no sense that he would have been here thirty years before. And as a *voordalak* he shouldn't be here now in broad daylight, unless that aspect of their nature truly was a myth.

The figure turned and walked purposefully away down the street, allowing Tamara the briefest glimpse of his face. She stepped back from the window and put her hand to her mouth, stifling a gasp. The figure was not Tyeplov, but it was a face she knew well. And she was now certain that it had been the same man, though much younger, who had maintained his vigil there when she was a child.

It was Dmitry.

They had one last passionate night together. Now it was over, and Dmitry lay in Raisa's bed, in her room in the brothel on Degtyarny Lane. He felt her warm body pressed against his, with scarcely a gap where their skins were not touching, from the point at which her temple pressed against his chest down to where their insteps lay gently against one another. Her breathing was quiet, but he felt her body moving. His own slow inhalation and exhalation matched hers exactly.

It was a rare treat; to be in bed with her like this, and to have the luxury of remaining still and silent for so long. It was a happy side effect of the danger they faced. Last night, after Tyeplov's visit, they had been able to stay together, and again tonight. Normally he would have been thrown out, just like any other customer, when the doors were finally locked in the small hours of the morning; it was the rule of the house.

After visiting Yudin, Dmitry had gone to see the Lavrovs, but he had been too late. Tamara was already there. He'd seen her, up at her bedroom window, just as when he'd looked up at her when she was a little girl. Then he'd believed what he was meant to believe – that she was the Lavrovs' daughter and that Domnikiia was merely her nanny. He remembered his loathing for Domnikiia then, for taking his father from his mother, and worse, for taking his father from him. But he had grown to realize that neither was true.

He was sure that Tamara had seen him and recognized him. Perhaps she even remembered him standing on that same spot all those years before, his eyes blazing with hatred for her mother. But when they met again that evening, Tamara had said nothing. Dmitry did not speak to the Lavrovs. It was better to leave their secrets undisturbed.

He had returned to Degtyarny Lane to be surprised how easy it was to convince Raisa to leave Moscow. Perhaps she had seen from the first that he was going to have his way, regardless of her objections. He'd have locked her in a trunk and thrown her into the luggage wagon if need be. In the end, he hadn't even needed to explain to her the full nature of the threat she faced. He'd discussed it with Yudin, and they'd decided it was best to avoid it if possible. She understood well enough that a vampire could kill her; there was no need to tell her that it could also capture her soul.

There was a knock at the door. Dmitry had been expecting it, but he didn't respond. The door opened slightly and the light of a candle shone in.

'It's nearly time.' It was, as he had known it would be, Tamara's voice. 'He'll be here soon.'

'We'll start moving,' he said, turning his head towards her. She left the candle on the table, along with a jug of hot water, and departed.

'Do we have to?' Raisa had been woken by Tamara's arrival, but she still sounded sleepy. She coughed heavily, but waved Dmitry away when he showed concern.

'You know we do,' he said, when she'd recovered.

'Then you come too.'

'You know I can't.'

She rolled over and pushed herself up with her arms, straddling him on all fours. Her loose, golden hair, translucent in the candlelight, hung down over him, tickling his shoulders and his forehead.

'Aren't you going to miss me?' she asked, rubbing herself up and down against his belly.

'Of course.' He pulled her down on to him and pressed his lips to hers, knowing that if she continued, he would not be able to resist her. They didn't have time. He rolled her over on to her back, so that he was now above her, then gave her one final kiss before standing up. He washed and dressed quickly, then went to the door, leaving her running a comb through her shimmering hair.

'I'll wait downstairs,' he said, then departed.

In the salon, Yudin was already waiting. He had in his hand a glass of tea. Tamara offered one to Dmitry. He sipped it.

'I should come with you,' he said. 'At least to the station.'

'We're not going to the station,' said Yudin. 'Not in Moscow, anyway.'

'What?'

'It's too obvious. I have a carriage. I'll take her to Khimki and she can get the train from there.'

'Can you trust the carriage driver?' asked Tamara.

'Oh, I think so,' said Yudin, with the slightest of smiles.

Then both Yudin and Tamara looked up, to the top of the stairs. Raisa stood there, wrapped in a light overcoat, her hair hidden by her hat, a small valise in her hand. She looked utterly demure – quite unlike the woman whose body he had caressed not twenty minutes before. He rushed up the stairs to take her case from her, but his ankle still slowed him. She was halfway down when they met, and brushed aside his offers of assistance.

She went to Tamara first, kissing her on both cheeks and then taking her hand. 'Goodbye, Toma,' she said. 'I hope you'll be able to carry on here without me.'

'You'll be hard to replace,' said Tamara.

Then Raisa turned to Dmitry. She said nothing, but merely raised her eyes up to his. He threw his arms around her and squeezed her as tightly as he could, as if it would keep her from going. She didn't even breathe but stood quite still, her face buried in his neck, until he finally let go of her. She gave him the most knowing of smiles, which told him everything about her. His own broad smile caused hers to widen. He leaned forward and kissed her lightly on the lips. Then they separated.

Tamara turned the key in the door and drew back the two large bolts, then opened it and stepped outside. Between them Dmitry and Yudin picked up Raisa's large trunk, which had been packed and brought down the night before, and carried it outside. They strapped it on to the barouche that waited there. By the time they were done, Raisa had already climbed aboard. Dmitry heard her cough again.

The coachman's seat, behind the two black horses that would pull the carriage, was empty. Yudin clambered up and took the reins. He grinned down at Dmitry.

'No need to let anyone else in on this, I don't think,' he said.

Tamara and Dmitry stepped back towards the house. In the early morning darkness, Raisa was scarcely visible, sitting back beneath the half-hood. Dressed all in black, Yudin perched above her and in front, leaning out over the two horses like the expert driver that Dmitry knew him to be. He flicked them with his whip and the two beasts began to move. Raisa was out of sight in a moment, hidden by the black canopy, but Yudin remained visible until the carriage turned the corner. He gave a cheery wave as he disappeared from view.

Dmitry felt Tamara's comforting hand on his back. He felt an almost overwhelming urge to embrace her, but for it to have made any sense she would have had to know she was his sister, and now, more than ever, that knowledge could only bring her danger.

'Are you coming back in?' she asked.

'No,' he said. 'I'll head off.'

She smiled briefly and stepped back inside. Dmitry waited until he heard the bolts drawn shut, and then walked away, wondering when he would ever see Raisa again.

CHAPTER XX

My dear little Mityenka,

It seems so long since I was last in your arms, and yet it was only this morning when we said goodbye. Everything went as you and Vasiliy Innokyentievich told me it would. We made good time out of Moscow and were soon on the chaussée. As dawn broke, I made him stop the coach and looked back on the city in the morning sunlight. It was quite the most beautiful thing I have ever seen, but it saddened me to think that somewhere among those gleaming church domes and clusters of buildings you were there, alone, and probably already back to sleep, knowing you.

We reached Khimki in plenty of time, and Vasiliy suggested that we should take a walk around the famous gardens, but I demurred. I cannot see this journey as any kind of a holiday, but perhaps one day soon we will be able to walk through those gardens together. We sat at the station and waited for the train, which duly pulled in a little before noon. I was surprised how many people got off when it arrived, but Vasiliy explained they would have come for the gardens, or to take lunch, or to listen to the orchestra that sometimes plays here. I'm sure you would adore it, though I don't imagine they play anything like as well as you do. He also said that some people come just because they enjoy riding on the train, and that this was the shortest journey they could take, but that seems quite silly to me.

There were only two others apart from myself who

boarded the train at Khimki, though both I and Vasiliy Innokyentievich verified that neither was Tyeplov or Mihailov, at least as far as you described him. How could they be? How could they know of our plans, and even if they did, how could they stand there on the platform, with the summer sun at its highest?

Vasiliy Innokyentievich had arranged a seat in a first-class carriage for me, and he waited on the platform until the train pulled away. There was only one more stop before we got to Klin, and we crossed a very large bridge, at which I dared not look out for fear of seeing just how far the drop was down to the river. The journey took a little over four hours altogether and when we arrived I looked out of the window to see a kindly lady standing on the platform who I just _knew_ was Mme Zhiglova. We took a little open wagon to her house, which overlooks the river Sestra. She is a widow who lost her husband when the French first attacked Sevastopol, back in 1854. I told her I have a friend who was in the city throughout the entire siege (I didn't dare mention to her exactly what _type_ of friend). I'm afraid I may have made rather more of your wounds than is strictly correct, but I know you love to do that too. I told her I would ask if you ever encountered Captain Zhiglov of the Tarutino Regiment. She has a daughter, Sofia Bogdanovna, who lives with her. She is fourteen years old and quite delightful. Her two sons, Ivan Bogdanovich and Lyov Bogdanovich, are both serving in the Caucasus.

Mme Zhiglova showed me straight to my room, from which I can just see the river, and as soon as the maid had unpacked and helped me change my clothes I sat down to write this letter to you. Mme Zhiglova has already brought me some tea, and now she has called me down to sit with her on the veranda and share some vatrushki, which she is keen to tell me she makes with apples from her own orchard, so I must say goodbye.

Write as soon as you receive this.
Your loving
Rasha

My dearest Rasha,

Vasiliy Innokyentievich has already told me your story up to the moment you left Khimki, though I must confess his telling of it was far less enchanting to hear than yours was to read, though somewhat more succinct. You'll be pleased to know he made it safely back to Moscow and I dined with him yesterday evening. If I had known, I would have eaten only vatrushki and thought of you. Even without them I thought of you.

My day has been as tedious as ever, reading reports from officers who have never been into battle and who believe the best way for a soldier to defeat his enemy is to dazzle them with his over-polished buttons. Tiresome though it is, I am beginning to feel a certain pride at the spectacle we shall see at His Imperial Majesty's coronation, and I feel sure that my small contribution towards organizing the parades of the cavalry will help to ensure they do not go unnoticed. It would be wonderful if we could find a way for you to be back in Moscow by then. I'm sure I could secure you the perfect spot from which to see all those mounted officers passing by (though I flatter myself to hope you would have eyes only for one).

On that front, Vasiliy and I have been discussing how we can finally be shot of the creatures that threaten you and thus allow your safe return. We disagree on precisely what their next move will be. Vasiliy suspects that they will abandon all plans to imperil you and will turn their attention once again to me. My belief is that they will attempt to make a further move on you at Degtyarny Lane. Thankfully we can combine our defences against both eventualities. If they do come for me, I am well armed, and Vasya has used his influence to ensure that two covert officers, similarly armed and ready to protect me, will be close by whenever I am out during the hours of darkness. Thus I will be watching Degtyarny Lane from without, while Tamara Valentinovna watches from within. If they come in search of you, or in search of me, the result will be the same.

I know you will hate the thought of my putting myself in danger, but in truth the danger is already there and if we don't act to precipitate events, then it will remain with us for the rest of our lives.

I'm afraid that I never encountered Captain Zhiglov, though I do have some friends in the Tarutino, so I will ask them when I see them. I'm sure he died bravely. The tragedy of the war has been that the same could be said of so many.

I count the hours before your next letter arrives.

I am yours,

Mitka

He hated to lie to her, especially in a letter. It was only over a small matter, but not so small that he chose to tell her the truth.

Yudin had indeed suggested the idea of providing officers to protect Dmitry, and Dmitry had initially agreed, but then his mind had gone back to 1825 and the plan he had hatched with Aleksei to kill the vampire Kyesha. They had recruited half a dozen good soldiers, but had understood that they would be laughed at if the word *voordalak* was ever mentioned in connection with their purpose. They had been careful to tell the men merely to follow Kyesha, never to approach him, but one of them had decided to show his bravery – why shouldn't he? – and had died for it.

He and Yudin had discussed whether they could conceivably tell the men what they would be dealing with, tried to find ways to make it sound less preposterous, but in the end they had agreed that it would be impossible to tell the truth. Yudin had still been prepared to take the risk and let the men protect Dmitry even though they were unaware of the danger, but Dmitry had refused to allow it.

In the end, he had only Yudin to protect him – and Tamara, though she was under strict orders to consider primarily her own safety. Each of the other two had furnished themselves with a cane, much like Dmitry's. He had shown them how to sharpen its tip to a point and then cover it with an extra length of wood. The three of them had laughed as they stood there, canes in hand, like desperate followers of some new fashion trend. But it made a good disguise for a good weapon. Aleksei had managed with only

336

a wooden dagger, modelled on the one he had made Dmitry as a boy. What, Dmitry wondered, had he made for Tamara when she was a child?

They also carried pistols. Dmitry had told Yudin how effective such a weapon had proved, however accidentally, in Sevastopol. It could not kill a vampire, but it could incapacitate for long enough for a weapon more familiar to folklore to do its work – the ancient augmented by the modern. Yudin, as ever, had gone one better than Dmitry and presented them each with American revolvers – Colt Dragoons – capable of firing off six shots before needing to be reloaded. Yudin would not say where he had got them, but all agreed that the vampires wouldn't stand a chance.

And then, they waited. Each evening, Dmitry had loitered around Degtyarny Lane, making himself obvious in the hope of attracting Tyeplov or Mihailov's attention, or in the hope of catching them trying to break in. Sometimes he noticed Yudin shadowing him, sometimes not, which proved that Yudin was doing his job well. Occasionally he would catch Tamara's eye through the window or as she opened the door, but they rarely spoke.

He and Raisa exchanged letters every day. She would write in the evening and her letter would be carried by the train from Petersburg the next morning, travelling with it for the last few versts of its journey into Moscow. The letter would be in Dmitry's hands by evening. He would write a reply that would go out with the morning train and be with Raisa in the afternoon – often as she sat down for lunch.

July passed into August, and neither of them once missed writing a letter. The warm days of August ran by and the coronation approached. Moscow prepared for the celebrations and Dmitry's work on the committee headed towards its conclusion.

And of neither Tyeplov nor Mihailov was there the slightest sign.

'All alone, Cain?'

Yudin looked up. He smiled, but at the same time he reached into his desk.

'As are you, I believe, Tyeplov,' he replied. The *voordalak* stood at the foot of the stairs to his office, tall and impassive. 'Mihailov cannot have survived what I did to him, and I've heard more than one account of what happened to Ignatyev. One by one, your friends have fallen by the wayside.'

Raisa had told him of the events in her room at the brothel even before Dmitry had come to him. He had hoped that all three of the *voordalaki* had perished in the fire at the church, but was circumspect enough to allow for other possibilities. From what Raisa could gather, Tyeplov and Ignatyev had been quite unaware of any connection between her and Dmitry when they came to Degtyarny Lane. Their desire was solely for revenge over her helping Yudin at Chufut Kalye. No one except she had noticed the look of surprise on Tyeplov's face when Dmitry burst in. But even as Raisa spoke of Dmitry's heroic rescue, a plan had begun to form in Yudin's mind. Now, with Tyeplov's arrival, he had the final piece that he needed to begin his gambit.

'Neither of us has had a friend for many years, Cain,' said Tyeplov. 'We both chose to abandon such things.' Yudin said nothing. Tyeplov filled the silence. 'What do you want with me, Cain?'

'What do *I* want with *you*?'

'You summoned me here.'

'Did I?' teased Yudin.

'With the blood – my blood.'

'You mean this?' Yudin lifted his hand and revealed the vial of red liquid which he had been clutching. 'You were willing enough to let me take it.'

'That was a long time ago.'

'True.'

'What have you been doing with it?' asked Tyeplov.

'Various things – exposing it to the sun, mixing it with acid. Anything to painfully destroy a few more drops of it.'

'Every week,' said Tyeplov. 'Regularly. For six weeks.'

'Ever since your little escapade with Raisa Styepanovna.'

'I felt it burn.'

'You were meant to.'

'But I knew it was a summons.'

'So you come in peace?'

'I want nothing from you now, Cain. Be happy – you have beaten me. I had already left the city when you called me back.'

'I, on the other hand, want something from you. I have a small job for you.'

'Why should I help?'

Yudin wiggled the vial of blood at him. 'I think you know why. And it's nothing difficult – just a little play-acting.'

Tyeplov considered, eyeing the blood, wondering just how much more pain Yudin could inflict than he had already. 'Then you'll leave me be?'

'I left you for thirty years, didn't I?'

The implied threat and the memory of his long entombment appeared to have the desired effect. 'What do you want me to do?' Tyeplov asked.

Yudin hesitated. There was not just Tyeplov to be considered. Whatever words were exchanged between them, Zmyeevich would be listening too. Mihailov had explained that. Tyeplov and Zmyeevich had exchanged blood when the one had transformed the other into a vampire and now they were linked. But there was no reason to suppose Zmyeevich would want to hinder Yudin's plan – more likely he would enjoy watching as it played out. Anyway, Yudin had no other choice. He needed a vampire.

'I want you,' he explained, 'to catch a train.'

They dined again at Yegorov's. It wasn't late in the evening, though Tamara was already beginning to notice that the nights were drawing in. But it was too early for there to be much business at Degtyarny Lane, and as the weeks had gone by, with no sign of the two vampires that they knew were still out there somewhere, they had grown more relaxed. Dmitry still never missed a night of his vigil outside the house, but he tended to arrive later and leave earlier.

Dmitry had his blini with cherries and cream. He didn't mention it, but Tamara remembered that it was what both he and Raisa had had here before, the first time they met. Tamara herself had chosen mushrooms, fried with onion.

'I'm going to have to go away for a few days soon,' she told him.

339

'What? And miss the coronation?'

'It's because of the coronation. There's worry about the security of the imperial train. The whole family's going to be on there. Yudin thinks that having a female agent on board might add some extra safety that a man would not.'

'How so?' he asked.

'I think the idea is that they might overlook a woman.'

'They?'

She shrugged. 'Whoever hates His Majesty sufficiently.'

'What is it that you do, exactly?' He sounded intrigued.

She leaned forward and glanced across the dining room, pretending to check that no one was listening. 'If I told you, I'd have to kill you,' she said.

Dmitry laughed and covered his mouth with his napkin.

'So I'll be back in time for the big day.'

'It'll be quite a spectacle.'

So Tamara had heard, but still she felt a certain trepidation. Konstantin would be there, and if she found herself a lucky place in the crowd, she would see him, but he would not see her. Or if he did see her, he would pretend that he didn't. It would be the first time that, in her eyes, he had been a grand duke rather than a man. She hadn't asked Yudin for the posting on the imperial train, and soon realized how Konstantin would see it. He would put her down on his list of women who had wanted too much of him; at his age, a short list – perhaps she would have the honour of being at the top of it. But she couldn't disregard orders. She could only hope that Konstantin did not catch sight of her.

'And it'll mean that you'll see your papa soon,' she said. 'Aleksandr will announce an amnesty.'

Dmitry nodded. 'It seems certain.'

'You're not pleased?' He certainly didn't sound it.

'I'd forced myself to give up hope. It's hard to revive it.'

Tamara had never given up hope of finding her parents, and the imperial decree that brought Dmitry's father back to him would bring her closer to the truth. Domnikiia, Aleksei's mistress and Tamara's nanny, would be returning too. Once Tamara had made the connection between them, it hadn't taken many hours in the archives to discover that Domnikiia had followed her lover out to

Siberia and was still there with him. She, if anyone could, would be able to tell Tamara the truth. It was Dmitry who had given her the clue, and yet they had not spoken about it since. With all the upheaval over Raisa, the moment had not occurred. Now was the time.

'What were you doing at my parents' house the other week?' she asked.

'When?'

'The day after you told me about Domnikiia Semyonovna.'

He answered smoothly, but she noted that he didn't comment on being told a name that he had claimed not to remember. 'I thought I'd pay them a call. Talking to you reminded me. I hadn't seen them for years.'

'Thirty years,' said Tamara.

'I suppose so, yes.'

'That's when you used to stand there and look up at my room, when I was a little girl. Why was that, Dmitry?'

He flushed and began to open his mouth, but this time no words came to him. She had been right to think he knew more than he had been telling. Perhaps she wouldn't need to wait for Domnikiia's return after all.

'Why, Dmitry?' she repeated.

She never heard his answer.

'Thank God I've found you!'

They both turned. It was Yudin. He was flustered, out of breath. He had a wad of papers clutched to his chest.

'What is it?' asked Dmitry, reflecting Yudin's urgency.

'I tried your rooms,' explained Yudin, 'then Degtyarny Lane, and they said Tamara was here, so I guessed you might be too.'

'But what's the problem?'

Yudin paused. He glanced at Dmitry, then Tamara, then back to Dmitry. 'Mitka,' he said with a sigh, 'I've never told you fully what it is I do for His Majesty, and I don't propose to now, but one of the tasks that falls to me, or my department, is the censorship of mail.'

He paused, waiting for Dmitry to respond, but the younger man took the revelation easily in his stride.

Yudin continued. 'Normally, I don't bother with the detail. I leave it to Gribov. But I can't blame him. We've never bothered with letters sent over such short distances. If conspirators wanted to communicate between here and Klin, they'd do it face to face.'

'Klin!' Dmitry pounced on the name of the town.

Yudin nodded. 'I happened to be looking over his shoulder, and I saw her name.'

'Raisa?'

Yudin placed the letter on the table in front of him. 'I knew that the handwriting wasn't yours.'

Dmitry snatched the letter up and began to read. Tamara saw his eyes darting back across the page as he took in each new line.

'It sounds like they've been corresponding for some time,' Yudin explained to Tamara while Dmitry read. 'But I can only guess what was said.' He glanced over at Dmitry, who had just turned to the second page. 'I only wish we could have intercepted one of the letters back from her.'

'She replied?' asked Tamara.

Yudin looked at her sharply, but answered her question. 'Gribov remembers the letters coming across his desk. He just never bothered to look at them.'

'It's from Tyeplov,' said Dmitry. He had finished reading.

'You're sure?' asked Tamara.

'He's signed the fucking thing,' Dmitry snapped. 'He says he's going to visit her. Tonight. He's taking the slow train. He wants her to meet him at the station in Klin, at four in the morning.'

'When does the train leave Moscow?' asked Tamara.

'In ten minutes,' said Yudin.

'What?' shouted Dmitry.

'You may still have time,' said Yudin.

'But if she hasn't received the letter, she won't go to meet him,' said Tamara.

'I'm not taking that chance,' said Dmitry. With that he was gone. The door out of the restaurant swung closed behind him.

'I've been a fool,' said Yudin, sitting in Dmitry's chair and putting his head in his hands.

'We'll be even bigger fools if we let him go after Tyeplov alone.'

Yudin looked at her. 'You're right, of course,' he said. He rose to his feet at the same time as she did. When he saw it, he raised his hand to her. 'No, Tamara Valentinovna, not you. This is man's work, and you can't be any part of it. That's an order.'

Tamara sat back down and watched him depart through the same door that Dmitry had just used. She waited for precisely half a minute, counting the seconds in her head. Then she threw some banknotes on the table in settlement of the bill, and followed them both out into the street.

Outside the restaurant, Yudin turned right. From the corner of his eye he glimpsed Dmitry, trying to hail a carriage in the street. He turned right again, into an alleyway, where his own coach was waiting, as instructed. He boarded it and told the driver to make for the station, as fast as possible. They were there within five minutes. Kalanchyovskaya Square wasn't busy, but as soon as he entered the station, he found himself buffeted from every angle. The train was at the platform and its steam was up, ready for departure. All around him men clambered on board. It was officially a freight train, but the cheap carriages for the slow journey were becoming ever more popular. Second-class passengers got covered wagons, but at this time of year, when the weather was usually fine, third-class travel meant a space on a bench on a flatcar, and the feeling of the wind rushing by.

He caught sight of Tyeplov, standing back just as Yudin had told him, waiting to move. It was a good job he was so tall, head and shoulders above most of the crowd. Dmitry was of a similar stature. There was no risk that they would not see one another. Yudin waved curtly and Tyeplov nodded in response.

Now they swapped roles. Tyeplov stepped out into the middle of the platform where he could be clearly seen, while Yudin ducked back into the shadows, close to the station entrance. The crowd seemed to part and move around the obstacle that Tyeplov presented, but if they felt any resentment towards his standing in their way, they did not dare show it.

Moments later, Dmitry arrived, pushing his way through the crowd and standing on tiptoe to make himself even taller than he already was. Yudin was about to follow him, ploughing through the crowd in his wake, when he noticed another figure had walked on to the platform – a woman. She was not distinctive by virtue

343

of her height, indeed there were few in the bustle around the train who were shorter than her, but what made her unmistakable was the flash of bright, auburn hair that shone through whenever a gap in the crowd appeared.

Tamara's arrival was an irritation. If she got in the way, he would have to deal with her, but it was unlikely she would be able to see what was going on. Yudin pressed on through the crowd, getting as close behind Dmitry as he could. He slipped his hand into his pocket and curled his fingers round the revolver. Tyeplov would not attempt to board the train until he was sure that Dmitry had seen him – and standing where he was, he would be impossible to miss.

Tyeplov began to move, heading for the second-class wagon with determined strides, pushing aside the teeming crowds. Yudin took a final glance around him, but could see no sign of Tamara. Tyeplov stepped on to the train and gave one final look down the platform so that Dmitry could not fail to understand where he was going. Yudin was right behind Dmitry now. He raised his hand, with the pistol in it, and brought it down heavily on the back of Dmitry's neck.

Dmitry slumped forward and Yudin managed to catch him before he even hit the ground, using the body to hide his hand as he slipped the gun back into his pocket. He slapped Dmitry on the cheeks lightly, as if trying to rouse him, but he knew it would take a few minutes yet.

The train whistle blew and the conductor on the end carriage disconnected the brake. Yudin heard the same sound from each wagon, and then from the distant locomotive came a whoosh of steam, and the train began its slow, relentless movement out of the station.

'How do you feel?' said the white blob in the middle of the red blur.

'What?' said Dmitry.

'It was Mihailov – Vasiliy Innokyentievich saw him.' The white blob seemed to grow a little and the red aura receded, both sharpening into focus and revealing Tamara's face looking down on him.

344

'Mihailov?'

'He hit you, from behind.'

'Where's the train?' asked Dmitry.

'It's already gone.'

Dmitry pulled himself upright, and pain surged through his skull. He squeezed his eyelids together and remained as still as he could. The pain receded, but didn't vanish completely.

'I saw Tyeplov get on it,' he said.

'You're sure?'

'Of course I'm sure!' Shouting made the pain worse. 'Where's Vasya?'

'I don't know. He said he'd be back soon.'

'I have to beat the train to Klin.'

'That's what he said.'

'Mitka, my God, how are you feeling?' Dmitry could not see Yudin, only hear him. He realized there was nothing but a dark haze on the right-hand side of his vision – a result of the blow. He turned his head and saw that Yudin had returned and was sitting next to him on the bench at the side of the platform.

'I'll live.'

'Fit enough to ride?'

'What?'

'I've found you a horse – a real beauty.'

'He'll never make it,' said Tamara. 'He can't beat a train.'

'An officer of His Imperial Majesty's cavalry?' said Yudin. 'Of course he can.'

'He can hardly walk.'

'I can walk,' said Dmitry. He stood up to prove it. Stars filled his vision, but then receded. 'And besides, who else is going to do it?'

Yudin led him out of the station, guiding him lightly by the arm. Tamara came too, ready to catch him at any moment. He walked like a drunk who was trying to hide the fact, but he managed to make it outside.

In the square a boy stood, holding the reins of a horse – a bay colt. It looked like it could gallop. 'How did you find it?' asked Dmitry. 'At this hour?'

Yudin rubbed his fingers and thumb together, the sign for

money. Dmitry mounted. Again his head stung, but once he was on the creature's back he felt more comfortable. Tamara handed him his walking stick.

'You know how to get there?' said Yudin. 'The chaussée is your quickest route – it'll take you straight to Klin.'

'I know,' said Dmitry. He wanted to be off, but Yudin had taken the reins from the boy and was holding them tightly.

'And even if you beat the train, don't go to the station. You're not there to fight Tyeplov on your own.'

'Is Mihailov with him?'

'No – I saw him run off. But the point is you must go to Raisa, make her come to her senses and at all costs keep her away from him. You know how to get to Madame Zhiglova's?'

Dmitry nearly laughed. He could picture almost the whole town of Klin in his head, Raisa had described it in such detail in her letters. 'I'm sure I can.'

Yudin handed Dmitry the reins. 'Then off you go, and God be with you.'

He slapped the creature on the haunch and Dmitry was off. From behind him he heard Tamara's shout of 'Good luck, Mitka!' He raised his hand in acknowledgement, but did not turn.

The slowest part was getting out of Moscow. The chaussée began over to the west, essentially as a continuation of Tverskaya Street. He rode a little way back into town and turned on to the Garden Ring, following it anticlockwise around the city until it intersected Tverskaya Street. Even then, his pace was slow. It was impossible to go any faster than a trot in the city, with so much traffic about. It was only once he was on the chaussée itself that he could gallop. He pushed the horse on for a few minutes, but realized it would be futile to attempt the long journey at that speed. He pulled back to a trot, occasionally breaking into a canter when he felt the beast could take it.

The road first crossed under the railway a little way beyond Khimki. Dmitry looked up and down the track. There was no sign of the train, but he had not expected there to be, not with the head start it had. He realized that he didn't know for how long after the train's departure he had remained unconscious. He should have asked Yudin. At full tilt a horse should be able to travel at twice the speed of a freight train, limited by the rules to go no faster than sixteen versts per hour, but a horse could not keep up that sort of gallop – or even a trot – for the ninety versts of the full journey. And with the rise of the railway, the number of hostelries along the way where he might find fresh horses was dwindling. On the other hand, the train would have to stop to take on fuel and water, so there was a chance that he might make it to Klin at around the same time. And there was always the possibility that the locomotive would break down.

After Khimki the chaussée ran roughly parallel to the railway line, a few versts to the north. Occasionally Dmitry caught sight of it when the embankment beneath the rails rose up above the surrounding land. The two thoroughfares began to converge once again as they approached the village of Solnechnaya Gora, where Lake Senezh – now dammed and turned into a reservoir – forced them together. He had been riding for more than three hours.

Dmitry's horse could barely trot now, but as they plodded into the town Dmitry's heart was lifted at the sight of a train just pulling out of the station, heading in the direction of Petersburg. It could only be the one Tyeplov was on. Miraculously, he found a hostelry that could provide him with a fresh horse. Tempted as he was to press on and not waste the few minutes it would take him to change, he knew that his current mount would never make it to Klin in time – if at all.

As he waited, he wondered if he himself would make it. He had not ridden very much since he had been wounded, or even before that, once the Siege of Sevastopol had settled into its moribund routine. His legs were stiff, particularly his right ankle, and his head still ached from Mihailov's blow, but he knew he could not rest, even for a moment. He mounted his new horse – it was not as fine a beast as the one that had brought him this far, but it was fresh. When he left the village he was able to do it at a canter.

The railway line veered away to the left, but the chaussée was almost a perfect straight line from here to Klin, while the tracks meandered to find the shallowest gradient. For Dmitry there was little more than twenty versts to go; on the route the train took, another three or four could be added.

In less than an hour and a half, Dmitry was entering the

outskirts of the town. He understood Yudin's advice about going straight to Raisa rather than trying to intercept Tyeplov, but the station was only the slightest of diversions. He didn't even need to get close to see the rear end of the train again as it pulled away. He didn't know how long it had been stopped there, but he knew that Tyeplov would have been out of it and on his way to Madame Zhiglova's as soon as it came to a halt.

Dmitry spurred his horse and carried on, picturing the route that Raisa had described to him in her letters, which she had taken two or three times a week, either in a carriage or on foot, to visit the shops and coffeehouses in the centre of town. The road led directly away from the station, crossing the chaussée at right angles. It was only a few minutes before he saw the house, with its distinctive white walls and the veranda on which Raisa had so often taken tea.

Raisa's room was directly above it. There was a light at the window, even though it was by now almost four o'clock in the morning. A signal for Tyeplov? Unlikely – with his final letter intercepted, she would not have been expecting him. That must mean she had awoken. He imagined Tyeplov below, calling softly to her, waking her. It would have been no challenge for a *voordalak* to climb up there.

Nor did it prove for Dmitry. His boot clunked against the walls and on the roof of the veranda, but that was all to the good. If he could raise the household, however much they might curse him, it would help put a stop to Tyeplov's plans. But he wasn't going to let the idea distract him. Once on the flat roof, he drew his revolver and pulled the cap off the end of his cane. He would give them no warning. He raised his boot and smashed it through the window, throwing himself through the gap created.

The room was empty. A single candle shone from atop the dresser. The bedclothes were rumpled. Dmitry peered at them, terrified that he might see blood, but there was nothing. The door was open. Dmitry went through it and down the stairs. It seemed that no one in the house had heard him. The front door was open too. He looked out. Across the dirt track that led past the house was a church; between him and it, a mass of gravestones, their shadows long in the moonlight.

Then came a flicker of white, only for a moment, close to the church itself, as though a ghost were running from its grave. Dmitry ran across the road and entered the cemetery, heading towards where he had seen it. He had to zigzag through the graves and tombs, some taller than he was, and soon became disorientated. He looked around and found he had veered far to the right of where he had briefly seen the figure. There was another flicker of white and he set off in pursuit, scarcely able to see where he was putting his feet among the shadows cast by the gravestones.

At last he reached the point where he thought he had seen whatever it was, but there was nothing: a patch of coarse grass, a few headstones. He turned a full circle, his cane and his pistol still grasped in his hands, looking around the churchyard for any sign.

And then he was face to face with Tyeplov. The *voordalak* had emerged from behind one of the graves. He was naked from the waist up. In his hand, Dmitry noticed the glint of a small knife, but that was merely a distraction. The feature that transfixcd Dmitry was the blood. There were two patches of it; around his lips and on his chest – just below his right nipple. It was easy to guess where the blood on his face had come from, but it took Dmitry a moment to see that the blood on Tyeplov's chest was his own, oozing from a long, straight, horizontal cut to his skin.

'She's ready for you, Mitka,' he said.

He stepped aside and like a butler guiding a guest into the drawing room, held out his hand to show Dmitry where to go. Dmitry had only to take a couple of steps for the headstone that had been obscuring her to be out of the way.

She was still beautiful, even in death. She had been laid out, or had lain there, in precisely the position of the body beneath her, lying in its grave, the stone just inches above her head, her arms by her side. She was wearing only a simple cotton nightdress, her hair down, spreading as a halo around her face and neck. Even the blood could not detract from the desperate yearning he felt for her.

As with Tyeplov, there were two areas of blood – blood from two quite different creatures, Dmitry realized. For many, it would have been the wound to her neck that was most shocking. It reminded Dmitry of what he had seen in the tunnel beneath the Star Fort – though this was far fresher. Blood still trickled down from it, some to the ground, some forming a little pool in the dip of her collarbone. It was enough to tell Dmitry she was dead. But that had not been his darkest fear.

There was also blood around her lips. They were parted slightly, and Dmitry could see it in her mouth too – black in the moonlight – not just stains but an actual mouthful, too much for her to swallow before she died. But he had no doubt that she had consumed enough. Tyeplov's blood. Yudin had explained the process. The *voordalak* had consumed her blood and, in the moment of dying, she had consumed his. And it had been done willingly, Dmitry could not doubt it. The only thing that Yudin hadn't told him was how long the process would take, but it was irrefutable that when Raisa Styepanovna finally awoke, it would be as a vampire.

'She's beyond death now.' Tyeplov was still standing just a few paces away.

Dmitry allowed his heart to fill with rage. He realized now that he had still held some slight affection for Tyeplov, even after discovering that he was a vampire. He supposed it was because in some way he had believed Tyeplov's story about being wronged – about seeking revenge.

Now that sympathy was all gone. What stood before him was a monster, an animal, an undead creature that had sold its soul to Lucifer. It didn't deserve pity or understanding. It deserved death. The whole of nature screamed at him that Tyeplov should die and die now at his hand.

Dmitry raised his pistol to the level of his shoulder, pulling back the hammer until it clicked into the cocked position and imagining what would become of Tyeplov's face when he fired – remembering the effect that a single, lucky bullet had had on Mihailov in the casemate in Sevastopol.

He squeezed the trigger and the hammer fell forward with a click. There was no explosion and no bullet. Dmitry tried again, but still the gun did not fire. And now, Tyeplov was walking briskly and purposefully towards him. He grabbed Dmitry's left hand before another shot could even be attempted, and then swung at him with the back of his fist. Dmitry felt the knuckles connect with his jaw, and then blackness came.

For the second time that evening, Dmitry fell painfully into oblivion.

CHAPTER XXI

TAMARA HAD HEARD NOTHING FOR ALMOST TWO DAYS. SHE had watched Dmitry as he heroically rode off across Kalanchyovskaya Square to save Raisa and then she had returned to Degtyarny Lane. Yudin had walked with her, but little had been said. All either of them could do was pray.

But Tamara should have heard something. If either of them had written on the day after Dmitry got to Klin, then she would have received it by now. She had not heard from Yudin either. She was tempted to go and see him, but it was late for him to be in his office. Anyway, she was busy. The coronation was only a week away and so the city was fuller than ever with senior officers and *chinovniki*. And many deemed that a fitting way to celebrate the accession of their new tsar was to visit a bawdy house and raise their own kind of salute with one of the girls there.

It was after ten o'clock now, just about their busiest time. Someone was knocking at the door again, softly but insistently. Tamara looked around the salon. She would have to turn them away. All the girls were occupied, and there were enough men here – sipping wine, some chatting, some avoiding the gaze of the others – to keep them busy for at least another hour. And Yudin would be pleased with some of them – there were men of real influence here, many of whom would more normally be found in the houses of Petersburg. Thus Yudin would be able to prove the usefulness of his organization here to his superiors in the capital. At the sound of the knocking Isaak stood up impassively and went to do his duty in opening the door.

Tamara waved him away and dealt with it herself. She opened

352

the little hatch in the door and clicked her tongue. The bright, shining blue eyes that stared back at her could belong to no one but Raisa. She quickly opened the door and let her in. A coachman followed, carrying her trunk. He tried to concentrate on his work, but eyed the salon curiously. The gaze of every one of the waiting customers fell to the floor.

'Put it in my office,' said Tamara. She went over to the door and opened it and he put the trunk inside. By the time she had shown the man out and paid him, Raisa had disappeared upstairs. Tamara knew she should not abandon her role as hostess, but she had to find out what had happened. She lifted her skirts and ran up the stairs, then went into Raisa's room. Raisa had already removed her outdoor clothes, and seemed to be preparing herself for a night's work.

'You're all right!' gasped Tamara. She stood still for a moment, then ran over to Raisa to embrace her. She felt her friend's arms around her, but their response seemed half-hearted.

'Yes, I'm all right,' she said blankly.

'What happened? Where's Dmitry?' Tamara sat down on the bed. Now that she knew Raisa was alive and well – albeit a little out of sorts – she was full of enthusiasm to hear the story of Dmitry's rescue mission.

'He made it in time,' said Raisa. 'He killed Tyeplov. It was quite' – she smiled – 'wonderful.' She continued with her make-up.

'Where is he now?'

'Haven't you seen him? I needed time to pack and take my leave. Madame Zhiglova has been so kind.'

'Raisa,' said Tamara, a little more sternly now, 'I saw the letter from Tyeplov to you, arranging to meet.'

'Yes, that was silly of me. But Dmitry made me see things properly.'

'After all you knew about him – about what he was.' Tamara was merely shocked, but in her voice it sounded like scolding.

'I know, Toma. I'm sorry.' Raisa's eyes filled with tears and she ran over to Tamara. This time her embrace was strong and sincere. 'I'm so sorry,' she repeated. 'But do we have to talk about it?'

'I think we all deserve to know,' said Tamara softly.

'You're right. You're right. But just not now. Tomorrow.'

'Tomorrow then,' said Tamara. As she spoke she remembered that she was off to Saint Petersburg tomorrow, but it wasn't worth pointing that out just now.

Raisa stepped back and tried to smile, blinking to clear the teardrops from her eyes. Tamara handed over her handkerchief, and Raisa wiped them away. She went back to her dressing table and resumed the application of her make-up, as ever without any need for a mirror.

'Now I must get ready for work,' she said.

'Oh no you don't!'

Raisa looked at her. 'Really, Tamara, believe me, it's what I need to do. I need things to be normal.'

Tamara stood and sighed. 'OK. But if you change your mind, don't think for a minute that you have to stick with it. Just give me a call.'

'I will,' said Raisa with a smile. 'I won't, but if I do, I will.'

Tamara left her and went back downstairs. There was an air of impatience in the room. Tamara circulated and refilled empty glasses. A year ago she would have taken one of them upstairs herself at a busy time like this, but now she was less keen. If one of them asked, she might, but none of them chose to. Did they think of her as old now, she wondered. Konstantin didn't see her in that way. At least she hoped not – it had been five months since they had laid eyes on one another.

It was only a few minutes after Tamara had left her that Raisa appeared at the top of the stairs and floated down them. Her eyes gleamed and her smile was small and knowing. Every man in the room preened himself. Some had been waiting for over half an hour, but the rule was generally not one of first come, first served. Raisa knew her regulars, and knew that it was they who merited special treatment.

Her eyes fell on a man in his late sixties, a General Maciejewski, though he wasn't in uniform and his full name would never be used. She stretched out her arm, pointing her index finger directly at him, and beckoned. He stood and came over to the stairs.

'Have you missed me?' she murmured to him. He pulled a face

354

that could be taken as a yes or a no, but said nothing. 'Well, we'll soon fix that,' she continued. She let him walk up the stairs ahead of her, one step at a time because of an injured leg. Tamara couldn't help but be reminded of Dmitry.

'And when you came round?' Yudin's voice was eager. Dmitry could not deny that it was a compelling story, but it was not the stuff of entertainment.

'It was morning,' he explained. 'Not all that late.'

'And I take it you were alone?'

'Utterly.' From somewhere deep in his subconscious, he had chosen precisely the right word. His voice almost cracked as he spoke it.

'So what did you do?'

Dmitry emitted a hollow laugh. 'I went to the house and asked after her.'

'You did what?'

'What else was there to do? Madame Zhiglova was very polite. She even guessed who I was. She was quite concerned when she went up to Raisa's room and found she wasn't there – and saw the broken window.'

'So why didn't you come straight back after that?'

'I don't know.' Dmitry felt he had been on the brink of insanity. Even what he told Yudin now was just an attempt to make sense of a kaleidoscope of recollections and emotions. 'I remembered what I'd heard in stories – about the undead lurking in graveyards close to where they died, so I booked into an inn and went back there every night. But there was nothing. And then this morning Madame Zhiglova came and found me, and told me that she'd had a letter from Raisa saying that everything was fine and that she wasn't to worry.'

'I see.'

'The letter was from Moscow.'

'My God!' exclaimed Yudin.

'I've seen her, Vasya.' There were tears in Dmitry's eyes now. 'She's back at Degtyarny Lane, as if nothing had happened.'

'At Degtyarny Lane?' Yudin raised his voice. 'What about Tamara Valentinovna? We must do something.'

'I know. I know. But . . . I can't. How can I chase across the country to save her one day, and then destroy her the next?'

'You must, Mitka. Think of what she's become.'

'I can't,' he moaned.

'Then I *will.*' The determination in his voice was unshakeable.

Dmitry looked up at him, his eyes glistening. 'I can't ask you to do that, Vasya.'

'I hope you don't plan on asking me not to.'

Dmitry shook his head. Yudin was right. It was not for him to force his cowardice on to others. 'No. No,' he said. 'You must do what you know is right.'

Yudin nodded, but did not seem to relish the prospect. Then he posed a question which Dmitry had already asked himself. 'Why do you think he let you live?'

'Tyeplov, you mean?'

Yudin nodded. 'It seemed like he had the perfect opportunity to have his revenge on you,' he said.

The answer was all too easy. 'You think he hasn't?' Dmitry wailed. 'You think that for me to die there quickly wouldn't have been a blessing compared with the state I'm in now? To go on living, knowing that the woman I love has been transformed into a creature like him?'

'Love?' asked Yudin simply.

'Loved. She's beyond any human affection now.' It was the most categorical lie he had ever spoken.

'Of course she is,' said Yudin. 'We found where Tyeplov was living, by the way.' He seemed happier now to change the subject, if only slightly. 'Gribov remembered the address where the letters from Raisa had been sent. It's not far from the theatre. There was a cellar, and a coffin. I burned it – he won't be able to return there. But . . . I found the letters.' He reached into his drawer and placed a bundle of papers on the desk. 'I suspect he destroyed the earlier ones.'

Dmitry ignored them. 'Have you read them?'

'I couldn't bear to.' Yudin paused, then spoke with an air of confidentiality. 'I take it you were unaware of her condition.'

'Condition?' The word drove through Dmitry's mind like a hot poker. 'She wasn't . . .' He couldn't bear even to imagine it. 'My child?'

Yudin looked horrified to have put the thought into his mind. 'No, no,' he said quickly. 'Not that. Almost the reverse. I've known for some months, I'm afraid – she was consumptive.'

'What?' It seemed so irrelevant now, after what had taken place, but somehow the idea began to penetrate Dmitry's mind – to infiltrate it.

'I don't know why she chose me to confide in – perhaps because it's I who knows you best. She didn't even tell Tamara.'

'She was dying?' gasped Dmitry.

'A few months at most, so they told her.'

For the first time in days, Dmitry heard music once again playing in his mind. It was the sound of hope. Dmitry felt as though he had been falling from a cliff and with flailing hands had grasped some thread of cotton dangling from above, something so fragile, so insubstantial, that only a fool would place hope in it, and yet which might save him. There was a chance that Raisa's actions in some bizarre way made sense.

He snatched up the letters and began to read them. They were not the billets-doux he had been expecting – far from it. They were precise and rational – almost clinical. Of course, it was only half of a correspondence; Dmitry could not see what Tyeplov had written back, but each subsequent letter from Raisa implied that she had received the responses she had been hoping for. There were fragments that spoke to him as if she had been in the room, standing beside him.

And what of any disease that a man or woman might have been suffering before the transformation? Would such an ailment go on to afflict them once they had become like you?

In the next letter, she pressed the point.

And so even if the person were to be on the very verge of death, they would, on reawakening, emerge into a life of immortality? You can assure me of that?

It all made perfect sense. He could not condone her for seeking to escape death by abandoning everything that was good, but it was at least understandable. It was not whim, caprice or mere vanity. But there was more.

You tell me of the changes that would take place; the new strengths and the new weaknesses. But what of those things that remain the same? Could I still laugh? Could I still enjoy the sensation of a man's arms around me? Could I still love?

And then:

You lead me to doubt you. I ask if I could laugh or love, or even cry, and you tell me that not only could I, but that those emotions would be a thousand times stronger than what I experience now. Why should I trust what you say? Why should you choose to help me? And yet, how will it benefit me to doubt you? You offer me my only hope.

Then there was the first mention, obliquely, of Dmitry himself.

Your candour can only do you credit. You are right; it is vain of me to think that you would do this for my benefit. I do not know what went on between you and Aleksei Ivanovich, but you clearly owe him a great debt and, I suspect, a little love. I can only thank God that you allow some of that obligation to be transferred to his son, and, through him, to me. I pray that he will choose to benefit from it as I do.

Dmitry glanced up at Yudin. His face carried that familiar, fatherly look of benevolence. He didn't probe or question or attempt to force Dmitry into revealing what the letters contained, he simply waited, knowing that he would be told everything that he deserved to know.

Dmitry read on.

You tell me of the acts which you and I must perform together for my salvation to take place. I will not hide from

358

you the fact that they terrify and revolt me, but I am not
so timid as to shy away from them merely because of that.
But the question on which everything must hinge is: will I,
once transformed, be possessed of that same ability to make
others (one other in particular) into a being such as myself?

It could only be that she received an answer in the affirmative.
Her next letter expanded on it.

You make it sound so beautiful. The Bible talks of a man
and a woman becoming 'one flesh' but what you speak of
might better be described as 'one soul'. And yet if that can
be the state that exists between Dmitry and me, will not the
same apply between me and you? If that one hurdle can be
overcome, then I can foresee only bliss for us.

Then came the final letter. It was dated 14 August – just two
days before the letter from Tyeplov arranging to meet her. That
one had to be a response to this.

You have convinced me. There is so much that I must take
on trust, but so much that I have to gain by trusting. It is
only the faithless who have no hope of heaven. I am willing,
more than willing, just as you tell me I must be. I can only
hope that, when the time comes, Dmitry will feel the same.
But I will not tell him beforehand. My act of faith must be
my own. If he chooses not to join me, I will not blame him,
he will be acting out of goodness.
*   Write to me and tell me when you will come. I am ready.*
I will be waiting. Come soon.
*   Raisa Styepanovna Tokoryeva*

Dmitry lowered the final letter. He had not put any of them
back on the desk, but let them rest in his lap. His face glowed
with a mixture of passion and shame. He felt tears pricking at
his eyes. He remembered what Tyeplov had said to him in Klin.
'She's ready for you, Mitka,' and 'She's beyond death now.' It all
made sense.

'No man likes to read of his own betrayal at the hands of the woman he loves,' said Yudin.

Dmitry shook his head. 'No,' he said. 'No. It's not that at all.' He tried to think what he should do, but in his mind there was only Raisa. He felt her pain, her indecision and her hope pouring out to him in every line he read. She had suffered so terribly, made so awful and profound a choice, and yet that did not mean that she had chosen correctly. He looked around the room. It was dark and dank and stuffy – no place to be thinking of her, of how he might regain her.

Yudin reached out his hand across the desk. 'Might I see?' he asked.

'No,' said Dmitry, snatching up the letters and putting them in his pocket. He knew that it was perhaps the most stupid thing he had ever done, that if anyone had the wisdom to tell him how to act then it was Yudin, but for that very reason he feared Yudin's opinion of what he should do might not tally with his own – even though, as yet, he had no opinion.

He stood up. 'I'm sorry, Vasya, but I have to sort this one out for myself.'

'You always have done, Mitka. And you've always come to the right decision.'

'And forget what I said earlier. I *do* ask you to do nothing with regard to Raisa. I'll deal with the problem, one way or another. Whatever happens, she'll be out of your way.'

He turned and headed for the stairs that would lead him up to the fresh air.

'Mitka!' Yudin called from behind him. Dmitry turned. 'Always act in accordance with your conscience. No man can ask you to do any more.'

Dmitry stared at him. It was as if he understood. Perhaps he had read the letters already – that would be like him. He would lie if it were necessary, but only to do good. Dmitry paced across the room and leaned across the desk to kiss Yudin on each cheek. Then he turned and left, knowing that he might never see his old friend again.

✳   ✳   ✳

This was the fastest Tamara had ever travelled. The freight trains went at about sixteen versts every hour; the passenger trains at forty. The imperial train was unlimited by anything but the power of the locomotive pulling it, and the impetuosity of His Majesty. A conductor had told her that they would reach speeds in excess of fifty-five, but moments later a colleague had added that that was only because Aleksandr was more in favour of a smooth ride than a speedy one. Under Nikolai, he told her, they had sometimes got up to seventy. But even at today's speed, the journey from Petersburg to Moscow would be completed in under fifteen hours. It was a quirk of tradition that even when Pyotr the Great moved his capital from Moscow to Petersburg, it had been decided that coronations would still take place within the Kremlin. Now that the railway had come, the decision seemed modern and far-sighted.

She had only had a few hours' stop in Petersburg. The scheduled train had got her in at the usual time of nine in the morning, and the imperial train had departed that same afternoon. There were more dignitaries on board than had ever been gathered together on a Russian train, more even than when the line was opened. The imperial ultramarine coaches – there were only two in existence – had been hooked together, but that was only sufficient for His Majesty, the tsaritsa, the tsarevich and the other children, the dowager empress and perhaps a few others. Tamara did not even know if Konstantin was included in that august group. The rest of the train, apart from the two kitchen cars, was made up of compartmentalized first-class carriages, specially cleaned and repainted for the occasion, though some of them seemed to be running without occupants.

At the very end of the train there was one coach – open rather than divided into compartments, but still first class – where the likes of Tamara had their seats. There were agents of the Third Section and the Gendarmerie, officers of the regular police and middle-ranking employees of the railway. None of them was worthy of sitting among the nobility in the other coaches, but the imperial train would not pull any carriage that was not at the very least first class.

For now, Tamara chose not to sit. She stood outside, on the iron platform at the back of the train, watching the track vanish into the distance. She exhaled and watched as the smoke that she had drawn in from her cigarette was caught in the wind and dragged away from her. It was dark, almost midnight, but the train would carry on through the night and arrive in Moscow in the morning, leaving the imperial family a few days to prepare themselves for the great, once-in-a-generation spectacle that was the coronation of the Tsar of All the Russias.

The locomotive whistle blew and the conductor, who had been standing a little way away, moved to apply the brake. Even an imperial train needed to stop for fuel. The station they rolled into was Okulovka. Tamara threw her cigarette down on to the track and stepped on to the station platform before they had quite stopped. There were only railway staff on it – no passengers. It wasn't a scheduled train, and even if members of the public turned up, they wouldn't be allowed on to the station. They were free to stand beside the track and cheer, which during the day they had, but not to get too close when the train stopped.

Tamara was not the only person to alight quickly. From every carriage at least one figure got off and looked warily up and down the platform just as she had. She was not even the only woman. Moments later, as if responding to the command of some unseen choreographer, a number of the passengers disembarked as a single mass. Tamara focused on the imperial carriages, but there was no sign of His Majesty or any of his immediate family. Okulovka was only a second-category station, and so they would not be staying long. She looked too for Konstantin, but did not see him. That did not mean he was not there. While the tsar, a typical Romanov, would have stood above the crowd, his brother could more easily get lost among it.

Everything seemed quite relaxed. She had spoken to a few of the Third Section's men who were based in Petersburg, and their opinion was that this was more for show than out of fear of any serious threat. The importance of a leader was reflected in how well he was guarded, and so a leader of Russia required the most guards of all. In her bag she carried the Colt pistol that Yudin had given her – for quite a different purpose – but she doubted she would have call to use it.

She walked up the platform, glancing at the faces she passed, and occasionally into the train. In the rear of the two imperial coaches she thought she caught sight of His Majesty, though she really only recognized his distinctive moustache. He looked pensive; for a man only three years older than herself, it was a great weight that had been thrust on his shoulders – but one he had been born to.

Then, on the platform, at the end of the very same carriage, she saw Konstantin. He was looking back up at the train, speaking to a woman Tamara could only guess was his wife, Aleksandra Iosifovna, who was looking down the platform, straight towards Tamara. Tamara was struck by how beautiful the grand duchess was. She had a reputation for it, but Konstantin had never described her. But then he wouldn't, not to his mistress. Tamara could almost see something of herself in the woman. Their faces were quite different, but her hair had a hint of red to it, though darker than Tamara's. Their builds were similar too – neither of them skinny, nor by any means fat; both with a full bosom and a body and limbs that curved gracefully. She was nine years Tamara's junior.

Aleksandra turned to face her husband and, seeing her in profile for the first time, Tamara could only be surprised at the size of her nose. It wasn't bulbous or even unattractive, just rather long. It was the only advantage that Tamara could see she had, at least in terms of appearance, but it was enough to cause her to smirk a little. At the same moment Konstantin turned and his eyes fell on Tamara. It was bad enough that he should see her at all, but that when he looked at her it was to see her sniggering at his wife's nose was appalling. Tamara felt her face redden and hoped he had not guessed her thoughts.

Konstantin was a model of calm. He had seen Tamara, she was certain, but he did not bat an eyelid or waver for a moment in his conversation with Aleksandra. Tamara walked past, perhaps a little closer to him than she should have, but neither he nor his wife seemed to notice. She walked all the way down to the north-western end of the platform, where the imperial waiting rooms were situated, but none of the royal family had chosen to make use of them at this stop. She looked inside the Kartsov Restaurant, which was reasonably full – the kitchen cars on the train served only the imperial coaches, and so by now many *chinovniki* and other attendants were feeling hungry and thirsty. She paid her ten copecks for a cup of coffee.

After about a quarter of an hour, the restaurant began to clear as passengers reboarded and the train prepared to leave. Tamara remained until almost everyone had gone, then walked down the platform towards her coach at the back. She passed the imperial carriages, and then the compartmentalized first-class carriages where, on a scheduled service, families and individuals could enjoy privacy for an extra charge. She had just passed an open window when she heard a familiar voice.

'Excuse me, mademoiselle.'

She took a step back and looked in through the train window.

'Yes?' she said.

'Would you, by any chance, be interested in becoming a member of a very exclusive group of people?'

She raised an eyebrow and smiled, but said nothing. The door opened and she stepped inside.

The locomotive blew its whistle and the train rolled slowly out of the station and onward towards Moscow.

It was an honour, but Titular Councillor Myshkin could see it only as a curse. He was certain that of all the people on the imperial train, he was of the lowliest rank – and that probably included the driver and the stoker. He had only been invited on board because His High Excellency, Actual Privy Councillor Laptyev, still had preparations to make for the coronation and needed a secretary to write down his thoughts.

It was Laptyev who had called it an honour, but now he had fallen asleep further up the train with a bottle of vodka in his hand and left Myshkin to write up letters to three dozen dignitaries explaining precisely what the limits of their duties would be on the day. And a moving train was not an easy place to write a letter, particularly when accompanied by the loud snoring of an Actual Privy Councillor, and the raucous shouts of others who had not yet succumbed to the drowsy numbness to which so much celebration must eventually lead.

Fortunately, Myshkin had noticed a few empty compartments and so, while the train was halted, he walked down the platform and got into one, and now he sat there alone, trying to write. The problem was the shaking of the train. If Myshkin had not been so busy with his work, he would have been interested to make notes on how the amount of vibration did not simply increase with the speed of the train. When they had been going slowly, it had been quite violent, and then they had reached a velocity at which the train itself had seemed suddenly comfortable, calm even. If only the driver could have kept them at that rate of progress. Now they had speeded up further, and the movement was worse than ever.

Suddenly there was a loud bang, and the whole carriage shook. For a moment Myshkin feared that a bomb had been laid on the track, but he soon realized that the train was continuing its swift, rocky motion. It had just been some kink or perturbation in the rails. The only thing that had been disturbed was the door that led through to the next compartment in the carriage. The noise he had heard had been its banging against the wooden partition.

He looked through, and his pen fell from his hand and on to the floor.

The scene was framed perfectly by the doorway. Its main element was a woman's naked back. Not quite naked; her underskirts were still on, but were dragged up and bunched around her waist, held there by the hands of a man whose face was obscured by the woman's body. Her own hands were raised and clasped behind her head, holding up a mass of curled red hair that would otherwise have hidden the beautiful – Myshkin could not deny it – curve of her back.

Her knees were up on the train seat, on either side of the man who sat there. His trousers were down around his ankles. While the rocking of the train might have been a hindrance to Myshkin's chosen occupation for the evening, it seemed to provide a convenient metronome for these two. Each time the wheels beneath the carriage crossed the join between two lengths of rail, which would have knocked Myshkin's pen across the page, the woman's body crashed down on to the man's, and even on flat sections of track they performed the same movement, maybe with a little less vigour.

Myshkin recovered his pen from the floor and put it on the table beside him. He was no stranger to the sexual act, as his wife would attest and his nine children demonstrated, but in the thirty-seven years of his life it had never occurred to him that anyone could – or should want to – perform it in so uncomfortable and precarious a position. A bed would prove far more suited to the activity, though it had to be admitted that there was no bed available in the carriage.

It suddenly seemed to Myshkin that the train was beginning to travel faster, though a glance out of the window showed the landscape outside rushing past at the same speed as before. He quickly realized that it was not the train that had increased its tempo, but the couple in the compartment opposite. Like an unruly violin section, they had broken free of the rhythm dictated by their conductor, and were racing ahead to the conclusion of their performance. The train could no longer keep up with them, and Myshkin might have been convinced that it was their intention to arrive in Moscow ahead of it.

Then the woman stopped moving. She tried to rise, but the man's hands, still at her waist, held her down on him. She leaned forward and slightly to one side, putting her arms around his neck, and in so doing allowed her red tresses to fall down and cascade across her back. The man's face peeked from behind her shoulder.

It was the Grand Duke Konstantin. Though his eyes were shut tight, his spectacles were still perched unmistakably on his nose. Titular Councillor Myshkin could not see the woman's face, but he felt certain that she was not the grand duchess. She certainly didn't behave as though she was.

Myshkin stood up and walked across the compartment to the door. He closed it quietly but firmly, and returned to writing his letters.

CHAPTER XXII

THERE WAS NO CHANCE THAT TAMARA WOULD HAVE BEEN granted a place within the Cathedral of the Assumption, nor would she have wanted it. It was a beautiful, warm day in late August, perhaps one of the last good days they would get before the autumn. Inside the cathedral it would be close and stuffy, and all there was to see would be stilted and formal. From here she could see Russia – not the entire land but, it seemed to her, the entire people, or a fair sample of them. Without even turning her head she could look out on what felt like half the population of Moscow.

She had found herself a spot among the crowds in Ivanovskaya Square, in the south-eastern corner of the Kremlin. It was evidently an ideal viewpoint; clustered in the same area were a number of artists, making sketches of what they saw before them, so that posterity might never forget the day. Behind her was the Church of Saints Konstantin and Yelena, nestling in the Taynitzkiy Garden, and beyond that the river Moskva, flowing below the Kremlin walls, spanned by the Stone Bridge to one side and the Moskva Bridge to the other. Stretching across the skyline, their domes glistering in the sunlight, were more churches than she could count, some tiny, others vast cathedrals. To her left, beyond the Kremlin walls, she could see the Cathedral of Christ the Redeemer, built to celebrate the deliverance of Moscow from Bonaparte, and still not complete. Diametrically opposite, in Red Square, stood the garish painted domes of Saint Vasiliy's; far older, and for her the true symbol of Moscow.

She had begun the day in the company of Rodion and Vadim,

but they had soon separated, her brother sensing her desire to be alone. She was almost at the back of the crowd, but the added height of the slope meant she had a better view. Ahead of her perhaps ten thousand people lined just this side of the path that His Majesty's carriage had taken that morning, having entered from Red Square through the Saviour's Gate. The crowd was held back and the pathway kept clear by three ranks of guards in their finest uniforms. On the other side, a similar cordon pinned back another huge crowd into the area in front of the Assumption Belfry. From where she stood, she could clearly see the Tsar Bell in its place in front of the bell tower, a huge gap in its side, big enough to walk through, where it had shattered in a fire.

The imperial procession must have been over a verst long. The carriages and mounted guards had come down from the Saviour's Gate, past the bell tower and the Cathedral of the Archangel and the Cathedral of the Annunciation, and deposited their charges outside the newly completed Great Kremlin Palace. After that, as the various members of the imperial family and other dignitaries had paused and waved to the crowds before going in, the carriages and horsemen had continued down to exit the Kremlin by the Borovitskaya Tower, in order to allow room for the remainder of the procession to pass through.

When Konstantin had climbed down from his coach he had looked distant and minuscule, but Tamara had still been able to recognize him. With him were his wife and his little son, and two daughters, the youngest only two years old. It was strange for her to watch him like that – much like the occasions in Petersburg when she had silently, distantly gazed upon her son Luka. Today she was just like any other Russian who had come to see the imperial family on this grand occasion, but she wondered how many of the women in the crowd around her could boast that they had slept with one of the men in the royal party. She smirked to herself. At least one or two others, she'd be prepared to guess. The Romanovs were not the most chaste of men. But she hoped it would be only she who could claim to be part of that elite group who had done it at a speed of fifty-five versts per hour.

She had been quite unprepared for the encounter, understanding that even to speak to Konstantin in such a public place as on the train risked their being discovered. But once they were alone in the carriage, he told her how he had yearned for her all the time they had been apart, and how the momentary glimpse of her walking along the platform had inflamed his passion. It was evidently true. Their brief liaison in the small compartment had been the most fervent she had ever known with him. She had left him at the next station, even before the train had come to a halt, so that no one would connect her to the fact that, a few minutes later, the grand duke had emerged from exactly the same door.

In the few days since then, since she had returned to Moscow, life had gone on very much as usual. Raisa had refused to tell her any more detail of what had happened in Klin between her and Dmitry and Tyeplov, but seemed to be back to her usual self. Tamara had not seen anything of Dmitry, despite calling twice at his rooms, but Yudin had assured her that all was well with him. The strangest thing was that Dmitry had not once called on Raisa. But that was their problem, not Tamara's.

Things had quietened down a little now that the entire procession had passed and all who were needed for the coronation had gone into the Great Palace. Tamara had looked, but not caught sight of Dmitry at the head of the Izmailovsky Regiment as it paraded past. She knew how easily she might have missed him. The crowd happily remained, knowing that the imperial family would soon re-emerge. The mood was one of light-hearted chatter. Cheering could often be heard above the sound of the bells that pealed from every church in the city. She scarcely remembered the coronation of Nikolai I. She had been only five, but had a vague image of watching from somewhere in the city, hand in hand with Yelena and Valentin – not with her true parents, they had gone by then, though it couldn't have been too long before. The Lavrovs described it as quite a solemn occasion – the most obvious noise from the crowd being the sound of their prayers for Nikolai's long life and safety. It was a sign of how times were changing.

Another cheer rose up, louder than the general hubbub. Tamara looked in the same direction as everybody else, and could just see a vague movement of figures, all but obscured by the multitude between her and them. But she knew what was happening. The tsar and his entourage were leaving the Palace of the Facets and stepping out on to the Red Porch, before descending into Cathedral Square and thence into the Cathedral of the Assumption.

Tamara held her breath. It was a sublime moment. A new tsar was about to be crowned.

Yudin peeped into the nave of the cathedral. There was some light shining in through the high windows, but he would be safe if he remained in the shadows. It was hard to say why he had come here, but the simple answer was that it was because he could. It would not have been possible for him to walk across Cathedral Square and enter the church by the normal means, but there were other ways through the Kremlin, known only to a few. An underground corridor had led him up to a small enclosure, just behind the right-hand Deacon's Door in the iconostasis. The most risky part was to move from there into the nave, but all eyes were on Aleksandr, standing in front of the Beautiful Gate; and in a church of this size, nobody's attention encompassed both that and the door through which Yudin now slipped.

But there was more to being here than proving that his inability to walk in sunlight was no bar to his attending this most important of occasions – Yudin also felt a sense of history. He had failed to attend the coronation of Nikolai – it being at a time when he was still coming to grips with his new state as a *voordalak* – but he had been instrumental in the ending of the reign of Nikolai's predecessor. There were powers in the world that would now be focusing all their attention on this new Aleksandr. Did Zmyeevich, Yudin wondered, know that he could not make his move on Aleksandr II until Aleksandr I, wherever he might be, finally died? It seemed likely. Yudin had his blood samples and his microscope, but Zmyeevich had his mind, and that would tell him in seconds what it might take Yudin months to methodically ascertain.

But Zmyeevich would not come in person to see this; it would be too great a risk. That did not mean that he might not send someone through whose eyes he could see. If Tyeplov had, like Yudin, found a way into the cathedral that avoided the sun's light then he might stand as a proxy for Zmyeevich, allowing one to bear witness to everything that was seen through the eyes of the other.

He glanced around the crowd that filled the nave – brows glistening in a heat that Yudin perceived but did not suffer from. Though the people stood shoulder to shoulder, still the great height of the building meant that it had a sense of emptiness. The pillars that supported the roof, ten times higher than the tallest man in there, soared upwards, the painted faces of the saints staring down on the proceedings below. The vast iconostasis filled the eastern wall. It was all as though it had been built as an antidote to hubris, a reminder to the new tsar that however powerful he might believe himself to be, he was puny compared to the one who gave him that power. Whether that one was God or Zmyeevich, the tsar himself would have to choose.

Yudin saw no sign of Tyeplov. The only unexpected face was that of Gribov, who caught his eye from his vantage point beside the South Portal. He seemed almost to merge into the biblical scenes that were painted on it. Yudin was surprised that someone so lowly would be invited here, to the heart of the ceremony, but he realized that Gribov had almost as good a knowledge as he did of the ancient passageways that ran beneath the Kremlin – perhaps better. If he did know of all of them, at least he did not have the keys to access the most important ones, beneath Yudin's office.

The tsar and his entourage moved away from the iconostasis and on to a raised platform closer to the centre of the church, where all could get a better sight of him. The tsar and the tsaritsa sat on their thrones. An elderly general approached them – Prince Gorchakov, hero of the Russian army and leader of the defence of Sevastopol. In his hands he carried a red velvet pillow, and on it sat the Golden Orb, the most important item of the imperial regalia. Gorchakov shuffled forward slowly and ceremoniously, his head bowed in deference. Then he appeared to stop dead in his tracks, before tottering, at first gently but with ever-increasing speed, to his right, overcome by the heat. The pillow dropped from his hands and the orb spilled over on to the wooden floor. The crack as it made contact filled the silent space of the cathedral. Yudin covered his mouth to hide a smirk.

Attendants stood in momentary confusion as to whether to rescue the fallen orb or the fainting prince. In the end, both were raised back to their proper positions, little the worse for wear. There was frantic checking to ensure that the diamond-encrusted cross, which was mounted above a huge sapphire at the top of the orb, was not bent out of shape, but it seemed that all was in order. The tsar said a few reassuring words to his general.

'It's all right to fall here. The important thing is that you stood firm on the battlefield.'

The words were spoken softly; at the distance Yudin was standing, a human ear would not have been able to catch them. Yudin had to admire Aleksandr's quick thinking, but it was a poor way to inspire confidence in the general. Some time later that evening the old man would play those words over again in his mind and remember that he had not stood firm – it was he who had ordered the evacuation of Sevastopol.

The ceremony continued with prayers and blessings from Metropolitan Filaret and then at last he handed the crown – more reminiscent of a jewelled mitre than the image of a royal crown that Yudin had grown up with in England – to the tsar. Aleksandr placed the Great Imperial Crown upon his own head, just as Bonaparte had done over half a century before. Today though, no denial of God's authority was implied.

Next, the emperor was to crown his empress, but again there was to be mishap. She looked pale as she rose from her throne and knelt before him. He lifted the Lesser Imperial Crown – distinguishable from his own only by its size and its slightly more modest jewels – and placed it on her head. Four attendants reached forward to clip the crown to her hair, but as she rose, it slipped to one side and was only just caught before it too fell to the ground. A look of horror filled the tsaritsa's face, but Aleksandr remained calm. He replaced the crown on her head and the same attendants, with hands that Yudin could only imagine were trembling, clipped it again. This time it stayed in place.

Now the cathedral was filled with sound, from within and without. The bells of the cathedral and all the churches around began to toll, and a salute of 101 guns boomed. The choir struck up the Polychronion. All in the church then knelt to pray, and

Yudin decided that it was best to follow suit. More hymns were sung and another salute was sounded by the guns outside. At last the tsar was led away by the metropolitan, through the Beautiful Gate and into the sanctuary where he would receive communion. It was the only time – and the tsar the only man – that someone who was not ordained was allowed before the altar in any church in Russia. Even the tsaritsa had to remain in front of the iconostasis, to receive the bread and wine together on a spoon in the normal fashion.

The thought of the consumption, however symbolic, of flesh and blood caused stirrings in Yudin's own stomach, and he could only smile at the mimicry that existed between the world of Christianity and that of the *voordalak*. It also gave him pause to wonder what was to become of Dmitry. It had been a week now since Yudin had shown him the letters from Raisa, which Yudin himself had so carefully dictated to her. And yet he had heard nothing of Dmitry going to Raisa to discover the truth. But he knew not to worry. Dmitry would act as Yudin had predicted he would act. He had no need to go back to his labour – to peek at it as it bubbled in the oven and give it an extra stir. Like any great chef he knew that that could ruin a recipe; he knew to trust in himself.

Aleksandr was back on his throne now, receiving homage from the closer members of his family, including his brothers, Konstantin, Nikolai and Mihail, and also his son, the tsarevich Nikolai Aleksandrovich. Perhaps it would be on to that boy – not yet thirteen years old – that Zmyeevich would now turn his attention.

Finally the dismissal was read and the tsar and his family began to process out of the cathedral to the strains once again of the Polychronion. Once they had gone, the rest of the congregation began to follow. But it was still light outside in Cathedral Square, and Yudin could only disappear back through the Deacon's Door and return the way he had come.

Raisa was alone. She was standing by the window, looking out at the moon that hung over Degtyarny Lane. She turned as he closed the door behind him. In her eyes he saw only terror.

'Hello, my little Mityenka,' she said softly.

Dmitry said nothing. He gazed at her, trying to take in what she was, and what she had been. The silence seemed almost painful to her. Tears began to form in her eyes and she took a step towards him.

'I know why you're here, Mitka,' she said. 'But I beg you, on everything we've ever meant to each other, give me a chance to explain first.'

'First?'

She laughed mirthlessly. 'Don't tease me. I've seen what you can do with that.' Her eyes flicked towards his right hand.

In horror he took in what she meant, and what she was looking at; the cane that he carried with him everywhere. He'd used it in front of her to kill Ignatyev – in this very room. He threw it aside on to the bed.

'I would never . . .' he began to say, but he knew it was untrue. It was still – just conceivably – where the evening might end. But there was another reason that the words would not come to him; a simple, visceral reason. He had not seen her – apart from the sight of her body in a churchyard in Klin – for many weeks; had not seen her, or put his arms around her, or smelt her, or kissed her.

He charged across the room and clutched her in his embrace, pushing his lips down on to hers and feeling them open to receive him. He felt her hands on his back, his shoulders and his head. There was nothing different here, nothing changed from what she had been before. It might be that she could no longer exist in daylight, that she would live for ever, that any wound to her body would heal, but to everything he cared about, that seemed to make not a jot of difference. Her kiss was still Raisa's kiss; her caress still Raisa's caress. What else was unchanged about her, he would discover as time went by, but for now, this was enough.

They separated and stared silently into each other's face. It was Dmitry who spoke first.

'Why didn't you tell me?'

She looked away from him, embarrassed. 'There's so much I haven't told you.'

Only then did it dawn on him that she could have no idea

what he'd discovered. He persisted with the point of his original question. 'About the consumption.'

'How would that have helped? Could you have cured it?'

'I deserved to know.'

'So you could cry over me and tell me how you loved me and how you would miss me?'

'Yes,' he said earnestly.

'And remind me every minute of my last days that I was going to die.'

He couldn't deny it. 'I saw you with him,' he said bitterly. 'With Tyeplov – in the cemetery in Klin.'

'What?' She couldn't conceal her surprise.

'I chased him there. We found his letter to you.'

'And you came to . . . to save me?'

Dmitry nodded.

'You fool!' she said. 'He might have killed you.'

'No,' said Dmitry. 'He let me live. And now I understand why.'

'I doubt that.'

'I read your letters, the ones you sent to him. Not until afterwards.' She looked at him, trying to fathom what precisely he might have gleaned from them. He explained. 'I know why you did it – so that you could live.'

'That was selfish of me.'

'So that I could join you,' he added.

She flushed. 'That was even worse.'

'No. No,' said Dmitry. 'It was wonderful – the most selfless gesture that anyone could imagine.'

'Selfless?'

'You did it for love.'

She turned away from him. 'I did it for *me*, Mitka. Not for love, not even for you. I did it because *I* couldn't bear the thought of living without you, or even of sharing you with your wife, and so I decided that *I* was going to have you – all of you and for ever.'

'So why haven't you come to me? Why haven't you asked me?'

She walked back to him and laid her cheek against his breast. 'I've tried. I've come close to you; I've watched you, but it's the same terror that strikes me every time.'

'What terror?'

'That you'll say no.'

'What would you do if I did?'

'I would pray for death.'

'Only pray for it?' asked Dmitry.

'I could not bring it about myself.'

'What if I were to?' he asked.

She turned and walked to the bed, then picked up the cane he had thrown there. She plucked off the protective cap and flung it aside, before handing him the now lethal weapon. She sat down and began to unfasten her bodice and then unbutton the blouse beneath. She lay back on the bed, the garments hanging on either side of her, revealing her belly and her breasts.

'If that's your choice, then I won't stop you,' she said. 'This isn't how I'd have chosen my life to finish, but from where I am now, I can conceive of no better ending than by your hand.'

She raised her arm to cover her face, either so that she would not see him or, more likely, so that he would not look into her eyes and be diverted from what he must do. He gazed at her body, as he had done so many times before, but now with very different thoughts. He had the weapon in his hand. He need only press it down against her skin, just below her breast. It would be doing her will, and the will of God. Afterwards, he still had the pistol for himself, but he need not tell her about that.

And yet what he saw before him was not the prone body of a *voordalak*, easier to be rid of than any he had before encountered. It was Raisa. Beneath that point on her chest where he would stab, her heart still beat. He could almost see it. Her kiss and her touch had been the same as before – why then should so much else be different? He fixed his eyes on her chest, watching its slight movement as she breathed. He felt the solid, firm shaft of the cane in his hand and imagined it penetrating her flesh, imagined her momentarily writhing as her skin ruptured and then . . . that was too much. He had seen two vampires die – both by his own hand – and though he had no idea what they suffered, the mere image of Raisa's beauty decaying so utterly and so suddenly persuaded him that he could not go ahead with this. Even when he had entered the room he had known he would not. He had been teasing himself, which was indulgent, and teasing Raisa, which was cruel.

He leaned forward and placed his lips on precisely the point where, in another life, he might have thrust with the blade.

'One final kiss,' he heard her say, 'to prove it as an act of love.'

But Dmitry chose to express his love quite differently. Quickly, and with the passion of weeks of separation, he began to remove the remainder of her clothes.

'You're a fool, my little Mityenka,' she said. It was a harsh word that she had chosen – *prostak* – as was her tone. She might almost have been crowing, like an adversary at Preferans who had tricked him into playing the wrong card and was now in a position to take everything he had. He knew it was not true, but he doubted he would have changed his course of action, even if it had been.

If there was anywhere in Moscow that wasn't celebrating, Tamara had been unable to find it. It was almost as light as day now, the sky illuminated by the most magnificent display of fireworks she had ever seen. She'd headed north-east, in the direction of the station, and was now caught up in the huge crowds that thronged the largely open spaces around the Red Gate, through which earlier that very day Aleksandr had made his ceremonial entrance into the old capital.

All through the city, stalls had been set up to provide free food and cheap drink for the people, paid for by the tsar. Vodka, beer and wine had flowed freely, and more than once a tankard had been thrust into Tamara's hand by a complete stranger. At first she had felt a little detached from these people, but as the evening had worn on it had become impossible not to be sucked up into the atmosphere of ecstatic joy. On top of that, she had to admit, she was a little drunk.

Not for the first time, she felt a man's hand grab her around the waist and attempt to squeeze her close to him. On any other day, he would have been walking away from her in agony, but today she extricated herself with a fairly gentle push. He was in no condition to hang on.

The air was filled with the sound of people's cheering, of the church bells still pealing and above all of fireworks exploding. Smoke blew across the square ahead of her, causing some to cough, but Tamara revelled in the smell of it – the taste of it. Bright rockets exploded across the sky, white and green. Three huge fountains of red sparks spewed into the air like volcanoes. An old man on a cart tried to drive his way through the crowd, but his horse took fright at the noise and reared into the air. Three men managed to grab it and calm it, but still the driver seemed intent on continuing, despite the terror of the beast. The men led them away – horse, wagon and driver – into a nearby courtyard, and soon four men emerged, all drinking, the driver abandoning his journey for now.

An arm draped itself around her shoulder, but it felt like someone who sought physical support rather than anything else from her body. He must have been sixty or more, and had hung himself from her and another woman.

'Just like in '12,' he said to no one in particular. 'We saw them off then – and we will next time.'

'What?' asked Tamara. Despite his drunkenness, the man seemed joyous, and Tamara could not help being infected by it.

'The French!' he shouted, freeing his other hand to wave it in the direction of the imagined enemy. 'Rostopchin burned the city to stop them. They never even made it this time.' He released her and staggered down the hill towards the flames, only to be caught by the crowd before he ever got near them.

Tamara walked on. Through the sounds of the fireworks and the crowd and the church bells, there came something else that she couldn't make out – an artificial sound that sometimes cut through the noise, sometimes was masked by it. She followed it, away from the fireworks. The crowd thinned a little and then grew more dense and the sound became clearer. It was music – two men played balalaikas, one a guitar. In front of them people were dancing, some very well – particularly the men – others less so.

Tamara began to push her way through to the front of the circle of people who stood and watched. Just as she reached it, the music came to its climax and the onlookers cheered. Some of the dancers, exhausted, fell back among their friends in the crowd, but others stayed, ready for the next dance. Two of the men had tambourines and started the music by striking them in time. The band struck up and then the crowd began to clap in rhythm. Tamara joined them. It was a slow song at first, but she knew it would speed up.

The two tambourinists were expert dancers. They threw themselves to the ground at strange angles, sometimes supported by both feet, sometimes by a hand and a foot, constantly swapping the hand in which they held the instrument, and beating it against their foot or knee or head. There were times when Tamara would have sworn they were standing on both hands, but she could not see how they could manage that and still keep striking the tambourines. Their movement was rapid, fluid and instinctive.

Tamara raised her hands above her head as she clapped, swinging her hips and shoulders in time with the accelerating rhythm. Soon she realized that she was no longer watching, but part of the dance itself. She did not know from where inside her it came. She had seen dances like this before, but never partaken. Her dancing had always been far more formal; western, French, the way she had been taught. This dancing was Russian. It was about feeling, not understanding. At another time, the thought of the crowd watching her as she gyrated before them would have embarrassed her, but now she was thrilled by it; she felt at one with them.

The two men with the tambourines had soon caught sight of her, and now they danced on either side, facing one another and with her in between. They continued the same strange motions, as though for them legs and arms were of equal function, and without even having to think, Tamara found her movements fitting in with theirs. As one did a cartwheel, his feet almost hitting her nose, she fell back instinctively and found herself caught by the other. Now off balance, she was under their control and they threw her back and forth between them, while her feet remained fixed to the ground at a single point. She could have stepped away at any time, but she enjoyed the loss of control; it was like being caught in a great storm that would lead her where it willed.

Then she found that she was upright again and the two men were on the ground, both on their backs, supported by their arms.

They seemed to be kicking at her legs, but never made contact. Once she had cottoned on she began to jump in time with them, and they now aimed their feet much closer to her, so that if she didn't keep her skips and leaps in exact time with the music, they would surely kick her. Tamara lifted up her skirts, revealing her boots and ankles, and was amazed to watch as the men's legs swung beneath her, as if gravity applied to none of them.

As the music sped up still further, she became a little giddy, and feared she would lose her balance. With one final leap she was away from the two men, but turned to see her place had already been taken by another woman, who continued the game of musical hopscotch with no less enthusiasm than Tamara herself had displayed. Tamara joined another group of dancers who held hands and circled around the central trio, occasionally letting go to clap at a slower beat than that with which the guitar and balalaikas and tambourines rushed on. But as the tempo increased, so they were forced to as well, and Tamara found herself circling round and round with ever-increasing pace. The sound of the music filled her ears, along with the explosions of fireworks that still lit the sky, their colourful sparks blurring before her eyes as she moved faster and faster, her hands sore from clapping, her breath short.

It was over before she even noticed. She had felt that the crescendo and accelerando of the music could never stop, but finally it did and the crowd exploded into cheers and applause with which Tamara happily joined in, while noting with not a little pride that some of it was directed at herself. She felt hands patting her on the back and arms embracing her and she did not resist them. Someone handed her a mug. She sniffed it and then gratefully downed the cooling ale inside.

Then, to a cheer, the band struck up again and, to an even greater cheer, Tamara stepped back out among the dancers.

The boom of the fireworks outside reminded Dmitry of the guns at Sevastopol, but he did not fear the sound any more. Soon he would be beyond all fear. The process had already begun.

There was little pain. Her playful bites during their lovemaking had in the past caused him more discomfort than this. The overriding sensation was the smell of Raisa's hair, which pressed against Dmitry's face. He could see nothing of what she was doing to him. Only the slight sound of her tongue lapping away at him and her occasional moans of pleasure gave any clue as to what was happening.

After they had made love, they did not speak. She had lain in his arms, just as ever they had done before. After what seemed like an eternity, she had asked one question.

'So, will you join me?'

'Yes.' Dmitry's answer had been a whisper, but he had always known what it would be. She wasted no time. First she had kissed him on the lips and then her mouth descended on to his neck.

She remained there, drinking from him, for two or three minutes, and although he could feel little at the point where she drew the blood, the effects of its loss were becoming clear. He felt light-headed – happy even, though that was not truly his mood. Then, just as Raisa's letters to Tyeplov had described, he began to share her mind. His first sensation was of his own blood. The taste itself was foul, though he imagined he would get used to it, but he also experienced the pleasure which Raisa took from it. He understood that soon he would know that pleasure for himself. He tried to explore other corners of her mind but found himself unable. Each door he came to was barred.

Raisa pulled away from him and looked into his face. Her expression was of a joy he had never seen in her. The blood smeared around her mouth – his own blood – should have revolted him, but the ecstasy to which it had driven her, as she ran her tongue around her lips to taste a little more, could only turn revulsion into hunger.

'Not yet,' she said. 'Not everything.' He knew that she was talking about those closed doors of her mind. 'First you must drink.'

She knelt up on the bed on one knee, her right leg up, so that her thigh was horizontal. In her hand she had a knife. She drew it across the inside of her thigh, just inches from the top, and blood began to drip down on the sheets.

'Quickly,' she said. 'Before it heals.'

Dmitry leaned forward and placed his mouth over the wound.

He licked at the blood on the surface. It tasted foul, as his own blood had always done on those occasions when he had had cause to taste it, but the joy he felt from knowing it was Raisa's blood, knowing that it was willingly given, was overpowering. He pushed forward with his tongue, using its tip to force open the tiny wound she had created in herself, trying to make it wider and deeper so that more blood could escape. Then, as though her heart had suddenly beaten more strongly, a spurt of blood forced its way into his mouth. He swallowed it in an instant and waited for more, but it did not come. He knew he would have to take it. He pressed his lips to her skin, sealing the wound, and then began to suck. The blood flowed smoothly, and he allowed his mouth to fill before swallowing each gulp.

Music came to him, music that was louder and more powerful than ever before. For all he loved the melodies and rhythms that he had created in his mind in the past, this was the sound of true genius. This would make Bach, Mozart and Chopin weep for their inadequacies. It grew louder with each gulp of her blood that he swallowed, and the harmony grew darker, more unnerving. There was a distinct moment at which he realized that the music was no longer magnificent, but terrifying. He wanted to make it cease, but could not. It filled his head with images of pain and torture and betrayal, as though it were played by an orchestra that had been damned to Hell. He tried to listen to the fireworks outside, to use their noise to make the music end, but he could not. And through it all, hiding behind the music but clearly there, was the sound of laughter; Raisa's laughter.

Suddenly, he could no longer taste blood. He pulled away. The wound in her thigh was gone – healed. He felt her hand on his hair, pulling his face upwards to look into hers, and stretching open the wound to his neck as she did so.

'That's enough,' she said. 'Now we need to finish you off.'

The foul music still played and images filled his mind. One predominated. It was himself – a little boy of about five – playing with a wooden sword, sparring with a grown man, who brandished a real sword; his father, Aleksei. Was this, Dmitry asked himself, how it was supposed to end?

'No,' he said weakly, but she did not listen. She pushed him down on to the bed with a strength he could never have guessed she owned. One hand pressed down on his forehead and the other on his chest as her mouth returned to the still-fresh wound that she had created and began to drink once more.

Still the music grew louder, as did the laughter, even though there was no chance now for it to escape her mouth. But it did not come from her mouth; it came from her mind. Dmitry felt her grip on him relax and tried to move, but he was too weak. He raised his hand just a few inches and looked down on it. It was pale and thin. He could not hold it there for more than a moment and was forced to let it drop.

He saw Raisa's face above him again. His blood was now spread over her cheeks and neck. She was panting – pleased with herself. It was only a respite. Her teeth went down on him once more and he felt her tearing at his flesh, turning now to that as his blood ran short.

The music grew ever louder, though the sound of her laughter was gone, and Dmitry realized that he had no feeling in his limbs. It was as if he had no arms and no legs, and the sensation continued to work its way up his body until only his head existed, then only his face, then only his eyes.

Then the music stopped.

CHAPTER XXIII

THEY FOUND THE BODY BESIDE THE RIVER, A LITTLE WAY OUT of town, downstream, two days after the coronation. He hadn't been that difficult to identify – he was wearing the uniform of a cavalry major, and the word was already out that Major Dmitry Alekseevich Danilov had failed to report for duty on the morning of His Majesty's great day. There was no clear idea of precisely when he had died, but the speculation was that it had occurred the night before the coronation. No one knew why Major Danilov might have wandered into a rough part of town, but there seemed little doubt that vagabonds had fallen upon him and had cut his throat – quite brutally, as reports were keen to point out.

Tamara knew differently. Nadia had told her that Dmitry had called on Raisa, and that she had seen neither of them leave – a puzzle in itself. But both were gone. The reason for Dmitry's absence was soon revealed, but of Raisa there had been no further sign. Until Tamara heard the news, she had suspected they might have eloped – hoped it at least. After she learned about the state of Dmitry's body her first guess was that the one remaining vampire, Mihailov, must have come upon the two of them in Raisa's room and slain them both. She had no doubt that before very long on some other riverbank or remote spot Raisa's body would be found, and that the newspapers would linger with similar glee over the details of the wound to her neck – though few would be smart enough to make a connection with Dmitry.

Then the letter had arrived.

Yudin had made most of the arrangements for the funeral.

It was to be in Petersburg, on Vasilievskiy Island. Then, on the evening before they were due to travel up, Yudin had announced to Tamara that he would not be attending the ceremony. He told her that he felt responsible for Dmitry's death, and that he could not put Svetlana Nikitichna through the agony of seeing him and blaming him. It seemed more like a way to assuage his own conscience than to save Svetlana pain, but there was nothing Tamara could do about it.

That morning, as she had been about to set out to catch the train, she had found the letter. It had been slipped under the door by an unknown messenger some time in the small hours. She picked it up, but did not have time to look at it until she was on the train to Petersburg. The text was not long.

My dear Tamara Valentinovna,

By the time you receive this, I shall be gone. Whether I shall be dead is a matter for fate to decide. And on this occasion, fate will take the form of our mutual friend, Raisa Styepanovna. I will not bore you with detailed explanations. Suffice it to say that I did not make it to Klin in time, and before I could reach Raisa, Tyeplov had converted her into a creature like himself. The fact that I was fully aware that such a transformation could only be enacted upon a willing supplicant made her actions all the more a betrayal. I was destroyed.

And yet out of my misery came hope. I learned of her consumptive state, and her plan to defeat it by allowing, more than that, by asking Tyeplov to make her into a vampire. I also learned of her hope, so I choose to see it, that I too would follow her down that path. I suspect that I will. I shall call on her and ask her what it is she wants from me. If I am right, then we shall be together. If I am wrong, then who knows? I cannot ask you to pray that I am right, but I do ask that you will pray for God to guide me.

You may ask why I should choose to reveal all this to you, an acquaintance whom I have known for less than a year, and who in that time I have met but rarely. As I think you guess, my dear Toma, I know your secret, even though you do not.

*I know who your parents are. I would dearly love to reveal
it to you here and now, but it is not my decision to take and
even if it were, I would not commit it to the same pages upon
which I have revealed an intention which, I have no doubt,
will make you despise me.*

*Suffice it to say that, as you guessed, Domnikiia
Semyonovna knows the truth, as does Papa. They will be
returning soon, thanks to His Majesty's pardon. Ask them
to tell you. Let them know that I insisted they hold nothing
back from you. But please, Toma, tell my father nothing of
what has become of me. He would no more accept it than
you do.*

*To have at last met you has been one of the greatest joys
of my life.*

Yours eternally,
Dmitry Alekseevich Danilov

It was a bizarre letter, from a man, Tamara deduced, with only
a tenuous grip on his wits. But his message was clear, the first
part of it at least. Raisa had become a *voordalak*. When Tamara
had met her on her return to Degtyarny Lane, when she had said
that Dmitry had saved her from Tyeplov, it had been a lie. Tyeplov
had made her into one of his own. Tamara had seen no change
in her, but what should she see? It was only by daylight that her
altered nature would be revealed.

But worse than that, she had tricked Dmitry. Where was the
need for such cruelty? Perhaps that was the tell-tale sign of her
new nature. But she could feed on anyone. Why pretend to him
that she would make him like her? Dmitry was right; Tamara was
revolted by the idea, and if she'd had the chance she would have
screamed at him to be revolted too. But Raisa had not allowed
Dmitry to live on by her side. She had waited until he had come
willingly to her, and then devoured him. Did that make his blood
taste all the sweeter, the fact that she'd played him for a fool in
order to get it?

The most generous light it could be seen in was that something
had gone wrong – that Raisa had tried to make Dmitry like her,
but had failed. Either way, Dmitry's corpse, drained of blood,

lying on the bank of the Moskva was ample proof that for him there was no life after death. Out there, somewhere, Raisa still roamed, still feasted upon the blood of the living, but for Dmitry there was nothing.

But it was the second part of Dmitry's letter that thrilled her. The knowledge he had of her parents. He had given her hope; hope that was more substantial than anything she had encountered on her long quest. The news of the pardon would have reached Siberia by now. Aleksei and Domnikiia might travel quickly or slowly, but they would come, Tamara felt sure of it. And when they did, they would know the truth. That had been Dmitry's promise.

The burial took place the day Tamara arrived in Petersburg. Dmitry's coffin had travelled by the same modern means as Tamara – the railway – a few days before. It had been carried over to Vasilievskiy Island by another example of Russia's surge into the nineteenth century, the Nikolaievsky Bridge. Konstantin had told her that his father had ordered it to be erected so far downstream so that the imperial family would not be able to see the endless funeral cortèges crossing it from the window of the Winter Palace. She thought he had been joking, but now was less sure.

It was a reasonable turnout; a good military presence, a large contingent of Svetlana's family, and even a few from Dmitry's – cousins with whom, she discovered, he rarely communicated. A few months before she would have had so many questions for them, but now there was little she did not know about the deaths in 1812 and 1825 and Aleksei's involvement in them. She could have told his family that, despite his exile, he was a hero, but soon she would have the honour of telling Aleksei himself, face to face.

Svetlana had been polite, almost effusive towards Tamara, considering how icy their last encounter had been. At least Tamara had bothered to come. There were few other representatives of Dmitry's friends in Moscow.

'Actual State Councillor Yudin asked me personally to send his apologies,' Tamara said, by way of explanation. 'He has so much to do with all the reforms His Majesty is putting into place.'

'I know. I know,' said Svetlana. 'He organized all this; paid for it. It's so like Vasiliy Denisovich to hide away from the occasion itself.'

It was a simple mistake over the patronymic – Denisovich for Innokyentievich. Svetlana had clearly been thinking of another absentee: Vasiliy Denisovich Makarov. One had organized this funeral; the other managed the rental of her former home. And yet neither had made it here.

The most surprising face Tamara saw was that of her brother, Rodion Valentinovich.

'You knew Dmitry?' she asked.

'Very slightly. Years ago, when he was young and I was younger – before you were born. He used to visit with his parents. Mama insisted I come here. To honour Grandpapa. He and Aleksei Ivanovich were so close.'

Rodion left soon after, saying he had to be back on duty. Tamara didn't even have a chance to thank him for giving her the name of her nanny.

She left Petersburg on the train the following morning. Konstantin was not in the city, but she would not have tried to contact him even if he had been. That could wait. For now there was only one thought on her mind: the return of the Decembrists.

There was no music. There was no light. There was neither cold nor warmth, neither pain nor comfort, neither pleasure nor sorrow. The only sound was that of a sudden, laboured breathing; of lungs that had lain empty for days at last filling. The only knowledge was the understanding of the mind of another.

The breathing was Dmitry's own. This had been no gradual restoration to life, no transition from death to slumber and from slumber to wakefulness. His body's need for air had arisen in the same instant as his mind's awareness of it. The first few breaths were desperate and deep, accentuated by the emerging sense of enclosure. An early thought was that there was little air for him to breathe; a later one that he had little need for it.

His next perception was Raisa's mind. A human child might look forward to a decade and a half in which his parents would pass down the knowledge learned from their own parents, plus a little more that had been accumulated during their lives. They might even employ others to assist in the process. A *voordalak* could not risk such a slow transference of information so vital to survival; it was like a newborn foal that must learn to stand on its own feet within hours, or perish. Thus the mind of the parent vampire was shared with that of the child.

Like him, Raisa was awake – newly awake as night had just fallen. She was in a dark place, as was he. She knew he was there. She was in a coffin. She hungered. The wood of the lid above her face meant that she could feel the warmth of her breath blowing back on her. Dmitry could feel the same. She pushed at it and it yielded. Dmitry pushed, but there was no movement. He tried again, but still his coffin remained a prison. He prepared for that awful sense of being trapped to come upon him – the claustrophobia he always felt when his sizeable frame could not stretch to its fullest. But the sensation did not come. Instead he felt . . . safe. He searched Raisa's mind for help, back to the time when she had first awoken as a vampire, after Tyeplov had made her into one. In understanding her first moments of this new life – her rebirth – he hoped to better make sense of his own.

Raisa was walking now, down a flight of stone steps and into a dark, low corridor. She offered no resistance to his mind, as she had done when last they had been together. Even that, she revealed to him, had been longer ago than he would have guessed. He had been dead for three weeks – buried for two. But his curiosity was directed towards the past, not the present. He searched her mind for the memory of her own rebirth.

Weeks turned into months and months into years, and yet still he could not locate the moment of her resurrection. He quickly found the cemetery in Klin where he had seen her dead. She remembered waiting there, standing beside Tyeplov as they both watched. Then she had seen him – Dmitry – and they had moved swiftly. Tyeplov had bitten at her throat and she had cut his chest. Each had smeared the other's blood across their mouths, steeling themselves against the repugnant taste of the blood of another vampire. Then Raisa had lain down on the grave, in desperate concentration to prevent her wounds from healing, waiting for Dmitry to arrive. She had heard noises, but could not make sense of them. It was only when Tyeplov had kicked at her prone body that she had opened her eyes and seen Dmitry unconscious beside her. She and Tyeplov had fled.

She had been a *voordalak* even then. She had been a *voordalak* when Tyeplov and Mihailov had confronted her at the brothel, when she had first met Dmitry, when she had first met Tamara, when she had come to Degtyarny Lane.

Years rolled back. 1848 – the cholera – the famine – the foreign revolutions. 1831 – the Polish uprising – a revolution against the Turks. 1826 – Nikolai's coronation. Even 1825 and the Decembrist Revolt; she remembered it, though she had not been there. And soon before that deep in a cave – a chain around her neck – his father's face! And then at last he found the moment: her sense of the new, her search for the mind of the one who had created her. Dmitry recognized him – Kyesha, the vampire he and his father had hunted in Moscow; the one who had transformed Raisa into a creature like himself.

And then knowledge poured in. Everything had been intended to deceive him. It was no lie that she was a vampire, but not for a matter of mere months; her transformation had occurred thirty years before. Everything that had taken place between her and Dmitry had been to that one end: to persuade him to become like her – persuade him because he could not be forced; only the willing would receive that which they desired. And yet, the prime motivation had not been hers. It had come from a man who had watched even as Kyesha had drunk her blood and she his; a man she had known as Cain. But now he was no longer a man. He was a *voordalak* too. And his name was no longer Cain; it was Yudin.

Dmitry had been deceived; tricked, seduced and exploited. Raisa had been the primary agent of it, but its cause and its motivation had been Yudin. His reasons were a closed book to Dmitry; Raisa did not know them, and Dmitry had no power to perceive what she could not. And yet he felt no sense of betrayal at any of it. He was not happy to be in his present state, but neither was he disturbed by it. It was what he was, and to reject it would be to reject himself. He knew with utter certainty that the Dmitry of before would have been sickened to know what had become of him, but that was not enough to make him care. The Dmitry of old was like a former friend; a friend who had been close, but for whom one little cared. If he despised the new Dmitry then it only demonstrated what a fool he had been.

Raisa had now come to a wooden door. She had a key to it, which she hesitated to use. Her hunger overwhelmed her, but she knew how wonderful the cessation of that hunger would be. She did not want to rush into it. Dmitry felt the same hunger, but had none of the desire to delay its sating. He kicked hard at the wooden lid above him, again and again, and eventually it splintered. He revelled in his new-found strength, and began to beat against the wooden lid with his feet and knees. Soon it was a mess of shards. Some of the earth above fell into the coffin, but it did not matter. In moments he was digging his way through it, ever upwards to the surface, pushing earth aside like a mole, unconcerned as to the lasting integrity of his tunnel.

At last he was breathing the cool night air. That it was cool was of no greater cheer to him than that it had been warm below – it merely gave him a greater sense of where he was, and of where his prey was. The scent of human blood wafted to him on the breeze. It was everywhere – a hundred odours merged into a single melange. He knew that he must learn to distinguish them.

In his hunger he had forgotten his exploration of Raisa's mind, but now it forced itself upon him in a single image – one that was both surprising and familiar. That Raisa should have held in her memory the distant image of Dmitry's father from years ago made some sense. They must have met. Dmitry felt confident that he would, on further reflection, understand it fully. But that his mother's aged face should at this moment be in the forefront of Raisa's mind was a matter of complete puzzlement.

It was of little concern. Hunger was an issue of greater immediacy. Through the tangled mixture of scents, the blood of one now stood out. Dmitry could only determine that it was human; male or female, young or old, he could not tell. He felt sure that such discrimination would come to him with practice, but for now the scent only told him that the body which carried that blood was close. And he was oh, so hungry. He paused, listening for the sound of any music that his mind might generate to accompany the sensation, but none came. It was unnerving, but he would get used to it. Hunger was a more beguiling seductress than any music he could conjure.

He scuttled across the graveyard, his nostrils leading him where they would.

'Did you have to kill him?'

Tamara remained on the stairway, fearful and ready to run. There was still some daylight up above, though whether it would be enough to protect her, Tamara could only guess. It was only a guess that Raisa could not throw herself across the room in the time it took for Tamara to climb but a few steps. Then there would be nothing to save her from the same fate that had already befallen Dmitry.

'Who?' asked Raisa. She was sitting in Yudin's chair, her feet up on his desk, reading some document she had picked from it. She didn't even look at Tamara.

'Who do you think?'

'I've killed so many,' replied Raisa.

How many was that, Tamara wondered. It had been only a month since Tyeplov had made her a *voordalak*. How many souls could she have consumed? One a day? It was conceivable. She had gone through men at a higher rate in Degtyarny Lane – though Tamara could hardly censure her for that. But it might hint at how Dmitry could be so easily forgotten among them – among either group.

Tamara had not come to see Raisa; finding her here in Yudin's office was as surprising as it was inexplicable. Tamara had come to see Yudin – or perhaps to see Makarov. She had little doubt now that the two men were one and the same. Svetlana's faux pas at the funeral had set off the train of thought. The fact that Yudin and Makarov shared the same Christian name could be mere coincidence, but the fact that they seemed to fulfil similar roles in Dmitry's life was more suspicious. Makarov had disappeared from the official record soon after the Decembrist revolt – just as Yudin had appeared. Yudin could be the same age as Makarov. He looked younger, but that merely went to show that he hid it well.

'Did all of them love you quite so much?' she asked.

'*Love* me?' Raisa's confusion would have fooled most. 'Do you mean Mitka?'

'Are you suggesting he didn't love you?'

Raisa shrugged. 'He thinks he did, but it's hard for him to know for sure. But I didn't kill him – not really.'

'Not *really*? I watched them bury him.'

'These things take time,' said Raisa. 'Or didn't you know that?'

'Time?'

'He's been reborn for a week.'

Tamara felt a sickness in her stomach – greater than she had been experiencing already. In the belief that Dmitry was dead she had been able to pray for mercy on his soul, and to pour her hatred upon Raisa. From somewhere she had convinced herself of the idea that the transformation from human to *voordalak* would be a rapid one, virtually instantaneous. So it had been with Raisa herself.

'You've spoken to him?' asked Tamara.

Raisa swung her feet down from the desk and stood up. Tamara tensed. Raisa began to walk across the room, not towards Tamara, but putting herself within easy reach. 'Spoken?' she said. 'There's no need for speech between us. We know one another's minds.'

'Then I pity him,' said Tamara.

Raisa cocked her head towards Tamara, but didn't rise to the bait. 'He used to pity you,' she said. 'But not any more.'

'Me?'

Raisa now spoke in a singsong voice, like a child. 'Poor lost little girl, looking for her mama and papa, all alone in the woods.'

She knew, thought Tamara. Of course she knew; she knew Dmitry's mind and Dmitry had written to Tamara that *he* knew who her parents were. That was if any of it were true. Even the fact that Dmitry had risen as a *voordalak* came only from Raisa's lips, and was therefore best treated with contempt; but that did not make it false.

'You know who my parents are?' she asked.

'Of course I do. Would you like to hear?'

Tamara considered. What value could anything that Raisa said have? She could throw out two names at random and Tamara would be in no position to judge whether they truly were her parents – the knowledge of them plucked from Dmitry's mind – or simply Raisa's invention, intended purely to tease. But whatever she said would at least be a starting point. If it were true, it might easily be verified; if false it might still contain some shadow of the truth.

'Tell me,' said Tamara before she had finished considering the possibilities.

'Come over here,' said Raisa, beckoning. 'I'll whisper it to you.'

In spite of herself, Tamara took a step forward. There was something entrancing about Raisa, almost hypnotic. It seemed that it would be so very simple and very natural to go over there and bend towards Raisa's lips. She saw the image in her mind: her own head tilted to one side, offering up her ear to Raisa and at the same time exposing the snow-white skin of her neck; Raisa's red lips opening, ready to impart the knowledge that Tamara had for so long desired. But that would not be the outcome. Raisa's lips would descend not towards Tamara's ear, but towards her throat. She could see the image of white teeth rupturing her skin, of her own red blood spurting forth.

Even as Tamara hesitated, Raisa had taken two steps across the room towards her, and was moving fast now. Tamara turned and fled up the stairs. She heard Raisa's feet behind her, catching up with her. The bright rectangle of the doorway above, filled with late afternoon sunshine, was only a few steps away. She could almost feel its warmth. A second more and she would be basking in its safety.

She fell forward. For a moment she couldn't understand why, but then she felt Raisa's grip around her ankle, tight as a vice, trying to pull her back down the stairs. At the same time, Raisa still managed to climb, her face closing in on Tamara, her teeth bared. Tamara twisted and managed to get on to her back. She kicked out and her heel caught Raisa squarely on the nose. Tamara saw blood, but the blow had little effect in deterring Raisa. Tamara reached out behind her, trying to find anything to grip on to before Raisa could pull her back down into the darkness and do to her what she had already done to Dmitry. Her hand found something and for a moment she felt hope; an instant

394

later despair. It was the edge of the door. It yielded as she pulled, and offered her no anchor against Raisa's remorseless strength.

Then there was a scream. From Tamara's ankle – from Raisa's hand – smoke began to rise. Despite her yelp of pain, Raisa was determined not to let go. Tamara felt her grip, still pulling, but her hand was disintegrating as Tamara watched. The slight movement of the door had allowed the daylight to shine a little further down the stairs, and it had caught Raisa's fingers.

The skin had blackened and split, allowing blood and a thick, yellow pus to ooze out. The smell was repellent. Tamara even thought she saw a glimpse of bone. It lasted only moments. Soon Raisa could resist the pain no longer and snatched back her hand. She gazed at Tamara sullenly from the shade and seemed about to speak, but Tamara did not give her the opportunity. Instead she turned and scrambled up the last few remaining stairs to the door. She stood in the corridor for a moment, safe in the sunlight, though still indoors. To her left she saw the faded tapestry in which the unicorn gazed at its reflection in the mirror, covering the door to the archives.

Then the unicorn itself began to move, turning its head as if about to speak to her. Doubts of her own sanity were banished as she realized that someone was emerging from behind the hanging cloth. Before she could wonder who it might be, the bald head and bushy eyebrows of her friend Gribov appeared.

She glanced back down the dark stairway to Yudin's office. Down there she could still see a vague movement which she knew to be Raisa; the smell of her charred skin still filled Tamara's nostrils.

'Don't go down there,' she said, turning back to Gribov, her voice croaking. 'Just don't.'

It was all she could do. She knew he deserved a better warning, but her fear for herself was overpowering. She turned and fled, running out into the fading daylight of the Kremlin, knowing that Raisa would not dare venture after her. But daylight would not last for long – already evening was drawing in. Tamara turned and headed away towards the Nikolai Gate; she had no idea where she would hide once night fell.

* * *

'Are you hurt?'

Raisa looked up. Yudin had been in the cellars below his office and returned to find her sitting at his desk, cradling her hand. He could see no sign of injury, but a slight hint of something unpleasant in the air suggested that her flesh might briefly have been caught in the rays of the sun.

'It's nothing,' she said. 'It's Tamara Valentinovna's fault.'

'Really?'

'She knows about me; knows about Dmitry.'

'And about me?'

Raisa shook her head. 'I doubt it, but she's still a danger.'

Yudin considered. Everything was becoming a danger. It was no surprise how much Tamara knew. Dmitry's letter to Yudin, sent before his death, had revealed that a similar letter had been sent to Tamara. From it she'd guessed the truth about Raisa. It wouldn't be a great leap from that to Yudin. It was already time to move on. He'd known for weeks that Prince Dolgorukov would soon be taking over command of the Third Section, and that could only lead to the discovery of what Yudin had been up to in Moscow. Down below, in one of the empty cells, he had begun packing his most treasured possessions into crates – his journals and scientific instruments being the most essential. He would have to find a place for them to be stored, to be sent for when he had re-established himself elsewhere. Where, he knew not. But Raisa was right about Tamara.

'Deal with her,' he said.

'That's what I was trying to do.'

'Then try harder!'

He went over to his desk, expecting her to vacate his seat, but she stayed where she was. He looked at her, but still she did not move.

'No,' she said.

'No?'

'No, I won't try harder. No, I won't deal with her. Not until you keep your promise to me.'

'My promise?'

'You know.'

'Ah!' His promise that he would find a way for her to look

upon her own reflection. He couldn't string her along for ever. He'd had the mirror for months, but had not dared show it to her, much as he was tempted to. He was eager – desperate almost – to discover how a *voordalak* would react to truly seeing its own image, but fearful as well; certainly too fearful to perform such an experiment on himself. But he was also afraid of losing Raisa – at least, he had been. Now, if he were to move away from Moscow, then it would be safer not to take her with him. Perhaps this was the best time.

'Move,' he said, flicking his hand at her. She stood up from his desk and walked round to the other side of it. He took her place and opened the top right-hand drawer. Out of it he took his latest journal. He wrote down the date, 26 September 1856, and then a brief heading in anticipation of the events he would so carefully note.

Effects of Iceland Spar mirror on voordalak *subject – Raisa Styepanovna.*

Then he reached into the lower drawer, and took it out. It was still covered in the old, embroidered shawl – an essential protection, not for the mirror but for Yudin. He did not want to catch sight of his own reflection in there. Raisa's eyes followed the shape beneath the cloth as he placed it on his desk.

'A few words of explanation first, I think,' he said.

'Very well.' Still she did not take her eyes from it.

'I've long known that a normal mirror does reflect the image of a vampire, but I believed that it does so in a way that somehow alters the image.'

'You've told me this before.'

'I have, and that was what I believed. But now I think I was wrong.'

'You?'

Yudin shrugged, happy to acknowledge his error. 'I'm now of the opinion that it is only by reflection that the true image of the *voordalak* is revealed. What you and I see in each other is the illusion, the shroud of humanity that allows us to pass among them undetected – and among ourselves.'

'But we don't see our true selves in a mirror – we see nothing.'

'Oh, we see it. We see it, but our minds cannot cope with it.

They remove it – censor it like a diligent and benign government. We see nothing because it is safer to see nothing.'

'But you have found a way to . . . avoid the censor?'

Yudin nodded. 'It's essentially an ordinary mirror, but instead of glass we have a sheet of a mineral that is well known for allowing the viewer to see two images of whatever they look at through it. In the case of a vampire, the mind is caught unawares. The first image is removed, but the second gets through.'

'You tested it?'

'On a human; a human looking at my reflection in the glass.'

'What did they see?'

Yudin paused, careful to phrase his answer. 'They wouldn't say,' he replied eventually. The memory of a woman's laughter, echoing in the chambers beneath them, filled his mind. She had been laughing at him; laughing at what she saw of him in the mirror.

'But you've never looked at yourself.'

'I felt that would be unscientific. But if you don't want to be the first, I'm sure I can find another way.'

'No,' she said quickly. 'Let me see.'

Yudin put his hand under the shawl and felt the mirror beneath, checking that the glass was facing down on to the desktop, keeping all risks to a minimum. It was. He held it still while he pulled the cloth away, and then slid it over towards Raisa. She put her hand on it, but did not lift it immediately.

'You may not like what you see,' he said. The words seemed decisive for her. She grasped the handle and held the mirror before her face.

For a moment her expression was calm. She stared at her image, obscured from Yudin's sight, with an air of fascination. A smile almost crept to her lips. She glanced over at him with a look of amused excitement, but only for a moment, before returning to look into the glass.

'*Also*,' he said, '*bist du die Schönste im ganzen Land?*'

She said nothing. She raised her hand to her face and touched her cheek with her fingertips. Then she moved her hand away and looked at it directly, then put it back to her face so that she could see its reflection. Now her expression was of ever-growing puzzlement. She looked at her fingers, flexed them, turned her hand around to see its palm. Her eyes flicked between the reality of her hand and its image in the glass, as if trying to find any difference between the two – or perhaps any similarity.

'Tell me what you see,' he said.

A tiny sound escaped her throat, the closest thing she could manage to speech. She returned her hand to her face and now, rather than simply touching it, began to probe and explore it. Yudin could see tears form in her eyes, and wondered if she could see them herself. One or two began to trickle down her face. Now her probing had become a clawing. Her nails scratched down her cheek, drawing blood, whose droplets mingled with the saltwater of her tears. She watched and waited and the marks on her cheek soon healed, but as soon as they had she began again, her nails digging deeper than before so that Yudin could see the skin hanging from her.

Now at last she found the power of speech. Her voice was mournful, deeper than Yudin had ever heard it. 'What have you done to me?'

'I don't know,' said Yudin, still hopeful of learning something from her. 'Tell me.'

She shook her head. Her nails continued to scratch at her face, creating new wounds faster than the old ones could heal. Her own blood caked her fingernails. Now she had them hooked into her lower eyelid. She began to pull mercilessly at it and the skin stretched and finally began to rupture. Her eye remained as beautiful as ever, its blue iris shining even in the dim lamplight, but below it her cheek came away, gripped tightly in her hand. It was a deliberate attempt to destroy her own face, to remove it in reality so that whatever she saw of its reflection might vanish too. But as she watched herself, her hand fell down to her side. The effort was clearly futile.

'Tell me,' Yudin repeated.

She let her other hand, still holding the mirror, fall and placed the two together like a ballerina with her arms *bras-bas*. The mirror was at about the level of her crotch, its back facing out towards Yudin. Her eyes were still tearful. The flap of torn flesh that hung down from below her right eye was only just beginning to heal.

'Why should I tell you?' she asked, her voice numb and empty. 'Why should I tell you, when it's so much easier to show you?'

As she spoke she lifted both her hands, raising up the mirror to face Yudin. He caught the reflection of his office wall sliding quickly past as the glass moved into place, and then, as he held up his hands to block the image and turned away, he caught the briefest glimpse of something awful sitting at his desk.

'What's the matter, Richard?' she said, using the name by which she had known him so long before. 'Aren't you curious?'

Yudin kept his eyes averted. He felt his heart pump. His fear was visceral and he could not entirely account for it. It came from her, and however much Yudin might think of himself as different, he was one of them; a *voordalak*. Just as one terrified ox could spread its fear invisibly to the entire herd, so Raisa's terror seeped into him.

'Don't you want to see what you've become?' Raisa continued. 'I was beautiful and I've faced myself. What do you have to fear?'

He could sense she was approaching him, but still did not turn to look. He searched the shelf behind his desk – the only place he could risk looking – trying to find something that might be of help.

'I'm curious too,' she said. 'I've seen me, but I haven't seen you. All I need to do is tilt the mirror, then I'll see your face. And if you look, you'll see mine.' There was a pause and then she began to laugh, just as the old woman had. Yudin could only presume that she had done what she threatened and was now staring at his reflection instead of her own. 'Oh, Richard,' she said. 'You really should look. You make me look quite, quite plain. It's you who's the fairest in the whole land.' She continued to laugh but it was the forced, cold laughter of madness, the only possible reaction to a situation that was beyond sorrow, beyond tears and beyond hope.

Yudin turned and took the briefest glimpse at her, just enough to judge the position of the mirror. He was an inverted Perseus, daring only to gaze upon the gorgon in the flesh, not in her reflection. He fired the revolver that he had picked up from the shelf. The shot rang out and Yudin allowed himself another glimpse of what was going on. The bullet had missed the looking glass, but had hit Raisa in the wrist. Her thumb was bent at a peculiar angle, its tendon severed. Raisa herself did not seem to notice. She continued to laugh and gaze into the mirror even as it teetered and fell from her fingers.

It hit the stone floor and shattered, its fragments flying in all directions. The harsh sudden sound of its fracture brought an end to Raisa's laughter. She gasped and fell to her knees, then picked up one of the small fragments of the looking glass and tried to peer into it, gripping it so tightly that it cut into her flesh and drew blood.

'No,' she moaned softly, and then louder, 'no!' She put the fragment back on the ground and reached out for others near her, placing them beside the first in an attempt to re-create the whole. 'Not yet,' she said. 'One last look. Just one more.'

Yudin fired the gun again. This time there was no inaccuracy. He hit the shard of crystal that she had put down and it shattered to powder. Those around it were flung away. Raisa turned and looked at him.

'Pity me!' she said. She looked around the room as if not knowing where she was, as if Yudin was not even there, and then she was on her feet and running up the stairs to the world above. It was dark now and she would be safe outside, but if Yudin had possessed the ability to pity her, he would have prayed that it was still day and that her misery would have ended in an excruciating but mercifully brief inferno.

He took a few steps towards where the fragments of broken mirror still lay – at least twenty of them – preparing to clear them up. Then he froze. They had fallen randomly, facing in every direction. Those that lay flat on the floor were no problem, but some were raised up at just such an angle that they reflected Yudin's image back at him, following him like eyes as he moved. None was large enough to see himself in clearly, but with every step he took he caught a glimpse of some dark creature slithering across the room. He saw shapes that he could make some sense of, but not relate to any part of his own body.

He reached out to pick up one of the fragments and saw his

hand reflected in it. He pulled back. That it was the image of his hand, he knew simply from the physics of the matter, but he would never have recognized it. And yet, as had been the case with Raisa, he yearned to see more. He reached out again and picked up the piece of crystal, curling his fingers around the edge so that he could just see them reflected, black and hard.

He almost raised it to look into his face, but then sanity prevailed. He threw the fragment to the ground and in the same movement flung himself back across the room. The temptation to see the truth still filled him, but he resisted. He grabbed the embroidered shawl from his desk and shook it out, opening it fully, then tossed it across the floor as though it were a tablecloth and it was his job to prepare for dinner. The shawl swirled and descended gently as the air caught it and tried to prevent it from falling, but eventually it settled, covering almost all of what remained of the mirror. Two shards of the Iceland Spar glinted in the light. Yudin stuck out his foot tentatively and kicked them under the cloth.

It was the best he could do. To clear it away properly he would need help – human help. He strode to the bottom of the stairs.

'Gribov!' he bellowed. 'Gribov! Get down here!'

But Gribov did not respond.

CHAPTER XXIV

I T WAS DMITRY'S FIRST NIGHT BACK IN MOSCOW. HE HAD BEEN forced to travel on horseback, riding along the chaussée by night and sleeping rough by day, burying himself beneath a light covering of earth. He knew from Raisa that she and Yudin travelled by train between Petersburg and Moscow, having themselves delivered as luggage to be loaded into one of the baggage wagons, but he did not feel sure enough of himself to risk it, nor did he know of anyone he could ask to help him. Every friend he had believed him to be dead.

He got into the city only just before dawn, and had found a churchyard with more than one tomb that was large enough for him to crawl into and sleep. It was the most comfortable night he had spent since slinking from his own grave. Physically he had lain upon the hard, stone floor of the vault, but that was hardly a matter of significance. What was good was to be lying among the dead. They could not communicate with him, they did not even know that he was there, but somehow they made him feel he was where he was meant to be.

Once darkness had fallen Dmitry emerged into the night, determining to sleep there again if at all possible. Partly through instinct, partly through the knowledge that Raisa shared with him, he understood it was necessary for a *voordalak* to have several places in a city where he could hide. This would be the first, and perhaps the favourite. He was not even sure if he would be staying in Moscow for very long. He might return to Petersburg – or go somewhere else entirely. He wasn't sure of anything – except for his hunger.

And that was why he had come to Moscow; to speak to Yudin. He knew enough from Raisa to understand that it was Yudin who had strung him along for all those years, that it was Yudin who had made the decision that he should at last become like them. Should Dmitry bear him any grudge? He did not regret the fact that he was no longer human, even though he knew he had been tricked into it. It was not now in Dmitry's nature to admire honesty in others, any more than to treasure it in himself. All he wanted from Yudin was advice on how to live his new life – it had to be more than mere hunger which drove him. Surely Yudin would not have brought him to this state if he had not planned ultimately to explain that. And yet Dmitry did not relish an existence like Raisa's, serving only as Yudin's abetter.

But for now, an encounter with Yudin was not Dmitry's primary concern. He had eaten only once since leaving Petersburg; a coachman who had dismounted and stepped into the woods to relieve himself. Dmitry wondered if he should have stuck around and enjoyed the coach's passengers too, but at the time one had seemed sufficient. He knew he would grow to better understand the cycles of his appetite.

Another thing he had to get used to was passing himself off as a human. Yudin, Raisa, Tyeplov, all of them seemed to do it so effortlessly. In reality there was little to it – he had the physical appearance of a man and years of experience of being one. The problem was his own fear; his own sense of being an outsider who would easily be spotted. For the first days of his new existence he had truly been a creature of the night, hiding in darkness and stalking his prey. Now, in Moscow, he dared to be seen. He walked down the street towards Lubyanka Square as any gentleman about town would on a cool autumn evening. It had not snowed yet, but it would within the next days or weeks – and the nights would grow longer. It was the perfect time to be here.

He had been tempted more than once to pop into a tavern or club; not one of his old haunts, for fear he might be recognized, but somewhere he could further test his ability to blend in. So far, though, he had resisted. He imagined the taste of alcohol – of any liquid other than blood – on his lips and of the feel of it slithering down his throat. It repelled him. It was a sensation he would have to overcome; Raisa and Yudin had managed it – he had seen them drink. But for now he had no stomach for it.

Neither did he have the need for it, not tonight. Tonight he would easily find himself a victim without having to go to any effort of ingratiating himself with strangers. He turned on to Kuznetskiy Bridge Street, taking the route he had so often followed in life, towards his Moscow lodgings. The memories of his former life came to him through a strange filter. The emotions, the love, hate, excitement and boredom of it all, were mere echoes, as though described in a badly written novel, informing him that they existed but not conveying how they felt. But details such as the names, addresses, habits and tastes of all those he had known were still utterly clear to him. Sometimes the memories of those things were more lucid than when he had been alive.

He knocked on a door just a little way down from his own former rooms. Behind it he heard the sound of feet running downstairs. The last time he had been here it had been to ensure the safe delivery of two letters, one to Tamara and the other to Yudin, in the event of his death. That was nothing compared with what he came for today. The door opened.

'Milan Romanovich,' he said with a smile that he hoped was not too broad, not least so that it would not reveal his teeth. He could see the blood draining from Milan's face – an unpleasant image considering the reason Dmitry had come here.

'Dmitry!' Milan exclaimed, his voice a mixture of shock and joy. 'They told me you were dead. What happened?'

'It's a long story,' said Dmitry, 'but well worth the hearing. May I come in?'

'My God, of course!' said Milan. 'And tell me everything.' He stepped back inside and indicated that Dmitry should enter. Dmitry took one glance up and down the street. It did not matter too much if he was seen, but it would be better if there were no witnesses.

He stepped inside and his friend closed the door behind them.

Tamara turned the doorknob and went into Raisa's room. It was dark outside now, but the curtains were still open and the moon shone in through the newly repaired window, augmenting the light from her lamp. All was as she remembered it: the bed, the two heavy wooden wardrobes; the doorway through to what had been Irina's room; the dressing table with no mirror.

That, of course, made sense now, if the folk stories were true. Raisa would not want the world to see that her image was not reflected in the glass. Tamara corrected herself. There had been no mirror in all the time she had known Raisa, not just in the weeks since Tyeplov had made her into a vampire. But it was oddly prescient that Raisa should avoid it even in anticipation of what she would one day become. It did not matter. What mattered was Tamara's overwhelming urge to remove every trace of Raisa from the room and from the building. It was irrational, she knew – Raisa had no further need of her worldly possessions – but Tamara felt that action was necessary, and this was all that she could achieve. This place had always been Raisa's – since before Tamara had even arrived. To clear it out would be one step towards erasing her memory.

She went over to the interconnecting door and unlocked it, and then the other just a little way beyond. It would be a shorter route to the stairs to carry things out through the other room – the room that had once been Irina Karlovna's – though why Tamara didn't just throw everything out of the window and into the street below, she did not know. Tamara pondered the details of the night of Irina's death. Irina had borrowed a set of keys to all the doors in the building from Nadia. Why would she have done that? She had her own key to the main door of her room, but not to these. Was it through here that she had let the vampire into her room? It seemed unnecessary.

Tamara couldn't doubt that it was a *voordalak* that had killed Irina. What would a year ago – months ago – have seemed a preposterous fantasy was now a rational, inescapable verdict. And yet there were still questions. Which of them had it been? Tyeplov? Ignatyev? Dmitry had spoken of his encounters with them in Sevastopol, but he hadn't been specific as to dates. He had travelled north in the autumn of 1855, but Irina was killed that spring. Could the vampires have left the city so long before he did?

Tamara paused before opening the second door. The space

between the two was as large as a small closet – enough for someone to hide in. The wall between the rooms was of the same thickness. That meant that the wall was also wide enough for a person to hide in.

It was an inescapable possibility. From her position between the two doors, Tamara tapped on the painted wall. It certainly wasn't made of brick or stone. That meant little. In a house as old as this – dating back to before the fires of 1812 – much of the construction was wood rather than anything more substantial. But it didn't explain why the wall needed to be so wide.

Tamara went back into Raisa's room and looked around. Her eyes fell on the tools beside the fireplace. Autumn was heading for winter now, and the fire would soon be needed, but that was not Tamara's immediate concern. She grabbed the poker and went back into the tiny space. It took only two determined blows for the iron tip to pierce the wooden panel beneath the paint. She pushed the poker deep into the hole it had created and encountered no resistance. She withdrew it and felt a light, cool breeze blowing at her through the gap, accompanied by a musty stench.

She hacked away again with the poker, making the hole bigger, and then used the hook on the end of it to pull away shards of the splintered wood. It wasn't thick, and Tamara soon realized that it would be easier to break through with her bare hands. Soon there was a large enough gap to peer through. She picked up the lamp and looked. Leading down within the thick wall was a staircase.

Within minutes, Tamara had created enough of a breach that she could squeeze through. She reached back to pick up the lamp and the poker. From inside she could see that the wooden panel had a latch and a handle with no corresponding partner on the other side. Instead, a length of cord was attached to it, feeding upwards before disappearing into the ceiling. Evidently this was a door rather than a wall, and was intended to be opened in a more civilized manner than the one that Tamara had come up with. Where the end of the cord secretly emerged, Tamara did not know – but she could guess who did. She turned and went down the stairs.

They ended at the level of the ground floor. Tamara imagined the salon beyond her, through only a few inches of wooden wall.

The space was no larger than at the top of the stairs between the two doors. This, though, was not the end of the journey. Now a ladder descended through a small, round gap in the floor. Tamara threw the poker into it and heard a thud as it landed on what sounded like earth. She put the lamp on the floor and began to climb down the ladder, allowing her skirts to ride up so that her feet could find its rungs. Just before her head disappeared, she retrieved the lamp and ducked into the cellar below.

It was a small space, barely high enough for Tamara to stand upright. The building had sizeable cellars – Tamara had been in them – but they did not fill quite all of its floor plan. This extra space explained why. It was inaccessible from the main cellars, but as Tamara glanced at the wall, she guessed it was a temporary barrier and that when the building had first been erected all the spaces beneath it had been interconnected. Both this area and the route down to it were relatively new.

There was only one object in the room – a coffin. Tamara walked over. It was open and empty – expensively made, with a silk lining. Its purpose – the purpose of the whole room – was obvious; it was the resting place of a *voordalak*. Raisa's job entailed that she work above during the night, but Tamara had never known where she lived during the day. She had said she had rooms across town, but now it was clear that it was into this cellar that she came each day as dawn broke, and in this coffin that she slept.

Tamara looked around again. Across the room, a dark tunnel led away to the north. Along there must have been some other exit, out into one of the gardens or perhaps the cellar of another house. It would explain how she had often seen Raisa arrive for work through the front door – always after dark – as if coming from her home. She had been, but her home was beneath that very building, and all she had done was depart through the tunnel and emerge elsewhere, disguising the fact that she could in reality have simply climbed the ladder and the steps back up to her room.

But the one striking realization that had come to Tamara as soon as her eyes had fallen upon the coffin, as soon, perhaps, as she had discovered the concealed stairway, was that all of this had been here for some time. It could not have been put together in the weeks since Raisa's encounter with Tyeplov, when she had supposedly become a vampire. It could never have been built without Tamara noticing: the wall had always been that thick; the cellar had always been missing this section. It must all have been there when Tamara had first arrived, over a year and a half before.

And that meant that from the moment Tamara had met her, from the moment that Raisa had first opened the door and invited her in, she had been a *voordalak*.

Did that really make much of a difference to things? For Raisa – no. If she had been such a creature for two years, or for ten, or for a century, it was of little import compared with the fact of what she was. But for Dmitry, it made all the difference in the world. He had believed that Raisa had become a vampire out of her love of him; that she had become undead to save herself from the certain death that consumption would bring and to save herself from the separation from Dmitry which would ensue. She had persuaded him that once she had led the way down that path out of love for him, he should follow out of love for her. But while his love had been real, hers was a lie. She had been a *voordalak* since before Dmitry had ever met her, and all of the events with Tyeplov, her journey to Klin to be safe from him and Dmitry's race out there to save her – so perfectly timed that he witnessed the very moment of her conversion – were part of the same web of deceit, intended to entrap him and make him willingly become a creature like her. It made him no less of a fool for falling for it, but it was clear that the whole thing had been expertly planned.

Too expertly for Raisa. She would not have had the wit for it, and certainly would not have been able on her own to hide her coffin beneath the brothel in this way. Had she had Tyeplov's help? Certainly in the deception of Dmitry, but Tamara doubted he could have helped her construct this. That would have needed to be organized by whoever owned the building. And that was Yudin.

It was Yudin who had suggested that Raisa go to stay in Klin, Yudin who had miraculously discovered the correspondence between her and Tyeplov, Yudin who had conveniently managed to hire a horse so that Dmitry could chase after the train. Was

Yudin a *voordalak* himself, or simply a human who had some kind of alliance with them? It did not really matter, though try as she might, Tamara could not recall ever seeing him in daylight, or seeing his shadow, or seeing his reflection. And Yudin, she already felt certain, was Makarov; and Makarov was very old. How well he hid it.

Tamara climbed the ladder and went back up the hidden stairs to Raisa's room, and then back down the main stairs to the salon to see Nadia about to knock on the door of her office.

'I'm here,' said Tamara.

Nadia turned. 'This was just delivered for you.' She held out a letter.

Tamara took it. 'Who by?' she asked, as she broke the wax seal.

'Just a messenger boy.'

Tamara read.

My dear Madame Komarova,

I am informed by my agents that Raisa Styepanovna is heading for the railway station with the apparent intent of catching a train to the capital. I trust this information is of interest to you.

Titular Councillor Gribov

Tamara walked briskly over to her office. She returned a moment later having acquired two items: a pistol hidden in her bag and a cane held in her hand. The cane's tip was covered, but beneath it was still sharp enough for its purpose. It might have been Yudin, as part of his intricate deception of Dmitry, who had suggested using that combination of weapons against a *voordalak*, but it did not mean that they would be any less effective.

Outside the house, she turned right and headed towards Tver-skaya Street. It was away from the station, but was the nearest place that she would be able to hail a carriage.

She hadn't gone more than three paces when she felt a hand tugging at her sleeve. As she turned, she heard her name being called. 'Toma!'

It was the old woman, Natalia Borisovna – or at least that was the name she had used when they had last met, at almost the same

410

spot over a year before. Natalia Borisovna's own son's testimony, that she was long dead, had proved that this woman was not who she claimed. But could Tamara be sure of that – or of anything? Yudin had spun an impenetrable web of deceit around Dmitry – might he be doing the same with her? Had that really been Natalia's son she had spoken to? Or perhaps all was true. Perhaps Natalia had died and this was her, risen from the grave? Bizarre though it was, it could prove the most plausible explanation.

But it was Raisa, not Natalia, who was Tamara's primary concern. 'Go to Hell!' she spat, and continued on her way through the darkness. As she walked down Degtyarny Lane, towards Tverskaya Street, she heard the old woman's shuffling footsteps, desperate to keep up with Tamara's longer, younger stride.

'I must speak to you,' the old woman called out.

This time Tamara didn't even turn. 'I've no time,' she shouted. She turned on to Tverskaya Street and saw a coach. She stopped and raised her hand.

Almost immediately the woman caught up with her. 'Toma,' she repeated, 'I have to tell you.'

Tamara turned, at the same time plucking the protective cover from the end of her cane and pointing the sharpened tip towards the woman's chest. 'I've no idea who you are, but I've got a pretty good idea *what* you are, so you'll be wise to be afraid of this.'

The woman was bewildered. She certainly had none of the arrogant self-confidence that Tamara had seen in Tyeplov and Ignatyev and even at times in Raisa. Perhaps she was mistaken, but still she had no time to consider. The coach pulled up and she climbed aboard.

The woman grabbed at her. 'Toma!' she cried. Tamara pushed her off, not strongly, but the old woman fell down. Tamara felt a pang of sorrow, but she knew she must not yield to it. She gave a brief, firm instruction to the driver.

'The station – quickly.'

The coach began to move off. Tamara looked back and saw with some relief that the old woman was back on her feet. She raised her hand to her mouth to shout and at the words, Tamara froze. 'Your father sent me to warn you!'

Tamara almost told the driver to turn back, but she would be

411

a fool to do so. She was being manipulated, just as Dmitry had been. She had to catch up with Raisa, had to stop her, had to punish her for what she had done to Dmitry. Thinking of it, as she sat in the coach, rattling through the Moscow streets, it sounded foolhardy, but who else was there to do it? Perhaps one day she would have to kill Dmitry too, but that would be an act of mercy, not vengeance. And what of Yudin? She did not know. All that could wait. First she must deal with Raisa – or try to. If Raisa were the victor then at least Tamara would die doing something good. Luka might never hear of it, but he would have a mother that he could be proud of.

She felt a pain in her stomach again and something rising in her gullet. She thought she was going to be sick, but it was only wind. She breathed deeply. Here inside the carriage she was safe and comfortable, if only for a few minutes. She had to ready herself. Even so, she had no idea what she was actually going to do. She could not stab Raisa in the middle of the station. Or could she? There would be no body left behind, she had seen that with Ignatyev. All she needed was to find some quiet corner where no one was looking and it would be as if Raisa had never existed. If such an opportunity did not arise, Tamara could wait. She had time on her side; in around eight hours it would be dawn.

Now the station was in sight, its clock tower, topped by the Russian flag, rising above Komsomolskaya Square. The coach stopped and she paid the driver, then rushed into the station. There was only one train waiting – a mixture of freight and passenger wagons. Winter was now close enough to merit boxcars for the third-class passengers instead of open, flat trucks. Tamara walked along the train, peering through the unglazed windows, but saw no sign of her quarry. Now she was passing the second-class coaches, and the windows had glass. A flash of blonde hair was all that was needed for her to spot Raisa, her head turned away, looking out of the far side of the carriage.

Tamara doubled back and climbed on to the metal platform at the end of that carriage, standing next to the conductor. She didn't go in yet – she didn't want Raisa to see her and have the chance to get off. Things would be much easier once the train was moving.

'Would you like to take your seat, madam?' the young man asked.

'When we get going. I just want to be able to wave goodbye.'

The conductor shrugged, but didn't object. Tamara kept glancing into the carriage, but Raisa was still there, and had not caught sight of her. At last the whistle blew. The conductor released the brake and the train began to roll out of the station. In keeping with her story, Tamara waved towards the people who were left standing on the platform, perhaps surprising one or two who had never realized that they knew her. Finally, when they were clear of the station buildings and on open track, she went inside.

Raisa had her back to her, and that really wouldn't do. Now that they were moving, it would be better if Raisa understood the danger she was in. Tamara walked to the front end of the coach, where there was a spare seat three rows along from Raisa. She took it and fixed her gaze on the vampire.

It was about two minutes before Raisa turned away from the window and saw her. There was no indication of shock or surprise, or even acknowledgement. There were tears in her eyes, but they had been there before she had noticed Tamara. Tamara suppressed the pity she felt at the sight. It was a human reaction to a human emotion, but she knew that whatever soul might lie within Raisa, it had long ago forgotten what humanity meant. Whatever tears she might shed now were nothing compared with what was to come. If she got off the train then Tamara would follow her and drive the wooden cane into her heart. If she remained on board then eventually the light of dawn would shine through that window and destroy her. Tamara had only to wait, but in doing so she still watched, her eyes fixed on Raisa, reminding her that there was no escape.

Raisa turned her face back to the window; as for so many of the passengers who looked out into the darkness of the night, there was nothing for her to see. At least for those others, their own reflection would be something to entertain them. In the window beside Raisa – though no one in the carriage seemed to notice it – there was reflected only an empty seat.

*   *   *

Dmitry was learning. It was not the taste of blood that was so wonderful, though that was pleasant. Neither was it the satiation of hunger, though that was necessary. Both of those would be reason enough to justify the depleted corpse that lay on the couch beside him, but they were not where the real joy of it lay.

He tried to pinpoint the moment, but realized that in fact there were several, each a little more pleasurable than the last. It had begun with the explanation that he had promised to Milan Romanovich.

'Milan, do you know what a *voordalak* is?'

His friend had laughed, and Dmitry was reminded of the laughter of Tamara and Raisa when he had first introduced the subject to them. Then there had been an equal deception, but the roles had been reversed. Then he as a human had been describing to Raisa what she already was. Now it was he as a vampire who was revealing his own nature to an innocent victim.

'Don't be an idiot, Dmitry. I'm sure you've caught out a few of your friends like that, but I think you'll find I'm not quite so gullible.'

Dmitry smiled. 'What would convince you?'

'A little more than your word.'

Dmitry let his lips open slightly to reveal his teeth. In honesty, they weren't much; only a little longer than they had been in life, though far sharper. It was the hugely increased strength of his jaw that made the real difference. Even so, he detected a slight pause – a moment of doubt and hence a little fear – before Milan spoke. That was the first moment of pleasure.

'And I think you're going to have to do better than that too. What are they – wooden? You could at least have made them look like fangs.'

Milan had taken a step closer to look, and it gave Dmitry an easy opportunity to swing at him with the back of his hand. It was not enough to knock him unconscious, though it might well have been – Dmitry was still poor at estimating his new-found strength. It threw him back on to the couch and Dmitry had seen the wounded look in his eyes – that was the second moment of pleasure. And then the look of surprised offence had been displaced by one of fear – a connecting of Dmitry's suggestion

414

that he was a vampire with the unnecessary violence of the blow. That was the third.

And then Dmitry had been unable to resist. He had fallen on Milan, holding him down easily without having to exert his full strength. Milan had screamed as Dmitry's teeth penetrated his neck, but Dmitry had quickly moved a hand over his mouth to stifle it. He had drunk only a little at first, enough to weaken Milan; enough to make him understand. There was some pleasure in it, but it was a cruel trick that nature played on the *voordalak* – to arrange things so that the primary mechanism of attack was one which also prevented a clear view of the victim's face. How was Dmitry meant to know the pain he was inflicting if he could not see it written in Milan's agonized grimace and in the expression of betrayal in his eyes?

Dmitry had taken a moment to pause – to pull away and look at Milan and enjoy what he saw. He doubted whether he was the first *voordalak* to understand that this was the true source of contentment, but not all would come to discover it. Yudin, he felt, surely had. What of Raisa? He tried to sense her mind, but found only confusion. It did not matter – Dmitry was quite able to enjoy this moment on his own.

Milan tried to speak, but the damage that Dmitry had already done to his voice box made it impossible. He could only guess that it was a request for some explanation, some understanding of why Dmitry had chosen to come to him. Even though the answer was simple – it had been a matter of Dmitry's convenience – the lack of knowing would increase his suffering. People liked stories – even the stories of their own short existence – to have endings, be they sad or happy, Dmitry remembered that much. It would be far better – for Dmitry – if Milan were to die still pondering the unanswered question: why me?

But die he would. Dmitry took one last look at the man's terrified face and then returned to his repast. He ate a little of the flesh around the man's throat, but mostly drank. The flesh was interesting, but it had none of the immediate appeal of blood. Dmitry suspected it might be an acquired taste. He had many years before him to acquire it. He did not notice the exact moment of death. Milan had fallen into unconsciousness some time before, and so the real fun had ended. When the blood began to taste sour, he knew that life had passed. He pulled away. The blood of the dead soon became repellent; he had learned that on his first night as a vampire. Old and young, male and female, each had their own qualities, but blood that lay stagnant, unquickened by a human heart, was like dishwater. He had sat back and gazed at Milan's body.

That must have been over an hour ago. It was a habit that Dmitry had got into, to contemplate his victims as their flesh first began its decay into nothingness. Perhaps he would grow out of it; perhaps not. Time would tell. It was a fascinating sight. Milan's flesh was pale – waxy. The blood around his throat was dry now, but still showed, both on his skin and on his shirt. The expression on his face was relaxed; his eyes were closed as if in sleep. That was a shame, a consequence of his becoming unconscious before dying. If Dmitry could learn to kill more quickly, then he would be able to see his victim's terror preserved on the face until nature ensured that no face remained.

A knock at the door disturbed his contemplation. It was late – past midnight – but perhaps Milan had been expecting someone. He stood and went down the stairs to the door. The knock came again.

'Who is it?' he asked.

'Katyusha, of course.' A female voice – young.

'Hang on!'

Dmitry looked around him. There was a mirror on the wall near to the door. He went over to it to check his face for stains of Milan's blood, but realized at once the futility of it. He pulled out a handkerchief and wiped his mouth, looking for traces of blood. Then he opened the door and peered round.

'Oh,' said the girl, surprised. 'I was here to see Milan.' She was young, certainly not twenty, and not dressed as though she was rich. She did not look like a whore, but it was no stretch of the imagination to guess why she had come here at this time of night. As far as Dmitry could guess, she was pretty; he certainly would have thought so before. It did not matter; looking at the girl now he found her attractive in much more compelling ways. And her revulsion at discovering what had become of her lover would only add to the pleasure Dmitry would take from her.

'He's here,' said Dmitry, his voice, he hoped, open and friendly. 'He's upstairs, waiting for you.'

Katyusha ascended. Dmitry closed the door and followed her.

The first stop had been Khimki, but Raisa had not moved from her seat. Neither had Tamara. She had remained where she was, watching. Someone, however, had got on.

It was the old woman – Natalia Borisovna, for want of a better name. She must have followed Tamara to the station and made it on to the train, but not the correct carriage. Khimki would have been her first opportunity to move up. There were no seats near Tamara and Natalia did not attempt to join her. Instead she sat at the far end of the carriage, staring at Tamara in much the same way Tamara looked at Raisa, though without the expression of hatred that Tamara knew was displayed on her own face.

The train pulled out of the station and continued on its slow journey to Petersburg. It began to shake, giving the impression of gathering speed, but Tamara knew it would never go very fast. She recalled her previous journeys on the route – all but one had been on the fast passenger train. The last trip had been to Dmitry's funeral and back. Before then, it had been with Konstantin on the imperial train. She allowed herself a slight smile. That would not have been nearly so much fun going at this speed. She had not heard from him since, though she felt sure he would write. But that was for the future, and today it was of little interest. After she had dealt with Raisa then she could deal with the future. She felt pain in her stomach again, like indigestion. There was one matter for the very near future that did count – Aleksei Ivanovich would soon be back in Moscow. She had not heard of him directly, but there was already gossip that another Decembrist exile, Prince Sergei Grigorovich Volkonsky, would be home within days. And he had settled in Siberia in the town of Irkutsk – the same place as Aleksei and Domnikiia.

Tamara was awakened from her thoughts by a disturbance further down the carriage. The conductor was standing, raising his voice to one of the passengers. Tamara craned her neck and saw that it was Natalia. She stood up, curious, and walked towards them.

'No money, no ticket,' said the conductor. 'No ticket, and you're off at the next station.'

'Please,' replied Natalia. 'I have to stay on board.'

She looked at Tamara as she spoke, as if her being on the train were Tamara's fault, which in some sense it was. She was following Tamara and Tamara had got on the train. For Tamara, even if she'd had no money, her official papers would have seen to it that the matter was ignored. Natalia did not share that privilege. Tamara did not like the idea of the old woman being dumped on the platform of a third-category station in the middle of the night. Besides, she still wanted to talk to her about Dmitry.

'I'll pay for her,' she said.

The conductor looked her up and down. With anybody else, certainly any other woman, he might have refused to accept the money, but he'd seen Tamara's passport, and knew the authority that she had behind her. 'Where to?' he asked Natalia.

Natalia could not answer. Instead she looked at Tamara. A smile almost passed between them as Tamara understood that since she was following Tamara it would be Tamara who knew how far they were going. But in truth Tamara didn't know. That question could be answered only by Raisa.

'Petersburg,' said Tamara, knowing they could go no further than the end of the line. The conductor took her six roubles and issued Natalia with a red, second-class ticket, then moved on his way. Natalia and Tamara remained looking at each other. Tamara wondered if she should sit down now and talk. It seemed wise. There was nothing she could do while Raisa merely gazed at the window. She turned and prepared to sit, glancing over towards Raisa as she did.

Raisa was gone. She must have been more alert than Tamara had given her credit for, and used the few moments of distraction to make her move. She could not have got past Tamara and the conductor as they stood in the centre aisle, so she must have gone the other way. Tamara ran along to the door at the end and opened it. In an instant she was out in the cold night air, standing on the metal platform at the end of the carriage. The moment she arrived, Raisa leapt. Tamara got just a glimpse of her hair and skirts as she landed beside the track and rolled away, but then she vanished from sight as the train moved on.

Tamara cursed her stupidity. For a human, such a jump might not prove fatal, but the risk of injury would be enough to put anyone off. For a *voordalak* there was no risk and no fear. Any injury would soon heal. She leaned over the rail and looked back. She could just see Raisa, bright in the darkness. She wondered whether she too should risk the fall, but watching the ground speed by she thought it too dangerous. Even if she survived, she might break a limb; or be knocked out, and find herself at the mercy of Raisa.

Then she heard the train whistle blow three times – they were stopping. She looked up and saw the green lanterns which marked the beginning of a bridge ahead; the one across the Skhodnya. Two trains were not allowed on a bridge at the same time, so it must be that another was crossing towards them, and that this one would have to wait.

She let the train slow, but did not wait for it to stop before jumping to the ground, running as she landed so as to keep upright. The conductor was too busy at the other end of the carriage operating the brake to notice her. The moon had set, but there was sufficient light from the train to see by, and Raisa made an easy target. She was only the train's length away, walking back alongside the track, as if hoping to return to Moscow. The train had halted completely now, and stood there, waiting until the bridge was clear. Tamara walked briskly. The ground was too uneven for her to run, but even so she would soon catch Raisa.

Tamara called out to her, but it had no effect. She waited until she was a little closer and then called again. This time Raisa turned, looking straight back towards her. Then Tamara saw her body drop down a little as she simply sat beside the tracks, waiting for Tamara to catch up. Tamara slowed to a steady walk. She reached for the cap that covered the tip of her cane and threw it to one side. Then she drew the pistol from her bag.

It was when she cleared the last coach of the waiting train that Tamara realized they were not alone. On the other side of the track, someone else was walking, mirroring Tamara's movements. For a moment she supposed that it was one of the conductors, come to see why two women had chosen to throw themselves from the train, but it was not. Once again, it was the woman who called herself Natalia, sticking to Tamara like a shadow.

'Get away from here,' Tamara called out, still walking, not looking at the woman, her eyes instead fixed on Raisa. 'It's not safe.'

'You think I don't understand that?' asked Natalia.

'You're not one of them then.' Tamara had not forgotten the possibility, given Natalia's supposed death ten years before, but it seemed increasingly unlikely.

'Toma!' It was a personal affront.

'But you're not Natalia Borisovna either.'

'No. That was just a name I borrowed.'

'Why?'

'Because I wasn't supposed to be in Moscow.'

Still Tamara marched on towards Raisa, knowing that she must not let these other matters distract her, but sensing also that this woman was vital to her understanding of what was really going on. 'I meant, why her?' she said.

'Because she was around in 1812.'

'And your ages matched?'

A pause. 'She was a little younger – a friend of a friend.'

Tamara remembered Oleg Ilyich's description of his mother's friends – and their names. 'A friend of Captain Petrenko?' she asked.

'Hardly.' There was a touch of bitterness.

'Then of Captain Danilov?'

'It's a long time since he was a captain.'

Tamara came to a halt. Raisa was now just a few paces ahead of her, still sitting on the ground. Tamara raised her hand to the old woman, indicating to her both to be silent and not to come across the tracks to them.

'Stand up,' said Tamara.

Raisa looked towards her. Her face was tear-stained. 'What?'

'Or die where you sit.'

'Leave me alone.' Raisa's voice was sullen. This was not what

Tamara had been anticipating. There was no fight in the woman, and without that, it was difficult to find reasons to hate her. Then she remembered one.

'You could have left Dmitry alone,' she said.

'He made his choice.'

'After you'd fooled him.'

'He still had a choice,' said Raisa, 'even at the end. Most men would have preferred to keep their dignity.'

Tamara considered. Raisa was right. However much the cards had been stacked against Dmitry, he'd still been in command of his own destiny. A stronger man would have turned back, however far he had gone down the path, when he realized where it would lead. But it did not matter.

'Dmitry's stupidity doesn't lessen your guilt,' said Tamara.

Raisa didn't seem even to hear the comment. Instead she stood up and smoothed her dress. She took a step towards Tamara and then stopped, examining her face closely, as if seeing it for the first time. But when she spoke, her thoughts, as ever, were focused upon herself.

'Am I beautiful?' she asked.

'I'd have said so, if I didn't know you.'

'So you see it?'

'See what?' asked Tamara.

'What I truly am.'

'I understand it. I don't need to see it.' As she spoke, Tamara heard in the distance a locomotive whistle. It was not the train from which they had disembarked, but one a little further away. It must have been the one for which they had stopped, now coming over the bridge.

'I saw myself in a mirror today,' said Raisa.

'How can you?'

'Oh, Vasiliy Innokyentievich is a very clever man. He can do anything.'

'And what did you see?'

'What you see,' said Raisa simply. She turned towards the old woman on the other side of the tracks, taking half a step towards Tamara as she did so. 'You!' she called out to her. 'You can be the judge. Which is the prettiest out of the two of us?'

'Toma,' said the woman, without a moment's consideration, as if she had been asked to verify that two and two made four.

'She understands, you see,' said Raisa, 'but we can soon change it. Look.'

She raised her hand to her face and pressed her nails against her cheek, drawing them down and dragging the flesh with them. She must have been applying a phenomenal force, for it was no mere scratch that she left behind. Tamara gagged at the sight of Raisa's teeth and tongue, visible through the gaping hole in the side of her face. Somehow Raisa got a grip on her cheek and tore it away, hurling it on to the ground. The edge of her lip came with it, so that when she spoke, the gap spread from the right-hand corner of her mouth almost to her left ear.

'Makes no difference, does it?' she said, her words slurred almost beyond comprehension by the inability of her lips to properly form them. Tamara presumed she was referring to the fact that she would heal, but Raisa's next words put a different interpretation on it. 'What does my face matter? It's not that which makes me ugly.'

'No,' said Tamara. 'No, it's not.'

The ground was shaking a little now as the train drew nearer. It was still out of sight, blocked by the rear end of the stationary train. Tamara heard another whistle, and that train began to move, the bridge ahead of it finally clear.

'It wouldn't be the same for you though, would it?' As she spoke, Raisa reached across and put her hand to Tamara's face. Tamara felt a searing pain as the fingernails pressed through the skin and dragged downwards, trying to do the same to Tamara's cheek as they had done moments before to their owner's. Tamara had been taken by surprise, and with Raisa so close to her, she could raise neither her pistol nor her cane to defend herself.

Then Raisa let go. Tamara's cheek screamed at her as though it were on fire, and she could feel her own blood running down it. The pause in Raisa's attack was down to the fact that the old woman had thrown herself upon her. She had little strength to fight the vampire, but it brought a momentary distraction. Raisa threw her off with a nonchalant swing of the arm, and she fell backwards on to the tracks. It was long enough for Tamara to raise her pistol and fire. She remembered Dmitry's advice and aimed for the face, but thanks to Raisa's self-mutilation there was little left to aim for. The bullet entered through the still-gaping hole of Raisa's cheek, penetrating somewhere at the back of her mouth. It did not have quite the devastating effect that Dmitry had described, but the impact threw her backwards and she had to take a few steps to remain on her feet. She almost tripped on the rail, but managed to keep her balance.

Behind Raisa, the old woman was lying on the track, moaning in pain. The ground beneath her was shaking ever more violently as the train from Petersburg approached, building up speed now that it was off the bridge. The woman sensed what was happening and rolled away to the other side.

Tamara had five shots remaining, none of which could possibly be fatal to Raisa but which together, so the plan had been, might just be sufficient to incapacitate her long enough for Tamara to use the cane. Now the plan had changed, but it would take some precise timing. Tamara fired again, still aiming for the head. The bullet hit Raisa between the eyes. Her head jerked back and again she took a few steps, but when her neck straightened, she was smiling – her lips already healed enough for her to do so. Blood oozed from the neat, circular opening in her forehead. Tamara fired a third shot and again Raisa backed away. She was between the two sets of tracks now. Tamara took a few steps forward, keeping as close as she dared.

'You always were a stupid woman, Tamara Valentinovna,' Raisa said, her voice a mixture of despair and spite. 'And now, thanks to me, you're a stupid, ugly woman.'

Tamara fired again, and now Raisa was in the middle of the southbound track. Still the ground shook.

'Two bullets left, and I'm not dead,' continued Raisa. Her cheek was completely healed now, as was the wound between her eyes. She took a step forward and was again between the two tracks. 'What are you going to do when those run out?'

Tamara needed only one. She waited a moment and then fired again, aiming for the middle of Raisa's nose. She didn't see where the bullet hit, but once again Raisa took a step backwards, and the oncoming train hit her.

She flew into the air and disappeared from view, falling on to the far side of the track as the engine steamed past, its pistons pounding in and out, driving its wheels ever onwards. The impact would have broken every bone in Raisa's body, but it would not have killed her. Tamara had hoped to dive on her instantly and administer a final, fatal blow, but the train, raging onward towards Moscow, kept them apart.

Tamara dropped down and lay parallel with the track to look under the train at what was happening. With luck Raisa's injuries would be severe enough that she would still be unable to fight back when Tamara finally got across the track. Wagon after wagon rolled by, causing Tamara's view to flicker as it was obscured by the train's wheels and then became clear in the gaps between them. Luck was not on her side; Raisa was already on her feet, though not steady on them. She was upright now; Tamara could not see her face, but only the lower part of her body, broken by the impact, her legs skewed like a cripple. Tamara could not even tell which direction she was facing.

Then Tamara saw another skirt and another pair of legs, running towards Raisa. It could only be the old woman, Natalia. Raisa must have been facing away from her, since she made no attempt to react to the woman's approach. Natalia's legs disappeared from view as she hurled herself through the air, and then both of them were visible, on the ground, close to the track, as still the wheels rolled by, alternately blocking and revealing what was happening.

Natalia was on top. Her hand was upon Raisa's face and her eyes were filled with hatred, enough to give her the strength that no woman of her age should possess. Even so, Raisa must still have been weak from the impact of the train – or from the strange melancholy that afflicted her – otherwise she would have easily thrown the old woman off. Tamara glanced down the line; there were only a few coaches left to pass now. The train hadn't slowed and clearly the driver had noticed nothing of the collision. Through the wheels she saw that Natalia had managed to raise herself up a little higher above Raisa and now had both hands over the younger woman's face. Summoning the last ounces of her strength she pushed forward, and Raisa's head hit the rail.

There was a clunk as some part of the train connected with one or both of them. Natalia was thrown back and vanished from view, but Raisa lay still, just where the old woman had left her. Within seconds the train had passed and Tamara rushed across the shaking tracks.

Raisa's body did not move, apart from a gradual collapse as her remains decayed within her gown. The only visible part of her flesh was her hands, and already they protruded from her sleeves like the arms of skeletons. The collar of her dress lay neatly level with the rail and had already closed up, with no neck to keep it open. Raisa's head, which the train's wheel had so neatly severed, was gone.

Tamara glanced along the track and saw it, rolling along with the momentum it had picked up from the train, like a ball casually kicked away when the child was called in for tea by his mother. It bounced a little as it hit each sleeper, becoming smaller as dust flew off it. By the time it came to a stop it was no bigger than a walnut, and even that soon withered to nothing.

The dress lay beside the track, flat against the ground now that the body had decayed, like some sick warning against the dangers of the railway. But as for its owner, Raisa Styepanovna was no more.

CHAPTER XXV

TAMARA DASHED ACROSS THE TRACKS AND LOOKED AROUND. The old woman had been wearing a dark dress and with the moon gone and the trains departed, there was little light to see by. Thankfully, she was not far from the rails, lying face down in the grass. Tamara ran over to her. Her arms were laid out on either side of her, level with her head. Her hands were covered with blood and it looked as though both forearms were broken, smashed by the train's wheel as she had held Raisa's head down under it. It was a miracle they had not been severed. On her right wrist was a heavy ring of dark, roughly forged iron – somewhere between a bracelet and a manacle. Tamara turned her over. There was blood on her face too, her grey hair matted against it, and her nose was broken. But she was alive. She was breathing, albeit with shallow, halting rasps. Only one side of her chest seemed to rise and fall. The other lay still – a physical reminder that the woman was half dead already.

Tamara knelt down and wiped the hair away from the old woman's face. Her eyes were closed and there seemed little trace of consciousness. Tamara pulled her head up a little and rested it on her lap, stroking her cheek. She still felt the pain where Raisa's nails had gouged at her own face, but she did not dare touch it and discover the damage.

'Toma.' The woman's voice was weak, but perfectly clear.

Tamara looked down and tried to smile. She felt tears begin to form in her eyes. 'How do you know me?' she asked.

'You think I'd forget you?'

'It seems I've forgotten you.' It was a simple statement of fact, but it was loathsome for Tamara to say it to this woman who had sacrificed her own life to save hers.

'You don't recognize me?'

Tamara looked hard into the woman's face, desperate to see what it seemed she was meant to see. The woman had been beautiful once, that was obvious, and in a way still was. And yes – much as Tamara wanted to believe it, it was true – there was something that she recognized in that face. Then she realized. There was a resemblance, slight and foolish though it might be, to the Duchess of Parma, once, long ago, wife of the Emperor Napoleon. Tamara had seen a portrait of her, painted not long before she died. Ten years on, this might have been her. She wished the memory had been more personal.

'*Bayoo, babshkee, bayoo,*
'*Zheevyet myelneek na krayoo.*'

There was a growl to the old woman's singing voice, brought on by her age and her injuries, but the tune and the words in an instant brought back memories far stronger than any Tamara had found in her face. It all came back to her. She was in her bedroom in the Lavrovs' house – not the main room but the tiny room off it, with the little child's bed. She could hear that same voice – the voice of her long-forgotten nanny – so much younger then, singing the same lullaby, a silly story about a miller and his children at carnival time. She picked up the next two lines.

'*On nye byedyen, nye bogat,*
'*Polna gorneetsa rebyat.*'

The old woman smiled perhaps the broadest smile that Tamara had ever seen. Except that she was not 'the old woman' any more. Neither was she 'Natalia Borisovna'. At last Tamara knew her.

'Domnikiia Semyonovna,' she whispered.

Domnikiia could not smile any more widely, so instead she nodded. 'You do remember!' she said.

'I do now. I didn't when I saw you before.'

'Neither did I,' said Domnikiia, 'not right away. We chose not to know. But when I came to Moscow . . . I only went there to remember.'

'Went where?'

'To Degtyarny Lane. I was on my way back.'

'Back?'

'To Irkutsk. I had to deliver a letter for Lyosha – to Tsarskoye Selo. Everything we sent was censored, so he said I should come. It was safer for me than him. I hated to leave him, but I knew it was a chance to see you – just to look at you.'

'A letter?' asked Tamara.

'When we heard about the tsar's death. Lyosha knew that Iuda would go after Tarasov. We had to warn him.' Her voice became urgent. 'Is he all right? Did Iuda get him?'

Tamara had no idea how to provide an answer to the question, but Domnikiia clearly needed one. 'He's fine,' she said soothingly. 'He's fine.'

'And then I set off back to Irkutsk, but I stopped in Moscow on the way. I heard about the murder – went to Degtyarny Lane. And then I saw you. I didn't know it was you, but the hair reminded me. And then when you said it was your birthday, I knew it must be you.' She coughed and Tamara saw blood on her lips. Domnikiia tried to raise her hand to wipe them, but it was impossible. She didn't seem to understand that her arms were useless. Tamara cleaned the blood away for her.

'Why didn't you say?'

'I wanted to, Toma. How I wanted to! But I was as much an ex-ile as Lyosha. If I'd been recognized, I'd have been arrested. And then what could I have done?'

'But now you've come back.'

'We both have. He's free again and we've both come home, to see Dmitry and to see you.'

'Aleksei's in Moscow?' Tamara felt a thrill deep inside her. The news was not striking in any rational way, but it was the event that she had been anticipating for months. It seemed too good to be true. So many questions would be answered.

'We arrived today. I came straight to find you, but he wanted to see Dmitry. You understand?'

Tamara felt the urge to squeeze her former nanny's hand, but she knew it would only cause pain. Instead, she stroked her face. 'Of course I understand,' she said. 'Dmitry's not your son. They deserve some time together.' Tamara quietly contemplated the horror of Aleksei's potential encounter with his son. She could only pray that it would never happen. 'But you saved my life by coming to find me.'

'I didn't understand why you ran. Then I realized you were following that woman. I guessed what she was, and when you shot her I knew for sure.'

'You've met them before?'

Domnikiia smiled again. 'Not like that,' she said. 'That was always Lyosha. Do you think he'll be proud of me?'

'Of course he will,' said Tamara, her enthusiasm only a little forced. 'He'll be so, so proud.'

'You'll tell him?'

'*You'll* tell him,' insisted Tamara.

Domnikiia chuckled, as best she could, and shook her head. 'You're a good liar, Toma, just like Lyosha. You always took after him more than me, but neither of you could ever fool me. I'm not going to be seeing him again; not here. At least I've seen you.' She closed her eyes and turned her head to one side, but Tamara was scarcely listening to her any more.

She had been blind, but now her mother – *her mother* – had explained it all. '*You always took after him more than me.*' More like Aleksei than Domnikiia – more like her father than her mother. Aleksei was an old friend of Vadim Fyodorovich – his closest comrade. Who else but Vadim's daughter, Yelena, would he choose to care for his bastard daughter? And little wonder she could not distinguish the hazy memories of her nanny and her mother – they were one and the same: Domnikiia Semyonovna. What better way to ensure that the mother could keep watch over the child, and yet never have the truth discovered?

It was only the Decembrist Uprising and Aleksei's exile that had spoiled things. Tamara recalled how she had once scorned the idea that her father might be a Decembrist, but the more she had learned about Aleksei, the more she had grown to see him as a great man, of whom any child would be proud. 'A brother and an unhailed hero of the nation,' that was how Prince Volkonsky had described Tamara's father in one of his letters. Tamara was still to discover precisely what he'd meant by that, but soon she would know. Soon she would speak to Aleksei himself.

A mother and a father and one other; a brother too – Dmitry. A brother no more – he had died before she had even known him for what he was. Now he was nothing to her. She pushed the thought from her mind. She already had too much joy and too much sorrow to bear. She threw herself down and hugged her mother, squeezing as tightly as she dared, scarcely caring about the pain she inflicted, knowing that she would gladly suffer the same and more to feel the warm body of one so long separated from her. She felt her mother attempt to return the embrace, despite her broken arms, but then she fell back. Tamara raised herself up and looked at the ancient, wrinkled, beloved face beneath her.

'I had to go with him, Toma.' Domnikiia's eyes flicked frantically across Tamara's face. 'You must understand.'

'I do. Of course I do,' said Tamara. She had not stayed with her husband in Petersburg, and had never seen him again. Domnikiia's was the wiser choice. 'You left me in good hands.'

'We knew they'd look after you. Because of Vadim.'

'I've heard all about Vadim,' said Tamara, feeling the sting of tears on her cheek as they infiltrated the wounds that Raisa had given her. 'And Maks and Dmitry.'

Domnikiia closed her eyes again, but her voice was still clear, if quiet. 'I don't think I ever spoke to Vadim, but I know that to Lyosha he was the greatest man in the whole world. I knew Maks, and Dmitry. Maks was lovely. Marry a man like Maks, Toma, not one like Lyosha.'

'I married a doctor – he's called Vitaliy.' There was no need to go into details.

Again Domnikiia's smile spread, and then descended into a cough. Now the blood that came with it seemed not to bother her, and there was too much for Tamara to wipe away. When she had recovered, Domnikiia spoke again, quieter than ever. 'Children?'

Tamara managed to produce the standard answer. 'Three,' she replied. Domnikiia said nothing, but nodded slightly, her eyes still closed. 'Milenochka is fifteen now,' continued Tamara. 'Almost a woman. She's so beautiful.' It was so easy, and so wonderful, to lie about it. Domnikiia would never know of the deceit, and Tamara could experience the pleasure of pretending to someone else; something that usually she could only enjoy alone. 'Stasik is thirteen. He wants to be a doctor, like his papa.' Would he have wanted that? Would she have been disappointed if not? Would she and Vitya have tried to force him down that path? It did not matter; she was liberated from all such worries. She looked down at Domnikiia, but there was no response.

'Luka's only ten,' she went on. 'The other two tease him, but I think they love him even more than we do. I took him down Nevsky Prospekt a few weeks ago.' The memory was blatantly stolen. 'He stopped at every toyshop, and pressed his nose against the window. We spoil him – me more than Vitya, though I think Vitya buys him things and makes him promise not to tell me.'

It was pointless now. Domnikiia was dead. Tamara wasn't quite sure when it had happened, but she was certain she had died happily with thoughts of her phantom grandchildren filling her mind.

Tamara continued to talk, telling stories about her children, Domnikiia's head resting in her lap. Some of them were true – taken from their infancy – but most were just elaborations on the imaginings that had run through Tamara's mind ever since. It was bliss to be reunited – mother with children. Domnikiia with Tamara, Tamara with Stasik, Milenochka and Luka.

At last she could speak no more. She hoisted the old woman up in her arms, surprised by how little she weighed. Then she began to trudge with her alongside the railway track, heading north-west towards the green lanterns, and the bridge, and the river far below.

It was the first woman he had consumed; Katyusha, if names mattered. Dmitry had followed her closely up the stairs to Milan's rooms, eager to sense her reaction when she found what was up there, wondering whether she would perceive first the blood, or would see her lover on the couch and presume him asleep. Or would she instantly see the wounds to his neck, and understand what had befallen him? And after that, what would her reaction be with regard to Dmitry? Would she cower from him in fear, and

431

soon discover her fear quite justified, or would she throw herself upon him for protection, only to find her trust in him betrayed?

What in fact resulted was merely irritating. She screamed; a loud, repeated scream that, whether by chance or design, was most likely to save her life by attracting the attention of neighbours. Perhaps he should have let them come, but instinct took him over and he hit her, his knuckles striking the line of her jaw and knocking it upwards into her skull. She fell to the floor like a pile of wet rags, and he saw blood trickling from her mouth. He knelt down. She was unconscious, but not dead. That at least would preserve the blood, but there would be little to enjoy in a victim whose awareness of her fate had lasted for so inconveniently brief a duration.

He dragged her over to the couch and hauled her up on to it, sitting her beside Milan. She didn't groan or offer any resistance, as he had hoped. She made no movement at all. He slipped his hand inside her blouse and rested it below her breast, feeling her heartbeat. It was slow, very slow, as though she were supremely relaxed, but there was still life. Her jaw was broken and dislocated, twisted at a bizarre angle. She was no longer pretty. He would tell her that when she came round. Perhaps there was a mirror he could use to show her.

He went into Milan's bedroom and soon found one – a simple hand-held glass in a wooden frame. He came back and sat next to Katyusha. He looked at her through the mirror, but she appeared much the same as in real life. Then he held it close to her face, so that her own reflection would be the first thing she would see when she came to. She remained oblivious to the world, but Dmitry noticed the glass become fogged by her breath. He waited, perhaps for an hour, in the hope that she would revive naturally. Perhaps she would awake only to scream again, but the pain of her broken jaw might persuade her to keep silent, at least until she realized what was about to befall her.

Eventually he became impatient. He took hold of her shoulders and began to shake her, hoping to force her back to consciousness. A strange scraping sound emanated from her broken jaw. Then at last he got some reaction; her body jerked from somewhere around her stomach, then again. A sound that he could not make out emerged from her throat, and then she convulsed again and retched. Unconscious as she was, and seated almost upright, there was small chance for anything to escape her body. A little of the vomit reached her mouth and dribbled down her chin. Dmitry could smell it, but he did not find the scent objectionable as he once might have done. In fact, there was much to be learned from it. He could tell that she had been eating potatoes, and cabbage, and a little chocolate.

Another spasm ripped her body, this time a cough. The reflex cleared her mouth, spattering flecks of half-digested food across the room. Afterwards she was still again. Dmitry had hit her too hard – he had been forced to act without thinking. She was, for most purposes, as good as dead. She would never come round and if he waited too long she might escape him for ever. In her current state, there was still some enjoyment to be gained from her.

He knelt beside her on the couch and pulled her hair to one side, away from her neck. Her face was now a parody of what it had once been, even Dmitry could tell that. Her jaw still hung loose and bent, but the rest of her face was limp, as if paralysed. Strands of bile still dripped from her lips. Dmitry pressed his face into her neck and bit, at first tasting the vomit that coated her skin, but then feeling his mouth fill with the warm, rich blood that spurted from her pierced vein. He drank deeply, and forgot his disappointments over the manner of his feeding.

Then, suddenly, nausea hit him. He thrust himself away from the woman's body, for fear that what he was consuming had poisoned him, but he felt no lessening of the pain. Her blood had not grown stale, as it would have done if she had died, though death was not far from her now. This was something far more horrible, more fundamental, more all-consuming than mere tainted blood. It was as though he had received the most terrible news and awoken the following morning to have forgotten the details of it, yet still to remember the horror.

He searched his mind, and it took only moments to understand what had happened: Raisa was dead. Her presence, sometimes close, sometimes distant, had been there since the moment he had first awoken as a *voordalak*. Tonight it had been hard to discern, obscured by confusion, but it had existed; even when she slept.

Now it was gone, and although as a vampire Dmitry was young and naive, somehow he knew that she was dead. There was much he had hoped to learn from her, but the opportunity was lost. There was only one that he could learn from now, with whom there was no such bond as there had been with Raisa, but whose understanding of Dmitry's new condition would be far greater.

He glanced at the clock. It was too late for it tonight – soon Dmitry would have to head back to his adopted tomb, but he knew he could no longer put it off. When night fell again, Dmitry would not waste time on feeding. He would visit Yudin.

It had taken Tamara all night and most of the morning to get home. She had carried her mother's body north-west along the railway track. It hadn't taken long for them to reach the bridge and beneath it the ravine stretching down to the river Skhodnya below; a little longer before Tamara had been able to find a path down to the water's edge. If anyone had seen her she would have cut a strange image, carefully clambering down through the clumps of grass, tenderly clutching the frail corpse as though it were the most precious thing in the whole world.

Then she had stood there, gazing at the flowing water, wondering exactly what she should do. She could think of no other way to lay her mother to rest. She would happily have carried the body barefoot across a thousand versts, but to what end? Tamara had no room in her life for further complications; not now. She scoured the riverbank until she found some wood – a couple of planks that she guessed were left over from the construction of the bridge that towered above her. Then she cut strips of material from the hem of her skirt and used them to bind the planks together. She laid her mother on the makeshift funeral raft. Finally she gathered leaves and foliage and covered the body. Before covering her face, Tamara had given her mother one final kiss on the lips, and then gazed at her, trying to remember any detail that she could of their life together when she was a child. The memories of the last few hours proved too strong, overpowering, for now, those that were more distant and more subtle. But even they were enough.

She pushed the boat out into the water and let the current take it, murmuring a prayer that she remembered from her husband's funeral. She did not know how long she stood there by the river's edge before turning away – it was more than an hour. Domnikiia's body had long since vanished into the distance.

After that she had walked back to Khimki. Day had broken by the time she arrived, but she still had a long wait. A freight train came through, but with no passenger cars. At last the daily express train came in, two hours later than it should have done, but once she was on board, the journey back to Moscow was rapid and direct. She couldn't have looked at her best, sitting there in the second-class carriage, after the night's exertions, but after twenty hours on the train neither did many of the passengers.

Moscow seemed unquantifiably different. Tamara knew that it was she, not the city, who had changed, but still she felt that everyone she passed was examining her. It was only later, when she saw herself in the mirror, that she understood the grotesque nature of the wound to her left cheek. At the time she had felt that every uneasy gaze was asking her why she had let Domnikiia Semyonovna die like that, why she had disposed of her body with so little propriety. They could all go hang, and yet Tamara knew that there was one man who could fairly ask those questions of her: her father. He, who had survived so much, who had covered the thousands of versts from Siberia back to the west in just a few months, would not expect that the woman who had stood by his side throughout his exile would be dead within hours of their arriving home. He would not expect that, on hugging his beloved son after three decades apart, he would find that Dmitry had been transformed into the creature that Aleksei had spent his whole life learning to despise.

But first she must find him. She could not begin to guess where he would go. It surprised her that he had come to Moscow, not Petersburg, but then she remembered what Domnikiia had said. Aleksei had been eager to see Dmitry, and evidently they believed Dmitry to be in Moscow. They had not heard the news of his death, and before that, Moscow had been his last address. She would go and find out if Aleksei had called at his lodgings – sooner or later he would. But first she needed to clean herself up and, above all, to rest.

The door was bolted from the inside when she arrived at Degtyarny Lane, just as it should be. It took two or three minutes before Isaak opened it, but when she entered, what shocked her most was the ordinariness of everything. Nadia was crossing the salon, carrying jugs of hot water to take upstairs to the girls' rooms. Few of the girls themselves were out of bed yet. Sofia was coming downstairs and wished Tamara a bleary 'Good morning.'

None of them seemed concerned that Tamara had been away all night; none had noticed that Raisa was not there at all; no one had even discovered the broken-down wall in the gap between Raisa and Sofia's rooms, nor the grim item that lay at the foot of the steps beyond it. They'd certainly never suppose what had become of Raisa – that her head had been severed from her body by the wheels of the Moscow train, and that her remains had in an instant wasted to nothing. It was hard for Tamara to believe it herself.

It was only as Tamara turned towards her rooms that she heard a gasp and the crash of china breaking on the floor.

'What happened to you?'

Tamara turned and looked at Nadia, and realized that she was reacting to the scratch marks that Raisa had left on her cheek. She hadn't even seen them herself yet, but judging from Nadia's reaction it was none too pretty a sight.

'You'd never believe me,' she said.

Then she went over to her rooms, through her study and into her bedroom, and collapsed on her bed, asleep.

It was dark when she awoke. There was a light, urgent tapping on her door. She was amazed that she had been able to sleep, with so many thoughts bouncing off the walls of her mind, but it had been over a day since she had last rested.

'Come in!' she shouted.

Nadia popped her head round the door. 'A gentleman asking for you,' she said.

'Tell him to pick someone else,' she snapped, then added, 'Tell him I've retired.' It was entirely an afterthought, but the very idea of it filled her with excitement.

436

'I don't think he's interested in that. He's not that sort of gentleman. He asked specifically to speak to you.'

Tamara leapt to her feet, all sleepiness banished in an instant. Could it be, at last? Had her father come to find her? She sped across her bedroom, into the study and through the salon to the front door.

Her face fell. She had no idea what Aleksei looked like, but this wasn't him. It was Gribov. She had never seen him at Degtyarny Lane before. She wasn't even sure if he knew the nature of the business that Yudin operated from there, but the very presence of the small, mild, bookish man seemed incongruous.

'I hope I haven't overstepped myself, Tamara Valentinovna,' he said, 'but given your researches, I felt sure you'd like to know.'

'Know what?'

'Aleksei Ivanovich. He has returned. He's in Moscow.'

That much was old news to Tamara, but she could only guess that Gribov had more to tell. 'Where is he?' she asked urgently.

'Actual State Councillor Yudin has shown an equal interest in speaking to him. That's why he's had him arrested.'

'Arrested? What for? He's been pardoned.'

'I fear Actual State Councillor Yudin regards that sort of thing as a detail. It was only luck that I was there when the gendarmes delivered him.'

'Delivered him? Where?'

Gribov swallowed visibly before answering. 'To Yudin's office. I saw them dragging him down the stairs, but they didn't stay there for long.'

'Where did they take him?' It was a stupid question, as Gribov made clear.

'I think, Tamara Valentinovna,' he said, scarcely raising his voice above a murmur, 'that you know that as well as I do.'

'Why?'

The word surprised Yudin, not in its meaning but in the fact that anyone had spoken at all. He had been expecting, on his return from the cells beneath, that his office would be empty. But then he had also been expecting, for some weeks now, that Dmitry would seek him out. It was an appointment that neither

437

of them could shirk. And of all the ways that it might begin, Dmitry's 'Why?' had always been the most likely.

'You object?' Yudin countered.

'How could I? But that doesn't mean that I wouldn't have objected if I'd known.'

'You're sure of that?'

Dmitry paused. 'It's hard to tell. It's as if I was another person.'

'Really?' Yudin was, as ever, curious.

Dmitry did not choose to elucidate. 'How long has it been for you?' he asked instead.

'Barely thirty years. You remember when you left me and your father in Senate Square to face Nikolai's guns? It was within an hour of that.'

'Who was it that created you?'

'I'm unusual,' explained Yudin. 'I created myself.'

'From nothing? Like God?'

'Not quite. I needed a vampire's blood, but he was already dead.'

'So you are an orphan?' asked Dmitry.

'If you want to put it like that.'

'As am I.'

'Raisa's dead?' asked Yudin.

Dmitry nodded. 'I don't know what happened. Her mind was confused, and then was no more.'

Yudin sighed. It was a shame, but it had been a risk worth taking. Perhaps a stronger mind – or one less vain – would have dealt better with what it had witnessed in the looking glass, but Yudin still wasn't going to risk experimenting on himself, or even on Dmitry; not for now. He wished he were back in Chufut Kalye, where he'd had the facilities, and the guinea pigs, to conduct such elegant experiments.

Dmitry turned away and walked over to the map drawers. He reached out and pulled away the blanket, revealing the dressing-table mirror that had always stood there.

'Raisa told you that was there?' asked Yudin.

'I learned it from her. She was obsessed by it – by mirrors. She thought you would be able to let her see her face.'

Yudin felt his muscles stiffen slightly, ready for action.

Voordalaki were emotionless creatures, but he had learned over the years that the regard held by one of them for the vampire that created it could be strong; enough to lead to the desire for revenge over whoever had killed the vampire parent. Yudin did not feel the emotion himself – how could he as a parricide? – but in Dmitry it could prove dangerous. Neither of them knew how Raisa had died, but her reaction to the mirror must have been at least in part responsible. And Yudin had shown her the mirror.

'I tried,' he said. 'But I could never find a way.'

Dmitry nodded. 'She thought you were stringing her along.'

For a moment, Yudin considered objecting to this untruth, but he realized it was wiser to let it lie. Dmitry seemed to bear no grudge over such minor trickery of Raisa and so it was best to have him go on believing it rather than hint that Yudin might ever have had the power to reveal to her her true likeness.

'We both benefited from our association,' he said.

'You still haven't explained why,' said Dmitry.

So many reasons. Some Dmitry would understand; most he would be indifferent to. One, however, was fundamental. 'I'd always planned it.'

'Always?'

'Since I first met you, a little boy of five, in Petersburg, in 1812.'

'That's a long time to nurture a plan.'

Yudin smiled, taking Dmitry's words as a compliment. 'Perhaps an option then, rather than a plan, but it was there from the beginning.'

'So why now?'

'Because you were on the point of working it out for yourself, and that would have made it far more difficult to persuade you. Then of course there was the fact that, with the amnesty, your father would be returning home soon.'

'And he would have stopped you?'

Was that a hint of pride that Yudin noted in Dmitry's voice? It was unlikely – impossible, even. The intonation merely reflected years of habitually speaking of Aleksei in that way.

'Hardly,' Yudin countered. 'He's an old man now, and it's been a long time since he had more influence over you than I did.'

'So what's he got to do with it?'

'My dear Mitka, he's the reason for it all. He was what was on my mind, back in 1812, when I first met you and your mother. I remember so clearly thinking to myself, I am going to destroy these people, and I'm going to make Aleksei watch it.'

'Why do you hate him so?' There was no rebuke in Dmitry's question, merely enquiry.

'Hate him? I wouldn't go that far. Now, of course, hatred is lost to me, but even then, even when a human, I don't think I ever hated your father. Perhaps on brief occasions, when he thwarted me, but on the whole, no. He merely stood against me. He offered himself as an opponent and I accepted him. If the stakes have become higher than he originally supposed, then that merely makes the game more exciting.'

'I imagine he must hate you.'

Yudin considered, and then nodded. 'Then I have won,' he said.

'You failed to destroy my mother in front of him.'

'Did I? You never knew that your mother and I were sleeping together, did you?'

'You surprise me.' Dmitry's words were uttered with none of the emotion that might be expected to accompany them. It was news to him, but he was not upset.

'We surprised Aleksei when he found us together. And then when he discovered the influence I'd had on you throughout your life, the set was complete. I had stolen his entire family.'

'Stolen, but not destroyed.'

'There was still time.'

'But with my mother, cholera beat you to it.'

'Really?' asked Yudin.

'I'm sure Papa was upset, but he could hardly have blamed you. He was more likely relieved she was free of you.'

Yudin smiled. 'Come with me,' he said.

He went over to the door by which he had entered his office moments earlier and opened it. Dmitry followed him as he descended the stairs. Where they forked, Yudin nodded to the right.

'There are two coffins down there,' he explained. 'One is mine; the other was where Raisa Styepanovna sometimes slept. You're welcome to it now. There's a tunnel beyond to the river, if you can't get through the Kremlin.'

Dmitry looked in the direction Yudin had indicated, but made no comment. Yudin felt no particular desire for company as he slept, but neither did he shun it. The suggestion was purely practical. It was in Yudin's interests that Dmitry lived, and any extra hiding place he might know in Moscow would increase the chances of it.

They continued down the stone stairway and were soon in the short, low corridor with the six cells leading off. Dmitry had to stoop to walk through it, his shoulders almost filling the arch of the ceiling. From the grille in the door on the far right, a light shone, but at the moment there was no sound from within, save for the ever-present dribble of water. They would go there soon, but not now. For now, Yudin's goal was the seventh door, the one at the very end of the passageway. He put the key into the lock and turned it, then drew back the three heavy bolts. It was built to be strong enough to hold a *voordalak*, though that was not its present use. Before opening it, he turned back to face Dmitry.

'Raisa and I lived in Moscow for many years,' he said. 'But no one ever sought us out. How much blood do you suppose we drank in that time? How many bodies did we drain? And yet where were the reports of missing persons? Where were the remains that revealed the tell-tale signs of a *voordalak* at table? Why did no mobs descend on the Kremlin, baying for revenge?'

'I imagine in your position you could suppress any such discoveries – prevent gossip from becoming widespread.'

'You overestimate me, though you're right in part. Those disappearances that were necessary were kept quiet. But there were few bodies.'

He opened the door and stepped through. Dmitry followed. Beyond was a room, no taller than the corridor from which they had come, but wider. In the centre was a table, with food on it – fresh food that Yudin had recently put there. Along the wall on each side were two doors, bolted shut. Yudin walked over to each of the four doors and drew the bolts, knowing that the noise they made would be enough to rouse those who were concealed

441

behind them. Then he went back and stood beside Dmitry at the main entrance.

It was the one nearest to them on the left that opened first. A man emerged. He glanced around furtively, seeing that Yudin and Dmitry were there, but also seeing the food. He was Yudin's most recent acquisition – kept down here for less than two years. He was somewhere in his thirties, and his blood was still rich and vigorous. He scampered over to the table, revealing the chain that stretched out beside him and back into his cell. Close to him, it split into three strands, two shackled to his ankles and one to an iron ring about his neck. It was just long enough for him to reach the table. He began to eat hungrily, stuffing the cold meat, bread, cabbage and beetroot into his mouth. It was a diet that had been carefully selected by Yudin and honed over the years to its present form. It was not intended to be flavoursome, or to provide strength. Its twin goals were merely to sustain life, and to sweeten the blood.

Once the first one had begun to eat, the others came quickly – as quickly as they could. They did not want to lose out on their meal. There were two more men, both older than the first, and from the far right-hand cell a woman, who was by a long way the oldest of all. All were fettered in a similar fashion.

'Occasionally they die,' explained Yudin. 'Usually of disease, although sometimes as the result of overindulgence on my part – or Raisa's.' He lowered his voice. 'And then there's always suicide.'

He took a step into the room and grabbed the chain of the youngest man, pulling him close. 'This one's called Bogdan,' he said. Bogdan had learned by now that it was futile to defy Yudin's strength and so did not try to struggle. Instead he grabbed a few last morsels of food and shoved them into his mouth. Once he was close, Yudin offered the chain to Dmitry. 'Hold him!' Dmitry complied.

Yudin grabbed Bogdan's arm and rolled up his sleeve. There were two wounds revealed on the inside of his forearm. One was almost healed, the other still had a fresh scab on it.

'The risk of death is too great if we drink from the neck,' Yudin explained. Bogdan eyed him as he spoke, quite able to understand him, but quite uninterested. He had heard it all before. Yudin made very sure that everything was explained. It was best if Bogdan and the others understood the reason that they were still alive.

Yudin pressed his lips against a clear patch of skin on Bogdan's arm, between the two wounds, and bit. In the early days, the man would have pulled away, hit him, tried to fight him off, but his spirit was broken now. Even if it hadn't been, the fact that Dmitry was there would dampen any thoughts of resistance. It was when Yudin came alone that they were most restive, thinking that they might be able to overcome him. That had been one of the benefits of having Raisa at his side. Those who did not know thought she would be weak – an easy victory. She soon disabused them of the idea.

Yudin drank, but not for long. He raised his head and took the chain from Dmitry, wrapping it once around his wrist. 'Enjoy,' he said.

Dmitry gave him a brief glance, seeking confirmation, and when he got it, he bent forward, sucking from the wound that Yudin had already created. As he did so, Yudin looked into Bogdan's face. This was another benefit of there being two of them here. The man's eyes were blank. They met Yudin's without fear, but without hatred either – though perhaps there was a little of that, or the memory of it, hidden in there somewhere. But most of all, it was a look of acceptance; acceptance both of his situation, and of his lack of power to do anything about it. It was the look of the dairy cow to the milkmaid – hiding the secret hope that soon it would be taken to slaughter.

Dmitry raised his head. He seemed unimpressed. 'I suppose you get used to it,' he said.

Yudin understood him. The experience was not the best. Drinking from the arm, or anywhere on the body other than the neck – and Yudin had tried most places in the never-ending search for a fresh patch of skin – was not the same. And the restraint of drinking but not killing was a tiresome burden. But this way was far less risky.

'It ensures that you live long enough *to* get used to it,' he said.

Dmitry nodded non-committally, and Yudin released the chain. Bogdan gave them each a brief glance and then hurried back to the table, eager to eat before the food was all gone. The four humans didn't talk to each other. Yudin had done nothing to stop them, but, with every one of those he had kept down here, it seemed to come naturally. They didn't want him to hear. When they were in their cells and didn't know he was outside listening, they would talk. Occasionally one of them – invariably a newcomer – would try and inspire the others with some plan of escape, but it was never taken up. Yudin was always careful. No one new was ever brought in until those there were well and truly broken.

Yudin began to walk around the side of the room, avoiding disturbing the four figures at the table, until he was behind the old woman in the far right-hand corner. Dmitry followed him. Yudin lifted up her chain and pulled her towards them. She offered no resistance; she had hardly been eating anyway. She would be dead soon; that was Yudin's guess. Even now she was too weak to raise her head and look either of them in the face. It was lucky that events had timed themselves so perfectly.

Yudin grabbed her arm as he had done with Bogdan, but this time offered it straight to Dmitry. 'I think you'll find this one interesting,' he said.

Dmitry appeared unconvinced, but even so he bent forward and placed his lips against her skin. He was right to be dubious. Yudin had not got much sustenance from this old woman in a long time. But that was not the point. And anyway, Dmitry seemed to be doing a good job. Yudin could see smears of blood emerging from beneath his lips, and could only guess that at least a taste was getting into his mouth. Still, there was no need for further delay.

'This one's called Marfa,' he said. Dmitry did not react. He continued to drink. 'Marfa Mihailovna,' Yudin added. He sensed the slight movement of Dmitry's head cease. For a second or two, all was still, with Dmitry remaining bent forward. If his lips had been touching the back of her hand rather than the inside of her forearm, it might almost have mimicked a formal introduction at a ball. But these two had no need to be introduced.

Finally, Dmitry straightened up and Yudin pulled on the chain at Marfa's neck to bring her head up and make her face Dmitry. For himself, Yudin did not know which way to look. He was like a child outside a toyshop window, trying to take in everything. His eyes darted between the two faces in front of him as one broke into an expression of amused surprise and the other, slowly emerging from a pall of broken acceptance, revealed that a woman who had learned to live with so many horrors could discover that there were still things in this world that could make her weep for her very existence.

It was a touching moment, and one which Yudin found delightful. They had not seen each other in a decade. One had thought the other to be dead. But now, thanks to him, mother and son were finally reunited.

CHAPTER XXVI

MARFA'S LIPS MOVED, BUT EMITTED NO SOUND. HER FACE was pale and the skin was drawn tight over her skull, hollow at her cheeks. She was seventy-one years old, though in her bedraggled state she appeared older. As a loving son, Dmitry should have recognized her the moment she stepped into the cell, however much she had changed in the ten years since he had seen her. But he was no longer any such thing. Whether or not he was her son was a matter of philosophical debate. That he did not love her was a fact of undeniable certainty.

It was only when Yudin had spoken her patronymic that Dmitry had even begun to guess the truth, but then realization had come to him quickly. When he looked at her face, it was obvious who she was, and as he gazed at her, impassively, he had the privilege of seeing two waves of understanding come over her almost simultaneously: the first that he was her son; the second that he was a vampire.

She seemed very small. She had been a plump sixty-year-old when he had last seen her, her girth increasing consistently with her age, but that was all gone now. She seemed smaller in every way. She kept her eyes on him as they filled with tears, her hands, once he had released her arm, hanging down limply in front of her. The little blood that Dmitry had been able to find in her had already ceased to flow.

'She didn't die then?' he said, speaking to Yudin but still looking at his mother.

'She wasn't even ill. She merely noted one day that I never seemed to age, and that could only lead to her realizing the truth.

446

I knew it would happen eventually, and with you in Bessarabia it was the ideal time. I suggested we take a trip to Moscow together, and she never came back. It was surprisingly easy to make everything official.'

'And she's been here ever since?' said Dmitry. 'Eight years?'

'I'm amazed she lasted, but something kept her going. Hoping that Aleksei would come along and rescue her, I dare say – or perhaps you.'

Dmitry spoke now to his mother. 'If it's any consolation, I'm sure I would have done, had I known.' He wondered why he should want to console her.

'And now?' she asked, finally finding her voice, a shallow whisper.

Dmitry shrugged. He could scarcely understand why she asked the question. Did she hope that there remained in him some vestige of the man he had been, which would compel him to play the gallant son? Her calm sorrow could only imply that she did not. And yet why shouldn't he? What rules were there to bind his behaviour?

Seeing that she would get no answer, she chose a different question. 'Why?'

Dmitry took a deep breath. 'A long story,' he said. 'Suffice to say I did it for . . .'

He stopped as Marfa closed her eyes – forcing the tears from them on to her cheeks – and shook her head. She opened them and spoke again. 'Why, Vasya? Why show him to me?'

Dmitry felt a sudden annoyance at being ignored. He was reminded of when he was a child and she had wanted to punish him. Her favourite trick was to talk about him to someone else.

'Why not?' said Yudin.

'Haven't you brought me enough pain?'

'You think this is about you?'

'I saw you watching me just now, squirming with pleasure at how you thought I'd react – just like you always did.'

'That doesn't make you the reason. You were always a means, Marfa, never an end. You know that.' Yudin raised his hand and stroked her cheek as he spoke, like an affectionate husband of many years.

'So it was to see Mitka react?'

'Again a bonus, though there was little reaction to observe. But you're right; this is for Mitka's benefit. You should be pleased.'

'Pleased?'

'He's become an immortal; stronger than ever he was before, and faster, and wiser. What mother could not be proud of that?'

'You forget, Vasya, I know you. How could I be happy to know he has become like you?'

'Have it your way,' snapped Yudin, taking his hand from her face. 'I hope at least Dmitry's happy with what I have given him.'

'And what's that?' asked Dmitry.

Yudin looked at him, as if the answer were utterly obvious. 'Self-knowledge! Self-awareness! Look inside yourself, Mitka. What is it you feel?'

Dmitry thought for a moment, doing just as Yudin had said; examining his feelings. He spoke as the ideas occurred to him. 'A little amusement; the situation is, I think we all have to admit, somewhat ironic. Also annoyance at having been tricked – with myself mostly, but also with you, Vasya. I should have realized she was not dead.'

'Anything else?'

'Disgust.'

'Disgust?'

'At this place. At what you do. Living off chained humans in a hidden cellar, letting them revive each day only so that you can feed from them the next night. The *voordalak* is a hunter, not a farmer.' He meant it. Yudin's way was not the only way.

Yudin grinned and nodded. 'Good. Good,' he said. 'I disagree, of course, but I understand your instincts. And?'

Dmitry thought for a moment longer, then shrugged.

'No sorrow?' asked Yudin. 'No sense of regret, or outrage, or affection? No pity?'

'No.'

'And so you have learned,' explained Yudin. 'Would you have thought it possible to feel so little for your mother, even if you had possessed the capacity to imagine her in such straits as these?'

Dmitry considered and then began to nod. 'No, you're right, I couldn't. Or, at least, I might have thought it, but I wouldn't have felt it. If you'd asked me, I'd have guessed I'd feel nothing, but I wouldn't have truly known. So thank you, Vasya. Thank you.'

As he spoke, Dmitry understood that those same sentiments – or the lack of them – applied equally to Yudin. Surely Yudin understood that too, and yet he seemed confident of Dmitry's loyalty.

'And so now you are ready,' said Yudin. He held his open hand towards the door and Dmitry set off that way, with Yudin closely in tow.

'Ready?'

'I have one other thing to ask of you.'

'What?'

'You'll see.'

They had made it to the door and Yudin began to open it. 'Aren't you going to lock them back up?' Dmitry asked.

Yudin shook his head. 'Let them eat. I can do it later.' He stepped out through the doorway. Dmitry bent his head even further to follow.

'Mitka!' He turned. Marfa had finally managed to raise her voice above a whisper. 'Do you still hear music, Mitka?' she asked.

He turned without offering a reply, but she had managed to ask the only question about his former life that had truly concerned him since becoming a vampire; and the answer was no. Though he had tried every night since awaking in his grave on Vasilievskiy Island, he had not been able to summon a single note of music to his mind. And he understood now, with little doubt, that he never would.

Again he had something to thank his mother for; she had taught him to discover a new emotion in himself, and to understand that it would not be a stranger to him. For the first time, and only very slightly, he felt regret.

Gribov had been mistaken. Yudin's office was not empty. As soon as Tamara stepped out of the stairwell, she saw the tall figure, gazing into the mirror on top of the map drawers. Even if she had not guessed who it was from his stature, she would have been able to tell it was Dmitry from his reflection in the mirror.

There was no reflection.

Tamara was alone. At the brothel she had told Gribov to wait, and it had taken her only minutes to prepare herself to come here, but in that time he had gone. She doubted he would have been much help anyway. This was something she had to do for herself.

'Why didn't you tell me?' she asked.

Dmitry turned, without any expression of surprise, eyeing her up and down. In her left hand she had the Colt revolver, now reloaded, that had proved so useful against Raisa. In her right she held her wooden cane with its sharpened end, its cap lost somewhere in the rough grassland beside the railway track south of the Skhodnya. She wondered why she hadn't plunged it into his back before he even knew she was there, but she hadn't yet learned to hate him that much.

'Tell you what?' he asked.

'That they're my parents.' Her next words scarcely managed to escape her throat. 'That you're my brother.'

'Would you really want to know?' he replied. 'That your mother was a whore? That your father was an adulterer and a traitor and an exile? That your brother was . . . me?'

'It wasn't your decision to take.'

'It was Papa's decision. Should I have gone against that?'

'I had the right to know the truth.'

Dmitry shrugged and Tamara realized it was a pointless conversation. She was arguing with a *voordalak* over a decision made by the man who had once occupied the same body.

'Is he down there?' she asked, nodding towards the open door to the dungeons. 'Papa? With Yudin?'

Dmitry nodded. 'It's quite a reunion.'

'Why aren't you with them?'

'Yudin's plan is that I make my entrance in a little while – the brave son galloping to the rescue of his long-lost father. Then the son asks the father what it was that Yudin wanted to know, and in his relief the father reveals all.'

'So he doesn't know what's become of you?' Tamara failed to hide the loathing in her voice.

'That is to be the final coup de théâtre. Not only will Aleksei discover that his son has betrayed him to his oldest enemy, but he will learn that I have become what he despises most in all the world.'

'Is that really necessary?'

Dmitry gave a tight smile. 'He has the right to know the truth.'

Tamara had nothing to counter her own words. 'You'd better get on with it then,' she said.

He remained still. 'As I say, that is Yudin's plan.'

'I'd presumed you were his serf.' The bile she put into the word would have shamed her in front of Konstantin.

Dmitry's smile widened a little. 'So did I, for a while.' He paused for a moment. 'I remember a long time ago, when I was eighteen, when I joined the cavalry, I came down to Moscow with Papa. The coach dropped him off at his lodgings and then took me to barracks. And once I got there, I can remember this sudden sense of being totally alone. For the first time in my life, I didn't have my parents to fall back on, to make everything right. I was unprotected.

'And then minutes later I realized that I might be unprotected, but I was also untrammelled. Everything that I had been prevented from even thinking of doing as a child was now open to me. I could be naughty and no one would stop me. I could go out and get drunk; find myself a whore. Anything.

'And then I realized that I was freer even than that. I *could* do all those things, but I wasn't obliged to. I could do whatever I liked.'

'And did you?' asked Tamara, wondering where this was leading.

He laughed. 'No. I was mistaken. I wasn't free – I was in the army. I have been ever since. But now I'm free again; freer than I ever was, though it's taken me time to realize it. I don't have to do what humanity thinks I ought. But equally, I don't have to do what Yudin tells me to. Whatever I do, I do by choice.'

'And so will you choose to help Yudin?'

'Let's wait and see, shall we?'

He seemed to revel in his own indecision, seeing it as something positive. It could be a bluff, but it was the best that Tamara could hope for. She couldn't abandon Aleksei. She doubted she could defeat Dmitry, armed though she was, and even if she did, it would attract Yudin's attention. All she could do was go down to those dungeons alone, and pray that Dmitry did nothing.

Where the stairs forked she took the left branch, just as when Yudin had brought her down here. Soon she was in the narrow corridor. Light shone into it from the far door on the right. This was the room Tamara hated most – the room that smelt of sewage and disease. She walked along on tiptoe and stopped outside to listen. There were no voices, but she could hear movement, and splashing, and the occasional grunt or gasp. She might have been listening to someone in the bath, straining to reach out to clean the tips of their toes. Then there was a huge splash, and the sound of a man gasping for breath. Then she heard Yudin's voice.

'Just a name, Lyosha, that's all I need. A name or a place. You must know one or the other.'

The fast, heavy breathing continued, and began to slow. Then it paused and she heard another man's voice – her father! A dim sense of recognition came to her at the sound.

'You're a fool, Iuda. He never told me, and this is why.'

There was another splash, and the sound of breathing stopped completely. Tamara was sure she had heard right – 'Iuda', not 'Yudin'. The betrayer. It was the same name Domnikiia had used; clearly the name that she and Aleksei had known him by, years before.

She turned and stepped through the doorway. The room was as she remembered it; the only distinctive feature the stone bath, with the lead pipe that constantly fed it with water. Next to it, Yudin was seated on a wooden chair, his jacket removed and his shirtsleeves rolled up. He was leaning forward over the bath, pushing his hands down into it. Tamara could not see what was in there, but she could guess. The floor was covered with spilled water, which gradually drained into the gutter and then flowed out through the little hole in the wall. The smell of filth was still there, but it was less than when she had last been in the cell; perhaps that was due to the time of year. Again she felt the urge to run, but today she knew she would resist it.

She was about to speak, when Yudin straightened up, pulling what he had been holding down back out of the water. It was an old man. Tamara thrilled at the sight of him. His white hair was quite long, and stretched out straight, thanks to the water, to below his shoulders. His fringe covered his eyes, dripping into them. As soon as he emerged, he shook his head and water splashed across the room. His beard was white too, and clung together in a point from which water dribbled. He looked strong for a man of his age.

Despite the circumstances, he was everything she had imagined her father to be.

'How does it feel, Lyosha?' asked Yudin, his teeth gritted and his face close to Aleksei's. 'For once it's you who is drowning, and me who's thrusting you beneath the water.'

'It feels even better than the last time,' replied Aleksei.

'What?'

'Last time I had to bite my tongue. I had to leave you thinking you'd won. Now I can tell you everything.'

'So tell me.'

'You already know. You know that we tricked you and Zmyeevich into thinking Aleksandr was dead. You know that he went off to live in hiding. You even know something that I didn't, until you told me, something that makes this one of the happiest days of my life.'

'I've told you nothing.' Yudin's voice was dismissive.

'You've told me Aleksandr Pavlovich is still alive – otherwise why would you be asking about him? I can only guess how you discovered that much, but it's a joy for me to know that he's safe. And while he lives, so is Aleksandr Nikolayevich.'

'So tell me his name and tell me where he is,' said Yudin slowly, repeating himself.

'I know neither. He'd be a fool to have told me. Just give up, Iuda. You've lost. Again.'

'You know what, Lyosha? I don't believe you. And do you know why not? Because I choose not to. If I'm right, and you do know, then eventually you'll crack and you'll tell me. If I'm wrong, then you'll die. Either way I'm happy.'

He reached out his hand and grabbed Aleksei by the hair, standing to get better leverage. This time, rather than pushing Aleksei back into the water, he pulled him forward, dragging him by the hair. Then he pushed down, forcing the old man's head between his knees and under the water. Aleksei tried to resist for a moment, but had no strength for it.

'Let him go!' Tamara's voice, cold and firm, filled the room. It had its desired effect. Yudin released Aleksei, who pulled himself back into a sitting position, breathing heavily, his sodden clothes clinging to him. He seemed oblivious to Tamara. He would not have heard her beneath the surface, and she doubted whether he could see clearly while his eyes were filled with hair and water. Yudin, on the other hand, turned to face her.

'My dear, how wonderful to see you,' he said, quickly recovering from his surprise. 'I'd forgotten how interested you were in talking to Lyosha. But I did find him first. You'll have to wait your turn.'

'I think not,' she said, taking a step forward to make sure he could see the two weapons that she carried. 'You know what I can do with these.'

Yudin considered, and then stood up. Aleksei sat still, his head looking down into the water, his breath harsh and gasping. Tamara gestured to Yudin with the gun, and he moved further away. Then she took a step towards Aleksei.

'Colonel Danilov?' she said. The urge to say 'Papa' consumed her, but this was not the moment for reunion – not in front of a creature such as Yudin.

Aleksei looked around, peering towards her. His wet hair hung down over his eyes. He wiped it to one side, but still his squint revealed that he could not see clearly.

'Who are you?' he said.

How she would have loved to tell him; but the time would soon come. 'I'm going to get you out of here,' she said. 'Can you walk?'

Aleksei began trying to pull himself out of the water. Yudin continued to eye the gun and the cane in Tamara's hands, but he did not attempt to move.

'I'm not alone down here,' he said.

'I know,' Tamara replied.

'You won't escape two of us.'

'He let me in, didn't he?' For the sake of her father, Tamara was careful not to mention Dmitry's name, but she saw in Yudin's face a twinge of doubt over the loyalty of that newest member of his species.

She was distracted by the sound of a splash, accompanied by a gasp. Aleksei had slipped. He hung over the edge of the tub, his legs still in the water. It was a heart-rending sight; the image of one who in her mind – and, in younger days, in reality – had been so strong, now struggling and needy, unable to perform the simplest of tasks. And yet there was a joy to it too: her father was in need, and she could help.

She rushed over to him, tucking the cane under her right arm but still pointing the revolver at Yudin. It was a preposterously dangerous way to face such a creature, but she had no option. She put her left arm around her father and tried to heave him out of the water. He braced himself against her shoulder and she hauled him upright, providing the strength which his aged legs could not. He was heavy. Tamara recalled how light the load had been when she carried her mother. Aleksei wore his old age better.

At last he swung his legs over the side and was out of the water. But it had been a strain for both of them. Tamara lowered his body to the floor, so that he could lean against the side of the bath. She hugged his sodden body to her.

Yudin didn't bother to intervene, knowing that he could wait until both Aleksei and Tamara were exhausted by their struggle for freedom. But still she had to try. She began to heave again, pulling Aleksei across the stone floor. He reached across her and his fingers pressed hard into her shoulder, but then slipped away to scrabble at her chest. He fell back. They had moved just a few inches. Yudin emitted a sneering laugh.

Aleksei still hugged himself to her, his feet paddling at the ground, failing to find any purchase. He moved his hand back across to her shoulder and his thumb became entwined in the thin silver chain of her icon.

Tamara glared up at Yudin. She raised the revolver and aimed it at him.

'Do you still not realize what I am?' he asked.

'You're the same as Raisa – and I dealt with her.'

As she spoke Aleksei's fingers found the icon on the end of the chain and pulled it close, towards his weak, failing eyes. It was

455

only then that Tamara realized its significance – both to him and to her. She was four years old, lying in her bed. Her father was leaning over her. Her mother stood a few paces away, looking on. He lifted the icon and its chain from around his own neck and placed it over her head, pulling her red curls up through it so that it finally lay cold around her neck. She had never removed it since – hardly ever.

Today, Aleksei held the icon in his hand again, peering at it. He glanced up at Tamara and then down again. His face became an entanglement of surprise and sorrow, of elation and regret.

'Toma?' His voice was still a whisper, but if ever so soft a sound could have expressed joy, then it did now. 'Toma?' he said again, looking up into her face, running his hand through her auburn locks, holding them close so he could see them clearly. 'It is you. It must be you.'

Tamara gazed into her father's eyes. She had for so long imagined this moment, but had never foreseen that it would be like this, and yet the expression of love that she saw in his face, the feeling that welled in her gut and spread throughout her entire being, were all she had ever imagined and more. Whatever the circumstances, she could not now deny him the truth.

'Yes, Papa,' she whispered. 'Yes, it's me.' She felt Aleksei's arms tighten against her. He tried to speak, but could not, nor did he need to. She understood everything that he wanted to say.

Yudin's laughter broke into the moment. This time there was no snideness to it. It was broad and hearty and – to all appearances – genuine. 'Oh, this is why I love you so, Lyosha,' he said merrily. 'You're always so full of surprises. Where did this one spring from?'

'My mother was Domnikiia Semyonovna,' said Tamara with pride, the gun still levelled at Yudin. Beside her she felt Aleksei begin to rise to his feet, filled with a new-found strength that she well understood. With only a little help from her, he was upright.

'Ah, the lovely Dominique,' Yudin replied. 'It's so preposterously obvious. And all this time, ever since you first came to work for me, you've been plotting revenge on your father's behalf.'

Tamara chose to say nothing. It would keep him wary if he

believed that there was any plan at all to this. She continued to edge towards the door, leading her father to freedom.

'It's another reason for you to tell me, Lyosha,' continued Yudin. 'If not for your sake, then for your daughter's. Just think of what I might do to her.'

Yudin fell silent. There was little to read in Aleksei's face, but Tamara could guess how his imagination was following the trail along which Yudin's words had pointed it. There was nothing she could say – no chance that he would ignore her pleas not to worry about her. But then she sensed that Yudin had let the idea hang in the air for too long. He had lost Aleksei's attention and indeed Yudin's own eyes were fixed now on neither the father nor the daughter.

And suddenly Tamara realized they were no longer alone. From the doorway came another voice.

'And whatever Actual State Councillor Yudin might achieve is as nothing compared with what we have planned.'

Even before Tamara looked, she recognized it. Yet the words made no sense.

In the doorway stood Tyeplov, stooping to fit in the enclosed space. But it was not he who had spoken. Beside him stood a familiar figure, small and unassuming, and yet possessing a new-found swagger that Tamara had not seen in him before.

It was Gribov.

'Tell us, Aleksei Ivanovich,' he said. 'It's what we're all yearning to hear.'

Yudin gazed at Gribov with consternation. In return, Gribov's expression was smug.

'Why should you want to know that?' asked Yudin.

'For myself,' replied Gribov, 'I don't. But I think you can guess who does.'

'Zmyeevich?' hissed Yudin.

'Zmyeevich,' Gribov confirmed. The name meant nothing to Tamara. 'I am his representative here in Moscow; his human representative. You might like to think of me as the new you.'

'For how long?'

'Since long before we met.'

'Why?'

457

'Because you were the most likely person to discover the where-abouts of Aleksandr Pavlovich – but the least likely to share that discovery with your former master.'

'What about him?' Yudin nodded towards Tyeplov.

'Yuri Vladimirovich has always been the creature of Zmyeevich, though perhaps not a constant one. Now he has seen the error of his ways.'

'So Zmyeevich can hear us, through him?' asked Yudin.

'I can,' said Tyeplov. 'And I'm intrigued.' The voice, as far as Tamara could recall it, was Tyeplov's, but the tone was different; deeper, more confident, as though an older and more terrible man were impersonating Tyeplov, but speaking his own words.

'Totally under his control?' asked Yudin.

'Totally.'

'And what do you want?'

'The name and whereabouts of the Romanov, Aleksandr Pavlovich,' said Tyeplov. 'Great-great-grandson of the traitor Pyotr.'

'And if I tell you?'

'You know nothing.'

'I was about to make him talk when you arrived,' said Yudin.

'Then thank you for making our task so much easier,' replied Gribov. He stepped forward and peered closely at the bedraggled Aleksei. 'This is the man?' he said, turning back to Tyeplov. 'The man who twice defeated you?'

Tyeplov walked forward. 'He did not defeat me, he defeated Iuda, my unprofitable servant.' As they spoke, Tamara noticed that Yudin was hardly listening. His eyes flicked around the room as he desperately tried to formulate a plan. After a moment's con-sideration, it seemed he didn't judge his chances favourably. He began to edge towards the door.

Tyeplov gazed closely into Aleksei's face. 'Do you remember me, Danilov?' he asked.

Aleksei's voice was hoarse. 'I remember you chained to the wall of a cave, the sun burning through your body. I gave you your freedom.'

Tyeplov shook his head. 'Look beyond the body, Danilov. We met not far from here, almost half a century ago. I came to save your country, and you laughed at me.'

'You had no plans to save Russia, but yes, we laughed. Aleksandr Pavlovich is still laughing, wherever he may be.'

Tyeplov's eyes flared in anger, but then he calmed. 'You will tell me where that is.'

'Never.'

Tyeplov's hand smashed down on Tamara's, sending the cane and the revolver sliding across the floor and knocking her away from her father. In a second she was on her feet, her knife drawn from her boot and in her hand. She knew how little help it would be against a creature like Tyeplov, yet it was all she had. She backed towards the far corner of the cell, taking a few swipes at the *voordalak* in the futile hope it would persuade him to keep his distance. His solution was simply to grab the blade. Tamara pulled it back rapidly and saw blood oozing from between his fingers, but it was no deterrent whatsoever.

All she could do now was retreat. Behind Tyeplov she could see the rest of the cell. Gribov had retrieved the revolver and was aiming it at Aleksei, who leaned against the wall, still weak. Yudin continued to attempt his slow journey towards freedom, edging step by step closer to the door. It had not escaped Tyeplov. As Yudin passed closest to him, he lashed out with his fist, scarcely looking at what he did. His knuckles connected with Yudin's nose, cracking the back of his head against the wall. Blood began to spill from both points of impact, and Yudin slumped to the floor. Tyeplov still loomed over Tamara, ever advancing, his teeth bared.

She heard Gribov's voice. 'Do you really love your daughter so little, Aleksei Ivanovich? You'd let her die like this, just to keep your paltry secret?'

'No,' said Aleksei quietly.

'Then you're prepared to tell us?'

The prospect of discovering what he had come for did not seem to distract Tyeplov from his current intent. His fangs descended upon Tamara's throat, but she felt no pain – merely the warmth of his breath and the odious moistness of his saliva on her skin. He was eking out his performance for Aleksei's benefit. But his movement did allow Tamara to see what was going on.

Aleksei straightened himself and stood away from the wall. It was the first time she had seen him properly. He was nothing like as tall as Dmitry, but was strongly built, even in his old age, with solid broad shoulders. His square jaw was unmistakably her own. She was surprised that no one other than Dmitry had made the connection.

Aleksei shook his head wearily, his eyes fixed on the floor. 'No,' he repeated. When he finally moved, it was with a swiftness of which Tamara would not have thought him capable. In three strides he was halfway across the cell, towards where she and Tyeplov stood locked in their embrace. His arm was raised above him, clutched in it the sharpened cane which his son had devised and his daughter had brought to him. In another two paces he would be able to bring it down on Tyeplov's back.

The revolver spat a bullet at him, then another. Gribov was no more slowed by age than Aleksei. The first shot caught her father in the left shoulder, the second in his stomach. Tamara saw a plume of blood issuing from his back as the bullet emerged. But neither shot did anything to hinder him. Tamara saw his left hand – its two smallest fingers missing, along with half of another – reach around and grip at Tyeplov's nose, trying to prise his face away from her throat and brace Aleksei for his attack.

Gribov fired again, but Tamara didn't see where the bullet hit. Aleksei's arm came down. The cane penetrated the right side of Tyeplov's back at a shallow angle, so that path took it across to the left. Aleksei knew precisely where he had been aiming. Tyeplov's grip on her slackened in an instant. Just as she had witnessed with Ignatyev at the brothel, and Raisa beside the railway, Tyeplov's mortal remains began to collapse to nothing. He fell slowly sideways, but with the weight of his body gone, the air caught his clothes and resisted their descent. It was like some ballet dancer, throwing himself across the stage, graceful and controlled, and yet, ultimately, there was no control to it. The clothes kept on falling, eventually to hit the ground and to flatten as the dust within was exhaled through every available outlet.

Aleksei took a step away, still grasping the cane, and Tamara got a clear view of Gribov. He held the pistol in both hands to steady it, aimed squarely at Aleksei, and fired again. The bullet hit somewhere in the chest, and Aleksei slumped backwards against the wall, dropping the cane.

Tamara did not know if the screech that spilled from her throat was supposed to be an articulate word or the primitive cry of a vengeful animal. Gribov turned towards her, his face frozen in shock, but the gun followed his eye more slowly – too slowly. She was across the room and upon him in a fraction of a second. The knife that had been of so little use on Tyeplov was still clutched in her hand, and would prove its worth. She stabbed upwards, under his ribcage, pressing herself so close to him that he had no chance to train the gun on her. She felt sure her aim had been true, but she stabbed twice more, desperate that with at least one blow the fine steel blade would penetrate his heart.

She stepped back. Gribov was already dead – only her strength held him upright. She pointed her arm and the blade downwards and he slid off it, his body collapsing in a heap on the floor with a quiet, heavy thud. It was almost a relief to witness the normality of human death, but there was no time to relish the sight of a body that did not instantly decay.

Aleksei and Yudin sat against adjacent walls of the cell. Aleksei was by far the worse for wear, but he was still alive. Yudin was just regaining consciousness. Tamara couldn't guess how much time she had. She grabbed her father around the chest and, ignoring the pain that it caused him, hauled him across the cell floor and out into the corridor. She slammed the door closed, but there was no key in the lock and no bolt on the outside. It wouldn't keep Yudin in for long. She looked along the corridor down which she knew she must drag her father if they were to have any chance of survival.

Dmitry blocked their way, his huge frame filling the low, arched tunnel.

There was only one other chance of escape: the seventh door, behind which Yudin had refused to show her. She looked at it. The key was still in the lock. It turned easily, and she began to draw the three heavy iron bolts that gave this door extra strength. She glanced down at Aleksei, propped up against the wall, his breathing shallow. Beyond him Dmitry still stood, as indecisive as

461

he had been when they had spoken earlier. Son looked at father, but father did not see son.

Finally, she pulled the third of the bolts across, and began to heave on the handle. At the same moment, the door to her right opened, and Yudin emerged. She had the chance to run forward into that last, unexplored cell, but she had no idea whether it would lead to freedom or death. And anyway, it was not an option. She would not be separated from her father. She took a step back, towards Aleksei and towards Dmitry.

Yudin stepped out into the corridor, standing framed in the doorway that Tamara had just opened. She had never seen him look so angry – so out of control. She heard footsteps as Dmitry finally made up his mind and began to approach. From behind Yudin there were sounds too – moans that could have been animal or human, accompanied by the clanking of chains. God knew what Yudin kept in there; it was too dark for her to see.

It didn't matter. She was trapped deep beneath the Kremlin in a tight, low tunnel with a vampire in front of her and another behind. This was the end. She slumped back against the wall and sat beside her father. She felt his hand grip hers.

'A bit late for the gallant rescue, Dmitry,' said Yudin, quickly becoming himself again.

At the sound of the name, Aleksei became suddenly alert. He raised his head, causing him to cough, but he brushed the hair away from his eyes to peer at the figure that, even after so many years, he could not mistake for anyone but his son.

Dmitry's voice would only confirm it. 'That's not why I'm here.'

'Dmitry?' Aleksei spoke in scarcely more than a whisper. His son showed no interest in responding.

'Why then?' asked Yudin.

'I came to say goodbye.'

'To your father?'

'To you.'

The conversation apparently over, Dmitry turned – difficult in the tight corridor – and began to depart. Yudin stared ahead blankly. Behind him, Tamara thought she glimpsed movement. Then he turned his gaze downwards.

'Ah, Lyosha. You keep your petty victories over Aleksandr

Pavlovich. You can die in the knowledge that he's safe; he won't be long behind you anyway. But there's one thing you must hear before you die.' As Yudin spoke, Dmitry stopped in his tracks and turned. 'One thing you really do deserve to know about your beloved son.'

'No, Vasya,' said Dmitry firmly. He took three steps forward and was now at a level with Tamara.

'Why not? You wouldn't want me to lie to him.'

Dmitry took another step so that he was face to face with Yudin, towering over his father, who stared up at him.

'Who'd have thought, Lyosha, that the little boy I first met when he was five years old – while you were hiding away with your whore – who'd have thought that one day he'd grow up to be someone of whom I could be so proud; would grow up to be . . .'

Dmitry raised his arms on either side of him, bracing himself against the close walls almost as though he were Samson about to bring down the Philistine temple. But that was not his plan. He raised up his legs, his whole weight supported on his arms, and kicked forward, his feet landing squarely on Yudin's chest. Yudin's words were cut short as he was forced to take a step backwards.

At the same instant, Tamara saw more movement in the cell behind him – human figures creeping forward apprehensively, awaiting their moment. As Yudin stumbled backwards, they pounced. Two of them grabbed his legs and one his arm, dragging him back into their domain, but it was the fourth who most caught Tamara's attention. It was an old woman, her flesh sunk tight into her cheeks. Between her hands she held a chain, which somehow seemed to be attached to her as well. She flung it around Yudin's neck and then twisted it behind him with a strength that Tamara could not have supposed she had in her. It would have killed any human in minutes. Judging by the look of triumphant hatred in the old woman's eyes, Tamara wondered if it might not be effective even on a vampire.

Dmitry kicked again and Yudin fell backwards into the cell, dragged down by his attackers. Tamara moved fast. She threw herself towards the door and slammed it shut, holding for one final moment the victorious gaze of the old woman as she tightened the chain around Yudin's throat. Once the door was closed, she slid the bottom bolt across. Dmitry rammed the other two into place and twisted the key in the lock, then pocketed it. He turned and marched back up the corridor without a word.

'Dmitry!' Aleksei called plaintively after his son. Dmitry turned and looked at his sister, then down at his father. For years after, Tamara would try to analyse what she remembered of his expression at that moment, to make some sense of it, but now there was no time. A moment later he was gone, his footsteps retreating up the stairs.

She looked down at her father. His shirt was stained with his own blood and his breathing was weak.

'He had to go,' she said.

'Why?'

She could not think of an answer.

'Can you move?' she asked. She knew he wouldn't get far, but she didn't want to leave him here, so close to Yudin, whatever might be happening to him in there and however sturdy that door might appear.

'I think so.'

She helped Aleksei back to his feet and forced him to walk with her towards the stairs. Aleksei had no strength to climb them in the normal way, but instead sat down on them and pushed himself up, one step at a time. It took them five minutes just to get as far as the landing where the stairs split, and then Aleksei insisted he could go no further. He sat with his back to the wall, one foot resting on the step below, the other leg bent and held close to his chest. Tamara sat beside him, her hand in his. It was dark here, and neither of them could see very much, but it hid from her his wrinkled skin and white hair and, though his voice was soft and faltering, she could easily picture him as the strong man she had always imagined her father to be. Likewise, he would not notice the horrible laceration that Raisa had engraved in her cheek.

They talked for hours. Tamara told him everything that she could think of, and he did the same – though his voice was weak and he frequently coughed up blood. She knew that his body was

464

beyond salvation, and she could think of no way that either of them would rather spend his final moments than together. He told her of his exploits in 1812 and 1825, and at Austerlitz and on the Danube. He showed her his hand, telling her of how he lost two fingers in Silistria, and half of the third as he hung from a ledge of the Winter Palace. Tamara had to laugh at his stories at times, but she knew that was his intention in the way he described things. He did not want her to have to know the terror of it, though she could well imagine.

He told her as much of his military exploits as he did of his dealings with *voordalaki*, and seemed to take a far greater pride in the former than the latter. Much of it tied in with what Dmitry had already told her, but there was more that Aleksei could add. She could not guess whether it was because Aleksei had kept it from his son, or that Dmitry had kept it from her.

In turn, Tamara told her father of her life, with none of the blissful deceit she had employed when speaking of it to Domnikiia. She told him of how her husband and children had died, and of how Luka still lived. Her description of her occasional sightings of her living child seemed to affect him more than the deaths of the others. She could easily understand why.

Aleksei was at his happiest when he spoke of his friends – of Vadim, Maks and Dmitry Fetyukovich and their adventures – and most of all when he spoke of Domnikiia and the thirty peaceful and strangely contented years they had spent in Siberia. In turn Tamara told him of her encounter with Domnikiia, of how mother and daughter had been reunited, and of how her mother had saved her life. When he asked, Tamara told him the little she knew about his wife, Marfa – that she had died in 1848. He seemed relieved she had not lived to see him like this.

It was over Dmitry that she deceived her father utterly. She said she had met him, said what a fine soldier he was, how brave he had been in Sevastopol, and even how he had fought against Tyeplov and the others. She relayed pretty much everything that had occurred up until Dmitry's ill-fated journey to Klin, and then made up a story about brother and sister coming here together to save Aleksei. She could never have brought herself to tell him the truth.

'Why did he have to go?' Aleksei asked.

'He went to get help,' Tamara extemporized. 'He'll be back soon.'

'What did Iuda mean, about how Dmitry had grown up?'

'Who knows? Dmitry's no saint, you know.'

Aleksei chuckled and that made him cough more. 'It doesn't matter. I wouldn't believe a word Iuda said anyway. He taught me that long ago.'

Eventually, they came to talk of the Lavrovs, and Aleksei wept again when he explained how they had decided to leave Tamara with them. 'Did we do right, Toma? We had to protect you. Iuda would have come for you – to get at me. We had to do it.'

It was the same question her mother had asked. 'We're together now, Papa,' she said.

He fell into silence. His breathing was shallow now, and it was obvious that he had only a short time left to live. The bullets had done their work, little though that had aided the man who fired them. After a few minutes, Aleksei spoke again, suddenly urgent.

'Where's Dmitry?'

'He'll be here soon,' she replied.

'There's something I have to tell you. The name that they wanted to know; I must tell you it.'

'I don't need to know that,' she said. Moreover, she did not want to. It seemed like dangerous knowledge. It was Yudin's plan, but with the daughter replacing the son as heroic rescuer.

'Please, Toma,' said Aleksei. 'He's our tsar. Someone must remember.'

Tamara bent forward and Aleksei raised his lips to her ear, whispering two words that were so quiet she could scarcely make them out. It was disappointing to learn that he had sacrificed so much to protect so little.

'Fyodor Kuzmich.'

His head dropped back and he was silent. His hand tightened momentarily on hers and she squeezed it back, feeling the stumps of his missing fingers and remembering doing the same as a child. Then his grip weakened and his arm fell away. She looked over to him and his face was still. A long slow breath escaped his lips, catching his vocal cords and producing a low, sustained sound, like a contented sigh. Then he breathed no more.

The carriage rolled jerkily over the unpaved road. There was no railway to take Tamara to where she was heading – not yet. That made it feel so much more like an escape. It was a public coach, and there were three others in it – a couple and a single man. There were few words exchanged, even between the woman and her husband. Occasionally they looked at her, and she wondered if they were staring at the scar on her cheek, however thickly she had covered it with make-up.

As with her mother, Tamara had committed her father's body to the river. A little exploration had revealed a room furnished only with two coffins – she could easily guess its purpose. She had been tempted to use one as Aleksei's final resting place, but it did not seem fitting. The room had had another exit, which led to a corridor, and beyond that a maze of tunnels spread out. She had taken the path that led her downhill, carrying her father's body as she went, and had eventually found herself emerging on to the bank of the Moskva, below the Kremlin's southern wall. She could find no wood on which to lay him, nor any leaves to cover him, but the river flowed fast and strong here. She pushed her father's body out from the bank, and whispered the same prayer she had said for her mother. It was the best she could do, and there was some little sense in it; the Skhodnya was a tributary of the Moskva and so, she liked to hope, with a little luck in the currents, the bodies of her father and mother might somewhere be lying side by side in a watery grave.

She had scarcely dared go back down to that short, low corridor with its seven doors. From the far right of them, she still heard the sound of overflowing water. The stench was stronger again now – or was that just an excuse for her not to linger? Gribov's body lay still. She stood beside the seventh door, resting her ear against the sturdy wood, and listened. Perhaps she heard slight sounds of movement, but nothing more. If those four sorry creatures she had seen were human, then Yudin would easily have dealt with them, but if he had, then he was still trapped. The door was solid

– perhaps so solid that he would never emerge. And what could she do about it? Dmitry had taken the key.

Then she had heard a muffled scream inches in front of her and something thudded against the far side of the door.

She turned and fled.

Now, a week later, she was still fleeing. It hadn't taken her long to prepare her escape from Moscow. She had withdrawn all her money from the bank, and that had been enough to get her out of the city and to begin making a new home somewhere else. Her own resources would not last for ever, but she still had, sewn into her dress, the diamonds and pink sapphires of the necklace Konstantin had given her. They would see her through. She had never worn the necklace since the day he gave it to her. She reached up with her hand and felt the small, oval icon that still hung from her neck, and always would.

The necklace was not the sole gift Konstantin had given her, and was only the second most precious. The dearest gift was with her now too, closer even than the sapphires; the carriage's fifth passenger.

In the hours before he had died, she had told Aleksei of it, and he had been overjoyed. He had asked her who the father was, but she had refused to tell him, and he accepted it. She did tell him that if he knew the man's name, it would make Aleksei immensely proud, and she was certain that was true.

But she knew that Moscow would not be safe for her, or for her unborn child, and so she left. There was nothing to keep her there. She gazed out of the window and watched the landscape trundle past, so much more slowly than it had done from the train on which her child had been conceived. She rested her hand unconsciously on her belly. It was too soon to feel any kicking; the bump did not even show yet, but she knew it was there.

She would be happy either way, but in her heart she hoped it would be a boy. As to what she would call it, she hadn't thought yet, not of a Christian name, but she knew the rest. The patronymic would be Konstantinovich or Konstantinovna – the father deserved that much at least. But the child would carry its surname with pride. In her last days in Moscow she had called on contacts in the Third Section and acquired a new passport. She could have chosen any name, and the one she decided upon was foolish for a woman going into hiding, but she could no longer live in denial of her true self. She had never been a Lavrova, much as she loved Yelena and Valentin. She had been proud to take Vitaliy's name, and to call herself Tamara Valentinovna Komarova, but now even that would not do, not any more. The name on her new passport filled her with a pride she had never felt before in her whole life. Sometimes, she sneaked a look at it, just to be sure of who she truly was.

She was Tamara Alekseevna Danilova.

1864

EPILOGUE

Fyodor Kuzmich died a happy man, in Tomsk, in Siberia, on 20 January 1864. As he lay on a straw bed, in a wooden shack, he knew that death was coming, but he had lived long enough. He had lived, in fact, three years longer than he needed to, but God had granted him those three years to enjoy seeing the fruits of his nephew's achievement.

In 1861, Tsar Aleksandr II had at last emancipated the serfs. All men in Russia were free. On Kuzmich's own accession to the throne, as Aleksandr I, sixty years before, it had been his fondest hope to achieve the same, but it had never come to pass. Bonaparte was to blame, at least at first, and then had come all the trouble with Zmyeevich and Cain and the Romanov Betrayal. They'd found a way out of that, he and Volkonsky, Tarasov, Wylie and Danilov. Only Tarasov was left alive now – and possibly Danilov. Kuzmich knew he had returned west when the Decembrists had been pardoned, but had not heard of him since.

It did not matter. They were all old men, and it was meet for old men to die. If he could die happy in the knowledge that he had left his country in a better state than he had found it, all to the good, even if the credit was to his nephew and not to him.

He heard a voice, but he could not make out the words. It was probably his friend Simeon Khromov, who had looked after him in his final months. He knew full well what the man was asking him – it was always the same. Simeon suspected something about Kuzmich, but his guesses were never close to the truth. Now he would never learn it, but Kuzmich knew that his friend deserved a response.

He lifted his hand weakly, remembering the first time he had died, in Taganrog in 1825. He realized now what a good impersonation of a dying man he had given then. But this was no play-acting. He pointed to his heart and whispered as loudly as he could.

'Here lies my secret.'

Then his arm fell to his side and he was no more.

Four thousand versts away, Zmyeevich's eyes flicked open. The connection was broken. He had never been able to read Aleksandr Pavlovich's mind, but Aleksandr could at times sense his, and thus Aleksandr's existence was always a presence for Zmyeevich.

And now that presence was no more, and Aleksandr was at last dead. He should have realized in 1825, but he had been fooled. By the time he had understood, Nikolai had been well settled on the throne, and the return of his brother would have been pointless. But Aleksandr Pavlovich's continued existence had acted to protect his nephew, by attracting whatever influence Zmyeevich could exert over the bloodline. If they could have found him, they would have killed him, but Danilov's silence had prevented that. Even so, Zmyeevich had known he had only to wait and death would come. Now it had done so.

And so now retribution could begin again and at last, in the fifth generation, the Romanov Betrayal would be avenged.

CHARACTERS OF
THE DANILOV QUINTET

Aleksei Ivanovich Danilov

Russian soldier and spy who defeated the Oprichniki in 1812 and saved Tsar Aleksandr I from Zmyeevich in 1825 by helping to fake his death. Sent into exile after the Decembrist Uprising

Dmitry Alekseevich Danilov

Only son of Aleksei Ivanovich Danilov

Marfa Mihailovna Danilova

Wife of Aleksei and mother of Dmitry

Domnikiia Semyonovna Beketova

Aleksei's mistress, who accompanied him into exile in Siberia in 1826

Iuda
also known as *Vasiliy Denisovich Makarov* and *Richard Llywelyn Cain*

The only human among the twelve Oprichniki who came to Russia in 1812. Under the name of Cain he experimented on vampires. Became a vampire himself in 1825

Zmyeevich

The arch vampire who brought the Oprichniki to Russia in 1812 and who seeks revenge for the trickery played upon him by Tsar Pyotr the Great in 1712

Vadim Fyodorovich Savin	Aleksei's commander, who died during the campaign of 1812
Maksim Sergeivich Lukin	Comrade of Aleksei, who died during the campaign of 1812
Dmitry Fetyukovich Petrenko	Comrade of Aleksei, who died during the campaign of 1812
The Oprichniki	The nickname for a band of vampires defeated by Aleksei in 1812. Individually they took the names of the twelve apostles
Yelena Vadimovna Lavrova	Daughter of Vadim Fyodorovich
Valentin Valentinovich Lavrov	Husband of Yelena Vadimovna
Rodion Valentinovich Lavrov	Son of Yelena and Valentin
Dr Dmitry Tarasov	Physician to Tsar Aleksandr I, who conspired with Aleksei to fake the tsar's death
Prince Pyetr Mihailovich Volkonsky	Adjutant general to Tsar Aleksandr I, who conspired with Aleksei to fake the tsar's death
Raisa Styepanovna Tokoryeva	Vampire who helped Iuda to escape Chufut Kalye in 1825
Margarita Kirillovna	A prostitute colleague of Domnikiia who was murdered by Iuda in 1812
Natalia Borisovna Papanova	Daughter of a cobbler; sheltered Aleksei and Dmitry Fetyukovich during the French occupation of Moscow in 1812

ABOUT THE AUTHOR

Jasper Kent was born in Worcestershire in 1968 and studied Natural Sciences at Trinity Hall, Cambridge. He lives in Brighton and works as a freelance software consultant. *The Third Section* is the third book in *The Danilov Quintet*. The first two acclaimed novels – *Twelve* and *Thirteen Years Later* – are available in paperback. As well as fiction, Jasper has also written a number of musicals. To find out more, visit www.jasperkent.com